On The Edge of Sunrise

of Sunrise

Book One of the Long-Hair Saga

For Elizabeth
Fellow writer and
friend. Best wishes
always! Keep writing!
writing!

Cynthia Ripley Miller

EARLY PRAISE FOR
ON THE EDGE OF SUNRISE

"On the Edge of Sunrise is a compelling epic, sure to appeal to fans of historical fiction. Forbidden love, a turbulent time period, and world-changing events combine to produce a real page-turner."
- India Edghill, author of *Queenmaker*, *Wisdom's Daughter*, and *Delilah.*

"On the Edge of Sunrise is a passionate and intriguing take on the often overlooked clash of three brutal and powerful empires: the Romans, Franks, and Huns. A Compelling read!"
- Stephanie Thornton, author of *The Secret History* and *The Tiger Queens*

"Cynthia Ripley Miller chooses A.D. 451 as the year of her romantic historical novel. Perhaps a fifth century recognizable name to readers will be Attila the Hun, who has invaded Gaul (France.) Roman commander Aetius enlists Arria, a Roman senator's feisty daughter, as a secret courier with a message to Attila, but she becomes a political hostage. A developing romance between Arria and Garic, an elite Frank warrior, entails avoiding her forced marriage to repugnant Tribune Drusus, Garic's attempt to rescue her, and his injuries by a vengeful witch and those suffered in the battle against Attila. Readers will be absorbed by a setting of barbarian Gaul and the constancy of Arria's and Garic's destined love amid the strife of a dying Roman Empire."
- Albert Noyer, author of *The Getorius* and *Arcadia Mysteries*

"From cover to cover a gripping read – in all senses of the word! Grips your interest and imagination, your held breath and your pounding heart! A thumping good novel!"
- Helen Hollick USA Today bestselling author & Managing Editor Historical Novel Society Indie Reviews

On The Edge of Sunrise

Book One of The Long-Hair Saga

Cynthia Ripley Miller

**KNOX ROBINSON
PUBLISHING**
London • New York

KNOX ROBINSON
PUBLISHING

34 New House, 67-68 Hatton Garden
London, EC1N 8JY

&

244 5th Avenue, Suite 1861
New York, New York 10001

ISBN 978-1-910282-44-1

Typeset in Baskerville

Printed in the United States of America
and the United Kingdom.

First published by KRP in Great Britain in 2015
First published by KRP in the United States in 2015

www.knoxrobinsonpublishing.com

For my sister and Venus muse, Linda Marie

Cast of Characters

Main Players

Arria Quintia Felix	The daughter of Roman Senator Quintus Felix
Titus Claudius Drusus	Senior Tribune and later legate and commander of Cambria
Marcus Furius Severus	A Roman tribune, equite and Marcian's best friend
Marcella	An Egyptian seeress and slave
Garic	A barbarian noble and First Counsel to the Salian Franks
Vodamir	A barbarian warrior and cousin to Garic
Luthgar	Chief of a Salian Frank tribe
Basina	Apprentice shaman and Hun healer
Aveek	Attila's chieftain
Samuel	Arria's beloved servant and slave
Karas	A Greek slave woman
Angelus	Karas' ten year old son

Romans

General Flavius Aetius	Master of the Soldiers of the Roman army
Senator Quintus Arrius Felix	Arria's father
Lucius Valerius Marcian	Arria's deceased husband
Senator Flavius Valerius Marcian	Marcian's father and future emperor of the Eastern Empire
Governor Publius Sergius Lucinius	Provincial governor of Belgica Secunda in Gaul
Tarvistus	A Roman centurion (lieutenant) under Drusus
Nepos	An Roman optio (sergeant)
Silas	A Roman guard

Legate Appius Livius Brucerius	Relieving commander at Aurelianum

Salian Frank Barbarians

Ingund	Luthgar's wife
Amo	A barbarian Wespe warrior
Muric & Bede	Wespe brothers and camp cooks
Rudiger	Retired Wespe and Amo's Father
Theudebert	A Wespe soldier
Witigis	A Wespe soldier
Denis	A Wespe soldier
Faramund	Garic's older brother
Tagus	Garic's younger brother

Huns and Minor Characters

Attila	Hun conqueror of the fifth century
Orestes	Advisor to Attila
Onegesius	Attila's chamberlain/vizier

*****

Tibatto	Counselor to King Sangiban of the Alans
Castor	A slave trader
Theobald	A Visigoth warrior
Sunechild	Vodamir's mother and a healer
Betto	Drusus' male slave

Atlantic
Ocean

BRITONS

Belgica Secunda

Cambria
(CAMBRAI)

Rhine River
(Rhenus)

Danube River
(Danuvius)

Paris (LUTETIA)

Somme River

Metz
(METTIS)

Catalaunum

Orleans
(AURELIANUM)

Troyes
(TRICASSES)

Strasbourg
(ARGENTORATUM)

GAUL

HISPANIA

Ravenna

ITALIA

Rome

Mediterranean Sea

THE WESTERN ROMAN EMPIRE

A.D. 451

Prima Lux
First Light

GERMANIA
Month of Junius, A.D. 448

Arria no longer possessed the strength to turn the bodies. Fighting nausea, she covered her mouth with the fold of her dress and staggered through the tangled corpses. Slaughtered men stretched across the battlefield of red-stained grass; their blood-matted hair clung to dented helmets. Fixed, empty eyes stared at the blinding sun, while flies claimed the banquet before them. *He is here,* she thought and steeled herself. Wounded or dead, she would find him and have him placed on his warrior's shield.

Ahead, a Roman soldier slumped against a dead horse, a spear stuck in his chest. *Is it Marcian?* No. Relieved, Arria wiped the tears from her eyes and whispered a prayer for her husband. A barbarian slave yanked at his dead master's boots, his blond plaits swinging with each tug. Arria stepped past, but kept the bandit in her sight. A horse snorted behind her, diverting her attention. Marcus Furius Severus, her husband's comrade-in-arms, appeared silhouetted by the burning sun.

"Come, Arria. My men and I will find Marcian. I promise you. No barbarian in all Germania and on this broken battlefield will keep Roman legionaries from finding our wounded, dead or.... dying."

Arria brushed a damp curl behind her ear. "I cannot stop. My husband lies waiting for me." She pushed forward, tears welling in her eyes. "He is my life, Severus. He lives."

A sudden reflection skimmed the mosaic of corpses and caught

1

Arria's attention. She wove her way toward a glittering helmet. A bright yellow plume matted with blood jutted from a tangle of bodies fallen on a lifeless horse. Beneath the shiny metal, a familiar shock of brown hair poked outward, wet and limp. Arria scrambled across bent and broken shields and dead men, toward the silver glow.

Severus slid from his mount and caught her arm. "Lucius Valerius Marcian led the VIII Augusta Equites. We rode side by side. I have the strength to free him."

Arria met his gaze and nodded. Severus heaved several dead Germans one by one to the side. The gap revealed the Roman soldier's back. Partially trapped beneath the horse, he slumped over its neck, his face buried in the shiny black mane. "It's Apollo," she gasped, "Marcian's horse."

Severus dragged the limp soldier onto his back.

"Husband," Arria groaned and rushed to his side. Gently, she lifted the helmet from his head and pressed her fingers beneath his jaw. Severus crouched beside Arria and watched. Oblivious to the blood pooled below his sternum, she laid her head on his chest. "He lives. Give me water!"

Severus bolted toward his horse.

"My love, I will help you. Stay with me," Arria implored.

Marcian's breath grew deep and fast. His eyelids fluttered open.

Arria caressed his brow and fought her fear. His eyes, so brown, glistened. "We will bring you to safety. Be strong."

Severus returned and knelt beside Marcian. He held a water pouch to his lips.

Marcian took several gulps then turned away.

"I will carry you to the physicians," Severus said.

"No time," Marcian rasped and clutched Arria's hand. "I love you. If heaven is kind, I will watch ..." he coughed and a red line tickled from the corner of his mouth, "over ... you."

Arria dabbed away the blood with her fingers. "You will live."

Marcian reached for her cheek, but his hand melted to his side, his gaze fading.

A tender breeze caressed Arria's face. She sensed his spirit rising like ashes from a dying fire. Marcian's eyes fixed skyward. Arria grasped his shoulders and her body shook. "My dearest," she sobbed and buried her face in his neck. "Don't go."

Severus tore her away.

"No!" Arria cried. Breaking from his grip, she returned to Marcian's side. Her fingers floated over his curls and his softened brow. She gently closed his eyes. Then one last time, she cradled his face and kissed his warm lips.

PROVINCE OF TUSCIA, ITALIA
Month of Julius, A.D. 450

"Lovely? Why do you not sleep?" Senator Quintus Arrius Felix stood beside his daughter in his villa's garden retreat, the moon a silent observer. "Does the battlefield and Marcian's death still haunt you?"

Arria turned to greet her father's concern and nodded. The night almost gone, the torches burned softer, casting a glow on his kind features.

"You and Marcian lived your lives undivided. When duty brought him to Germania, you followed. These dreams may disconcert, but do not despair. He rests peacefully."

Tiny beads of perspiration covered Arria's brow. She took a deep breath, wiped her forehead and knelt, dipping her hand into the marble fountain. Cool water welcomed her, and she quenched her thirst. Unbound, her hair fell in dark brown waves about her shoulders and her sleeping robe clung to her body. Sitting on the garden bench, she rested her palms on its edge and gazed at the stars.

Her father sat beside her and wrapped his arm around her shoulders. "These dreams will ebb or one day comfort. Your mother has been gone almost twelve years; and yet, there are times when we meet in the realm guarded by sleep."

Arria clutched the cross hanging from her neck. Nothing could bring her husband back from the dead.

"Now Lovely, you must rest. Tomorrow is your birthday, a time of celebration and perhaps, some thought to a new beginning, a betrothal."

Arria sighed. "I will consider your wish Father. Return to your bed. Allow me just a few more moments alone."

Her father rose, but paused. "Do you still desire to represent me in Gaul as Rome's envoy?"

"Your health will not permit your travel, and I seek a purpose."

He bent and kissed her forehead.

Arria fondly watched as her father walked the path to his chamber. In an hour's time, she would be twenty-two. Perfume from the roses along the passage mingled with the night and tangled her in an invisible web. Tears spilled down her cheeks and she covered her face with her hands. *Another sunrise without you, my love.*

Part One

"...And Mighty and measureless now did the tide of his love arise.For their longing had met and mingled, and he knew of her heart that she loved,

And she spake unto nothing."

The Fostering of Aslaug

Chapter One

Terra Aliena
Foreign land

GAUL
A Roman field camp en route to Fort Cambria, AD 450

A sudden blast from the sentry's horn sounded the alarm. Awakened by the call to arms, Arria tossed her blanket aside and jumped from bed. Clad only in her linen nightdress, she grabbed a cloak and stepped outside the tent. Soldiers scattered half dressed from their sleep, while some ran for their horses, mounted and drew their swords. Centurions shouted orders. Legionaries braced themselves behind a line of shields and waited. A clamor rose and rolled toward the human barricade like an approaching storm. War cries screamed from the barbarian horde as they clashed through the barrier. Their silver axes ablaze in the sun, they trampled the Roman line and moved past the perimeter.

"My lady, take cover inside the tent!" Arria's guard, Silas, shouted.

Without question, Arria obeyed and watched him wrench the flaps closed. Sharp cries, hoarse grunts and metal ringing on metal forced her back. She crouched behind the bed. The canvas shelter billowed toward her with shadowed movement and she heard a guttural cry. The din roared like an angry beast, then rolled away and pitched toward the heart of the camp.

Arria stood, crept toward the opening and cautiously raised the flap. Silas lay crumpled on the ground, gaping in shock at his partially severed arm. Only sinew and battered bone clung together.

6

Arria froze. A horse shrieked and galloped past, jolting her senses. She scrambled for Silas' bloodied sword and knelt beside him. The soldier's fear-filled eyes gave his consent, and he pointed to beneath his bicep. Between gritted teeth, he forced, "Tie ... ." He touched his fingers to the strapping on his chest. His eyelids fluttered. "Chop," he hissed. Arria understood, the widow of a cavalry officer, she had heard many accounts. Even worse, she had searched for and found her dying husband on a battlefield. She could do this. Arria cut two leather strips from his armor and tied the thinner piece around his damaged arm. The thicker one she wedged between his teeth. Arria murmured a quick prayer, then took a breath. With both hands, she raised the sword high and swung. Silas screamed and his eyes rolled back.

Arria dropped the sword. Her arms trembled as she braced the bloody ground. Her stomach clawed on the inside. The severed arm lay pooled in blood and red dust. Arria retched and wiped her mouth with the back of her wrist. She forced herself upright and stripped a piece of cloth from the hem of her gown. With shaky hands, she bound the stump. Summoning all her strength, she grabbed his shoulders and yelled, "Silas! Silas!" No response. She slapped his face. "Silas!"

His eyes flickered. He moaned.

"Get to your knees, quickly! We must take cover."

Silas scratched the dirt with bent and bloodied fingers and pulled himself to his knees. Arria wound her arm around his waist and they crawled into the tent.

With all the strength Silas could lend her, Arria helped him onto the bed, then gently removed his helmet and covered him with a blanket. She tore extra strips from the hem of her gown, bound his wound tighter and wiped his face. "I will bring the physician. Lie still, and you'll be safe."

Arria rose and pushed back her fear. Her gown wet with blood and clinging to her legs, she stepped from the tent. Ahead, barbarians and Romans swung axes and swords against one another. Riderless horses whinnied in confusion and darted about, while traders and slaves ran for the borders of the camp and safety. With a wary step, she edged forward.

On the fringe of the chaos, a slave's child sat crying. Arria bolted, scooped the girl into her arms and joined several slaves, racing toward a line of soldiers.

"Doria!" screamed a woman, running towards them.

"Mama!" the little girl cried, arms outstretched. The mother tore the child from Arria's arms and fled toward the field camp's crude stronghold.

Arria attempted to follow, but a swirling dust blurred her vision. She stopped. Battle sounds raged around her, while the haze sifted and settled. Two barbarians slid from their horses with blood-smeared axes in hand. Splattered with gore from helmets to boots, an odor rose from them that rivaled the sewers in Rome. Arria's nostrils flared and she stiffened. They circled her like hungry wolves stalking a young deer.

The bearded and barrel-chested one stuck his axe in his belt and leered. The second was taller and dark. His deep scar sliced from temple to cheek and a toothless grin conveyed his intention. Arria backed up and dashed to the right, but the scarred one grabbed her.

"Let me go!" Arria cried, fighting him.

He put his axe to her throat, stifling her protest and dragged her towards his mount. Both barbarians heaved Arria across the saddle. The scarred one barked in a guttural command, then leapt onto the horse. He galloped out of the camp with Arria, while his companion stayed behind.

The horse's gallop pounded Arria's belly, forcing her breath in short gasps. Not willing to be a passive captive, she wrapped her arms around the barbarian's leg and called out, hoping a Roman soldier would hear her.

"Quiet!" her captor yelled roughly in Latin. He slapped Arria's bottom and slowed his horse.

Arria punched his calf, but his leg was tough and her fist weak. He laughed and drew the horse to a halt. Clenching her hair with a rough hand, he pulled her head back and brushed his knuckles over her neck.

"Shall I cut your throat Roman—or kiss it?" he said and pushed her from the horse onto the dry grass.

Arria sprang to her feet and bolted. His laugh boomed as she heard twigs crunch under his landed feet behind her. She sprinted up an incline toward the cover of the forest. She would find a low-limbed tree and take cover in its branches and leaves—the only plan she could think to save herself. Her heart pounded as she struggled for breath, her gaze fixed on the trees.

The crush of trampled leaves grew louder, closer. She scrambled faster, clawing her fingers into the dirt and grabbing handfuls of grass. Brambles cut her feet and legs. *Fight!* The thought raced in rhythm with her breath. His panting curse and rapid steps forced her scream as a hand clenched her nightdress. Arria tripped, rolled onto her back and kicked his scarred face.

"*Canis*, bitch! Now you'll pay!" he growled and rubbed his jaw.

Freed from his hold, she sprang to her feet and dashed for the trees. Branches scraped her arms, but his iron hand gripped her neck. Arria cried out. The barbarian's arm snaked around her waist and yanked her back. With a grunt, he threw her over his shoulder.

"Let me go!" she yelled, pounding his back. "I'm a Roman envoy!"

The barbarian ignored the blows and laughed. "You're a wild one, but I will tame you."

Arria pummeled him and kicked her legs violently. He threw her face-down and her head slammed the ground, barely missing the edges of a sharp rock. Her lip split open and she tasted blood and dirt.

He dug his foot into her back, "How does *this* feel, *Roman envoy*?" he mocked.

A sharp pain shot through her spine. She groaned.

He grabbed a leather cord dangling from his belt, yanked back her arms and wrapped her wrists. Arria squirmed, but he flipped her over and ordered, "Lie still and I will make you my slave. Fight me and you'll feel my axe cut your throat!" The sun beating down on them, he put his hand to his belt and stood over her. His eyes locked on her fear and he smirked. Opening his breeches, he exposed himself, hard and erect. "Spread your legs and know a real man."

"You're no man," she spat, "You're an animal!"

He threw his head back and laughed. A swift and sudden hiss sliced the air and wiped the menace from his face. The barbarian froze, but his eyes widened. His arms began to shake, and a trickle of blood oozed from his mouth. A vacant stare filled his gaze as he dropped on his knees and fell forward. Arria rolled out of his path. A silver axe jutted out from between his shoulder blades.

Arria stared at the dead warrior and then around in wild confusion. Two long-haired barbarians stood a few paces away. They looked as hard and savage as the man who'd abducted her.

The taller one walked over and wrenched the axe from the dead man's back. "Don't be afraid, woman. We won't hurt you," he said easily in Latin. He knelt down and cut her bonds. His golden hair fluttered in the wind.

The second barbarian whose hair shined copper in the light moved beside him.

Bruised and fearful, Arria sat up. Slowly, she rose to her feet and brushed the blood and dirt from her mouth. The two long-haired warriors watched, axes in hand. In all the mayhem, she had lost her cloak, and was mortified to realize that blood and sweat had rendered her nightdress transparent. From the look in the golden-haired warrior's clear blue eyes, she might as well have been naked.

I am a Roman woman. I will not cower in front of these barbarians. She had woken into danger beyond her experience and almost become the victim of the dead man lying at her feet. She refused to surrender to exhaustion and fear. Arria bent her head as she fought back tears. She wiped her hand across her eyes and took a slow breath. "Thank you," she said, but despite her resolve, her voice shook.

"Woman, it is over." Her rescuer pulled off his cloak and handed it to Arria. "I am Garic. You have the courage of a Frank," he added.

Clearly Garic thought his name alone should reassure or impress her, so Arria nodded her thanks and wrapped the cloak firmly about her. "I have heard your women follow you into battle." She was pleased her voice was steady now.

"Yes, and die by our sides," Garic said. "We honor our women and ourselves by being buried beside them."

His companion added in a smug tone, "Unlike Roman men, who are afraid to be buried next to theirs."

"Do not jest,Vodamir," Garic said. "Now come, Roman lady, we will take you—"

"You will not take me anywhere until I know more about you." Arria pushed her tangled hair from her forehead and removed the grass clinging to her face. Summoning anger, she pointed to the dead man and demanded, "Why did Franks attack us? Rome is here seeking allies. We came in peace."

"Rome comes in peace?" Vodamir said in apparent astonishment, and Garic regarded him sternly as Arria glared.

"Excuse Vodamir, if you can," Garic told her. "I am First Counsel to my tribe of Salian Franks. People know us as Long-Hairs. Vodamir is my kin and tribesman." Garic smiled and suddenly looked less fierce. "We did not attack your camp. We're on our way to the Assembly of Warriors. That"— Garic pointed at the dead man— "is a Chamavi warrior from Ingobar's tribe. They are Franks as well, but hostile toward all, so I assume they attacked your camp." He bent, wiped his axe-blade on the corpse's leg and stuck the weapon in his belt.

"Why did they attack us?" Arria asked. "They were plainly outnumbered."

Garic held out his hand to her. "Ingobar's men attack to frighten and weaken their enemies—and to steal women. His Chamavi warriors are not our brothers."

Arria ignored his hand and stepped forward, only to trip over the cloak wrapped about her and fall against Garic's broad chest. Given the choice between falling or clutching Garic for support, she would have fallen, but he swiftly set her back on her feet. She'd forgotten she wore Garic's cloak and not her own, and he topped her by a full head. Oddly dizzy, she found herself staring up into Garic's eyes. Was that laughter or admiration glinting there? *And why do I care? Of course I don't...*

Vodamir barked at Garic in Frankish, then kicked the dead man lying at their feet and added in Latin, "Ingobar's men don't travel alone. We must go. I will get the Chamavi's horse for her."

Realizing that she and Garic stood so close she could see the slow rhythmic beat of blood beneath the sun-browned skin of his throat, Arria stiffly pushed away from him. She felt her face burn, and saw Garic's cheeks redden.

"My apologies," Garic said, "I must remember to be more gentle with a Roman lady." Vodamir rode up leading the dead man's horse and tossed Garic its reins. Garic caught them and turned back to Arria. "Let me help you mount."

"I probably ride better than you do, Long-Hair!" Arria snapped. "I can manage."

"As you wish," Garic replied unruffled and reached into a bag tied to his horse's saddle. He pulled out some bread and offered it to the horses, who greedily devoured the treat. Patting the black steed's neck, Garic handed her the reins. "Does my lady have a name?"

"Arria Felix, daughter of Senator Quintus Arrius Felix." She expected Garic to aid her onto the horse, but his firm grasp around her waist sent a tremor through her body as he lifted her effortlessly. Heat seemed to radiate from his hands as he swung her up. By the time Arria had settled herself in the saddle, she was flushed and out of breath. From the shocks she'd endured during the past hour, she told herself.

Garic looked up, amusement glinting in his handsome eyes. She turned the horse around and urged it to a trot, but looked over her shoulder. Both men rode behind her, grins on their faces.

"Take care, Lady Arria Felix. One rescue a day is enough." Garic warned.

She recklessly urged her unfamiliar mount into a canter. "You needn't worry, barbarian," she called over her shoulder. "On any given day, I can outride you!"

Garic laughed a hearty laugh and yelled back. "My lady, I will accept your challenge on any day you choose."

ASSEMBLY OF WARRIORS
GAUL: Luthgar's Camp

Gaul, land of rich pastures and grapes, forests and cool rivers, was in danger of being overrun by Huns. Garic, first counsel to his tribe of Salian Franks, loved this land. Roman rule was bitter enough to bear, but the prospect of a Hun master was intolerable. The Romans were anxious to create an alliance with the Franks. Gaul under Attila's control would threaten the Roman Empire. Emperor Valentinian had sent envoys to strike an alliance with the barbarians, and Garic knew Valentinian needed them to fight Attila.

This autumn day, the Assembly of Warriors was to meet. Garic entered the council chamber prepared for a verbal battle wrapped in the mantle of diplomacy. Tensions were high between the Franks and Romans, but Attila was converging on their land. He looked around and sought a seat among the Franks. Wooden planks creaked beneath his doeskin boots as he slid onto a bench facing a low burning brazier. The Romans, newly arrived from Cambria, sat across the center fire, facing them. Garic swiped a few long strands of hair behind his right ear and brushed his knuckles over his chin. He was lost in thought when he heard a woman's voice, cool like the waters where Freya, goddess of love, croons to her lover. Garic looked around. The Roman woman, Arria, the daughter of the respected Senator Quintus Felix, was among the Roman envoys and seated beside Tribune Drusus. She greeted a newly arrived representative on her left.

Intrigued, Garic stared. Arria was more striking than beautiful.

Her almond-shaped, sea green eyes shone. He watched as she conversed with her fellow envoy. An unconsciously seductive quality lived in her smile and direct gaze. Like many Roman women, she was shapely, with round breasts and curving hips. Captivated, Garic gazed at hands adorned with jeweled rings; and thick chestnut hair coiled in an intricate style bound with gold ribbons. Arria glanced in his direction. Their eyes met, then she looked away.

Garic's heart quickened and he envisioned her in his arms, imagined kissing her full soft lips. She whispered his name as his touch carried them to a place beyond circumstance, beyond time .... A servant addressed Garic, and the fantasy vanished like morning mist.

"First Counsel, may I bring you some refreshment? First Counsel?"

"*Ja*," Garic answered staring at Arria. Had she felt anything when she had looked at him? Anything at all?

"First Counsel?" the servant repeated and stood waiting.

Garic glanced toward the servant.

"What shall I bring you, my lord?"

"Mead," he replied tersely, gazing at Arria.

A sudden hand on his shoulder startled him. "Garic, how goes it?" Luthgar, chieftain of his tribe, interrupted his thoughts. "You seem transfixed. I hope I haven't disturbed your thoughts."

"I was considering our terms for discussion at today's forum," Garic lied. He watched as Luthgar sat beside him, his long black hair trailing the sides of his face.

"I understand your concern," Luthgar offered. "These damn Romans want all they can get and give little in return."

Garic's voice lowered. "Yes, and may *Wodan* be with us. The price we pay to keep this land could be costly. Attila is a great leader. With help from the Ostrogoths and Gepids, he will be a formidable force. We have no choice but to join with the Emperor Valentinian and his Master of the Soldiers, Aetius."

"What if we chose neutrality?" interjected Luthgar. His brown eyes held a speculative look. "Would not the Huns look upon that as a favor to them?"

Garic shifted in his seat and gave a sidelong glance in Arria's direction. She was looking at him. Their eyes locked and he saw a blush rise in her face. She turned toward Drusus.

Garic looked at Luthgar. "*Ja*, maybe so, but much depends on King Theodoric and his Visigoths. If Theodoric unites with Rome against the Huns, then I say we align with them. Theodoric tolerates the Romans and they him, but he will bow to no man and neither will his son Thorismund. We're small in relation to the Romans, but together we have a chance against the Huns. We know the Romans, know their ways. We've held our ground against them, and from them learned many things."

"King Meroveus honors Aetius. He will want the Franks and other tribes to support the general in battle," interjected Luthgar.

"Of course," Garic replied. "We are at peace with the Romans. This is good. But, what if the Huns were to win? Can Franks live under a worse tyrant?"

Luthgar stroked his beard. "As always, your counsel is sound. I'm in agreement. I will inform the Assembly of Warriors that it would be wiser to unite with the Romans than try to remain neutral. We would be crushed between Hun and Roman forces, killed and enslaved. As soon as we reach equitable terms with the Roman Council, I will order the preparations for battle."

Garic and Luthgar noticed that others were moving to their places. Luthgar leaned toward Garic and said, "It seems we'll soon begin. I will go and inform the rest that we're of one mind. If any of the noble warriors should differ in their opinion, we'll ask for a recess to confer."

"Oh, and Garic?" Luthgar smiled, then whispered, "Arria Quintia, the beauty who fascinates you, is betrothed to Drusus. Be careful, my friend."

The entry flap to the leather tent was lifted. From the other side of the partition, a girl servant announced that Garic, Counsel to

Luthgar, was requesting an audience with the honorable Lady Arria Felix. A slight trepidation hid itself beneath Arria's calm demeanor as she approved his entrance. Since arriving at the assembly, she had learned that all the nobles and tribesmen acknowledged her brave rescuer as second in command.

Garic stepped in. His black cloak, fastened with red garnet brooches, signified his authority. He bowed, then smiled. Blue eyes, like a pool in a primitive forest, met her gaze. High cheekbones flanked a long nose that reflected his Teutonic heritage and defined his ruggedly handsome face. His forehead proudly displayed the peak of his wheat-yellow hair, and his stubbled beard outlined a square jaw and a cleft chin. Arria noticed his full lips beneath a border of pale-gold hairs.

"Lady Arria, it has come to our attention that your voice is admired in Rome. Will you honor us this evening by singing for our tribes and the Roman regiment at the celebration of our peace accord?"

Arria hesitated. It was difficult to concentrate on his words. His handsomeness was distracting. And his lips. Kissing them .... Quickly, she dispelled the improper thought.

"Lady, will you accept our invitation?" He looked at her intently.

"Yes, First Counsel. I'd be honored," she answered slowly, but her heart raced.

Garic towered over her, making his amber tunic stitched with bold, black stars even more impressive. An animal hair shirt could not hide his muscular arms, and a sword hung from his fur belt. Like Luthgar his chief, he wore a gold amulet set with a golden bee, the emblem of the Frank king, Meroveus.

"Thank you, Lady Arria. I will..." Grinning slightly, he glanced briefly away, "*we will* anticipate this evening's festivities and the pleasure of your singing." Stepping toward her, Garic gently lifted her hand to his heart, then to his lips. With a nod, he moved past her out of the tent.

Arria sat down. Garic's manly scent still hung in the air and her senses tingled. His kiss lingered on her hand. Her thoughts reeled.

She must erase this barbarian from her mind. She was betrothed to Drusus, whose touch left her cold, but in time this might change. *The marriage is what father wants. It has been arranged.*

The crisp breeze embraced Arria as she stepped from the tent. She raised her eyes skyward. The moon smiled down like a silver disk set in a mosaic of stars. The burning torches throughout the camp shed an eerie illumination on the surroundings. Luthgar's enclave was different from Fort Cambria. A Roman fortress, Fort Cambria was square, structured and built to endure long periods of warfare. The barbarian dwellings were crudely made from logs and trees. This rustic camp was merely a meeting place for the Assembly of Warriors with opportunities for trade and entertainment.

Arria's manservant, Samuel, approached with the horses ready to escort her to the main lodge. Samuel handed her Syphax's reins.

"I must warm my voice. See that the accompanists are ready," Arria instructed Samuel as they mounted their horses.

"Upon our arrival, I will make the preparations, my lady."

"Sour notes will only offend the officers and chieftains."

"Impossible. The Roman elite applaud the beautiful voice of Arria Quintia."

"You are kind, but I am far from a senator's salon." Arria smiled at him and Samuel smiled back, his brown eyes warm. "My lady, I've never known you inferior in any matter, especially a performance," he replied and wrapped his cloak tighter.

Wisps of hair streaked her face as she fought them back and raised her hood. The wind carried pungent smells risen from the fires and animals in camp. Arria took a deep breath. It was *October*, the month of change and movement.

"Samuel, I wonder what the night will bring," Arria mused, while Syphax nickered calling for her attention. She ran her hand over her horse's mane.

"What do you hope for, my lady?"

"I'm not sure. I've never been in such a large camp. I feel caught up in the commotion of this assembly. All around are Romans, Franks, and the *foederati*. I know of them, but I never imagined so many German regiments fighting for the Roman army. *Foederati*—the word sounds strong. Don't you agree?"

"It does, my lady. Why do barbarians join these German regiments?"

"Money always entices or the desire to marry a Roman woman. Others, the *laeti*, are prisoners of Rome. They earn their freedom through military service. Some just prefer the Roman way of life. Do you remember the barbarian, Danicus, who spoke at the assembly?"

"The large man who resembles a Roman bear?" Samuel quipped.

Arria laughed girlishly. "Why do you call him a Roman bear?"

"He's a big barbarian with heavy brown hair, but dresses and acts like a Roman."

"Exactly. He prefers our style of living and is now a Roman. Most likely, he was able to convince his tribe to welcome Roman occupation and fight against the tribes who will never accept the Roman way. This assembly has made it clear that the northern tribesmen of the Alans, Franks, and Burgundians, along with the eastern Visigoths and Gepids realize that money and luxuries reside with the Roman way of life."

"Rome is mighty," Samuel said, "but the growing barbarian regiments in the military may be its downfall."

"Possibly," Arria answered, and pulled her cloak tighter.

Vodamir looked around the main lodge in the center of the Frank camp. This night, soldiers, tribesmen and women were gathered at long tables eating and drinking. The Romans had been hospitable enough to bring barrels of light red wine from central Italia and the deep red wines from the vineyards in Hispania. Tonight everyone was gathered to enjoy the festivities and to hear the Lady Arria sing.

Vodamir felt excited at the prospect of seeing Arria again. Taking a seat at a nearby table, he grabbed an empty cup and filled it with wine. Its sweet taste helped him recall the morning the Chamavi swooped down upon the Roman camp and took Arria hostage.

Fate intended that Garic and I rescue her from that Chamavi pig! Vodamir spat on the ground; he hated Ingobar's Chamavi. He often told Garic that even a dead warrior from Ingobar's camp was one too many. He wished to Wodan he had killed the last breathing one of them that day in the field. The Chamavi were aching to fight on the side of Attila. Called by Romans, "The Scourge of God," Attila was bent on destruction and conquest. Unfortunately for the Franks and Romans, they were in Attila's path.

A low hum began to spread across the room. He spied Garic conversing with a warrior but glancing at the door. Vodamir wondered what distracted Garic's attention and swung his gaze toward the entrance. In the doorway stood the woman he had rescued, transformed into a vision of beauty. *Is it Arria, or Sif, the love of Thor?* Vodamir shook his head, fearing the wine was too strong. He was definitely in the mood for some excitement.

Vodamir quietly approached Arria from behind. Golden twine wove through dark brown ringlets and a thin gold band encircled her brow. Accustomed to fair-haired women, this dark luster sprinkled with a hint of gold dust made his loins ache.

The manservant beside Arria looked at him with a steady eye. Arria's betrothed, Drusus, was nowhere in sight. *Just as well*, Vodamir calculated. He wanted time with Arria. Was she vain or haughty? He'd been taught that most Roman women were frivolous and spoiled. Was the Lady Arria the same?

With a seductive tone that could spin the head of most Frank girls, Vodamir spoke softly in her ear, "Will you be singing with one of your savior barbarians in mind?"

Arria turned and looked Vodamir straight in the eye.

"I doubt that, Noble Vodamir. You are a Frank noble, aren't you? Or am I in error? Should I be addressing you at all?"

"Well, my lady, the last time I looked, I was—very noble; the last time I saw you, my nobility helped save you."

"True enough, Noble Vodamir," Arria retorted, but a blush tinged her cheeks. "I welcome your company, and if I smile while singing, I may be thinking of you, in gratitude."

"Then I petition the mighty Thor that having saved your virtue, you'll save my heart and think of me."

Standing close to Arria, Vodamir was unaware of the impending threat approaching from behind until too late.

"*Barbarian*," Drusus confronted Vodamir. "It's not our custom to approach a lady of status without a formal introduction."

Vodamir faced Drusus. "Forgive me, Tribune. I'd ask you to honor me with an introduction, but the lady and I have already met in battle. I think comrades in arms need not follow such formalities," Vodamir glanced sideways at Arria as she stepped beside him.

"Surely you jest!" Drusus snapped in disbelief. "The Lady Arria has never fought a battle in her life!"

"With respect Tribune, I know a dead Chamavi warrior who might disagree." Vodamir gave Arria a flashing smile.

"My lord," Arria interrupted, "this is one of the Franks who saved my life. He came to wish me well before the performance. Certainly you can understand the valiant Vodamir inquiring about my well-being."

Drusus gave Vodamir a hard look. A sarcastic twitch found Vodamir's grin. Their eyes locked like dueling swords; each regarded the other in deadly silence.

"Your deed is appreciated," Drusus said tersely. "I trust now that you've spoken with my lady and reassured yourself about her well being, you'll join *your people* and enjoy her performance."

Vodamir clenched his hands and steeled his gaze.

On the other side of the council lodge, Garic tensed. That damned Vodamir was beside Arria charming her with his sly fox ways. Garic poured himself another glass of mead. *This woman is trouble and betrothed to that Roman snake, Drusus.*

Unable to control himself, Garic moved across the hall in his cousin's direction. Up ahead, he saw Drusus' blood red cloak moving through the crowd toward Arria. The frown on Drusus' face matched his black hair and alerted Garic. Drusus was not pleased. Garic sensed a volatile situation and circled the newly formed trio. Drusus now stood beside Vodamir. Hearing Arria refer to his cousin as "valiant" made Garic want to roar with laughter. The only valiant thing about Vodamir was between his legs, and he loved sharing his courage with as many damsels as possible. Garic must intervene for the sake of Arria, Vodamir, and the assembly.

Garic's unexpected arrival broke the tension. Arria gave Garic a grateful smile.

"Tribune Drusus. Hail and Welcome." Garic nodded and watched Drusus return the gesture. "I'm Garic, First Counsel to Chief Luthgar. We're honored to have you join our celebration. I see that you have met my cousin, Vodamir." Garic shot Vodamir a stern look. "Good fortune allowed us to rescue your lady's honor when your field camp came under attack."

"Thank you, Noble Garic," Arria added quickly. "I cannot imagine my circumstance if you both hadn't come along when you did."

Drusus regarded their words like a cat watching birds fly around their nest, and Garic was quick to notice. He knew to be wary of Drusus and his subtle ruthlessness.

"My Lady, Tribune Drusus, will you excuse us? Vodamir and I must meet our comrades." Garic wrapped his arm around his cousin whose eyes were still fixed on Drusus. "We no longer will keep you from the performance. Everyone awaits. Goodnight to you, Lady. Tribune." Garic looked directly at Arria and she nodded. "Come Cousin, Luthgar is waiting, and it's time for Lady Arria to sing."

Vodamir understood Garic's underlying message. He stepped free from Garic's grasp and bowed to Arria and gave Drusus a smirk. Vodamir bumped shoulders with Drusus as he walked away like a mountain ram fighting for dominance—and the female.

Drusus stood firm, a stiff smile on his lips, his look dark and foreboding.

Chapter Two

Nox
Night

ASSEMBLY OF WARRIORS
Luthgar's Great Hall

Luthgar, brother to King Meroveus' mother, and chief of his own tribe, escorted Arria to the front of the hall. A musician plucked the strings of a small harp. The lyre's soft tones mingled with a second musician's kithara. Arria turned and faced the crowd.

"Tonight, my friends," Luthgar announced, "the Lady Arria will sing several poetic songs about love and valor. Afterward, she will delight us with a German ballad taught to her by her late husband, Lucius Marcian." Luthgar turned to Arria and bowed.

At the front table, Garic sat next to Vodamir, both of them watching Arria. "Thor take me! She's a beauty," Vodamir's smooth voice proclaimed.

Garic silently agreed. It wasn't her subtle beauty that held him prisoner, but her sensuality. It had hit him harder than Vodamir's axe ever could, and this unnerved him. *She's a widow not an innocent girl. Perhaps she's a vixen, a complement to Vodamir's foxy nature.* The thought annoyed Garic, and he stirred uncomfortably.

Vodamir glanced at him and grimaced, "Cousin, sit still. A Valkyrie will sing, and yet you thrash about like a playful pup."

Garic gave him a disapproving look and mumbled a curse.

Vodamir laughed. "Isn't she remarkable! That day in the wood,

22

when we saw her from a distance. She ran like a deer with that Chamavi on her heels. My blood raced as we galloped to her rescue. Another Roman woman would've screamed in terror or begged for her life. Arria would die fighting than be any man's slave."

Garic turned his gaze toward Arria. His cousin admired fine horses, or a beautiful sword, but women were seldom venerated. "Yes, she is indeed remarkable," Garic whispered, his words lost in the surrounding crowd. Romans and barbarians, some with arms around women, huddled closer together. Foreign words, warm smiles and laughter resonated throughout the hall.

Vodamir prodded Garic. "Did you say something? Speak, so that I might hear you."

Garic continued a little louder. "We are fortunate. Such a woman in our presence and her contribution to our political affairs is immeasurable."

"*Hel*, queen of the underworld!" Vodamir shot back. "I wasn't thinking of Arria's diplomatic contributions. It's her lively spirit. And what she might contribute beneath the bed furs." Vodamir smirked and leaned closer. "Those green eyes holding me captive and her satisfied purr in my ear."

The coarse image offended Garic and he snapped, "Quiet Vodamir! She begins."

Arria scanned the room as her voice rose high and strong. All around her, torches blazed a bold amber as a breeze careened through rush and straw embedded in the roof's timbers. Fire from the great hearth cast a heavenly aura on her frame. Garic leaned forward, his impassioned eyes intent on her every movement.

Arria sang and looked into the audience. She glanced past the elegant Drusus and the courageous Vodamir, but sweetly met Garic's gaze and smiled.

Garic would never forget this moment. Her smile called him and charged him with fire. He knew now that she would be his no matter the cost. Arria was his destiny, and may all the gods and Drusus be damned!

The last note diminished, held and then was gone. The audience sighed. Arria smiled radiantly. Men and women clapped and cheered their approval as she curtsied and bowed her head. Drusus joined her, beaming with admiration. He pressed her hand to his lips in a lingering kiss, then he held it up to the crowd who stood in a final tribute. She smiled gratefully and bowed one last time.

When the accolades subsided, Arria sought to leave the hall. Samuel waited by the door, holding her cloak and kid gloves. Drusus escorted her to the servant and brusquely ordered, "Make haste! Return my lady to her tent before she catches a chill." Bending his lips to her ear, Drusus whispered, "I will come to you tonight if it pleases you, my love. I leave for Cambria, but I could stay."

Arria's cheeks burned. "It would please me, my lord, to have you come to me if we were wed, but as yet, we're not, and so my father... and I, would deem it only proper that I refuse you." Their eyes and lips inches apart, she continued in a firm but careful manner. "Surely, the honorable and brave Drusus can understand. The Lord our God teaches us restraint in the matters of our bodies and abandon in the matters of our hearts. I think you would choose the latter for the benefit of your soul and character. Would you not?"

Drusus was silent. Arria forced a weak grin.

His stony stare held only a moment; then, an enchanting smile filled his lips. "I would choose you, dearest Arria, to benefit all aspects of my life. If I must wait because it is your wish, then I am your servant when it comes to our love. I only pray that my wait is not *too* long. Arria, my body is yearning and my heart is full."

Ordering his servant to assist him with his cloak, Drusus added, "I leave for Fort Cambria within the hour. There are matters that require my attention. Return to the fort in the morning. I will anxiously await your arrival."

Arria lifted her hand to his kiss and walked into the night, unconvinced that his love was genuine, though his lust was clear.

Vodamir slapped Garic on the back at the close of Arria's performance, catapulting him from his dream. "Ha! What a voice—so powerful and yet as smooth as a Byzantine wine. Cousin, I will have this woman!"

"Has Loki stolen your brain?" Garic bristled. "Her betrothed, *the Senior Tribune of Cambria*, hovers around her like a stallion protecting his favorite mare."

Beneath his words, Garic felt the sting of hypocrisy. He wanted what Vodamir wanted and more. He wanted Arria's heart, but he must know hers. This seemed a desire beyond his grasp and one compounded by his reckless cousin. Garic was certain that Vodamir viewed Arria as a conquest and a way to taunt Drusus. It was a foolish game for Vodamir. Luthgar had warned Garic that Drusus was dangerous. He took what he wanted—by any means.

Vodamir smirked. "Drusus bleeds like any man. Come Cousin, a drink before we depart; a notion has struck me." He found them an empty table near the fire. "A heat burns within me and I itch for a challenge." Vodamir called a slave who brought them a flask. He quickly poured himself some wine. Without a breath, he drank it down. "Let's raise a cup to Arria. To her voice, beauty, and—love." Vodamir locked eyes with Garic. "And may the best man win!" A grin tugged the corner of his mouth as he filled their cups. He handed the wine to Garic who took it without hesitation.

Had Vodamir noticed his exchange with Arria while she sang? "Why do you push me, Cousin?"

"If the lady does not interest you or the wrath of Drusus is daunting, refuse," Vodamir dared, his cocky grin growing wider.

Garic gripped his cup tighter and restrained himself from turning the table. Now was the time and Thor's strength filled his voice, "To the Lady Arria!" he proclaimed. In one gulp, he downed his wine, rose and flung his cup into the hall's stone hearth, shattering the clay vessel to pieces. Vodamir sprang to his feet, the challenge vibrant in the glow of his features as he hurled his cup against the fireplace, shouting, "To Arria!" Shards flew in all directions.

Garic watched the fragments sprinkle the floor. *What will her love cost?* he wondered.

The hour was late. Men searched for places to sleep, while some played games of dice. Drunken laughter filled the camp. After forty days on the road and despite their discipline, the Roman soldiers welcomed some respite and the Franks and barbarians were willing to match them. Unruly and unsettled, drunken and sleepy soldiers from both sides roamed the camp, searching for a place to rest.

Arria left the hall deep in thought. She slipped on her riding gloves as she walked toward the corral. She wanted to clear her head. Drusus' proposal, Garic's smile, and Vodamir's defiance all seemed to blend and rain a storm upon her thoughts. Shadowed by the glow cast from a distant torch, Samuel met her with the horses. Arria placed her foot into Samuel's cradled hands to climb onto Syphax's saddle. A sudden wind and a cluster of field mice swept by Syphax's hooves, making him shy. Arria lost her grip and fell sideways. Samuel reached for her, but was knocked to the ground, Arria upon him.

Late-night reveler and Roman centurion, Tarvistus, happening upon slave and mistress, stopped to help Arria. Beside him his *optio*, Nepos, swayed on his feet, a burning torch in his hand.

His voice thickened by drink, Tarvistus slowly stammered, "Let mmme help you mmma lady." He wobbled and extended his hand, "Let your slave—that *dog*...pppay for his lack of attention."

Tarvistus helped Arria to her feet then turned and kicked Samuel as he rose to his knees. Samuel groaned, clutched his ribs and fell to the ground.

Arria screamed as Nepos joined his centurion and kicked the writhing Samuel from the right. "Stop! Stop, I command you!" Arria cried. Her protest ignored, Nepos pummeled Samuel several more times, stumbled and fell to the ground, dropping his torch. Syphax tossed his head up and bolted away. A frenzy mounted in Tarvistus and he redirected his assault. He grabbed Samuel's collar and punched his face.

A dark red stream oozed from Samuel's nose. The sight of her servant's blood horrified Arria, and driven by impulse, she jumped on the centurion's back. "Let go of him!" she cried, pounding her fist on his head and pulling his sweaty hair.

Tarvistus let go of Samuel, reached back and grabbed Arria's shoulders. Her cape came loose in his hands. Tarvistus cursed and tossed it to the side. "You ssstupid bitch, just trying to help," he blurted out.

Exposed to the night air and shaking, Arria stubbornly clung to the centurion's neck. She was shocked by her own actions, yet fearful to let go. Tarvistus clawed her arms and staggered in drunken confusion. He whirled about and shouted for help. From the darkness and shadows, a drunken soldier answered his centurion's call and joined the fracas. The soldier gripped Arria's waist and wrenched her backward.

Arria struggled for balance, but from the corner of her eye, she spied a flashing sweep—an arm. It shot through the dim light. The sound of the soldier's jaw cracking filled the air. His grip loosened, he fell to the ground. Arria watched as Luthgar knelt over his victim, striking him again and again.

Yanked from sleep by comrades, others roused from the commotion, barbarians and Romans trickled toward the assembly hall near the corral. The skirmish growing, a call-to-arms from both sides rang through the camp. Weapons given in trust and locked away, warriors and soldiers rammed head on, punching, kicking, and wrestling one another. Fists smashed noses, faces and jaws. Guttural sounds flew all around Arria, and the smell of blood and sweat made her vision blur.

Overwhelmed and weakened, her legs trembled, but a sudden, steady grip on her arm and Garic's voice from behind reassured her as she fell back into his arms. The stars floated above her as he hurried to a small, tent-shaped hut just beyond a line of trees and hidden from view. He laid her on a bed of straw.

Arria reached for his hand. "Samuel ... help him," she pleaded.

"Don't move and stay quiet. I will find your slave. You'll be safe here. We fight and I must go back," he whispered.

Arria closed her eyes. She felt the gentle touch of lips. Garic's strong hands and heated breath filled her senses, then—he was gone.

Garic returned to an all-out brawl. The call to arms had awakened most of the men. Half-dressed and naked fighters ran through the barbarian camp. Romans and barbarians, asleep earlier side-by-side, choked and grappled one another. One barbarian clutched his groin as his legionnaire opponent followed up with a fist to the back of the neck. A Roman soldier, head-butted in the stomach, fell to his knees and vomited his wine. A Roman lying beside him clawed at the hands choking him. Warriors and soldiers rolled on the ground covered in blood, dirt and excrement.

Vodamir had dragged Luthgar away from the young centurion to ensure that Luthgar's punches wouldn't destroy matters beyond repair. This fight could not afford any deaths.

Tarvistus approached Garic, and swung a feeble blow. Garic ducked and knocked Tarvistus flat on his back. Tarvistus lay moaning. One more fallen man on a heap of men. The few who were left standing staggered with fatigue. Some were Roman, but most were barbarian. Garic felt a hand touch his shoulder and swung about with a ready punch.

"It's me, Cousin!" Vodamir shouted. He rubbed his jaw with his right hand. There was a bloody cut above his eye and his shirt was torn to his navel. "Give me to Hel that ugly bitch of the underworld," he spat. "What just happened here? I thought Luthgar was going to kill that Roman ass."

Garic shook his head ruefully. "Nothing good can come from this. Drusus will be as wrathful as a wounded boar. Luthgar knows better, even under the influence of drink. He must have felt truly provoked to vent his rage."

"All will pay for this in some way," Vodamir replied, running his fingers through his coppery hair. Bending over, he grabbed a wine flask from the belt of a Roman soldier sprawled at his feet and took a long slow drink. Wiping his mouth with the back of his hand, he asked, "What started this anyway?"

"I am not sure, but it had something to do with Arria's slave. Go find him, quickly," Garic instructed Vodamir as he hoped to return to Arria alone. "Find Luthgar as well. Make sure he is alive and—Wodan help us—unhurt."

The sun was above the horizon. The thick sounds of groaning men filled the camp. Some retched over sprawled and unconscious bodies; others limped back to their tents.

Garic alone knew where Arria rested and this excited him. He knelt by her side and listened to her soft breathing. He gazed at her for a moment, then bent and kissed her. Arria stirred beneath his touch and her eyelids fluttered. Her right arm glided gently upwards and rested on his neck. Arria's lips responded with a fervor Garic never expected, nor could he resist. "Don't let go," he said huskily. "I want to hold you." His lips brushed Arria's ear as he spoke, making her powerfully aware of his accented speech. His words and touch moved her, and she began to cry.

"Why do you weep, woman? No harm will come to you—while I am with you."

"I was afraid, but anger came over me when I saw Samuel attacked. I couldn't let him be hurt ... or die. Is he alive?"

"I've sent Vodamir to find him. You are as Vodamir says, a woman warrior, a Valkyrie who will fight beside her man." Garic could barely control himself. He was exhausted, but lying beside her made him feel stronger. He knew they must return, but he couldn't pull himself away. Her arm around his neck, Arria blushed as he gazed into her eyes.

Garic continued. "Pray to your Christian God there are no deaths. Drusus will be as difficult in this matter as Luthgar."

Arria sighed. She brushed her fingers across one gold armlet, then across the soft blond stubble covering his jaw.

"Was I dreaming or did you kiss me?" she asked.

Garic caressed the corner of her smile with his thumb and smiled back. "Was I dreaming or did you kiss me? Or perhaps we both kissed, my lady," Garic moved closer, his lips inches from hers. "But dream or kiss, it was our destiny."

"Then kiss me again, so I am sure," she whispered in his ear.

Garic's ardent kiss found its haven, a place where pain washes away. Arria's fingers tangled themselves in his hair and he kissed her deeper. The spark between them was fierce, he knew he loved her. He wanted her by his side and in his bed. "Arria, do you want me?" he asked, his voice husky with desire. His fingers stroked her temple and he searched her eyes. "Tell me," he repeated softly, brushing his lips over hers, then kissing her again, hungry and urgent. "*Mellitula,* I must know."

"Why do you call me "little honey?" she asked softly.

"My heart names you," he replied and kissed her again. "Our path is dangerous, so I must hear it from your lips. Do you want me?" Intent on her answer, Garic failed to notice the approaching footsteps.

"Fool, stand up! Let go the betrothed of Drusus! You are mad and will surely condemn us to our deaths!" At the shelter's entrance and visibly fatigued, Luthgar, the Frank chieftain, shouted at Garic.

Vodamir, Garic's copper-haired, cocky cousin who only the night before had tangled with Drusus, stood frowning beside Luthgar. Behind Vodamir stood Samuel, her most loyal manservant. Garic rose and helped Arria to her feet. He placed his cloak around her shoulders and they stepped out. She rested for a moment on his arm and then stood tall with her chin raised. No one would make her feel what passed between them was wrong. But in the light of day, standing in the midst of their judgment, she doubted that loving Garic was possible. She saw Vodamir's blue eyes, sullen and dark. Luthgar's face shone with incredulity. And Samuel, beaten and bruised. She smiled at him and nodded, relieved that he was alive and not seriously hurt, but she did not speak a word.

Garic stepped forward and addressed the three men. "I will escort the Lady Arria back to the Roman fort. No harm will come to her. I will also inform Drusus of the night's events if he hasn't already heard."

Arria moved beside Garic. "I too will inform Drusus about the altercation, and I will praise Luthgar's warriors for my defense and rescue and the defense of Samuel."

"How will my lady explain the gallant Garic to her *betrothed*?" Vodamir's last word dripped with sarcasm.

Garic shot Vodamir a warning look. Vodamir blanched, but his gnawing envy was apparent. "What the Lady Arria does or says is not for us to question."

An impish smile spread across Vodamir's face that hinted his intent, "Since your arrival, my lady, life has taken an interesting turn of events. I look forward to the coming days and the pleasure of your company. Let it be known, I love a good gamble and a good ride. I am at your disposal."

"Noble Luthgar," Arria gathered herself and addressed the chief without looking at Vodamir. "Thank you for coming to my rescue. Please, do not worry. First Counsel Garic will escort me back to the fort in the company of Samuel. I assure you that although there may be some strain between our people, it will soon clear. Tribune Drusus' main concern is to build alliances. Attila is more of a threat to him than a drunken brawl. Besides, Roman soldiers are to blame for this fight."

Luthgar scowled, "Lady Arria, the day is upon us and your return, I am sure, is much anticipated. I was informed that a messenger awaits you in the council hall. Most of the soldiers involved in the fight have gone back to the fort. The few left behind have more serious wounds and will be moved when they are stronger. Please make haste. It's the wise thing to do."

"I agree," she replied and looked at Garic.

The bustling camp signaled they must hurry. Vodamir placed his hands on his hips and addressed Arria and Garic. His weary tone reflected the night's events. "I will gather the horses for the ride to Cambria. I think it best that I accompany you both back to the fort. The reckoning that awaits your return, Lady Arria, may be difficult. Drusus will not be pleased in this matter, and I will not leave my cousin to meet his wrath alone. Drusus will want answers. Garic, you will need a witness to this debacle and its outcome."

"Wisely spoken, Cousin," Garic agreed, glancing in Arria's direction. "How long before we must ride?" he asked, his tone wistful.

Vodamir read Garic's thoughts and answered, "We should leave as soon as possible."

Arria looked at both men and a dread swept over her. The edge of a vision gripped her. A Roman standard toppled over blood-soaked ground. She breathed deeply. These Franks were different from what she'd been taught. She felt embarrassed but rebellious; to defend a trusted friend seemed worth the price of humiliation.

Arria gazed at Garic. He was magnificent. Could she forget that he was a barbarian? A Frank noble he might be, but could they bridge the chasm between their worlds?

Luthgar, growing impatient, now spoke with authority, "Vodamir, ready the horses and supplies for your journey. Lady Arria, Garic will attend to any of your needs and provide you with some refreshment before your departure." Luthgar stepped directly in front of her. "Remember, the messenger from Cambria awaits you. If you'll excuse me the night has been long, and I must draft a letter to Senior Tribune Drusus and to Commander Lucinius explaining the situation." He bowed and turned to leave. He asked Garic to join him a few paces away for a last minute counsel.

Seizing the opportunity, Arria moved to Samuel's side. "Are you well?" she asked.

"I am hurt but alive," Samuel said. "I thank the God of my fathers for his protection and yours." He touched his ribs and winced.

Tears blurred Arria's lashes. "I cannot believe those men were so cruel," she said, fiercely. "It seems my attempt at rescue only created more trouble." Arria gazed at Samuel, his brown curls matted with blood. It was fortunate for Samuel that Luthgar and his warriors intervened. How this skirmish would be viewed by Drusus and resolved was another matter.

Samuel smiled at Arria reassuringly, "Don't blame yourself. Those soldiers were looking for an excuse to fight. Their drunkenness hardened them and clouded their vision."

"Even so," Arria replied, "it was cruel. And I will not have my servants attacked!"

"During our long journey, I've been honored by our conversations on matters of life and the Empire. Last night, you witnessed how men most often are, intolerant—barbaric." Arria noted the irony in Samuel's words. He added, softly, "Roman or barbarian, the capacity for cruelty lies chained in the heart of every man and woman. Whether we keep it prisoner or let it free is what defines us."

Arria nodded and drew her cloak tighter. For the first time, she viewed her own kind in a manner that reflected the attitudes of the Franks towards their conquerors. Exhausted and overwhelmed with emotion, tears ran down her cheeks.

Garic and Luthgar stood several paces from Arria and Samuel. They discussed Arria's return to Cambria and a plausible explanation for the brawl to Drusus. Garic noticed Luthgar's gaze move past his shoulder. He turned and watched the tender exchange between Arria and her slave. Garic looked briefly at Luthgar who shook his head in confusion, but Garic understood. He didn't need years with Arria to know her. Garic knew her by the way she spoke, her manner, and her eloquence at council. He knew her by the way she sang and what she sang, how she looked at him, touched and kissed him. He knew her by her strength and determination, her character. Arria's compassionate response to her servant only confirmed what he already understood; and in this instant, Garic's heart was forever hers, locked in loyalty and undying devotion, regardless of where the path would lead.

Chapter Three

Cui bono
Whom does it benefit?

FORT CAMBRIA

Marcus Lucinius occupied living quarters adjacent to the administrative headquarters in the center of the fort. This central location not only made his administrative center easily accessible, but it also provided him a layer of protection in the event the fort came under attack. He packed some final documents and scrolls in a large wooden chest as Drusus entered the library.

"Ah! Drusus, I'm glad you were able to make it back from the council meeting last night. How was the ride?" Lucinius closed the lid of the box and secured it with a metal pin.

"As well as could be expected, given the growing chill of these Gallic nights. It's the damn marsh grass that one has to be mindful of come dark. If a man ventures from the trail chances are he'll find himself in the midst of mud and water."

"Come sit and feel at ease. I have important news for you."

Drusus' eyes narrowed. Casually he sat and reclined in a posture that portrayed his sophistication.

Lucinius walked to the window overlooking the open courtyard. A table to his right held a bowl of pears. A loaf of bread sat beside a decanter of wine.

"Let me offer you some repast. What would you like?" Lucinius asked.

"Wine and one of those pears will be enough." Drusus answered.

Handing the fruit and drink to Drusus, Lucinius leaned back on the edge of the table and crossed his arms. "I expect you received the good news last night, otherwise you wouldn't be here. My hearty congratulations."

"The same to you, Governor Lucinius. That does have an appealing sound to it, don't you think?"

"I told you, Drusus, hard work and diligence provide opportunities and open doors, and I dare say one has just been opened for us both." They laughed and Lucinius continued, "but there are a few details that you should be apprised of now before my departure, hopefully in the next hour."

Taking a long, slow drink, Drusus calmly waited, relishing the thought that soon this portly, aging dignitary and ex-commander would be *out of his way*. Drusus found it difficult to conceal his excitement.

"It has come to Rome's attention that a party of Attila's border scouts have been seen close to Artesia," Lucinius said. "My superiors suggest that you solicit Luthgar's men to investigate this situation, seeing that these Franks know the terrain."

"I think I know two of Luthgar's men that I might engage in this matter." A sardonic grin tugged at the corner of his mouth. "You need not worry. Anything else?"

"Yes. The diplomatic seal is in that box on the shelf, and oh, there is one other matter; it regards my slave woman, Marcella. She's my gift to you. A token of my gratitude for your hard work as my senior tribune, and in recognition of your advancement to legate. It grieves me to give her up." Lucinius glanced away and drummed his fingers on the table's edge. "She's a slave-girl of remarkable abilities, but I think she'll serve her purpose better under your command."

Drusus smiled and replied, "Thank you."

Lucinius nodded, "You are welcome. Well, I think that addresses everything," he said resting his hands on his legs. "If you ever need anything from me don't hesitate to ask." He walked back to his desk, picked up some final papers, looked at Drusus and smiled. "As the new provincial governor, I'm sure, I will be able to help."

Drusus was silent for a moment, then he replied, "It has been an honor to serve you. Forgive me, but I have no token to offer you except my friendship." He lifted his glass in the air and said, "Salute. Live a long and healthy life."

Drusus' promotion came sooner than he anticipated, but was no real surprise. Before his departure for the council meeting at the barbarian camp, Lucinius had called him in to explain that changes might occur that would satisfy Drusus' desire for advancement. Ambition lived inside Drusus like a hunger. He had gone to Luthgar's camp focused on a positive result. He understood that an alliance with the Visigoths and the Franks was crucial. King Meroveus' traitorous brother and the Chamavi, Ostrogoths, and Gepids were aligning with Attila. If an agreement with barbarians sympathetic to Rome wasn't reached, Rome would suffer.

A consummate diplomat, Drusus cleverly negotiated and fraternized with these tribesmen; but secretly, he lacked respect for all barbarians. In his opinion, they were uncivilized, undisciplined, and untrustworthy. It was a twisted irony, he thought, that Imperial Rome believed it beneficial to civilize and pander to these tribes and their leaders. Drusus wondered what Rome must have been like when legions were pure and the old Republic was strong. A glorious time to live, he thought. Then strength and honor had meaning and power.

Aside from an occasional philosophical reflection about the glory of Rome, Drusus didn't care very much about who he dealt with, but how he dealt with them and how it would best serve his own interests. With the help of Arria and the other dignitaries, he had managed to forge an agreeable alliance with the Assembly of Warriors. The terms were set. Both sides wisely calculated that without the other, each was weak. But together, they were strong.

It was during Arria's performance at the Frank camp that a messenger arrived with the news of his promotion. Drusus had not confided his advancement to Arria. He thought it best to wait until she was within the safe and settled confines of the fort. He wished to tell her in private, to relish the look of surprise and awe that would surely come to her face on hearing of his good fortune, and hers as well. She would be a commander's wife, and he speculated that this idea alone might move her more quickly toward marriage. He felt confident that his elevation in status would win her heart. She would forget that horse soldier, Marcian, who left her widowed; she would have him, Drusus, legate and commander.

Drusus inhaled and scanned the view before him. He was the new master of the commander's luxurious quarters near the fort's center. The open courtyard, the heart of the house, nestled a small but elegant garden decked with lavender and wild hyssop. Even after a night's chill, their early morning perfumes rose from sprigged leaves and complemented the smell of fresh baked bread emanating from the kitchen. He loosed a hearty laugh. He was the commander of Cambria.

Having conducted the customary change of command before the legion, and seeing Lucinius off with ceremony, Drusus found relief in the warm bath of the *tepidarium* and pondered his good fortune. Things were going according to plan.

Drusus relished the water's heat rising around him. His gaze sought the mirror set on a small easel near the pool's edge. Drusus delighted in his image. His black wavy hair and handsome face lent him power and enforced his status as a soldier and daunting adversary.

A smug grin reflected his thoughts, and he reached for the oil flask lying on the tiles. The *arybolla* was partially filled with a sandalwood scented oil. Drusus called to his new slave. She was the gift from Lucinius. "Marcella, rub this oil on my body, while the water is still hot," he ordered. His falcon eyes watched her move toward him. Drops of water beaded off his chest and arms and dripped into the water as he sat upright.

"Will my master want me to scrape the oil and dirt from his skin with the *strigil*, or would he prefer my nails?" Marcella asked

37

seductively as she descended the marbled stairs one long, bare leg after the other. Her tunic reached only to her hips. She swayed into the pool with the blunt blade and moved to Drusus' side. Taking the flask from his hands and laying both items on the edge of the bath, she circled the new commander as his gaze followed her. "Master, I am now yours, and I care only to please you in whichever way you desire." Trailing her fingers over the surface of the water, she smiled beguilingly. "I've been schooled in the art of pleasure. My many gifts and talents are for the pleasing."

Enlivened by Marcella's seductive manner, Drusus uttered a lusty laugh. "I've no doubt of your ability to please. Lucinius *was* reluctant to give you up."

"His wife was jealous of me," Marcella coyly replied. She moved close to him and slid her fingers gently up and down his arm. "How may I serve you, Commander Drusus?" her dark brown eyes and sultry tone invited.

Drusus raised strands of her cat-black hair in his fingers and grabbed her waist, pulling her to him. He kissed her with a pent-up hunger and she dug her nails into his shoulders in a way that roused him even more. His second kiss bit and bruised her lips with fervor. Marcella rubbed her palms firm and slow over the hollows of his buttocks. Drusus crushed her against his chest and swept a kiss across her shoulder and up her neck. "Mmm, *Carissima*, you taste as sweet as a Tuscian peach," he whispered lustily. Marcella raised her eyes to him. Her gaze was sharp with desire not subdued as he'd expected. *She understands me.* Drusus trembled. The sensation that she was his counterpart ripped through him, but a warning seized him. Arria's face flashed in his mind.

His instincts urged caution. The parting between Marcella and Lucinius was possibly rooted in trouble and trouble is what she might bring, but a good servant was more than a comfort, she was a haven. Arria seemed adamant in following propriety. Despite her appeal, Arria's love-making might prove as boring as warm milk in a ceramic bowl. He was a man who preferred a hot, spiced wine. Marcella seemed like a woman who would give her master her all, just for the pleasure of pleasing him and herself, of course. Trouble or not, Marcella looked worth the risk.

A servant entering from an adjacent alcove poured water on the heated tiles. Steam rolled across the pool and clouded Drusus' view. He wiped the mist from his face and opened his eyes. Marcella's tunic clung to her curves. A mysterious aura, hinting ancient origins radiated from her.

"Where do you come from my exotic beauty?" Drusus asked, fondling her firm breasts proudly sculpted by the wet cloth. Brazenly, he rubbed her small orbs. They hardened and rose beneath the sodden linen.

Marcella rested her hands on his shoulders, savoring his touch and answered, "I was born to an Egyptian priestess who served Isis and was abandoned by her lover, my father, a Roman soldier. At twelve, I was sent as a gift to the Emperor Valentinian by the Alexandrian elders. They made gifts of children, animals, goods and spices for his favor." A pensive glance filled her eyes, but then faded.

Drusus observed Marcella's brief departure into thought and ripped the tunic from her body. He marveled. Her small waist and ample breasts, wet with steam, charged him with desire. "You are a rare beauty," he drawled, his lust rising.

Marcella smiled seductively, then cajoled, "Turn please and brace your arms against the edge of the pool, Master. I will rub your strong, handsome body with oil to cleanse you, and by my expert and devoted attention, bring you certain ... satisfaction."

Bending to kiss her one more time, Drusus obediently turned his back to her and braced his arms against the tiled rim. She took the oil from the pool's edge and poured some into her palm, brought her hands together, then to his back. She ran her hands sensually over his skin, massaging downward until like vipers hungry for conquest, they snaked over his pelvic bones. Drusus winced and licked his lips. Marcella's hands burned with heat and slid toward his loins. He stiffened and caught his breath. His head fell back.

Marcella pressed her lips against his ear, "When I am finished, you will move to the cool rinse bath, totally refreshed and relaxed," she said with confidence.

A laugh burst from his throat. "Whatever you wish, Marcella. This morning, I am your slave—but only for the morning. This afternoon, I will be your master once again—do you understand?"

Marcella purred her agreement. Grasping his phallus, her hand moved rhythmically to his pulse. Oil and friction pushed over him. Drusus groaned. Marcella rested her head on his sweated back and quickened the tempo as his legs tensed and spasms racked his body.

"Come, my handsome soldier," she cooed, kissing his shoulder blades. His hoarse cry signaled his passionate and ardent satisfaction.

Marcella reached for the arybolla and poured new oil in her hand. She gently massaged his shoulders. "With me, you will always find delight."

His head bent, his arms braced weakly on the edge of the pool, Drusus sought a calming breath. "What will you have me do now, Marcella?" he asked submissively. "Should I move to the cool bath?"

"Am I still your master, Drusus?" she asked, her tone daring.

"For now, yes. What would you have me do, Carissima?"

The water swirled slightly below her thighs as she stepped closer. Placing her hands on his hips, she leaned in and commanded, "Turn Drusus and kneel. Now, please me."

Chapter Four

De Mortuis Nil Nisis Bonum
Let Nothing But Good Be Said Of The Dead

THE ROAD TO FORT CAMBRIA

Arria felt safe and comfortable riding between Garic and Vodamir. Their skills gave them the ability to meet any challenge. Even Samuel found a new friendship with the least likely of the pair, Vodamir. Arria was amazed when Samuel prompted his horse beside the wild and unruly warrior, and asked Vodamir when he first learned to throw the *francisca*, his battle axe. Pride radiated in Vodamir's face and he fell behind Arria in order to converse with her servant.

Garic whispered to Arria, "Samuel's beating has roused his interest in the skills of self-defense."

"I hope he'll benefit from Vodamir's tutelage. Although a slave, he should know how to defend his life," Arria replied with conviction.

"Good men die because they lack the ability to protect themselves," Garic agreed. Sounds of thunder rumbled in the distance and he turned his face toward the clouds rolling across the gray sky. "The rain will come soon. We must find shelter."

Arria gazed at Garic's profile as he checked the sky for signs of lightning. His long blond hair, freshly washed from his river bath near Luthgar's camp, was tied back with a leather string. A woven black tunic over his doeskin leggings made him appear every inch the noble barbarian. She suddenly felt compelled and asked gently, "Garic, what is it like to kill a man?" Garic locked eyes with her.

41

Arria sensed that she breached a secret place. He shifted the reins in his hands as if they needed some adjustment, but then, he turned toward Arria. "Do you really want to know?" he asked, a heavy-hearted warning in his voice.

Arria hesitated. Should she take back her question? His question hinted she might venture there—if she were brave. "Yes, I would hear. Will you tell me?"

"The first time—is the hardest," Garic said, searching thoughtfully for words. "I was fifteen years, but already strong. Small bands of Visigoths were raiding our farms. I was one of the young warriors ordered to drive them off. Elation filled me; yet, a tension gnawed my stomach. I wondered if it would be the time of my first blood."

Garic gazed at the trail ahead. The shallow and muddied crevices were imprinted with reminders that animals and travelers trod this rustic road. Like the path, his trust was marked with apprehension. Sharing this dark part of himself required a separate courage. Arria knew how to reach inside of him, but could she tolerate what he would reveal? For some inexplicable reason, he still wanted her to know.

"We tracked them to a grove. Vodamir was with me. He growled they were near because he could smell them. I told him, 'Be silent, man. You're only smelling yourself!' As we laughed, our enemies attacked. They screamed and bore down on us with their axes raised. One red-haired Visigoth raced in full fury toward me with a blood-curdling cry. He saw my fear and came in for the kill. I stood transfixed, my feet rooted to the ground.

Behind me, Vodamir braced for his own attacker and screamed at me, 'Lift your axe!' and I tried, but my arms felt like tree limbs weighed down by heavy snow. My legs trembled as the Visigoth drew closer. Then, on my right flank, I heard Luthgar's sudden and strong voice shout, 'Lift your axe or perish! Lift your axe—now!' And I obeyed. I lifted my axe, stepped to my aggressor's right and crouched. I sliced his middle with the blade of my axe. The Visigoth sank to one knee and fell forward, a whispered curse on his lips. I rose and stood over him. His eyes stared at the sky."

Thunder rolled and rumbled from the west like anxious warriors readying for battle. The horses raised their heads and their ears twitched nervously.

With a melancholy grin, Garic turned to Arria. "I believe I felt his spirit rise toward Valhalla, where the gods meet the fallen warriors. In those seconds, I realized if I didn't fight, I would follow him on his journey. I quickly rejoined Vodamir and Luthgar who were occupied with three remaining Visigoths and we slashed our way to the wood. We fought fiercely and ran the remaining Visigoths off." Garic paused, "I was born a warrior that day."

Arria looked at him intently.

He cleared his throat and continued, "While Luthgar and the others collected weapons from the dead men, I walked deep into the woods and retched, my guts turned inside out. The Visigoth's final breath and empty eyes left my heart numb. I think, one day, it may be my life rising to Vahalla."

Garic patted his horse's mane. "In little time, I matured as a fighter. Strong warriors kill with force and fierceness. It keeps them alive. A warrior seldom welcomes death; and yet, he hears death's whisper in every skirmish and every battle.

Bravery siezed him and he continued. "A few times, I've dreamt about battle and death. I am wounded. My body trembles from the cold. I sense if I open my eyes, I will begin the warrior's journey to Valhalla. I struggle for escape, but I'm drawn upward. My eyes open. An apparition, perhaps a Valkyrie, floats above me. It feels pure, sacred. Then, I awake."

"Your dream speaks of your strength," Arria said. "I believe guardians in the next world watch over us in this world."

Garic smiled. "Maybe so. Warriors live to fight, but Franks believe that the spirits and gods surround us. We can only ask that they stand for and not against us."

Lightening flashed on the horizon, and Garic's stallion tossed its head.

"Who longs for death?" Arria interjected, "Did the warriors killed by your hand want to die?"

Garic frowned. A warrior's life wasn't easily explained, especially to a Roman woman. Yet, he felt compelled to speak. If given the chance, he would bring Arria into his life. Straddled between two worlds, both violent and unpredictable, they would encounter many obstacles.

"The Franks are a wild and strong people," Garic answered. "We hate our enemies and they hate us. These enemies would steal our land and enslave us. For this reason alone, we fight." Garic leaned into Arria. From their saddles, their legs brushed and Garic rested his hand on her hair, lightly cupping her head. "Look at me," he said, "I am not a murderer. I protect and defend, and for this I risk my life. Does that answer your question?"

Arria nodded. He moved his hand to the rear horn of her saddle and she rested her hand gently on his arm. "If I sounded impertinent, my lord, forgive me. I shouldn't ask such a question of a warrior. I was driven by my curiosity and not my good sense."

"Everything about you is good and your curiosity is what appeals to me. If you find my life offensive it's because my world is untamed."

Dogs barked in the distance, interrupting their silence. Garic quietly said, "*Mellitula*, listen to me, a man changes inside when he kills. He changes because he knows he must. He changes in order to live and survive. Most soldiers accept this and push it away somewhere deep inside of them. They harden themselves."

Garic reached and placed another fallen curl behind her ear. "I have a question for you," he said. "A question you never answered."

His presence was strongly upon her again, and she had no telling what he would ask, but at the same time she intuitively knew.

"Knowing what I have done and how I live, tell me Arria—will you have me?"

Arria looked at him. Desire and fear mixed and overwhelmed her. The two emotions ran together at full speed, coursing through her and clouding her mind. Without a word, she kicked Syphax and broke into a gallop traveling towards the sound of the dogs and away from Garic's powerful presence.

Startled by the sudden movement ahead of them, Vodamir and Samuel watched the galloping horse. They glanced at each other, then Garic. He stared after Arria, discontent shadowed in his face. Vodamir seized the opportunity and pulled his horse from the line. Rain stabbed his face, but he only welcomed them as he pursued Arria down the trail. Steadily he gained on Syphax. Arria glanced back and saw Vodamir's advance, but to his surprise she lashed her horse faster. It was provocation enough. The race was on and he would win, even if it cost every breath in his body and his horse. Arria was the prize. This was his chance, and he basked in the challenge.

Tree branches hung low over the trail. Up ahead, the wood broke into a wide clearing, where he would gain ground. Lightness on her well-bred stallion gave Arria an edge. But his battle-toughened horse and knowledge of the trail enabled maneuver and recovery from unexpected ruts and obstacles. Arria burst into the meadow first. Vodamir followed just two horse lengths behind. He grinned as her cape whipped in the wind, and her hair flew like a battle flag on a stormy day. His cheek brushed his horse's mane as he drew beside her.

Arria glanced over her shoulder and cried out, then urged her horse faster. Syphax tried to please his mistress, but Vodamir's horse was swift. An expert horseman, Vodamir lunged and gripped Syphax's reins and gradually brought him to a stop. "Leave him, I say! I command you Vodamir! Let go!" Arria yelled and slapped at his arms.

Vodamir, surprised by her response, shouted, "Have you gone mad, woman?"

Rain fell violently upon them as Arria, gasping for breath and totally drenched, dismounted and found Vodamir right beside her. Before she could recover her equilibrium, he swept her up and carried her to a natural shelter of smaller trees and bushes. He placed her on her feet and clung to her. His hands cupped her face. Arria's tears mingled with the rain as he placed a slow burning kiss on her lips. Vodamir's hips pressed hard and firm against her chilled, wet body. Arria pushed him away. "No, Vodamir. This isn't right."

"Why?" he responded adamantly. "Because of Drusus or my cousin? You're like me, Arria. Wild and free. You just don't know—not fully, but you feel it when you look at me. Admit it."

"It's not right ... *between us.*"

Vodamir pulled her close to him. "Is it right between you and Garic? Tell me!" he demanded.

A sudden clamor of hooves and the thudding of splashing water alerted them to the presence of another. Vodamir and Arria watched as Garic jumped from his horse, equally drenched. With a fierce look and an angry growl, he grabbed Vodamir and yelled, "What do you think you're doing?"

"Nothing that the lady doesn't want," Vodamir smugly answered in Frankish.

Garic punched Vodamir, and Arria yelled out in protest. Vodamir fell on the ground but did not rise. He rubbed his jaw.

"Stop it!" Arria screamed. "This is nonsense. Stop it right now, you're acting like—*barbarians!*" she cried, her hands clenched at her sides.

Arria's words rang in the wet hollow. Garic standing with tightened fists, lowered them. Placing his hands on his hips, he looked at Arria and roared with laughter. Then he helped Vodamir to his feet.

Clothes saturated and bodies chilled, the traveling party of lady, slave, warriors and soldiers made their way to an abandoned cottage known to Vodamir a few miles off the main trail. Arria was thankful as it loomed in the distance wedged between dusk and earth. She anticipated the men would hunt for game to settle their empty stomachs, a comforting thought. Soon she would wrap herself in one of the fur blankets Garic and Vodamir carried with them.

Layers of mist encircled the empty cottage as their horses cut through the airy shroud and halted in front of the wooden door. Garic dismounted and went inside. He returned shortly and announced the cottage contained enough wood to build a fire. The Roman soldiers, accompanying the Lady Arria, did not dispute when Garic decided they would hunt in pairs for small game and swiftly. They relied on Garic's knowledge of the terrain and needed to change their clothes and warm themselves before nightfall. Garic enlisted Samuel's help as well, and tossed him a javelin.

Samuel looked uncertain.

"Throw it straight and aim for the heart," Garic said.

The optio heading up the escort party asked, "Who will guard the lady Arria?"

"She will guard herself." Arria's voice informed from behind them and they watched as she turned on her heel and marched towards the cottage and through the door.

Garic smiled briefly, but ordered, "Go now." And swiftly they dispersed each in his own direction.

Welcomed by the blazing fire Garic built upon their arrival, Arria's toes extended toward the warmth of the fire, while her soft, leather shoes lay drying close to the heat. Her hair combed and changed into a pale-blue Frankish dress she purchased in the camp, she leaned back and gazed into the flames. Arria watched yellow and blue tips dance upon the blaze. When the creaking door broke her spell, she looked up and gasped. A man's gray silhouette stood in the doorway. Arria recognized Vodamir as he stepped in and chuckled softly.

With three dead rabbits held high and an impish grin on his face, he boasted, "Who is the hunter in this group, Arria? You will eat well." He walked into the room like a victor and laid the rabbits by her very warm and exposed feet. He squatted and tickled her right sole with triumph and laughed.

Arria quickly dropped her hem over her feet and snapped, "Vodamir, your impropriety is unbecoming. This is not the way a noble should tend a Roman lady and dignitary."

47

"It's the way long-hairs treat their women."

"I am not your woman!"

"You could be. Or perhaps you prefer my cousin, Garic," Vodamir added slyly.

Arria frowned, while Vodamir grinned.

Vodamir stood and removed his wet shirt, exposing strong muscular arms and a sunburst tattoo, its blue rays reaching toward his collar bone.

Arria slid herself farther down the bench and asked him, "What does your tattoo signify?"

"The eighth month, the time of full sun. The Romans call it *Augustus*. I was born and became a warrior in that month. My patron god is Frey, the god of sunshine and fertility," another grin captured the corners of his lips.

He was very bold and sure of himself, Arria thought, but she couldn't help admiring his playful manner. It was obvious, Vodamir was trouble.

Vodamir stepped toward her. His body exuded a masculine vitality and she watched as his strong hands moved to the waist strap of his breeches. Slowly he began to untie it. Arria caught her breath.

"Don't worry my flower, I won't compromise your gentility nor my honor." He chuckled and sauntered toward a corner of the room. "But I suggest you turn around. I must shed these wet clothes before I take ill."

Arria turned her back, and heard the door open. She glanced over her shoulder. Samuel and Garic entered.

Garic froze. "Is my lady all right?" he asked, immediately.

Arria's eyes reassured him.

Garic barked, "Vodamir! Have you killed any game?"

"Naturally, Cousin. Look beside the Lady Arria's feet." Vodamir said, in dry breeches and donning a fresh tunic.

Garic's wrinkled brow relaxed as he set two rabbits and a few small birds on the crude table beside the bench. "If you're in such a hurry for food and warmth then clean these animals while Samuel and I change into dry garments."

The voices of the Roman soldiers announced their arrival as they marched through the door carrying their kill.

Arria decided it best to step outside so the men might change. She would welcome a few minutes alone. So many men around her was overpowering, but she reminded herself that she was in Gaul for a purpose. She had come to the assembly as Valentinian's envoy to the Franks. Rome needed their support. There was also the 'delicate matter' the emperor had requested she handle when the time was right. Yet, what did she desire? A new beginning, a challenge and adventure, they all called to her. And love? She was betrothed to Drusus, but Garic possessed her heart. She pushed these thoughts aside. She needed to breathe, rest.

Daylight just about gone, Arria found a tree stump in the clearing and sat down. Infinite stars speckled the night sky, while she absorbed their magnificent beauty. The cottage door opened and an amber glow pierced the shadowy darkness then disappeared. She watched Garic come towards her guided by the rising moonlight. Her heart raced; he made her feel this way.

He stopped before her and extended his hand, "Come Arria, the night is brisk and the meat will soon be cooked."

"The sky is breathtaking and gives me peace. Will you sit here a moment with me?"

"Rise and let me sit," Garic said, his tone firm.

"Will I sit at your feet?" Arria retorted, rising suddenly.

Garic laughed and grabbed her to him. "Your Roman temper can be quick and fiesty. I meant you for my lap. My body will protect you from the breeze and keep you warm." He seated her across his knees, and cradling her face in his hands, he kissed her. His tongue parted her lips and caressed hers with long, smooth thrusts. Arria responded to his touch and kissed him deeply.

"Love me, Arria," he murmured fiercely.

"This is madness!" she protested, and jumped up. "When I am near you, I forget who we are. Tomorrow we will arrive in Cambria where Drusus waits. If he suspects that we are intimate, he will kill you, of this I am sure."

"Do you think he can?" Garic gruffly replied and stood. He reached his hand to her, "I will fight him. But you must answer the question, I've asked more than once. You cannot ride away from me now."

Arria accepted his hand and rose. "After my husband Marcian's death, I thought I'd never love again, not even Drusus. Yet, when you're by my side, I feel alive and protected, but I am not free. If you were to die at my expense, I would perish or fade away. Let us part now, before our love deepens. Does that answer you?"

"Arria, you are my destiny, and Drusus cannot scare me away. I will fight to be with you, even if it takes years," Garic said.

"Drusus will want to wed come June. My father expects it. My world is different. I am an obedient daughter to both father and Rome."

Garic reached for her palm and slowly traced the lines with his finger. "When I heard your voice at council, and saw you once more, I knew that if it were possible you would be mine. Tell me you want a life with Drusus and I will protect you, but I will never touch you again. Do you want him? I must know."

Arria shook her head, "No, but a Roman betrothal is a serious matter. I see no peaceful way out. Drusus will never release me."

"I understand your fear, but my feelings are true. Tonight, my heart pounds with joy," he said shyly, touching the hair fallen loose from her ribbon, "but my happiest moment will come when we are free to lie in one another's arms."

Arria rested her head against Garic's shoulder. "For me as well, but as the counsel for your people, you know there cannot be discord between the Romans and Franks—not with Attila so close. If I commit to you, can I be free from Drusus without bloodshed?"

"I will think of a way."

Arria sighed and covered his lips with her fingertips, "*We* will think of a way."

Light shot from the cabin door, interrupting the moment. Vodamir

50

stood in the doorway shadowed by the glow behind him. His whistle signaled food was ready. He stood for a minute and peered into the night; then he went inside.

Arria reached down and claimed the slender gold chain that rested around her neck. A cross hung from the links and was decorated with three vertical pearls set in the middle of the stem. Straddling the pearls were two gold Greek letters.

"What do these letters mean, Arria?"

"They are the Greek letters Alpha and Omega, the beginning and the end, eternity."

"Like our love," Garic replied.

She smiled. "This cross was a gift from my father. Tonight, it's my pledge to you. No matter what happens, you are in my heart and thoughts. Let no one see this token, especially Drusus." Arria placed the gold necklace in his palm, folded his fingers over it and kissed his hand. "Tell me the word for warrior in your language," she said.

"*Krieger*," he answered.

"Garic, you are my *krieger*. Any messages you receive with this title will be from me." Arria kissed him, cherishing their embrace. She believed his word was true; he would never leave her. Live without him she might, but he would live in her heart. In the bright moonlight, Arria reached for a fallen twig. On the bare earth, she wrote *Semper,* always._

Garic kissed her one last time. "On my word, I will never leave you."

"I know," she answered, trembling slightly, moved by his words. Together they walked into the cabin filled with the aroma of roasted rabbit and the faces of the men turned their way.

Chapter Five

Infra dignitatem
Beneath one's dignity

THE MARKETPLACE
Fort Cambria

Cambria's marketplace teemed with merchant stalls, soldiers with money to spend, and tradesman offering services. Potters, blacksmiths, cobblers, cloth makers, glass blowers and metal workers of fine weapons as well as taverns and brothels all provided the necessary sustenance required for frontier life. Riding toward the center of this small village, Arria gazed at buildings that lined stone block streets. Striped and colored awnings projected from the walls of the buildings over market stalls, providing shade from the sun. On the far side of the western wall, small houses built for the "unofficial" families of legionnaires nestled between a few shops and play areas for the children. It was unfair, Arria thought, that active duty soldiers were denied the right to marry. Even if Rome did not recognize these marriages, the people did.

"Arria." Garic reined his horse closer. Their arrival meant their time together was limited. "Will Drusus be with Commander Lucinius?"

Arria gave him a heartfelt smile that he returned. "Yes, it's customary for the first tribune to assist the legate commander with new arrivals of a diplomatic or political nature."

Garic grew pensive. "My heart will stand strong as metal and the love that burns within me will remain hidden, but speak with

Vodamir. He cannot betray his admiration for you to Drusus."

Vodamir sensed the seriousness of their conversation and moved his horse closer. "Cousin and lady, is this conversation private?" His eyes spoke mischief and his smile dazzled.

Arria couldn't help notice his devil's grin. "Vodamir, take care when we see Drusus today. Do nothing to incur his wrath. When Drusus is angry, he listens to no one. I might not be able to intercede."

"Lady Arria, your green eyes sparkle, even though you scold. They are the most beautiful I've ever seen in a woman of warm complexion," Vodamir drawled playfully.

Forgetting her warning, Arria smiled sweetly. "And in women of a fairer complexion, you've seen as equal a beauty, I'm sure."

Vodamir grinned but his tone was sincere, "In my eyes, no greater beauty exists than you—my lady."

"Stop it, Vodamir!" Garic snapped. "Be serious, man. An angry or jealous Drusus means trouble for us, if you aren't wise."

"I am wise in the observation of my Lady Arria's eyes, and I am very serious," he snapped back, then lapsed into Frankish. "Jealousy doesn't suit you, Cousin. Perhaps you don't care for how I entertain the lady's attention and speak to the betrothed of *Drusus*, but she seems willing to engage me. Besides, I can make her laugh."

"My lords, please," Arria interjected, sensing their discord, but not understanding the words that passed between them. "This is not the time nor place for such disagreement. We are almost there. Let us enter on good terms with each other," she ended calmly.

The crisp *October* breeze mingled with the afternoon sun, making the atmosphere pleasant as the riders approached the heart of the market square. Samuel rode to Arria's side and pointed out an impending slave auction. Without a word, she broke from their rank and rode to where horses were tethered, dismounted Syphax, then handed the reins to an attendant.

Alarmed by her sudden departure, Garic followed while the others stopped to watch the lady and the noble, as well as the preparations for the auction. Garic swung down from his horse and pulled Arria aside, "What are you doing? Shouldn't we report to the fort commander, Lucinius?"

"He can wait. I am in need of a personal attendant, and one of more mature years than the girls assigned to the envoys. There might be a woman here that I can buy and possibly save from a life of cruel servitude."

"A wise idea," Garic answered. "A woman attendant might move unnoticed through a household easier than Samuel, and we will need someone we can trust." Garic turned and looked in the direction of her slave. "Let Samuel purchase your attendant. You need not draw attention to yourself."

Samuel worked his way to the front of the crowd followed by Arria and Garic. Those gathering formed a semicircle around a wooden stage as a gruff looking auctioneer climbed the steps and announced that the sale would soon begin. To the left of the platform men, women, and children stared toward the crowd from large iron cages.

In a smaller pen, they spied a woman and a boy huddled together. The young woman rested her cheek on the boy's curly, brown hair and held his hand. Drawn to this tragic pose, Arria moved closer for a better view. The woman's eyes passed over her to linger on Samuel's face. She smiled.

Samuel looked at Arria and she nodded. He stepped up to the iron bars and said in Latin, "What are your names?"

The boy answered, "Why do you want to know?"

"This woman—can she speak Latin?"

The boy eyed Samuel suspiciously, "If she can?"

"She might become the attendant to the Lady Arria Felix, the daughter of the Roman senator, Quintus Felix."

"She can speak a little," the boy said quickly. "This is Karas, my mother. I am Angelus." The boy whispered into the ear of the sandy-haired woman.

Angelus and his mother approached the bars. She spoke rapidly to her son.

"My mistress speaks Latin, not Greek," Samuel objected, understanding a little of what Karas had said. He glanced at Arria who continued to study Karas.

"I ... can ... speak, yes," Karas said in a slow and thickly accented Latin. To Angelus, she said, "Ask him, please."

With the look of determination in his brown eyes Angelus said, "Would your lady buy the two of us? We would work very hard."

"How old is your mother, boy?"

"Twenty-six years, sir."

"And you?"

"I am almost ten," he said "so I can do a man's work. I'm strong and don't tire. I eat and sleep little. We would work day and night for the great lady. Please sir, ask her." Angelus drew close to his mother. "My mother ... she is all I have. *Please*, sir."

Touched by the boy's words, Arria reached through the bars. Karas seized her hand to kiss it.

"It appears you are buying two servants." Garic said, standing behind Arria.

Arria withdrew her hand and turned to Garic. "You are right. How could I part these two?"

"You couldn't. Your heart wouldn't let you." Garic grinned. "Besides, Samuel seems taken with them as well. Buy the pair."

"I will!" Arria felt a thrill of joy as she wrapped her cloak tighter against the breeze. "Samuel could never refuse a woman and her child, and neither could I."

A glance passed between them as Garic secretly took her hand and held it in his strong but tender grip while feigning a protective stance as her escort.

A bell rang three times at the front of the stage. The dealers began to shout that the bidding would begin and lined the slaves for sale. Inspired by purpose, Arria and Garic followed Samuel through the crowd to a second row facing the center of the platform.

Samuel shifted nervously beside Arria. "My lady, the hour has grown late. What about Drusus ...."

A final peal of the auction bell signaled the bidders make ready.

"Not now, Samuel," Arria whispered. "There is time enough. Drusus will wait."

"As you wish, my lady," he said, his eyes riveted on Karas and her son.

The first lot for bidding was a set of twin girls from Dalmatia. Girls just past puberty were considered valuable slaves. Eager buyers were willing to pay a premium price.

Samuel informed Arria that Castor, a Greek ex-pirate, was the auctioneer. The girls cried as Castor approached them, his whip in hand. With the leather handle, he flicked their shoddy cloaks from their naked bodies, leaving them huddled and shivering in the biting air. Castor grinned and fondled their breasts to heighten their appeal. He pushed them toward the edge of the platform. Castor tapped the girls under their jaws to raise their faces to the crowd. His coarse Latin demanded, "Who has seventy-five silver *denarii* for these beauties?"

"Seventy-five!" a merchant waved his hand.

"Seventy-seven *denarii*," yelled a dark burly man, who leered at the girls, licking his lips.

Arria glared at the last bidder. It was clear why he wanted the girls.

"I will give you eighty-five," called the strong voice of a man dressed as a baker. Beside him stood a woman and child.

Arria prayed the baker and his family would win the twins, and they did.

Groups of slaves and individuals crossed the platform over the next hour. To Arria's anguish, one family was separated. Cries from the children and parents brought tears to her eyes.

After this sale, Castor announced a short break. The crowd drifted off, searching for wine, fruit, and roasted chestnuts. Samuel went to the cage where Karas and Angelus waited. Vodamir appeared with a newly purchased horn filled with mead, but on Garic's direction left to procure lodgings at the local inn.

Garic asked Arria. "Does my lady require any refreshment?"

"No, my lord, but your thoughtfulness is appreciated. My appetite craves only to purchase those slaves."

Garic's blue gaze penetrated her heart. "May all your desires be fullfilled, Arria, now and later."

"It will be so, my love," she whispered.

Criers ran through the market proclaiming the auction was on. Arria watched Samuel hurrying through the crowd to join her and Garic.

Samuel whispered to Arria, "Karas and Angelus will be sold as a couple. The starting bid is high.

"For me to bid is inappropriate," Arria told him, "so you will speak upon my signal. Are you ready?" Samuel nodded.

Barbarian warriors from Pannonia went to a farmer. From their expressions, they appeared glad to escape the arena. Next, Castor called for Karas and Angelus.

They mounted the platform wearing only thin cloaks and placards with their names and skills. Karas' lean frame stood four to five inches taller than Arria.

Castor pointed his whip at Karas, "Who will start the bidding for this mother and son of many abilities?" He ripped the worn fabric from Karas' body.

A shiver shook Samuel. "The humiliation she suffers is more than I can bear," he hissed. Garic's hand on Samuel's shoulder cautioned him against action.

Castor moved on to Angelus. With his whip's handle, Castor prodded the boy to turn, while announcing that manhood would make him strong and pleasing to the eye.

Pitch complete, he barked, "Who will offer forty *denarii* for the pair?"

Arria nodded to Samuel who raised his hand, "Fifty!" A gasp rippled through the crowd.

Castor grinned. "We have fifty. Do we have fifty-five?"

"Fifty-five!"

The curious crowd shifted their direction toward the newest bidder, the leering man who had wanted the twins. Arria caught her breath and Garic cursed.

The crowd whispered that he was a foreman from a nearby farm as he moved closer to the platform. Karas cringed. Angelus' eyes pleaded with Samuel.

"Never!" Arria spat, and tapped Samuel's arm.

"Sixty *denarii*," Samuel called.

Garic leaned toward Arria and whispered, "How far will you go?"

"Until I win," she replied.

"Will anyone pay sixty-five?" Castor crooned with delight. It was obvious to all that this bidding war excited him. The mother's natural beauty and the boy's handsome innocence shone in the sun beating down on them.

A barbarian in the crowd shouted, "Sixty-seven!"

"Sixty-eight *denarii!*" was the immediate counter from the foreman.

"Seventy!" Samuel yelled, when Arria prodded his back.

Shaking his head, the barbarian walked off. He was out.

The burly foreman raised his hand, "Seventy-five!" he countered, glancing toward Arria with a pompous smirk.

Her adversary's arrogance shot fire down Arria's spine, and she shouted, "Eighty-five *denarii*, and—one gold *solidus*!"

The crowd fell silent. *Oh, what have I done*, she thought and looked around. All eyes were upon her. By adding the gold *solidus*, she had raised the value another twenty-five *denarii*.

Castor queried, "Will anyone top this offer?" No one answered. "Done!" he crowed.

Almost hopping with joy, Castor unchained both slaves and led them before Arria. "My lady, may these slaves bring you the satisfaction that your purchase has brought me." He dipped his head.

"I expect they will," Arria told him. I will send my servant with the money. Where can he find you?"

"*I* will see the dealer is paid," a commanding voice declared. Arria turned toward the sound. Seated on his black stallion, Drusus led a troop of soldiers. His brass helmet and chest corselet gleamed in the last rays of the sun.

"My ... my lord," Arria stammered, "what are you doing here?"

"I might ask you the same, lady? I was informed that you arrived at midday. Yet, I find you at a slave auction. Too long in the company of barbarians has caused you to act like one. Have you lost your manners?"

"Drusus," Garic interjected. Drusus raised an eyebrow to Garic's informal address, but Garic continued. "Please do not hold the lady responsible. I urged her to buy the attendant she needed before continuing on to the fort. I offer apologies to you and to Cambria's commander."

Drusus threw back his head and laughed, "Nobles and my beautiful lady, you've been so busy *shopping* it seems that you haven't heard."

"Heard what, my lord?" Arria asked.

"I *am* Cambria's commander."

Arria glanced at Garic. In that moment, they kissed good-bye.

Chapter Six

Divide et impera
Divide and rule

THE MARKETPLACE
Fort Cambria

C ome Arria, gather your belongings, while I have one of my men fetch your horse," Drusus commanded from his mount. Arria stole a glance toward Garic who wisely took his leave into the crowd along with Vodamir and Samuel; but as quickly, she swung her gaze back to Drusus and acknowledged his demand with a nod. "My lord, I have my belongings. To which do you refer?"

"Your slaves, of course," Drusus answered impatiently. "The barbarians, do they carry any of your things?"

"Yes, in fact they do," Arria replied stiffly. "I will collect them, and Syphax. He responds best to me. If you will, my lord, arrange my payment to Castor the dealer for the woman and boy." Arria handed Drusus a pouch. "The money will be safer in your possession."

"Arria, whatever possessed you to buy both woman and child? Do you need all this help? I have plenty of slaves to assist you. In fact, I recently acquired a slave girl from Lucinius who could have been your attendant."

"I prefer choosing the woman who will assist me. This Greek woman, Karas, is exactly what I require."

Drusus' eyes narrowed. "From what I observed, it seemed your servant, Samuel, was quite influential in procuring these slaves."

"Samuel knows what I value, and he obeys without question,"

Arria answered, matter-of-factly.

"Nonetheless, take care about whom you trust. Avoid a common friendship with those barbarians as well. Negotiations or not, they are primitive and uncivilized, even though they call themselves *duces* and nobles. Their blood is only royal in their world, not ours. Please *Carissima*, don't forget this." Pensive for a moment, Drusus added, "And the boy, your new slave woman's child? What do you need from him?"

"I miss the presence of children in my life. They bring me joy."

"I can bring you joy, Arria, and children."

Arria suppressed a shudder. She wondered what joys she would experience locked in his possessive embrace. His arrogant nature would most likely experience all the *joy* for himself.

"*Carissima*, have you no response?"

Carissima, fell so easily from his lips. Arria knew he shared this endearment easily with other women who crossed his privileged life; apparently, she was no different. Was she really a match for his ambitious plans? With a reluctant confidence, she answered, "My lord, I am struck by your devotion and desire to please me. Come the month of *Junius*, we will wed and discover the joy that awaits us." She flashed Drusus a pretty smile and continued, "I will join you shortly. I must collect my *belongings*, and invite Nobles Garic and Vodamir as our guests for dinner this evening. This will allow for discussion, concerning the necessary preparations to ready our defenses against Attila."

"Yes, Arria. There will be discussions." Drusus replied, his look grown stern.

Eager to find Garic, Arria clutched her cloak around her and casually scanned the crowd.

"In fact, the first discussion concerns a fight that took place at Luthgar's camp. My centurion, Tarvistus, brought me a complaint and reported that drunken barbarians attacked them and dragged you into the brawl as well."

"My lord, may we discuss this later when explanations can be made?" Arria pulled her hood over her head and gathered up her skirt, "I will meet you by the auction platform."

"Very well, Arria." Drusus chuckled, amused by her assertive stance. He ran a lustful gaze down her skirt clutched in her hands. Her slender leg showed between her ankle boot and hemline. "Don't be late. I am eager to return. It draws close to the twelfth hour, and another Cambrian sunset." Drusus signaled the small detachment of men posted behind him, and headed his horse in the direction of Castor, the slave dealer.

The crowd of people dispersed as the last slave was led from the platform. A final glance at Drusus caused Arria concern. She hurried to find Garic and Vodamir. Even a moment alone with Garic would be precious. She spied him among the horses in a paddock beside the stable and went to him. "Our time is short. Are we alone? Where is Vodamir?"

"Drusus puts him in a foul mood. He went to the tavern for a cup of mead."

"And Samuel?"

"Samuel is with the woman and child still held by Castor. The dealer won't release them until he is paid."

Garic pulled Arria's saddlebag from his horse and placed it on hers. Arria moved beside him.

"The wind carries your lavendar perfume and entices," Garic said, facing her. "One day, I will bring you oil scented with rose petals, and I will be the one who caresses you with its fragrance." He smiled and gathered up the sleeve of his woolen shirt. He pulled the gold armlet engraved with royal bees from his bicep and held it in his hands. "I am not certain I can pretend ... you mean nothing to me. Today, for awhile, I'd forgotten about Drusus. Those moments were robbed from me when I heard his voice."

"My love," Arria whispered, gazing into Garic's deep blue eyes. "Anguish twists inside of me as well, but caution must guide our actions."

Garic winced. "How is it that I am First Counsel, when you are the one who speaks wisely."

Arria felt herself blush, but held Garic's gaze. "*Krieger*, your passion makes my loyalty stronger. We *will* be together one day. Do not let go of this dream."

Garic stepped closer and with a quick glance around, he raised the armlet between them. "*Mellitula*, this band symbolizes my heritage. I am a long-hair, a Frank noble. We are a proud and loyal people. On the blood of my ancestors, I vow that one day, we will marry. Keep this safe. If we are separated, know that my love rests on the wings of these golden bees. Always carry this close."

From his belt, he pulled his knife and on the inside of the band, he scratched the word *Semper*, for always. Returning his knife to its sheath, he closed Arria's fingers over the circle of gold and brushed her cheek. "Do I dare kiss you one more time?"

Arria sighed, "We cannot risk it, but instead, close your eyes."

Garic obeyed.

"I am kissing you now. Do you feel our lips touching?" she asked.

"I do. And you are in my arms, as well," Garic answered, his stance strong and his face tranquil.

"Don't forget this kiss, and neither will I," Arria whispered.

The sun almost down, Arria knew Drusus would look for her if she didn't arrive shortly. Drusus waited for no one.

Garic opened his eyes and gazed at her with an intensity that caused Arria to tremble. Quietly she said, "Leave me now and fetch Vodamir. I must go for Samuel and our new slaves. Remember to carry my cross close to your heart, and your armlet I will carry near to mine."

"I am always with you, *Mellitula*," Garic held her hands in his and bowing in the event they were being watched, he placed a passionate kiss on her fingers. Stepping back, he turned and walked towards the inn. Arria brushed her fingers across her lips. Sudden tears filled the corners of her eyes. *Is my love walking away and out of my life?* she wondered.

FORT CAMBRIA

Arria was surprised to find the atrium so attractive and pleasing. When she first heard of the Cambrian fort and the journey she would make, she envisioned Spartan and primitive accommodations. She did not expect Drusus' household to be warm and inviting.

Drusus, leading the way for his guests and betrothed, removed his helmet and cloak and handed it to a slave girl just arrived at his side.

Arria removed and handed her cloak to the girl introduced to all as Marcella. Marcella folded Arria's cloak over her arm and went to take the small satchel that Arria held tightly.

"There is no need for you to take this, Marcella, I will carry it myself."

"I would not burden your arms with the weight of this bag, my lady."

Arria stared at Marcella and answered, "It's no burden. Lead me to my room."

"As you wish, my lady," Marcella answered, her feline eyes expressionless.

Arria climbed to the second floor, and entered the room prepared for her under Drusus' supervision. The windows held broad blue shutters painted down the center with a spiral of pink and red roses, blooming from thorny stems. Drusus knew she loved roses, Arria mused, and thought her sharp and sweet like the flowers she grew. This choice was no accident, and she accepted the humor in his subtle message.

Marcella moved through the room and lit the oil lamps that sat on marble pedestals and flanked the sides of the heater for light and additional warmth. Arria sat on the bed and fell into the soft down pillows. She closed her eyes. It felt divine to be finally at Cambria.

"This room is wonderful," Arria commented happily.

"My lord decorated it just for you. He remembered that you love roses," Marcella said.

Arria smiled. She had been right about the roses, but a sudden thought occurred to her and she asked Marcella, "My lord, Drusus, shared his observation with you?"

"He did," Marcella replied, her slight grin harboring the hint of a secret.

Arria looked keenly at Marcella. There was an unusual quality of power and assurance about her that caused Arria to tense. She felt wary. Sitting up, Arria looked with apprehension toward her satchel. Delighted and taken by the room's beauty, she had dropped it after entering. Now it lay open on the floor, her wooden box peeking from its rim. Arria rose quickly and reached for the bag. At the same time, Marcella scooped it up. Surprised by Arria's action, Marcella dropped the satchel. The box fell to the floor and cracked open. Garic's golden armlet wobbled across the tiles.

"I am sorry, Lady Arria. Let me get this for you," Marcella said quickly.

"No, don't!" Arria cried with impatience, unable to stop her.

Marcella looked curiously at the gold armlet already in her hand, and then at Arria.

From where she stood, Arria could see the word *Semper* etched on the band.

Marcella looked closely at the band, but Arria quickly grabbed her talisman.

"This was my mother's," Arria said. "It's very private and special to me."

"Oh, I see," Marcella answered with a knowing smile. "Is there anything I can get you, my lady?"

"Yes," Arria replied. "Send my slave woman, Karas, to me that I might dress for the evening meal."

"At once, my lady," Marcella bowed her head and walked toward the door, but at the entrance, she stopped and turned, "My lady?"

"Yes, what is it?"

"Was your mother a beekeeper or a lover of bees?"

Arria replied coldly, "Both. Now fetch my slave woman."

"Yes, mistress," Marcella answered, a glimmer of triumph in her eyes.

Arria sat on the bed after Marcella's departure and gazed at the band. *How could I have been so careless?* Footsteps in the hallway alerted her, and she quickly placed the armlet in the small box, secured the lid, and placed it under the down-filled mattress.

Karas entered and smiled. "Lady Arria, you want I should help you?" she asked.

"Yes, Karas," Arria smiled and pointed to her bags. "I will need my white linen tunic, and my lavender *stola.*"

Karas looked confused, but proceeded to open the bags and remove her mistress' garments.

Arria showed Karas her array of Roman dresses that tied just above the waist and pronounced the word, "*Stola.*"

Karas nodded her understanding and arranged Arria's clothes in the wardrobe and chest.

Handing Karas the green barbarian style dress, Arria noticed Karas' side glances toward the door. Following her gaze, Arria spied wisps of chestnut brown hair peeking past the door frame.

"Boy, come here," Arria commanded.

Angelus stepped around and stood in the entrance. "I am sorry, Lady Arria, but I want to help my mother."

"Well then, you may go with her to the baths. Make sure all is ready for my arrival. I would like verbena scented oil for my skin and rosewater for my hair. I would also like a strigil that is not too dull or sharp to scrape the oil from my skin. Can you and your mother see to this?"

"Oh, yes, lady!" Angelus replied, happily.

"Karas, I will only need a fresh tunic to wear from the bath to the room. I will dress here. Now go. Hurry, I am very hungry and the hour grows late. Oh! Angelus, where is Samuel?"

"He's with the barbarian lords in the bathhouse helping them to bathe and dress for dinner."

Arria was amazed how Samuel had taken to the two Frank nobles.

These long-hairs possessed a power that reached further than she ever expected.

"Lady Arria?" Angelus ventured.

"Yes, Angelus."

"Thank you for buying the two of us. We will always be grateful and loyal to you."

"Lady, our ... hearts serve you, always," Karas added, putting her arm around Angelus. Tears welled in her eyes, but she smiled at the same time.

Arria felt her own tears, but quickly said, "Go now. Make the bath ready for me, and tell Samuel to stay close to the barbarians and to keep a watchful eye."

"These Romans live a life filled with comforts," Vodamir sighed, refusing a slave's help and drying himself, while Samuel stood by holding his clean clothes.

"It will be the ruin of them," Garic responded as he finished putting on his boots. "They've allowed themselves to get soft. Their men don't even want to fight to protect their land. They hire foreigners to protect their interests because they prefer to stay at home."

Fully dressed and waiting, Vodamir answered, "This may be true, but at moments like this, I don't mind taking advantage of their hospitality, even if it's from this snake, Drusus. I feel like a new man."

"You will feel even better after we dine, but remember, we still have to deal with Drusus and the fight at the camp. I hope all goes smoothly." Garic buckled a dress belt over his tunic and stood straight.

"I hope you're right," Vodamir said. "If we have to fight alongside the Romans, it would benefit us to be on civil terms, rather than harbor animosity towards them."

Upon their arrival, Drusus rose from behind his desk. He directed the long-hair nobles toward several chairs nestled comfortably around the fire. The centurion, Tarvistus, already in attendance and leader of the Romans involved in the brawl, perched on a nearby couch, his helmet in hand.

Vodamir sat quietly next to Garic. He seemed willing to let his cousin handle this affair. After all, Garic was the ambassador for their tribe. Drusus surmised Vodamir acted as added protection.

"First Counsel Garic," Drusus said sternly as he returned to his seat, "the letter of explanation from Luthgar is sufficient, but this incident involving Lady Arria does warrant some concern."

"That's to be expected, Commander Drusus," Garic replied with some caution. He glanced at Tarvistus, who sat with a sour look on his face. "It's a delicate matter, but considering the importance of our alliance, it's essential that there be a harmony between our soldiers. Luthgar, my chief, has explained the situation completely and with honesty. If you have doubts, I feel confident that the Lady Arria will support our contention."

"She already has," Drusus replied, picking up the stylus from his desk and rolling it between his fingers. Looking at the centurion in front of him, he said, "Tarvistus, this letter claims that you and several of your men, in a drunken rage, fell upon and beat the slave, Samuel. Consequently, the Lady Arria was attacked when she tried to help her servant. Is this an accurate account of what happened?"

"No, Commander," Tarvistus replied shaking his head adamantly. "I saw the Lady Arria on the ground with the slave trying to defile your lady."

"How much did you have to drink, Tarvistus?" Drusus asked bluntly and gave him a penetrating look.

"Quite a bit, but not enough to be so mistaken, sir."

"Not enough to be so mistaken, you say, and yet, you *mistook* the Lady Arria for a man, is that not correct?"

Sweat gathering at the top of his brow, Tarvistus paused before he answered. His eyes projected a wariness. "I felt someone jump me from behind, but I couldn't see."

Drusus gently tapped the stylus on the desk and gave Tarvistus a doubtful look.

"I... I... I could never mistake the Lady Arria for a man," Tarvistus stammered.

"Unless of course, you were very drunk," interjected Drusus.

Tarvistus glanced sideways at Garic, then said reluctantly, "Yes, Commander."

"Yes, Commander, what?"

"Yes, Commander, I must have been very drunk," Tarvistus said slowly, as if he were reciting a lesson, "and unfortunately, I mistook the Lady Arria for a man—I mean an attacker, a *Frank* attacking me, and I tried to protect myself." Visibly distressed, Tarvistus paled.

"I hardly think you had to protect yourself against the fragile Lady Arria and her weak slave, Samuel, which leads me to believe that you were very drunk indeed." Drusus paused and stared sternly at Tarvistus. "I will grant you clemency only once, but you must apologize to the Lady Arria, and to First Counsel Garic. He will bring your apology to his leader, Luthgar."

"Yes, commander." Turning to Garic, Tarvistus rose and crossed his arm across his chest, his hand in a fist, the Roman salute of respect. He gave a slight nod and said, "My deepest apologies to Chief Luthgar, and his soldiers, and to you, First Counsel Garic." His face somber, but his cheeks flushed, Tarvistus turned to Drusus and nodded to him as well.

"You may go," Drusus said. "Find the Lady Arria at once. Apologize to her, and remember, you are not to harbor any ill feelings against our new allies, the Franks. They will be your brothers on the battlefield. Now, go!" Drusus ordered, waving the centurion away.

Tarvistus stood at attention, saluted and barked, "Strength and Honor." His face red as the cloak draped from his shoulders, he turned on his heel and walked briskly from the room.

Drusus turned to Garic, trying to hide his contempt for the Franks. "I think this should resolve this mishap. I was sorry to hear that the Lady Arria was involved. She could have been severely injured." Drusus avoided looking at Vodamir. He disliked the barbarian, especially since the celebration at the barbarian camp. Drusus found the familiarity Vodamir expressed with Arria disgusting. This barbarian needed watching, or better yet, a challenging mission from which he might not return.

"Commander Drusus, my cousin and I would fight to the death to protect the Lady Arria, your betrothed," Garic spoke the last word softly.

Caught in suspicious thoughts about Vodamir, Drusus barely noticed the quiet sadness in Garic's tone. "In any case, it's over and settled," Drusus replied, his attention returned to Garic.

An older manservant quietly entered the room and approached Drusus. "Commander, your guests await you in the dining room."

Drusus nodded and turned toward Garic and Vodamir. "Please excuse me, I must welcome everyone. I hope you enjoy the meal this evening, and the entertainment." Smiling with the reserved poise of a diplomat, Drusus instructed the servant to escort the two nobles to the dining room.

Arria stood at the arched entrance. The dining room sparkled with golden warmth. A long, dark wooden table held burning candles and swags of pine branches mixed with wild herbs and berries. Large platters heaped with fruit, nuts and cheeses graced the table to welcome the guests, while servants paraded past her carrying steaming dishes of mussels, boiled eggs and Lucanian sausages. Lively discussion filled the room and the soft sounds of music echoed in the background. Drusus was known for his hospitality and his good taste. For the Romans living in Cambria, an invitation to an evening hosted by the fort's legate was an honor and recognition of their social status within the Cambrian community. The mood of the diners was relaxed and congenial; their laughter and chatter added to the ambiance that greeted Arria as she stepped into the room.

Arria had arrived later than she hoped, but she dutifully joined the women and made her greetings. In a nonchalant manner, she looked for Garic. Taller than most men, he stood out in a white, short-sleeved shirt beneath a dark-blue tunic over deerskin breeches. A brown leather belt, encrusted with garnets, was tied at his waist, and his gold amulet with the Merovingian royal bee hung from his neck. His other gold armlet shown above his bicep.

Arria drank in every detail. She loved looking at Garic and listening to him talk. His voice was deep and soothing, and his accent lent a charisma to his words. As Garic finished relating to Drusus and his officers the difficulty in organizing the tribes, one of the officers said something humorous and all the men laughed. Garic, caught in this laughter, inadvertently placed his left hand above his right elbow and touched his armlet.

Arria focused on Garic's gold band etched with bees and recalled her encounter with Marcella. Horrified, she stared as the slave girl served Garic and Vodamir.

Garic's armband caught Marcella's eye as she rested a plate of fruit in front of him.

"What do you look at girl?" Garic questioned.

"It's nothing my lord, just ... your band is so beautiful. Those bees, do they have meaning?" Marcella asked, her manner unassuming.

"They are the talisman of our tribe and King Meroveus. I keep bees on my farm near the upper Somme river, not far from the sea."

"The bee is a symbol of loyalty and love, yes?" Marcella responded, looking him in the eye.

Such bold conversation from a slave surprised Garic, but nonetheless he answered, "The queen bee is the one loved and served; the rest are her soldiers who live only to provide for their mistress." Intrigued by her demeanor, he asked, "Where do you come from, Marcella?" Garic had noted that Drusus often called Marcella to his side. His cup raised for her to fill, he'd watch her intensely. She served modestly, but caught the attention of every man there.

"I came to Rome as a young girl from Egypt. Like you my lord, I am a stranger and subject of the Roman world."

A drunken Roman, holding a wine cup wove toward a couch and stumbled into Marcella. Figs from a second plate she held toppled into Garic's lap.

Garic pulled back in surprise and began to retrieve the fruit.

"My lord, please let me. I was careless," Marcella purred. As she gingerly collected the fruit in his lap, very gently, her hand caressed his groin. Garic's manhood hardened. Marcella smiled beguilingly as she removed the final fig and moved away from him.

"Marcella!" Drusus called sternly from across the table, "Get more wine!"

Marcella brought her master his wine, but not before she looked pointedly at Arria.

Garic swallowed his wine and met Arria's waiting eyes. He blushed. He had not seen her enter, having been in conversation with the men and then Marcella. He gazed at Arria embarrassed, but tenderness filled his heart. He slid his fingers over his gold armlet, clasped the band and smiled at her.

Arria politely bowed her head toward Garic, yet dangerous thoughts filled her mind. His blond hair spilled over his shoulders, and his white blond stubble hugged his weathered skin. Garic was truly handsome, but his embarrassed look caused her to wonder. She'd watched him down his drink in haste. Arria looked from Garic to Marcella. What had Marcella said to cause Garic's loss of composure? And the armlet? Had Marcella recognized it as the same one she claimed was her mother's? Arria decided to warn Garic and moved toward him on the pretense of engaging him in diplomatic conversation. She was stopped by Drusus in a festive mood, having had plenty to drink.

"Ah! Arria, when did you join us?" Drusus said, grabbing her hand.

"A short while ago. I was greeting the ladies, and now I would welcome the Franks and see to their comfort," Arria replied calmly.

His voice slow and thick, Drusus said, "Arria, has my comfort no meaning for you? Would you leave your betrothed until last?"

"Drusus, your comfort is everything to me and that is why I save it for the last, so that I might give you my full attention."

"Well then, sing for me, Carissima," Drusus emphatically entreated.

"I've gone too long without the pleasure of your beautiful voice."

"My lord, please let me fulfill my duties and offer your guests any comforts that they might require. Afterward, I will graciously sing for your pleasure."

Drusus pointed to his cup and a slave eagerly filled it. He stared at the cup and caressed the rim with his finger; he frowned then looked at Arria. "Sing for me now. Is there any reason or person more important than this request, my love?"

"My wish is only to please you, and if my singing is what you desire then I shall do so now."

"You please me very much, Carissima, and your beauty is only matched by your grace."

Bowing to Drusus, Arria moved toward the musicians to choose a song.

Garic felt miserable. The Egyptian slave girl had taken him by surprise. At the same time, he wondered how much Arria had seen or understood about his encounter with Marcella. He knew Arria had meant to greet him, but Drusus had a way of always coming between them.

A brooding temper crept over Garic. Tomorrow he would leave for Luthgar's camp. He hoped his return to the Franks would clear his head. He would hunt with Vodamir and Luthgar and place his love somewhere in the back of his mind and heart. His desire for Arria was strong; and yet, had he betrayed Arria when he responded to Marcella's touch? Guilty or not, Arria was not his, and Drusus was a powerful man.

The savory richness of another wine weakened Garic's will. He doubted their future together, but longed for Arria at his side. He had vowed to free her from Drusus, but how?

Vodamir ended his conversation with the Visigoth warrior beside him, then turned to Garic who was looking in Arria's direction. "Here, Cousin, take this mead and drink. Leave that Roman wine alone. This local mead is much better. You're far too thoughtful and quiet, and Arria will sing."

Garic gratefully downed the mead. "Pour me another cup, Vodamir."

Amused, Vodamir poured Garic a second cup, then spied the distress in his eyes. "What ails you, Cousin?" he asked.

Garic started to speak, but the music interrupted his words. He glanced at Drusus and felt twisted with envy. A slave passed him carrying a tray with mead, and he snatched another drink hoping to chase away his jealousy.

Drusus seated himself directly in front of Arria, his admiration apparent. Many of the guests moved closer to get a better view of the senator's daughter.

The light from the hanging lamps created a warm and festive atmosphere. To highlight Arria's performance, bronze braziers of burning coals circled the floor where she stood. Ferns, brought from southern territories, filled large clay pots painted with pictures of dancing maidens, nestled nicely between the bronze pedestals of light. The aromas from the foods and the libations helped create an ambiance pleasing to all the guests.

Music filled the room and Arria sang. Her voice transported Garic to the time when he first heard her sing at the Assembly of Warriors, when she had first captivated his heart. He closed his eyes and listened. Arria's clear, pure notes rose and resonated with passion. For him, Arria's voice was as beautiful as a Valkyrie who, the stories told, sang the dying soldier into Valhalla.

A tinkling bell, then a movement passed Garic's side. He opened his eyes. Drawn to the column just ahead of him, he realized the body of a woman etched the darkness behind the marble pillar. Arria's voice dimmed into the background as he focused on the mysterious figure standing in the shadow. He sensed that the woman was staring only at him. Garic felt a tingling sensation prick the back of his neck, a warrior's danger signal, but the shape held him captive.

Arria's voice climbed. She reached her final note and it shattered Garic's spell.

In this moment, from the column's edge, Marcella stepped into the amber light, shining from the lamp above. Her beautiful and seductive eyes lured his barbaric heart deep into her darkness. Garic held Marcella's gaze, then broke free.

Shaken, he glanced at Arria. Her beauty glowed as she sustained the last note, then let it fade away. Garic filled his cup, eager to escape his confusion. Unable to resist, he looked toward the column where Marcella had beckoned him from the shadow. Only lamplight filled the empty space.

Chapter Seven

Cave Felem
Beware of the cat

FORT CAMBRIA

Seated beside Garic, Vodamir yawned and filled his cup. Over the rim, he watched Arria across the table as she laughed. A gruff, older centurion, toughened by years of service, was telling her a humorous story.

Arria reached for a honey cake, and glanced in Vodamir's direction. Vodamir brazenly gazed at her. His roguish and impudent grin made her laugh, and she returned a dazzling smile.

Seated beside Arria, Drusus noticed their exchange and scowled, "Must you constantly entertain that ape barbarian with your attention?" Drusus' voice, loud and thick with drink, betrayed his jealousy.

"I am just being a gracious hostess. Roman hospitality is an important political tool. I know you understand this." Arria picked up her cup, and brought it to her lips. "Besides, he's a friend," she said, and took a slow drink.

Drusus rolled his eyes and shook his head. "Arria...Arria, you can be so naive. These are warriors out to profit. You are merely a woman, an object of their primitive lusts and appetites."

"Would my lord say there are no Roman men who see women as mere objects of their lusts and *refined* appetites? If so, who among the Roman men here can say that they hold women in such high regard?"

"Would my lady imply that *I* am no better than these barbarians?"

Drusus' hissed, his anger piqued.

Arria responded cautiously, guests were listening. "What I am saying is that barbarian or Roman, it's my duty to play the part for which I have been chosen. If it means smiling and talking with them, then I must. It's my duty." Arria took another slow drink, then pulled the cup from her lips and gave Drusus her most beautiful smile.

Garic found it difficult to ignore the interaction between Arria and Drusus. Maybe it would be better for him to leave. He would go back to the Boar's Head Inn and escape this longing ache by seeking reprieve in a lonely night's sleep.

Garic rose to leave, but Vodamir grabbed his arm.

"Do not go. There is but one more drink to finish the night," Vodamir said persuasively.

Garic reluctantly sat and downed the remainder of his wine.

"My lord, may I suggest a night potion that will help you sleep and dream a beautiful dream?" Marcella stood at Garic's side. Her sultry beauty emanated a confidence that was difficult to ignore.

"Why do you ask me this, girl?" he replied, turning his cup in his hand. "Does it seem like I need one?"

"My lord, your honor and kindness is known by many. I sense a heaviness in your heart. I possess the knowledge that can remedy this, at least for the night, and I am most willing to be of service to you in any way that I can."

Wine and sadness loosened Garic's tongue, and he ventured suspiciously, "You would help me? Are you not Drusus' woman?"

Marcella knelt beside Garic, lowered her eyes and whispered, "I serve Drusus, this is true—in all matters that please him, but I rule my own heart."

Frustrated by her enticing boldness, Garic snapped, "The servant rules a heart to which her master is a slave. Go away girl—leave me!" His command cracked like a whip in the air.

An icy chill invaded Marcella's eyes and her smile dimmed. "As you wish, First Counsel, but at least allow me to fill your cup for the last time tonight, the same as all the guests."

Regretting his harshness, Garic answered, "Very well. It cannot hurt."

"It won't, my lord, I assure you." Marcella rose and crossed to a table against the wall, which held several flasks of wine. Emptying one to half-full, she carefully poured a liquid from a glass vial hidden in her wrapped linen belt. She added a touch of fresh wine, gently shook the container, then went to Garic's side and filled his cup. Marcella bowed. "Rest well tonight, my lord," she said and placed the flask on the table.

As Marcella started to leave, a drunken Visigoth, Theobald, grabbed her onto his lap. He pulled Marcella close and growled, "Your beauty haunts me. I want you in my bed!"

Marcella's face blanked and detachment filled her eyes.

The Visigoth howled, then tore Marcella's dress, exposing a breast. With no mind to the guests around him, he ran his tongue greedily over a nipple.

Marcella turned a pleading gaze toward Garic. Her words about his honor echoed in his mind and yanked him to his feet. He tore Marcella from Theobald's lap. Marcella clutched Garic's tunic and clung to him.

Garic's action jolted Vodamir to his feet.

Theobald rose, spitting curses and knocking his chair behind him. He drew a knife.

The sudden commotion brought the evening's music to an abrupt halt. Voices went quiet. Garic and Theobald held everyone's attention.

"Would you steal the woman? Come on!" Theobald thundered with beckoning fingers. "Tell your pretty boy cousin to back off! This is our fight. Winner gets the slave."

From the head of the table, Drusus rose and called to the Visigoth, "Noble Theobald, this is my home and no place for fighting. If you have a quarrel with the Franks, save it for outside the fort."

Theobald wrenched his gaze from Garic and faced Drusus.

"My lord, Drusus, I would have this *cat* woman in my bed. All night her cold, black beauty has mocked my desire and I itch for her."

Theobald shot Garic a belligerent look and accused, "This Frank has rescued the slave for his own pleasure. Give her to me! Or... must I go to Attila's camp for what a man needs. And a leader who rewards his warriors."

"Theobald," Drusus said firmly, "if you're a man who *needs* the company of a woman, then as your host let me offer you the very best." He beckoned a waiting servant, gave him a quiet instruction and the slave left the room.

Disgruntled, Theobald sneered, "What about your lap dogs, these Franks?" and spat towards their feet.

Shock coiled through the guests. Vodamir took a step toward Theobald, but Garic grabbed his arm and held him back. "Think!" Garic warned.

Vodamir smirked at Theobald, but kept his place.

All eyes shifted when the dispatched servant hurried into the room followed by a woman.

A gasp escaped Arria's lips. Garic and Vodamir stared in confusion. Behind the servant was Karas. Wakened from sleep, her sandy hair hung unbound past her shoulders. Her soft, pale beauty bathed in waking sleep contrasted the dim faces weary from laughing and drinking deep into the night.

Karas looked around and then at Drusus. She tilted her head inquisitively and gazed at Arria, risen and standing next to Drusus.

Theobald's satisfied grunt signaled his approval.

Drusus spoke with authority. "As you can see this slave is a beauty. I am sure you'll find her most pleasing." Drusus ordered his slave to bring Karas before Theobald.

Karas looked fearfully at Arria.

"Titus, this is my servant," Arria intervened. "She was not purchased to entertain your guests or allies."

"Arria, she may be your servant, but she is under my rule. Is she not?"

79

Arria lifted her chin higher and her brow arched. "My lord, I believe that Karas belongs to my father. It was his money that paid for her." Arria stood taller.

Drusus' eyes narrowed and he lifted a small pouch from beneath his robe. He took her hand and dropped the leather bag in her palm. "I have fifty *denarii* in this purse, and I will double it for your *father's* slave."

Guests looked wide-eyed at one another. An extravacant sum for just one slave. Garic placed his hand on his sword hilt. Vodamir moved closer beside Garic and deftly gripped the knife hanging from his belt.

"My love," Drusus, continued in a honeyed tone before Arria could answer, "will you give your betrothed, Legate and Commander of Cambria, the sale of your servant as a gift? It would please me immensely."

Arria contemplated the bag of *denarii* in her hand, a glimmer of distress in her clear green eyes.

She glanced briefly at Karas, then Garic. She looked at Drusus and spoke with conviction. "I cannot give or sell what my father owns. Surely, you understand."

Drusus steeled his gaze and was about to speak when Garic interrupted, "Commander Drusus, if you'll excuse my interruption into this matter, I think I have a solution—a gift."

The guests swiveled their attention toward Garic.

Garic bowed and glanced toward Theobald, "One far more pleasing than a night with an ordinary house slave." His strong voice and confident manner revived the growing drama. Only a stifled cough floated somewhere in the room.

"On my farm up north, I have a horse that Vodamir and I have groomed for battle. On my word, he can outrun the fastest horses in the land and was bred from the best. I call him, Tiwaz, god of war. He is a rare prize. His sire is an Iberian from Hispania. I would give this horse as a gift to Theobald. In exchange, the Lady Arria will keep her servant. And for you, Commander Drusus, I would be honored to present you with the sire, the most magnificent stallion one will ever lay eyes upon. Even Attila cannot boast of such a horse. I named him Iberian after his breed."

An approving clamor exploded among the guests, and they began to cheer.

Drusus appeared to relish the value in the offer. Garic knew that Karas' purchase would have been won only at the expense of Arria's displeasure and a public witness to their disagreement.

Drusus raised his voice above the clamor. "Noble Garic, I will accept your gift. What say you, Theobald? This is a more profitable alternative, don't you agree?

Undone, Theobald grunted, but his expression conceded that a prized horse was far more valuable than a few hours in the arms of a slave girl. "Drusus, I will gladly accept this gift, and accept my apology for the mention of Attila. Your hospitality is far more generous than that greedy warmonger to the east."

Drusus nodded with a bland smile.

Theobald bowed toward Garic, but could not supress a smug grin. "Thank you, First Counsel Garic for the generous gift."

Beside Garic, Vodamir bristled under his breath, "Let me kill him."

"Not today, Cousin," Garic answered.

A political disaster avoided, a satisfied Drusus addressed his guests, "Please finish the last cup for the night and then my servants will escort you to your quarters."

Drusus turned toward Arria and cradled her chin. "Are you happy now? You can keep your slave. Let me escort you to your room. You never said if you found it to your liking?"

"It's quite beautiful," she replied tightly. "I will thank Noble Garic and bid him and Vodamir a goodnight before I retire. Please don't wait for me. Attend to your guests and their needs. Karas will accompany me."

"As you wish, Carissima," Drusus replied stiffly. Kissing Arria's hand, he walked toward Theobald.

Garic sat down and drank the wine Marcella had poured for him before the encounter with Theobald. Vodamir crouched beside Garic and shook his head. "Cousin, you always surprise me. I will get our horses, but first I will find Samuel to tell him of the night's events." Garic nodded and watched as Vodamir left.

Garic swallowed the last drops of wine and noted its sweeter taste and thickness. A long night of conflicting emotions and plenty of drink took its due from him. He felt spent.

"Garic." Arria sat beside him. The guests gone, they were alone. Karas waited in the hall on Arria's orders. She placed her hand on his hand, which rested on his knee.

Garic grasped her slender fingers.

"Krieger, why did you sacrifice your prized possessions? I might have been able to save Karas from that *bastard*." Arria's passion filled her words.

Garic grinned. This harsh word from Arria's lips amused him. "*Mellitula*, what do you think I sacrificed? A prized possession? The horses are valuable and beautiful, yes, but you and Karas are worth a hundred horses. I wouldn't see you bent to Drusus' will and humiliated in front of even one man or woman no less these guests, nor would I have Karas raped by that pig, Theobald. Besides," Garic looked around the room and leaned closer, "I would give all my horses to be free to hold you in my arms at night. The two of us alone."

The wine seemed to rock Garic's senses and he felt his ardor rising. "The pleasure I would give you would make you plead for more." Taking her face in his hands, he brushed his lips on hers, and his husky voice resonated down her spine. "Our cries of satisfaction would ride on dawn's first light into day; only then would I allow you to sleep." Garic brushed his hand across her bosom and felt her nipples harden. "Kiss me!"

Arria pushed Garic away, fighting her passion, and frightened. "I long for our kiss, but shadows house spies that sell secrets for profit."

Garic closed his eyes, grasped the bridge of his nose and shook his head.

"Are you ill? Too much wine?" she asked tenderly.

"No," he answered, his eyes still closed. "My head feels clouded. My blood...races through me. I need to sleep." Garic's brow wrinkled and he placed his hand briefly over his face, but made an effort to waken himself.

"You will not leave tonight. You are too tired to ride. I will find a room for you, and send Vodamir to the Inn. He can come in the morning with your things."

Garic made an effort to smile, "I cannot resist your orders. Will *you* show me to the room?"

"Yes. Can you follow me?" Arria watched as he rose to his feet. For a moment, he wavered, but righted himself and let her lead the way.

Garic and Karas followed Arria down a corridor leading to the guest quarters. Moonlight drifted through a high, round window, but vanished on the path lit by Arria's lamp. Snores and sudden bursts of laughter escaped from the rooms ahead and floated around them. Arria held the lamp high and found the door at the far end of the connecting hallway. She entered with Garic behind her, while Karas remained in the hall.

The crisp smell of juniper filled the room.

"It's cool in here." Arria remarked. She rested the lamp on the table, then turned to help Garic. He snatched her in his arms and kissed her with a fury. Arria lost her breath, but yielded overcome by his fierce demand. Breaking from his lips, she protested, "We shouldn't ..."

"Shh," he whispered, cradling her face in his hands. His tongue parted her lips and probed deeply, caressing hers. He swept her from her feet and laid her on the bed beside the wall, and lowered his lips to hers with burning kisses. "Don't leave me, Arria. Don't go to Drusus. My temper burns when he touches you." Garic whispered

83

hoarsely.

Arria pressed her palms against his chest. Garic's desire grew stronger with every kiss, each caress. Afraid of discovery and his fierce sexuality, she implored, "I must go. This is not like you."

Garic reclaimed her mouth, his tongue sweet from the wine. His kiss billowed through her like a sultry wind. The impulse to give in to his embrace taunted her, but approaching footsteps warned her to break free. "Listen to me! No!" she demanded and with all her strength shoved him away.

Garic fell to the side and rolled onto his back. He seemed dazed and beset by a strange trance. "*Mellitula*," he murmured and reached for her. His eyes fluttered and closed.

Freed from his embrace, Arria jumped from the bed. She hastily adjusted her dress and hair. She heard the soldiers approach. "We cannot be discovered, and I cannot love you like this." Arria looked at Garic. Her senses reeled. She felt uneasy. "What has possessed you?" she whispered. "Are you all right?

Garic slowly shook his head and tried to raise it. "For...give me, I would...never force ... never you. My love is real...re ..." Garic's sudden slow breathing told her he was asleep.

The soldiers entered the hallway. On the other side of the door, Karas knocked softly. "Lady Arria?" Karas whispered. "Lady, the night guard is coming!"

Arria straightened her dress one more time and lifted a few fallen tresses over her ear. Composed, she opened the door. Centurion Tarvistus, brushed past Karas and entered the room.

Tarvistus looked at the bed and the sleeping Garic suspiciously. Then his gaze landed on Arria, looking her up and down. "Lady Arria, what is wrong? Has this barbarian attacked you?"

"Not at all. He is ill. He passed out and fell. I caught him but couldn't hold him. We toppled and landed on the bed."

Tarvistus eyed her disheveled hair and wrinkled gown. "Lady, we will attend to the barbarian. A slave will come and sit with him in case he requires assistance."

"Thank you, Centurion. A thoughtful remedy. We must take care of our foreign guests, especially in these times." Arria made sure to remind Tarvistus of the politics at stake, in case he had some *special assistance* in mind that might prove detrimental to Garic's well-being. "I will inform Commander Drusus about your concern for his guest and that he's in excellent hands."

Arria looked at Garic fast asleep.

"Centurion?"

"Yes, my lady?"

"Remove his sword, boots and undress him. Cover him with the blanket."

"As you wish, my lady."

Arria walked toward the door, her mind racing. She had never seen Garic so forceful and what about the dizziness that plagued him? Arria paused, turning her head slightly, "Centurion, leave the lamp burning and tell the slave who watches over him to find me if the Frank shows illness. Is that clear?"

"Very clear, my lady."

Hidden behind a marble column, Marcella waited for Arria, Garic, and Karas to leave the Commander's private dining room for the sleeping quarters. She surmised Arria would make him stay the night. Marcella had guessed their secret. Garic's armlet the key. The band that circled Garic's powerful arm was twin to the band in Arria's satchel. The etched *Semper* had caught her eye, a word for lovers not daughters. The bees engraved on the surface of both armlets had convinced Marcella that they were a pair, separated only as a token of trust and love. She had discovered their secret, and joy raced through her body.

The setting moon cast an eerie glow down the hall as Marcella followed quietly behind them. The potion was more potent than she had hoped. Garic had needed some assistance from Arria. As the trio neared the room intended for Garic, Marcella stepped into a alcove, housing a shrine. She hid in its sacred darkness and gloated.

Tonight, she would seduce the golden long-hair, the man of passion, whose pure heart had sacrificed his prized possession for love. Tonight Isis, the goddess of power, passion, magic and moonlight would deliver the long-haired warrior into her arms. And soon, she, Marcella, the concubine slave, would rise above them all and rule them or destroy those who dared get in her way.

Marcella stepped deeper into the darkness as Arria and Karas swept down the hall and out of sight. Marcella reached for the string purse tied at her waist. Taking a small vial from the bag, she drank the contents and leaned against the wall, closing her eyes. Waves of euphoria intoxicated her senses. The potion was working. Once again, she reached into the purse and retrieved a small, round metal box filled with charcoal ash used to paint her eyes. She dipped her finger lightly into the dust and raised it to her forehead. With an invocation, she drew a small crescent moon. A balmy intoxication nipped her senses and resolution inspired her grin. It was time. Whispering a prayer to the goddess for strength and victory, she lifted her veil and stepped into the hall. Arria's orders to find an attendant for Garic had filtered into the hall and furthered Marcella's plan. She presented herself to a guard.

Tarvistus coming down the hall, stopped. "Is this the slave meant to watch the Frank?"

"Yes sir, she was sent by the Lady Arria."

A confused look crossed Tarvistus' face for a second, but he shrugged. "Escort her to the room. Leave her the means to light a second lamp in case she has a need for it, and make sure there is a blanket to warm her or she might be forced to join the barbarian." The guards chuckled along with Tarvistus as they moved past Marcella towards the barracks.

Marcella turned to her escort and quietly cooed, "Don't trouble yourself. All guest rooms have plenty of blankets and reeds to light lamps and candles. Go now to your rest."

The guard finding no reason to disagree, bid her goodnight and left. His retreating footsteps faded down the silent corridor, allowing

Marcella's chance for conquest.

Marcella slowly pushed open the door and pulled the scarf from her head. A dull light and soft breathing permeated the room as she stepped in, closed the door, and leaned against it. Garic's deep sigh drew her toward the bed as she clenched her silk night dress. He lay there defenseless. A low chuckle rumbled from her throat. Marcella, Roman slave, and worshiper of Isis would reign in her realm. In the end, she would rise higher than the waning moon. Drusus' desires, fulfilled by her, would make her master of a commander's heart. Garic's nobility, weakened by her, would make her master of a warrior's guilt. She would destroy the woman Drusus wanted and Garic loved. A path would open and elevate her above them.

Garic moaned some words in Frankish. Marcella gazed at his handsome face and his hair the color of light. She gently touched the strands clinging to the side of his face and moved them aside. Her lips beside his ear, she whispered the words that would awaken the love potion dormant in his blood. It waited to be kindled by her magic words, the words of the goddess.

Marcella breathed deeply and whispered the words into Garic's mouth, touching his lips with hers. She felt him stir. Her breath caressed his skin. A strong hand touched her flank and moved up beneath her open tunic and firmly over her buttock. A chill tingled through her; the potion worked. Slowly she slipped the blanket from his naked body and stared. A perfect man, Garic slept.

Like a cat, Marcella crawled on top and straddled Garic's legs. Nestled in hair the color of blond wheat, Garic's manhood woke from its sleep. Marcella laughed a low, victorious laugh and dragged the palms of her hands up his legs. Fever coursed through her blood. The power of the potion and Isis enlivened her and she raised herself and bent over him.

Garic waited ready for her. Marcella nipped and suckled his hardened nipples. A guttural cry escaped Garic. He grabbed her hair, clutched her waist and pulled her beneath him.

His eyes, prisoners of the potion, flickered and he ran his tongue over her breasts. Marcella opened herself to him. A lover's rhythm beat in his loins as Garic raised himself poised and ready. Marcella, her breathing labored, urged him on. Digging her nails into his shoulders, she spread her legs wider and her voice, lusty and urgent, rasped, "Take me! I am your goddess and you are my god."

Garic lowered himself and slid toward her fulfillment and conquest...

The lamp light dimmed and the candle on the shelf flickered. A cold breeze ran rampant over Garic's back, shaking him. A shiver passed through him and his waking focused on a face before him. He saw a woman. "Arria," tumbled from his lips. He thought it was Arria's smile, but his vision sharpened. He stared at Marcella; her cat eyes beckoned him. Bewildered and dazed, he looked at his naked self above her, his long hair brushing her chest and his manhood, a sword ready to impale.

A sudden, hollow cry erupted and rang in Garic's head jolting him. Like a thief caught by surprise, he turned and stared into Arria's wounded eyes. Garic sat back on his haunches and pushed Marcella away. He stood, and looked into Arria's face, stricken with shock and betrayal. His words stumbled from his mouth as his arm reached out, "Arria, I thought ... she was you." Garic looked down at his nakedness, and shook his head; he raised his eyes to hers. "I don't know how...You must believe me," he pleaded.

A sudden peal of laughter rang through the room. "Fool!" Marcella spat. "He would say anything *now* to keep your devotion. He desires real women, not girls. You cannot please him as I can. Besides, you're the betrothed of Drusus. I wonder what he would do if he knew about your *love*?"

Marcella rose from the bed naked and unashamed. She tossed back her hair, grabbed her shift and shawl and strutted from the room. "Arria." Garic begged and moved toward her.

Arria staggered back, running her hand across the table to steady herself.

Garic was immediately beside her, "Do not believe what you see or hear. It's not real. The witch poisoned me with something." Tired, but resolute, he insisted, "I thought I was with you. You must believe me." He reached for her hand, but she withdrew around the table's chair.

Arria looked upon Garic's nakedness. He was a lion of a man, brave and fierce. From the first moment she had seen him, she had loved him, but now she could see into his barbarian heart. A fearful instinct had prompted her return. A moment longer, he and Marcella would have been one. The cat and the lion, claiming their lust. Two wild animals meant for lies and betrayals—predators. They deserved each other. Hate flashed through Arria. She had never known such jealousy. She beat her fists against his chest, crying words that lovers never say.

Tears ran down her cheeks and Garic stood there, letting her pound on his heart. When she slowed, he held her wrists and said, "I love you and you alone. Believe me."

His eyes showed pain, but she dropped her gaze to her cross hanging on his neck. She ran her fingertips over the gold letters alpha and omega and stared.

Garic gently brushed her hair with his fingers. "Arria, say you believe me."

The sound of footsteps down the hall signaled the final rounds for the night guard and kidnapped their last moment. Arria raised her head, her gaze defiant with anger. "Liar," she hissed. "Go to her! She waits for you with open arms."

Arria moved to the door already ajar and slipped into the painted hallway. From inside the room, she thought she heard a muffled cry. Arria lifted her head and wiped her tears. A broken heart had little pride, but she was no man's fool.

Chapter Eight

Errare humanum est
To err is human

FORT CAMBRIA

aric stood alone in the center of the atrium. A mist rose from his breath as a crisp breeze danced around him. He waited for Vodamir, or so he told himself, but glanced at the high shutters closed against his fixed gaze. Would Arria come to the window before he rode away? He wondered if he would ever return now that she had rejected him. Garic stared boldly at the blue wooden shutters. They blocked Arria from his only hope—that final look when her eyes would speak the truth. The thought tormented him.

Vodamir approached and placed his hand on Garic's shoulder. "We must meet with Drusus before we leave."

Garic wrenched his gaze from the window. "Is Drusus waiting?"

"*Ja*. What happened last night? Arria said you were not well and could not travel. She gave me your sword and I returned to the inn without you. Early this morning, the boy, Angelus, came to fetch me. His mistress urged that I not delay."

Garic scowled at the closed shutters.

"Is it Arria's window that draws your attention?" Vodamir asked. "Was she not happy with the gift of prized horses given to Drusus and Theobald? I cannot believe that whore's son of a Visigoth will own the powerful, Tiwaz." Vodamir paused and looked earnestly at Garic. "Cousin, I realized last night as I laid in my bed that you must really love Arria. Why else would you give those horses away? You barely know the woman, Karas, and you understand the life a slave must lead: woman, man or child. You are wise, shrewd and honorable, but to give Tiwaz and his sire to men you despise, there can be only one reason—love."

A sudden noise burst into the courtyard. Angelus, dressed only in leggings and tunic, ran toward the barbarians. The early sun could not protect the boy from the late autumn chill. He shivered as he announced that Drusus was ready to see them.

Vodamir tousled Angelus' hair and indulged the boy's request to hold his axe. He pulled it from his belt and cautioned Angelus about safe handling, then raised his hood and folded his arms beneath his cloak to warm them. He turned back toward Garic, whispering, "You cunning wolf! Earth mother, Erda, would be proud of your worship and virile obsession for this woman." Vodamir's weak grin implied a slight apprehension. "Tell me. Did you have her? Is she yours?"

Garic looked back at the shutters. "I lost her, Cousin. I was tricked by that witch, Marcella, and I lost Arria."

"What did Marcella do?"

"She drugged me—the wine, I think—and later came to me as I slept. She beguiled me, twisted my perceptions. I believed she was Arria. I was about to take Marcella when Arria discovered us together and cried out, breaking the trance that held me. I tried to explain, but she did not believe me. She watched me rescue Marcella from Theobald, who accused me of wanting Marcella for myself. Now Arria thinks the same."

Vodamir whipped open his cloak. Strapped across his shoulder, a brown leather baldric held Garic's sword. Vodamir plucked the weapon from its scabbard and held it out to him. "I say we find the witch and make her confess this trickery."

"Marcella will never tell the truth, she has much to lose." Garic replied, taking the sword from Vodamir's hand. He began to speak again, but hesitated.

"Speak, Cousin?" Vodamir pressed him.

91

"Arria and I exchanged tokens of love the night we rested in the wood on the road to Cambria."

Vodamir kicked a cluster of stones beneath the evergreen hedge, lining the path and snapped, "Hel, take me! That night in the wood, I thought you might be vying for her ... I underestimated your intentions. Your serious nature and sense of honor always confuses me. Love can grip and weaken even the strongest man." Vodamir smiled candidly at Garic, but with resignation. "I understand your love for her. She stirs me as well; however ... it is you that stirs the Lady Arria."

"Not anymore. Arria is done with me. Marcella blinded me. I did not see the danger in that witch." Garic attached his sword to his belt, fastened the brooch on his cloak and raised his hood. He would not be undone by a slave, albeit a witch or her Roman lover commander.

Anger brewed hot and deep in Garic's heart. *The witch will not win. Who does Marcella hate?* She had captured Drusus' lustful attention. Drusus had slyly manueuvered Karas as the prize for Theobald. But Marcella had tempted and offered herself to him. It was his refusal that had challenged Marcella. She used her magic and defeated him, proving herself a formidable enemy. *What does Marcella want? What if I had desired her?* These thoughts whirled through Garic's mind. The answers caught in the puzzle. Marcella had won. He was in the darkness banished from the light of Arria's presence and her love.

Garic heard the latch on the shutters lift.

The shutters creaked and pushed open, exposing the pink roses adorning the interior blue slats. Arria stood framed by the flowers like a rose set amidst a wreath. Her thick, chestnut hair cascaded loosely over her one shoulder, and her green eyes roamed the courtyard.

Garic waited, but Vodamir fixed his attention on the window and called out, "Lady Arria, your beauty shines summer on this winter morning. It rivals the sun!" He pulled back his hood, revealing his coppery strands and smiled.

Vodamir's handsome confidence brought a grin to Arria's lips. "Thank you, Noble Vodamir," she called. "The day would seem colorless without your pleasant smile." Arria briefly glanced at Garic and her smile disappeared.

Garic stepped forward, Arria's name on his lips, but a shadow crossed his path. "Noble Garic?" he heard and turned to Marcella's triumphant smile.

"My lord," Marcella bowed with a smirk, "Commander Drusus waits for you and Noble Vodamir. He insists you come, *now.*" Marcella's eyes sparkled smugly as she gave a sideways glance toward the shutters.

Garic scowled and turned back toward Arria. The window stood empty.

LUTHGAR'S CAMP

November came and left Cambria with full force. The winds blew their bitter gusts around the fort and through the barracks. For soldiers and slaves, settled and comfortable, the fires warmed the awakened winter nights and harbored all in tranquil anticipation for the coming of spring.

Garic and Vodamir spent several days traveling back to the Luthgar's camp from Fort Cambria. The first snow fell and blanketed the ground with a silvery powder. The two cousins traveled quietly, each absorbed in his own thoughts. Garic was distraught. The loss of Arria's trust and possibly her love made him want her all the more. It was a bitter resolution to a convoluted problem. Arria had refused to see him before he left. He knew physical pain, but a wounded heart ached worse. A torment that would not die, it gnawed hollow and hungry. He filled the journey home with long hunts, during which he deliberated the offer made by Drusus to track the Hun raiders, and how he might win Arria back into his arms.

Vodamir rode beside his cousin. The situation reminded Vodamir of Garic's first kill. Garic the boy, with bloodied axe in hand, had looked at him that afternoon in the wood, fighting against the

Visigoths, stunned, but transformed. Like a drowning youth beneath life's rapid river, Garic had summoned his courage and resurfaced a man, sure and resolved. Garic's pain left Vodamir reflective. Garic was valiant and nobler than he. Despite what might have occured, Garic must truly love Arria, and he would rise to the surface again.

Garic and Vodamir arrived at the camp the same day as Luthgar. He and Garic had grown up together and weathered many trials as comrades and protectors. Their reunion brought Luthgar a feeling of deep comfort. At the river's edge, they praised the gods, Wodan and Thor, for their safe return, offering the choicest fish from the day's catch, a plump hare, a bronze amulet engraved with the royal bee, and three of the finest arrows among the warriors. They buried these gifts beneath the willow, its branches cascading toward the earth, and thanked the gods for their protection.

"Tell me once again, Garic, what does Drusus want from us?" Luthgar sliced a chunk of roasted pig from a platter, resting on the table in Luthgar's log shelter.

Garic poured a hearty mead in Luthgar's and Vodamir's cups. "He wants Vodamir and I to lead a small group of men to the northeastern border of Belgica to search for a party of Attila's raiders. They've been stealing and spreading havoc on the farms and terrorizing the neighboring Roman outpost."

"Why us?" Luthgar persisted.

"He believes the Franks are best suited to track the Huns. We know the land. However, he did recommend a tribune by the name of Severus on his way to Cambria and the centurion Tarvistus join us. So much for our choosing others. A recommendation from Drusus is as good as done."

"Tarvistus." Luthgar stroked his cropped beard and repeated, "Tarvistus ... The name sounds familiar."

"It should. He was the centurion who attacked Samuel and Arria. We gave him a good beating, especially you, my chief." Garic smirked and glanced at Vodamir who grinned back.

Luthgar chuckled. "I remember the fight and also the waiting arms of my wife. A good fight can ready a man for powerful lovemaking!" He grabbed another chunk of meat and chewed briskly. "Have you seen this Tarvistus since the fight?"

"*Ja.* He brought a complaint against us, but Drusus maneuvered Tarvistus' account into an apology. I judge, Tarvistus wasn't too happy about this outcome, but he submitted to Drusus' will."

"If we accept Drusus' request to track these Huns, what is the benefit for us?"

"He's assured us that in addition to granting us a greater portion of land between the Somme River and the northeastern border of Gaul, he will commission three centurion positions to anyone in our tribe who wants to be part of the *foederati.* Also, if any Huns are captured and brought back as hostages, he will pay fifty *denarii* a man, three times the value of a slave. And..." Garic paused.

"You hesitate," Luthgar said and leaned back in his chair. "Why?"

"Drusus' final gesture—he would return my stallion, Tiwaz' sire, if Vodamir and I accompany this tracking mission."

"Ah, your prized horse traded for a Lady's honor and a slave's dignity. An unexpected twist to a masterful plan on Drusus' part. With your answer, he'll see how much you love this horse, your tribe, and possibly—his betrothed?"

"No. I believe the condition that Vodamir be part of this mission reflects Drusus' jealousy. He and Vodamir clashed right from the start." Garic responded.

Vodamir let out a low laugh. "That arrogant, Roman bastard has a wolf's cunning. I would welcome meeting him in battle or at least running my boot up his backside!" Vodamir's insolent smirk sparked Garic's and Luthgar's laughter.

When the laughter died, Garic's eyes met Luthgar's.

"Those serious eyes, Counsel, spark my concern," Luthgar said.

"Many have heard that the Lady Arria was stolen by the Chamavi from Drusus' field camp, while on her journey to the assembly and Cambria. Vodamir and I, Frank barbarians, returned her untouched and alive. Drusus' pride was injured. I suspect he hates Vodamir for his gallantry and knows he can only get to him through me." Garic's contempt was evident. "On the other hand, if the *witch*, Marcella, has shared with Drusus how she poisoned me with her magic and what passed between me and Arria, then Drusus hates me as well. He may welcome both our deaths." Garic ran his fingers through his hair. "I am not sure who I should fear most, the Huns or Drusus?"

"I agree. What an opportune venture for Drusus to bring back hostages, and while on the way home, arrange for one or both of you to meet with a—fatal accident." Luthgar leaned forward, his smile grim. "What say you, First Counsel, will you accept Drusus' mission?"

Garic grabbed the hunting knife resting on the table and held the tip of the blade between his fingers. "I will accept this mission for the Franks and prove myself to Arria. And let the Roman soldiers, whoever they may be, sleep with their eyes open. Like the fox knows the wolf, the long-hairs know the Romans." Garic hurled the knife through the air. "We were *born* warriors!"

"And victors!" Luthgar bellowed, throwing his knife toward a second peg.

FORT CAMBRIA

Several nights after Garic left, Samuel, knowing why Arria turned away from Garic, brought her outside Drusus' quarters. Bidding Arria hide with him in the shadows and behind one of the columns surrounding Drusus' door, they waited. Arria wrapped her shawl tighter. Apprehension trickled beneath her skin. Samuel, standing beside her, sensed her unease and reassured her. It struck Arria how content Samuel seemed these days. Had he and Karas become lovers? On occasion, she had noticed tender glances and gentle touches pass between them. "Samuel," she whispered. "About Karas ... are you friends ... or lovers?" Even in the dim light, his smile radiated.

"We are friends and lovers, my lady," he whispered back.

"I am pleased and happy for you both," she answered, resting a hand on his shoulder.

"Thank you; I am relieved you feel this way. I will tell Karas."

Arria smiled and they settled back into the quiet watch. *My servants have found happiness*, she thought. *Will I?*

Soon after the darkest hour, a glow shone into the hall. Marcella emerged from Drusus' room, her candle held high. Drusus followed right behind her, his body naked and lean. He grabbed her. "Come back, *Carissima*. One more time. I am able." He laughed and rubbed his lips on her neck. Marcella turned to face Drusus. Her low, lusty moan careened through the hall as Drusus caressed her throat with his tongue, and ran it slowly up to her parted lips.

Marcella took hold of Drusus' manhood. She leaned against him and gently began to stroke him. He quickly stiffened. Fueled by his ardor, Drusus swept Marcella from her feet and carried her back into his room. He slammed the door behind them, while Marcella's haunting laugh hung on the air.

Arria leaned against the wall. Samuel rested his hand on her shoulder. "Do you see things clearly now? This woman wants more than Garic's and Drusus' love. She wants power! I am sure of this, and possibly—something more."

Arria's face reflected the glow from a low-burning torch as she stepped from the shadow. "What else could she want?"

"She wants something from you," Samuel whispered.

Arria echoed, "From—*me*?"

"Yes."

"What would she want from me? How can I help her?"

"I am not sure, but she has no power over you. This makes her fearful. My lady, please be cautious around her."

"The night I found Garic and Marcella together, he claimed he was drugged, intoxicated. I believed he meant by Marcella's beauty and seductive ways. Could it have been something more? Does a potion exist that breeds the wild abandon I witnessed between the two?"

Samuel said, "If one desires such an aphrodisiac there are potions that render a man raw and senseless in his passions."

"Come Arria, we should leave before we're discovered. You must decide what is lie and what is truth, but Marcella is evil. I am as sure of this as I am sure of the scar that runs from my eye to ear." Samuel traced his finger across the thin, coarse line.

Arria caught his gesture with her hand. "I trust you. And I will be careful, I promise."

"Be wise," he urged and squeezed her hand.

Slave and mistress traversed the shadows back to the blue room of roses where Karas, with Angelus asleep on her lap, waited patiently.

A fortnight has passed since you have gone, Garic, Arria thought. She stretched her limbs beneath the warm, soothing pleasure of the heated bath. Arria gazed at her hair trailing in the water. Lost in her thoughts, she wished these strands could reach to the warriors' camp and wrap themselves around Garic. Filled with the vision of her banished warrior, Arria's eyes closed, pulling her deeper into his embrace. The abruptness of water lapping against her face forced her eyes open—the dream gone. Arria looked into the face of Marcella and gasped, "What do you think you're doing? How dare you approach me in this manner! I will call the guard on you."

"My lady has nothing to fear from me," Marcella purred. "I relieved the bath attendant, so I may serve you." Marcella moved to the side of the pool and brought Arria a towel.

"As you serve everyone else in these quarters?" Arria spat back unable to check her temper. She yanked the towel from Marcella's outstretched hand.

Marcella smiled a little too boldly, causing Arria to curse under her breath at her own stupidity. She needed to control this situation, and fought the impulse to slap Marcella's smug face.

"I will serve you in any manner I can, if that is what you wish, my lady."

Marcella's words had an odd ring that ran a shiver down Arria's spine. "Marcella, my robe," Arria ordered.

Marcella wrapped the robe around Arria's shoulders. Taller than Arria, she passed her lips over Arria's ear and quietly commanded, "Sit mistress, so that I might comb your hair and run the strigil's blade across your skin to make it pleasing for our commander."

Arria stepped forward, then faced her. "Is our commander pleased by skin cleaned and oiled, Marcella?"

"Many things please him, but yes, that is one."

"Tell me. What else pleases him?"

"What pleases our commander is a woman who is willing to satisfy him in every way."

"Oh, I see." Arria pursed her lips, then asked, "And is there such a woman in our midst?"

Marcella smiled. "I would think it would be you my lady, his betrothed."

"And if it weren't, who might it be? Could it be someone like you, Marcella?"

"My lady, I've been trained to please."

"Yes. It seems you are quite versed in the pleasures that entice men."

"My lady, what you saw that night with the barbarian, Garic, was only what I was ordered to do. He threatened to steal and sell me if I didn't love him."

"Really? I remember you were quite eager to boast how much *you* pleased *him*."

Marcella shook her head. "No, it was horrible. He forced me to take a drug that would make me love him. I was a victim, my lady." Marcella walked to the chair used for grooming, and beckoned Arria to sit.

Arria hesitated a moment, then sat down. She needed to know more—the truth. Marcella rubbed the towel through her hair and Arria replied,"You didn't seem like a woman forced or drugged that night. In fact, one would think you might feel a deep sense of obligation toward Noble Garic. He saved you from the crude roughness of Theobald, who I am sure would be quite predatory in his lust."

Arria relaxed as Marcella's hands moved to massage her neck and shoulders. "My lady," Marcella broke the silence. "I have said nothing to Drusus about you and the Noble Garic. It was Garic who forced me to his pleasure, and my heart aches for you mistress that you were taken with him."

Arria hid her misery and calmly responded, "Your words speak impudence and error. I am taken with no one, Marcella. I advise caution. You are sleeping with my betrothed, are you not?"

Marcella's hands tightened on Arria's shoulders. She paused, "Yes, this...is true." The words tumbled from her mouth and her hands resumed their work, "But it has been at my commander's orders. He finds it vexing to wait so long, and he knows that until you are married there are proprieties that must be observed."

"How convenient for him then that you are here to lessen his suffering. One would think a veteran soldier such as he could tolerate *pain*."

Marcella laughed. Her hands moved over Arria's shoulders and caressed her below the nape of her neck. "My lady, you've been a widow for a while, and having known the pleasures that love brings, feels no pain herself?"

Arria did not answer.

"My lady doesn't answer."

"I choose not to answer."

Marcella placed her lips beside Arria's ear. "My lady," she whispered, "if it is pleasure that one needs, I can satisfy. I know many ways to delight both man—and woman. Let me show you." Marcella slipped her hand under Arria's robe and massaged Arria's naked breast.

Shocked by the boldness of Marcella's actions, Arria bolted from her seat and spun toward Marcella. "How dare you presume that I am ruled only by my desires!"

Marcella recoiled. Her eyes emanated a black hatred. "Oh, yes!" she spat. "A privileged Roman bitch like you is ruled only by money, or cock, or both! I know, I have served many of you."

Arria felt brimmed with fire and trembled with outrage. "What rules *me* is nothing *you* will ever understand. "You're a dark mistress, Marcella. You might control others through their desires, but you'll not control me. I have known lust, but love runs deeper."

Marcella spoke, her voice low and threatening, "You're a fool! We shall see how *deep* your love is—and your betrothed shall see as well. I am his mistress, not you. I desired you as a child desires a toy, but I can vanquish you and those who stand by you just as easily. You will see, *my lady.*" Marcella hurried from the bath toward Drusus' quarters.

Arria stood stunned, her heart racing. *Have I said too much? Is this a battle waged against a slave? Samuel believes Marcella is evil and wants to destroy me and the men in my life. Why?*

Moving to the edge of the pool, Arria dropped her robe and stepped into the water. Submerging herself, she held her breath and lay peacefully still. A childhood habit, she took pleasure in the peace that came with suspended silence. It helped to clear her mind and think for several glorious seconds. Then rising up, she wiped the water from her face. She called for Angelus posted outside the bath to bring Karas, who came running to answer her mistress' call.

"Hurry and dress me! I must see Drusus before it's too late, and I must look beautiful. Garic's safety and my well-being depends on the outcome of this meeting."

Chapter Nine

Re Vera
In Truth

FORT CAMBRIA

Arria reminded herself that she was a diplomatic envoy as she entered the ante-chamber leading to the commander's office. Chosen by Rome to protect its interests in this part of the world, surely then, she could safeguard her own. Never would an ambitious and cunning slave control her destiny. Announced by Drusus' private secretary, Arria swept into the room in her most stately manner.

Drusus sat before a burning fire, languid in a white toga that enhanced his raven black hair. The flame held his gaze. He gave the impression of a king lost in the concerns of state, but Arria sensed his dissatisfaction. He raised his head and smiled. Handsomeness was his weapon, and she wondered if she was a fool, as Marcella had accused. Power, position and an attractive husband could be hers, if she accepted Drusus.

Instead, she had chosen to love a barbarian, a foreigner, and a man she was unsure she could trust. Had her jealousy closed or opened her eyes to the truth about Garic? It didn't matter now, he was gone, but she longed for him.

"Arria I've missed your presence." Drusus' words hushed the voice within her. "You look beautiful this evening. Blue becomes you." Motioning for her to sit beside him, he ordered his slave to bring wine.

Arria sat close to Drusus, trying to read his thoughts. She looked boldly into his eyes. "My lord flatters me. It's my favorite color. I delight in the shades of blue, each unique, as the experiences that touch our lives."

Drusus' eyes narrowed and a seething look sent a flutter to her heart. His tone held contempt. "It seems experience is something you seek in all matters, my lady."

"As you, my lord," Arria shot back. "I seek to live my life as fully as possible and to serve my country."

"Then we both should be admired," Drusus laughed and lifted his wine to his lips, but his displeasure was evident. Draining his cup, he placed it on the table and sensually leaned in toward her. The scent of verbena clung to him, and his full lips, red from the wine, said slyly, "You sent word that you wanted to see me. Is there a matter that concerns you?"

"There is. It's your slave woman, Marcella. She offends me."

"*Really*? In what way?"

"The slaves say she's a liar who's out for her own gain. I find her to be a liar as well. Today, she tried to take liberties with me that were lewd and above her station."

"Lewd? Above her station? What do you mean?"

"Titus, hear me. Marcella's lusts are insatiable and she is driven by her desire for power."

"Arria, what would you have me do?" he asked, his words brittle.

"Send her away, Titus."

Drusus moved his hands in a bewildered gesture. "Away to where?"

"Anywhere—to Lucinius. Was she not his?"

Drusus chuckled. "That's out of the question. Marcella was a gift from our governor, and there is no civilized place or person where she could be sent or sold."

"Sell her to Attila," Arria fired back. "She would be the perfect spy. I am sure her lies would befuddle even his head as they've befuddled yours." Arria held a steady gaze, but a stream of fear ran through her. To brashly challenge the commander of Cambria was not wise.

Drusus smirked. "So, now I am befuddled by a slave, and as I've heard from Marcella, cuckolded by a barbarian. Is this true?"

Beneath her placid expression, Arria burned indignant. "It is a lie. Marcella's allegation is false and beneath me. You forget, my lord, that I am a patrician and a senator's daughter."

"No, my love, it seems you've forgotten. In which case, an affair with a barbarian would be disastrous not only for your reputation but also for your father's. I am sure Emperor Valentinian would disapprove of barbarian blood mixing with pure Roman blood such as yours. Even my blood isn't as pure as yours."

"Drusus, what did the slave tell you?" Arria asked calmly.

"I see we're back to Drusus again. Why is it that you use my given name only when you feel desperate? You've always kept me at a distance. Marcella has not." Drusus reached for Arria's hand and pressed his lips to her fingers. His mocking kiss feigned a reverence, then he continued, "Nonetheless, quite miraculously, your visit has coincided with another. I would like you to stay. The scouts I'm sending against the Huns are waiting for my attention, and I've decided to include you in these matters, seeing that you're the diplomatic envoy." Drusus called his secretary. Turning to Arria he said, "Oh, I nearly forgot. Another person arrived early this morning who is eager to see you. *Carissima*, are you ready?"

Drusus smiled brilliantly, his grin filled Arria with dread.

Twelve days after their meeting with Luthgar, Garic and Vodamir left the Frank camp on their two day journey to Cambria. Outfitted with food and furs, Garic and his cousin prepared for what dangers lay ahead. They knew the road well and were eager to finish this task and get to their homes for the winter. Garic's home was northwest of Cambria, a day's ride from the great sea and the bay of the Somme River.

Vodamir lived up river a few miles from Garic. Both men knew they were riding into danger, even their deaths, but their land and families, and their people needed protection, and Garic needed to see Arria. His choice had already been made on the day he carved *Semper* into the armlet he gave her at the slave auction. Arria owned his heart.

Vodamir and Garic reached Fort Cambria in the late afternoon. Immediately, they were escorted to Drusus, giving Garic little opportunity to see Arria. Garic's only hope was that the commotion made by their arrival would be noted, and perhaps, Arria's curiosity would draw her to him.

The corridor leading to Drusus' quarters smelled of pinewood and the resin that fueled the torches. Unsure of what awaited them, they happened upon Samuel.

"Nobles Garic and Vodamir, welcome back to Cambria!" Samuel said with a bow.

"Greetings Samuel, how fares my lady?" Garic asked without hesitation.

"She is well, but I am often pulled from her service. Just now, I was informed that I will serve the Tribune Severus, newly arrived at the fort. He was a close friend of Lady Arria's dead husband, Marcian." Samuel shook his head, then looked about. "I don't have time to explain, but Marcella practices her magic on Drusus and sought to seduce Arria into her web of deceit."

Garic tensed. "If Marcella harmed Arria in *any* way, I swear... ."

"No!" Samuel protested, raising his hands. "The Lady Arria is safe. She's young, but clever.

Samuel looked down the hall. Approaching soldiers signaled the end to their conversation. "I must go," he said, and hurried down the corridor, away from the oncoming soldiers.

Garic bristled, "I swear, if that witch or Roman dog commander harms Arria, my revenge will be powerful!"

"Calm yourself, man! Drusus cannot suspect any discord on our part. We are committed to this expedition. Must I remind you, we're outnumbered."

Garic and Vodamir waited outside of Drusus' administrative

office. Two soldiers guarded the door, while two stood together in conversation. Garic recognized one as Tarvistus, and the other, a tribune. Having just arrived in Cambria, the tribune spoke of his journey from Rome and the hazards he met along the way.

From the tribune's appearance, one could see that he was a veteran soldier of distinction. His uniform clean and polished, he was an *Equite*, a cavalry soldier. His brown hair hung straight over his brow and fell just below his ears. Not as tall as Garic and Vodamir, his stocky frame conveyed a sword-wielding strength. The soldier stared momentarily into Garic's eyes, then returned to his conversation with Tarvistus. Garic wondered if Tarvistus and the tribune were the trackers chosen for the scouting party. He glanced at Vodamir, who watched the soldiers as well. Vodamir looked back toward Garic, his eyes said, *be wary*.

Drusus' secretary stepped into the hall and announced that Commander Drusus would see them now. Tarvistus and the cavalry soldier entered first. Garic heard a woman gasp. "Severus!" It was unmistakably Arria. Garic shot Vodamir a quick glance. The two cousins hid their emotions and walked through the door.

Arria rose quickly from her seat and crossed the room to Severus. Extending her hands to him, she said, "Severus, I am delighted you're here! You look as valiant as when you fought at Marcian's side. When did you arrive?"

Her ecstatic greeting made him smile easily. "Just this morning. It was a long journey, especially in this cold climate. It makes me long for Tuscia. This weather is definitely fit only for barbarians."

Tarvistus and Severus stood in the center of the room where they held Arria's attention.

"Ah, yes. Barbarians, please join us," Drusus invited Garic and Vodamir just inside the room. "Maybe we should ask our guests how they fare in this weather?"

Severus dropped Arria's hands and turned to acknowledge their presence, which allowed her to view Garic with Vodamir beside him.

Arria's heart leapt, unprepared for this surprise. She gave her most gracious smile and extended her hand. "Welcome Nobles," she said, "your company is unexpected. What brings you back to Cambria?"

Garic stepped up and pressed his lips to her hand. His blue eyes locked with hers and proclaimed the depth of his love. "My lady, this biting cold brings us to the place where we know we will find warmth." He squeezed her hand, so only she would notice and moved aside to let Vodamir pay his respects.

Vodamir nodded and lightly brushed his lips over her finger tips. "Lady Arria, it's always a pleasure to see you." He stepped back and smiled impishly.

Arria's heart pounded. Could Severus beside her hear it beating? Garic watched her with confidence. Standing among Drusus, his soldiers, even Vodamir and acting indifferent towards Garic was difficult. All she wanted, needed, was time alone with him—to hear from his lips once more that he had not betrayed her.

Drusus watched the barbarians greet Arria. Both warriors seemed calm and unmoved. Vodamir, the cocky bastard, was his usual self. He stood there with a lopsided grin plastered on his face.

According to Marcella, Vodamir wasn't his rival after all. She had revealed Arria's infatuation with, surprisingly, the Franks' first counsel, Garic. In order to save Drusus' honor, Marcella had come between Arria and Garic and proved herself worthy.

Garic's quiet strength and authority were daunting, Drusus admitted to himself, but Garic and his impudent cousin would be no match for Severus and Tarvistus together. He would proceed as planned—wed Arria in June, bed her and seed her with child. Her fortune would be kindling for his political ambitions, and she just might prove to be more of a vixen than he expected. Maybe Garic's roughness excited her. In any case, in another week, the two barbarians would be food for the wolves.

"My lord Drusus, I will leave you to your business. I must see that there is food and wine for all." Arria smiled, "Dear Severus, we will catch up on past news at dinner."

"Until that hour comes, Lady," Severus graciously nodded and smiled.

"Lady Arria?" Garic's resonant voice filled the room. "Please excuse us from the gracious offer of dinner, but Vodamir and I have made plans to dine and lodge at the inn this evening. However, we brought the two stallions that were promised to Commander Drusus and Noble Theobald to the fort. They rest in the stable. Would you see them later? Given your excellent riding skills, perhaps in the morning, you might honor us by riding Tiwaz' sire, Iberian. I know I will have to ride Tiwaz one more time before I give him to Theobald. Please don't refuse us. It's our custom." His bold manner defied all onlookers as he waited for her response.

Arria hesitated, looked at Drusus, then turned back toward Garic. "Nobles. It's our habit to honor the customs and wishes of our guests and allies. When your meeting is concluded, Samuel will be waiting for you at the stable. Send him to escort me and I will join you. I would be pleased to see the stallions that saved a young woman's honor." Arria bowed her head and walked from the room.

Drusus bristled as he watched Arria leave. Was Marcella lying? Arria seemed calm and Garic seemed no different than any other time they were together, but Drusus' instincts gnawed at him. He would ensure Tarvistus made a trip to the stables. Let Garic enjoy his horse. Where the first counsel was going no horses were needed, only demons to carry the pagans to Hades. Drusus would order Severus and Tarvistus to bring him a lock of Garic's long hair once he was dead. From the golden strands, he would have a belt crafted and present it to Arria, as a token of what unfaithfulness cost them both.

"Commander, if I may, what amuses you so?" Severus asked.

"Only the delightful beauty of my Arria. I would venture that a man would lose his life for her. What say you, Noble Garic? Would a Frank lose his life for a woman like the Lady Arria?"

"A Frank would fight to the death for the woman he loved, and if a woman like the Lady Arria commanded his love, then to save her, he would die," Garic fired back. "I will ask the same question of you, Commander. Would you die for the Lady Arria?"

"Not only would I die—I would kill." Smiling directly at Garic, Drusus withdrew to a chair by the coals and sat down.

Severus sat beside Drusus who prompted Tarvistus to an adjacent chair.

Garic and Vodamir stood together in the center of the room.

"Come Nobles! The hour grows late and we have much to discuss. Please, be seated," Drusus invited. "Nobles Garic and Vodamir, excuse my bad manners, but I have yet to introduce Tribune Marcus Furius Severus of the VIII Augusta Legion. Severus rode with Lucius Valerius Marcian, the Lady Arria's late husband. Marcus was at Marcian's side when he was killed by barbarians in Germania."

Severus nodded, "Nobles."

"Severus and Tarvistus are just two of the four who will join you on this mission." Drusus reached for his wine. He signaled his slave who filled the cups on a marble sideboard and served the men. "We must track these Huns and stop their raiding. In the summer months, Aetius will arrive, so we must prepare for battle."

Garic and Vodamir, accustomed to the cold, sat farthest from the fire. Garic's suspicions grew deeper as Drusus spoke. This was more than a tracking mission. He was convinced that Drusus knew that he loved Arria.

"Severus, explain to our barbarian friends why you've come to Cambria." Drusus popped a grape in his mouth from a silver platter filled with fruit and sweets on a low table before them. Wisps of pink-gray smoke rising from the braziers hung in the air.

"I was sent by Senator Felix, Lady Arria's father, to check on her welfare and to make sure that she is not discontent. He thought that if she were homesick, she might advance her wedding plans and then return to Tuscia for a short visit. Of course, if her political duties demand her presence, it may not be the time, and her father is reconciled to this possibility. In the meantime, I am at the Commander's service and will help track the Huns."

Garic thought it wise to speak; though the thought of Arria's marriage or her return to Tuscia made him want to rise and steal her away. "Cambria without Lady Arria would be like the land without light. I regret that a barbarian stole her husband from her, but many German women have lost their men to the Roman sword. It's the price we *all* pay to live where we were born, and to keep it from those who would take it from us." Garic grasped his knees with his hands and addressed the Romans firmly. "Today, Attila is the aggressor, and we must band together to stop him, or we will all die or be enslaved." Anxious to meet Arria at the stable, Garic drained his cup and placed it on the table, while Vodamir followed his lead.

Garic felt the weight of the commander's calculating stare. "Well spoken," Drusus answered. "Make ready by midday tomorrow. My men will also make ready. The kitchen will provide food for the journey; extra blankets are stored at the stable. Help yourselves."

"We will make use of your generous offer, Commander and will take our leave," Garic replied. Rising together, Garic and Vodamir nodded and left the room.

The barbarians gone, Drusus and his two soldiers helped themselves to handfuls of raisins and small honey cakes.

"Severus, the barbarians should not return from this mission. They've insulted Arria with their brutish attentions." Drusus wiped his hands with the warm towel offered by his elderly male slave. "Tarvistus, you will serve Tribune Severus in all matters required."

"Yes, sir." Tarvistus responded.

"Good. What do you think, Severus? Will it be difficult?"

"It won't be easy. They're big men and trained warriors, but we have the element of surprise. Two less barbarians in this world suits me just fine." Severus pulled his sword and cradled the blade. "Their demise avenges Marcian."

"Excellent," drawled Drusus. "Don't mention any of this to Arria.

It would distress her if you or anyone might be hurt protecting her honor."

"Commander, I am a veteran. This mission rests in capable hands," Severus said.

The two soldiers and Drusus brought their cups together and Drusus pledged, "To the success of your mission. Kill the Hun raiders *and* the Franks who would defile a lady's honor. "*Salute!*"

"*Salute!*" both officers chimed.

Garic and Vodamir crossed from the headquarters to the stable. A luminous moon stretched tall shadows across their path as they spoke.

"After what we saw and heard, I suspect Drusus intends to have us killed," Vodamir confided.

Garic scowled. "I don't die so easily and neither do you."

Saying Drusus is a son of a bitch is too kind. He's the whelp spawned from Hel's cold loins," Vodamir hissed.

Garic laughed, "Cousin, as usual your words describe what my heart feels, but with more brutality."

"Drusus the black-hearted dog," Vodamir cursed again.

"He's a man out to win," Garic said. "Arria's the prize, but he has some heavier concerns, right now. Attila advances deeper into Gaul. Attila is dangerous—very dangerous, and a much bigger threat to Drusus and Cambria than you and I. Drusus makes the mistake of an arrogant man. He puts his own desires first and believes himself invincible."

"That well may be," Vodamir said. "I just hope his jealousy isn't our undoing. How will we protect ourselves?"

Seized by the need for levity, Garic replied, "Remember Uncle Benno? He'd disguise himself with leaves and tree branches and lie in wait for some unsuspecting Chamavi or Visigoth. Cunning runs in the family."

"What's gotten into you, man?" Vodamir piped, exasperated. "It's that trickster, Loki, again. It seems he's also the god of ill-humor." Vodamir stopped and ran a hand through his hair. "This mission

111

screams ambush and death and you're ranting about Uncle Benno and arming ourselves with tree branches against the Romans," he paused, "What bothers you—seeing Arria again?"

Brought to a halt, Garic faced Vodamir. His boyish humor gone, the warrior was back in place. "One thing must not happen—*never* let the Romans separate us. Alone, we are vulnerable. Do you understand? And Cousin, seeing Arria again is what prompts my *good* humor, not Loki. Come!" Garic playfully nudged Vodamir forward.

The walls of the stable loomed before them, and light seeped through the hinges and cracks of the closed doors. The earthy smells of horses and dry hay mingled with the cold air and drifted into their path as Vodamir swung one door open and entered with Garic behind him. Red-gold light shone from a lamp nestled in the stone alcove near the entrance and illuminated the front stalls of the long stable. On the straw covered ground was Samuel, wrapped in a blanket, waiting expectantly.

"Young Nobles." Samuel started to rise, but Garic stayed him with his hand and both cousins crouched near. Samuel said just above a whisper, "The Lady Arria sent me to wait for you. She knows not that we spoke previously and that I shared my concerns."

Garic grabbed a handful of hay and pensively let it sift through his fingers. "Samuel, you spoke of some danger to my lady. Tell me, what is her danger?"

Samuel straightened and glanced around before he spoke. "I only know that Marcella made a seductive gesture toward Arria. When my lady refused her advances, Marcella in anger went to Drusus."

"Did Marcella tell Drusus about Arria and me?" Garic asked. If Samuel didn't know he and Arria shared an admiration and love, he would now. Garic's drugged and drunken blunder with Marcella had unleashed their secret. Were the gods against him? In spite of this thought, he believed in Arria. He loved her, and he prayed she loved him, too.

"I am not sure what Drusus knows," Samuel answered. "Only Lady Arria can tell you. On my mistress' command, I've informed the stablemaster to take his dinner and to wait for her summons. I must also inform her you have arrived. If Vodamir agrees, we will guide her safely to you." Samuel glanced at Vodamir who nodded his approval.

They stood and Garic said, "Tell her, *Krieger* waits. Bring her, but let her enter alone. You and Vodamir will keep watch." Garic extended his hand.

Vodamir understood and placed his hand on top of Garic's. Looking at Samuel, Garic said, "Will you join us in brotherhood and loyalty?"

Smiling like a schoolboy with newfound friends, Samuel placed his hand on theirs and said passionately, "I will!"

Then disappearing into the night, Samuel and Vodamir left in search of Arria.

Along the stable wall, a hooded Tarvistus watched cloaked from view.

Arria slipped through the moonlight, her blue gown hugging her legs. A thick wool *palla* was wrapped around her, protection against the brisk air. The golden cord, crisscrossing her breasts tightened with every footstep closer to the stable. She stopped a few feet from the door, caught her breath and calmed herself. She nodded toward Vodamir and Samuel who left her side and flanking the entrance melted into the dark. Should she speak first to Garic? What should she say? Unsure, she urged herself forward, lifted the latch and stepped from the night into the stable. A tall, broad figure with axe in hand and silhouetted by dim amber light confronted her, Arria recoiled; but the word, *Mellitula*, fell from the dark stranger's lips and caressed her ears. Arria stepped with confidence into Garic's waiting arms.

Garic dropped his axe and crushed her to him. Arria sought for a reason to pull away, but he wouldn't let go. Like the forest that encircles each tree, one in part, one in all, he enveloped Arria, and his warmth radiated through her making her forget everything else.

"You feel good," he said, tilting her chin to his gaze and looking into her searching eyes. "A day hasn't passed that I haven't thought about you."

Arria blushed and attempted to pull away.

Garic secured her in his arms. "Arria, kiss me."

She squirmed. "Is this your barbarian way! You'll just take me and I will forget everything I saw? I cannot," she protested and turned her face.

"You can," he answered, as he laid his fingers on her cheek, guiding her gaze back to his longing eyes.

"*Krieger*, you hurt and betrayed me."

"Arria, listen to me. The witch drugged me. She hates me, you—us. I don't know her ambitions, but she will not hesitate to destroy all who stand in her way. I am sorry I hurt you. I never suspected deception from Marcella. That she would employ a potion—magic to seduce me. An oath on the grave of my parents, I didn't understand what I was doing!"

"But she's beautiful. Drusus cannot resist Marcella. He acts like he's her slave. And now you."

"I am not Drusus and Marcella is evil! Besides," Garic ran his fingertips through the wispy tendrils fallen from her hair and said huskily, "the most beautiful woman I know is in my arms. Believe me, Arria. I speak the truth." Garic touched her face, her eyes, then her lips with his fingertips. "Let me kiss you now." He pressed himself closer and slid his hand over her shoulder.

Arria caught her breath and Garic grinned.

"*Mellitula*, let me kiss you. I won't—until you tell me."

She dug her fingers into his broad shoulders and felt she would faint. She believed him and trusted his goodness. These virtues lived in Garic, barbarian or not. Arria gazed into the blue passage to his soul and what she saw, she loved.

She pulled him closer. "Kiss me now, or I will die," she whispered.

Garic kissed her tenderly.

Arria's eyes welled with tears. She had missed his touch and the taste of his tongue on hers. It hurt to be away from him and she ached with the pain of wanting him.

Garic's sun stained fingers brushed her tears aside and then his lips kissed them away. "Come away with me." He bit her lip, then nipped her neck and moved his hand over her breast.

"Not now," she could barely speak. "We won't run like the guilty."

He gently unfastened her *stola's* golden cord and tugged the bodice, freeing her to the warm shadowed light. Arria stood unashamed. He swept her up and laid her on a mound of hay and possessed her with his heated kiss.

She felt caught in a whirlwind driven by desire and unable to suppress a moan as his kisses roamed her flesh.

"Tell me you want me, there is no other," he said softly.

"I want you. There is no other," Arria whispered, her fingers digging into his broad shoulders.

"Do you love me?" Garic asked and ran a gentle hand beneath her gown.

"Yes," she gasped.

"Shall I take you now?" His voice was urgent.

Arria roamed her lips over his soft stubble until she found his mouth and lavished his tongue with her caress. Driven but wary, she uttered between kisses, "I am afraid...Drusus...he'll hurt you." She shuddered, spurred by her desire.

"Only you can conquer me," Garic said hoarsely. "Trust me," he whispered. "Believe we are one." Garic looked into her eyes. "I will please you. My Roman girl."

Arria kissed his lips, but seized by a sudden fear, she pushed him away. "Now isn't the time for us to possess each other completely," she said, her tone wistful. "If we are together, it should be unencumbered and free from Drusus and his revenge.

Garic sighed, reconciled to Arria's wish. "I want you more than all the riches of Rome, but even more than that, I want what you want." And pulling Arria close, he caressed and kissed her one last time and held her close.

A loud creak in the floorboards stopped them. Arria felt the blood ebb from her face and she gasped, "*Krieger!*" They turned toward the sound. A woolen cloak swept past the edge of the wall. Steps retreated into the dark toward the rear of the stable and a door shut.

Garic jumped to his feet and reached for the axe lying by his side. His ardor turned to anger. " A spy sent by Drusus, no doubt. We must leave Arria. Samuel will walk you to your room. In the morning, we will meet for one last ride together as planned." Arria nodded. Quickly and silently they dressed.

Beside the entrance, Garic wrapped Arria's wool *palla* around her shoulders. He cradled her face in his hands and kissed her forehead, her lips. "Come, we must hurry. Please, be careful. The snake and his magic mistress wait for you. Pray to your God for protection, and know that my heart and breath is with you as long as I live. Meet me here at sunrise, and we shall ride. For appearances sake, Drusus cannot stop us, but his spy will have much to tell. I will inform Samuel of the possible danger and will give him a knife to hide beneath his tunic. Stay close to him on the walk back to your quarters." Garic read the apprehension in Arria's expression. "*Mellitula*, are you afraid?"

Arria drew a breath and straightened herself. "I am only fearless when you are beside me, but I am strong and will holdfast, my lord."

"Your bravery surpasses all the women I have ever known. Believe in me! We will marry one day." Garic kissed her again.

"Promise me that you'll return from this mission," she said, fighting to hide her worry.

"I have no choice, *Mellitula*. I am your captive."

"No my love, you're my life." Standing on tiptoe, she flung her arms around his neck and kissed him with abandon.

Garic straightened and spun her around. "Yes, Lady Arria, I am," he replied.

Into the cool, pale darkness they stepped. Vodamir and Samuel stood nearby.

"What a beautiful night," Arria said and choked back her tears.

Chapter Ten

Promitto
I promise

So, my little Arria has run back to the first counsel's waiting arms. If Garic was such a wise counselor, he would advise Arria leave him and return to her betrothed, don't you think, Tarvistus?"

Tarvistus nodded and smirked.

Drusus, his face taut as a death mask, glared at a row of shelves. His fingers crushed the document he held and flung the ruined parchment toward the glowing brazier. "How dare that *barbarian* caress Arria's beautiful skin and possess her for even a moment! Garic's fate is planned, but more challenging, what shall I do with Arria?" In an odd sort of way it excited him to think of Arria crossing the conventions of her culture; but at the same time, how repulsive that the woman he would wed and bed craved the barbarian's crude lovemaking—a bestial act. After all, barbarians were only animals in men's bodies. Drusus shut his eyes and slouched deeper into his chair. His dark side rose. A vision of Arria entwined in Garic's naked embrace made him cringe. He imagined himself driving a dagger in Garic's back at the moment Garic reached his ecstasy. Drusus smiled, and relished his fantasy. Arria had rejected him, Drusus, the lover and politically powerful, for a barbarian misfit.

Tarvistus standing quietly by ventured, "Commander? What shall

I do?"

Drusus rose, paced several steps, then crossed toward a couch draped with a leopard skin, a spoil from an earlier campaign. He sat and gazed at the mural on his library wall, Achilles slaying Hector at Troy. His thoughts ran rampant and he bristled with anticipation. In just a few days, his soldiers would confirm Garic's demise. He would savor the news and expect a piece of Garic's golden hair as proof.

"The preparations for tomorrow's departure up north. Completed?" Drusus snapped.

"Yes, Commander. Everything is ready."

"And Severus stands *ready* as well?"

Tarvistus chuckled sardonically. "Severus claims dispatching the barbarians to Valhalla will sweeten the mission."

"Ah, yes, Valhalla. The word rings pleasantly. I am sure the first counsel and his impudent cousin will be most welcome in the hall of warriors. May you speed them on their journey, Centurion. Ensure that Severus cuts a lock of hair from both men, especially the first counsel as proof of their death. I must have my prize. As for my betrothed, it's time Arria learn her place in the order of Roman life. Her father has spoiled her and raised her like a son, but she isn't a son. It's time she came to accept Roman conventions and her woman's position. Do you agree, Tarvistus?"

Tarvistus wisely nodded, "Yes, Commander."

"She is to serve her husband first, then her God, if she chooses, and then anyone else she deems worthy of her help. However, I don't think my little songbird has realized this as yet, but she will. Soon, the Lady Arria will understand that she belongs by my side, or in the hell I will create for her. It's quite simple."

Drusus grabbed his wine cup from the table beside him and downed the drink. His eyes burned from fatigue and fury. A deadly jealousy shackled his heart. "I may need your help in matters concerning my lady, but that's for another time. First, you will handle this situation with the barbarians."

A soft knock at the door brought their conversation to a halt. "Come," Drusus responded. His manservant entered and bowed. "What is it" Drusus asked impatiently.

"My lord," replied the elderly slave, "dinner is served. Everyone awaits you."

Severus entered the dining hall and looked expectantly around the room. He hoped to find a place tonight at Arria's side. Several years had passed since he last saw her, but time had flown quickly. The many nights he had supped with Marcian and Arria at their villa in Tuscia loomed before his eyes. He had missed his good friends and the long summer nights spent on the outer verandah, overlooking the hills where they shared stories and pleasantries over a sumptuous meal. What was she like now? A young widow stationed on the frontier, betrothed to the arrogant and ambitious Drusus couldn't possibly be the carefree young girl who rode by Marcian's side. The young wife who held her dying husband in her arms.

Severus spied Drusus reclined on a couch near a low table. A plate perched in his hand, Drusus plucked at dried fruits and nutmeats. Upon seeing Severus, he beckoned to the tribune.

Severus approached, "Good Evening, Commander."

"Ah, Severus, join me." Drusus invited and pointed to the neighboring couch. Lazily, he tumbled two figs in his mouth. "I questioned if I would see you tonight."

"Why is that?" Severus signaled a girl carrying several cups of wine. Taking one from the slave, he drank and waited for Drusus' reply.

"I wondered if your sense of discipline forsakes social opportunities the night before a mission, or if you're the kind who allows no anxiety or worry to trouble him." Drusus smiled. "A good field soldier is generally wrought from iron, is he not?"

"I would say that my attributes are less noble and my desire to visit with an old friend stronger."

"You can only mean Arria." Drusus pensively shook his head. "What a hold she has on men."

"Excuse me?"

Drusus laughed. "Of course, you're curious to see how the widow of your dead friend fares."

"Absolutely. Marcian would expect it of me, and I from him, if I were buried and she were my wife."

"So many expectations from the dead," Drusus replied dryly. "Only to be compounded with the needs of the living. God help us. Tell me, Severus, you never thought of Arria in the way men sometimes fantasize about the wives of their friends?" Drusus narrowed his eyes, his smile bland.

Severus clenched his jaw. Drusus appeared willing to unnerve or uncover a weakness in him. Why? Severus understood why men approached Drusus with a guarded respect or loathing. He was a cunning dealer in human emotion and seemingly without boundaries. "Arria was committed to Marcian, and I loved him like a brother. Besides, my sexual appetites run more toward the strong women from Pannonia. They will fight you in and out of bed. I am a tough man who likes a strong woman. Have you ever *known* a woman from Pannonia?" Severus looked Drusus directly in the eyes.

Drusus threw back his head and laughed heartily. "Those barbarians will be no match for you. Just remember not to say anything to Arria. She has been insulted and upset by their constant badgering, but for diplomatic reasons she's suffered their company. I, however, will not. A quick dispatch of this matter and the proof of their demise will pay you handsomely and at the same time relieve my lovely lady of their unwanted attentions."

A small commotion at the room's entrance interrupted their conversation. Arria entered and was quickly met by several slaves who asked for further instructions for the evening.

Severus noted that her Jewish slave standing behind her quietly took a place at the serving table where servants came to refresh their pitchers with new wine.

Arria, dressed in white with a scarlet *palla* cascading from her shoulders, never looked so beautiful. Severus couldn't help gaping.

A dark look crossed Drusus' face. "She is beautiful, even if she's marred."

"What do you mean?" Severus asked defensively. "She is most virtuous. A rare thing in Rome. Some would say that you, Drusus, should know this better than most. After all, your reputation for *appreciating* the most fashionable women of Rome, married or single, is occasionally a topic of conversation at the emperor's festivities."

Severus' words shot through Drusus who quickly replied, "I would know better than most. A tarnished woman is not hard found in Rome, but never mind my words, my cynicism overshadows me. Arria cannot help that she was married."

"If you believe widowhood damages a woman then indeed your cynicism thrives. I only hope for the sake of your marriage and for the generous soul I know Arria to be, that you'll forget such a derisive notion."

Arria finished directing the slaves and glanced around the room. Upon seeing Severus, she approached him, but first acknowledged Drusus with a strained tone. Drusus seemed as cool as always, but a slight sulk gripped the corner of his mouth.

"My lady, it's been too long." Severus stood, took her hand and gently kissed it.

"Oh, Severus, how wonderful that you are here! What brings you to Cambria?"

"You, my lady, and other matters, but most important, your father has sent letters and presents and has urged me to discover if you're homesick and if your diplomatic duties are completed. He misses you dearly, and I am afraid your absence has been difficult on him."

"Is my father well?" Arria touched Severus' arm.

"Don't be afraid," Severus answered and took her hand. "He's quite healthy, despite his ailing knees, and even a little heavier around the waist. He just misses you."

Arria sighed, "Thanks be to Christus, he fares well. I miss him so much, especially now." Arria slipped a glance in Drusus' direction.

Drusus watched her with his falcon eyes.

"Especially now? Is anything wrong?" Severus asked concerned.

"Not at all," she smiled. "The news of my father made me want his company all the more. Forgive me."

"What's to forgive? Any loving child would surely feel the need for a loving parent's company. Come, let us walk the corridors and talk a while before dinner." Severus turned toward Drusus, "Of course, with your permission, Commander?"

"Of course, catch up on the news from friends and family, but do not trouble Arria this evening with business, Severus. Can I count on you?" Drusus' broad smile flashed strong white teeth. His voice was friendly.

"I assure you, the last thing I care to think about, while in Lady Arria's company, is business." Severus graciously took Arria's arm and escorted her from the room into the coolness of the narrow corridor.

"You've changed, Arria. You're no longer a carefree young girl. An aura of sophistication surrounds you and you seem more serious," Severus offered.

"A serious viewpoint is neccessary in such a rustic and dangerous place." Curled up on a corridor bench under a torch sconced on the wall, Arria wrapped her *palla* tighter around her shoulders.

Severus retrieved a blanket from one of the guest rooms and tucked it around her legs. "Arria, are you happy?" he asked, sitting beside her.

"Yes, Severus, I am." She did not say that it was Garic who filled her life with love, but Arria knew she could not tell him this secret. He would think she was mad. The only reality Severus understood was the Roman way. To a Roman tribune and veteran soldier there was no alternative.

"Do you miss Marcian?"

"I do. Sometimes, when I see a young soldier resembling Marcian mount his horse, tears come to my eyes. I have an urge to saddle

Syphax and chase after him. That sounds foolish doesn't it?" Arria smiled weakly. She was totally spent. Her emotions and all the events from the day had left her fatigued.

Severus grabbed her hand. "Arria, Marcian was my friend and more like the brother I never had. You and I grew up only children, but he tied the three of us together. It will take time. I see him too, riding at the head of a column or at the days end when we sit around the camp fire. I see him in a soldier's laugh or in one approaching from the distance, shadowed by the firelight. His spirit will always be with us and we honor him by seeing him in different people and in moments of solitude. Nothing that ever involves the memory of Marcian is foolish. Besides, you've never been a foolish woman."

Arria laughed at this irony. "Some would say that I am."

"If you're referring to your betrothal, I can only say that Drusus is a powerful and shrewd man and will not be in Cambria very long. If he can successfully help Aetius in the matter of Attila, his future will be very bright and you will be back in Rome in no time. These times dictate protection that only wealth and good politics can bring. Take heart, in time, you may be able to care for him and he for you. He is a lustful man, but with marriage and children, a settled way of life might begin to suit him better. Have faith that good will come your way."

Arria squeezed his hand and only smiled. "You will leave tomorrow to search for Huns. For what reason?"

"This is the business Drusus asked I not speak about."

"That will not stop me. Tell me Severus, has the Hun raiding been so vicious? Why do you need the barbarians?"

"We bring the barbarians because they're better trackers, especially in the marshlands. In the months to come, Attila will move his army further west into Gaul, but while it's winter, he waits. Cold weather isn't for fighting. His men cannot live off the land, but small raiding parties can rob farms, villages and towns to bring captured provisions, valuables, and horses back to Attila's very strong, large camp. Raiding also keeps their warriors active and able."

"How dangerous is this mission?"

"No more dangerous then facing five thousand screaming barbarians with raised axes." Severus quietly chuckled at Arria's horrified expression and squeezed her hand. "Don't be afraid for me, lovely. I will be safe. I am a proven soldier who wishes to find my way back to Tuscia and grow peaches and lemons with a strong woman by my side."

Arria shrank inside. She loved her friend, and his life was precious to her, but Garic's life meant even more. Her long-haired warrior would be riding with Severus, and it pained her to think that Garic might die and Severus would return to her with the body of yet another fallen lover. A bell chimed in the dining hall. "We must take our leave, Severus. Dinner is ready and Drusus awaits my presence." Arria clasped his hand. "My dear friend, I pray your mission is successful and *you all* return.

"Come my love, I will race you to the wood!" Garic challenged as he rode beside Arria in the morning light and across the barren meadow.

Arria laughed into the newly risen gust dancing around them. "My lord, you will leave today disgruntled for I can guarantee my victory."

"Win or lose, my lady, I will never leave your side disgruntled," he smiled and answered with conviction. "A sore defeat is only for those who lack confidence." Tiwaz, Garic's black stallion, and Iberian, Arria's mount, pranced skittishly about anxious to start.

Garic reined his horse harder and added, "The only regret I will know is that for a space of time you eluded me and I was not in your reach." With a quick grin, he loosened the rein, dug his heels into Tiwaz' sides and broke into a gallop. Looking behind, Garic laughed upon seeing her shocked expression.

Arria recovered quickly and yelled a starting cry to Iberian. Her command set the stallion in motion. Undaunted, though trailing behind, Arria bent low to Iberian's mane. This felt like the life she used to know. This race, the challenge, the outdoors, her love, it all felt like a place in time she once knew.

In a full run, Tiwaz' shadow skimmed the ground, magnificent and ahead by two lengths. His hooves dug pieces of turf from the frosty grass, while Arria's horse inched closer, synchronizing their strides and pounding the ground.

Garic's long blond hair streamed in the wind. Gaining on him was a moment without comparison for Arria. Only a horse length behind, she approached Garic steadily. Iberian's breath trailed behind him like the wind rippling Arria's hair as he gained on Tiwaz.

Garic looked back and whipped his rein across Tiwaz' neck.

Arria focused more intent, her victory in sight. The dark edge of the wood loomed rapidly near with Garic only a few feet in front. Employing all her skills, Arria loosened the rein, giving him his head and shouted in his ear, "Fly my brave boy! Faster!"

The stallion responded to his rider's plea and pushed harder, coming head to head with Tiwaz.

Garic glanced at Arria, yelled and dug harder into his mount.

"Now! Iberian! Now!" Arria screamed. Filled with fire, Iberian shot past the snorting Tiwaz and disappeared into the wood.

The narrow path wound itself on a soft incline deep into the forest. A perfect spot to call a victory, Arria reined in Iberian who slowed and snorted. She turned to await Garic and sat smiling with exhilaration, her wind streaked hair settling on her cheeks and the nape of her neck.

Left in the rear by two lengths, but now only paces away, the long-haired warrior reined Tiwaz to a walk. Garic looked serious as he approached and halted beside her. His face held a slight flush and he conceded, "My lady has won, and therefore deserves a prize."

"What sort of prize does my lord have to offer?"

Garic dismounted and grinned. "Come meet me in my arms and I will tell you," he said.

Arria swung down from her saddle and stood before him.

He crushed her to him and murmured in her ear, "An unpretentious prize my lady—a kiss."

Arria wrapped her arms tighter around his neck, hoping this

moment wouldn't be their last. "I feel on fire," he said huskily. "I've never felt like I belonged to a woman but with you it's different. We belong together."

Breathless, she whispered in his ear, "*Krieger*, you belong to me and I to you. This I know now ... more than ever, but I am afraid. I couldn't bear to lose you. Do not go on this mission."

Garic cradled her face in his hands and gazed into her eyes. "I will come back to you. No matter what you may hear or are led to believe—wait for me."

"What might I hear, love? What do you suspect?" Arria could see in his eyes the secret he shared the night before: how he longed for them to flee to Hispania or the ocean to the north where it would carry them to Britannia.

"Drusus knows of us I am sure, especially after last night and the spy in the stable. He needs Vodamir and I to track for him, so all will be well. But, if I don't return, unless you see my dead body, believe only what your heart and instincts tell you. Do not marry Drusus. Wait!"

"I will wait. Promise me you will return."

"I promise. I want to live, and even more, to be with you. I will come back." He removed the glove from her hand and kissed her fingers. Then he kissed her open palm and the line that their Frank priestesses called the line of life. Tracing the line with his finger, he said, "This is what will tie us together as man and woman, today, here in this wood. I, Garic, First Counsel to Luthgar's Tribe of Salian Franks, promise to be true to you, Lady Arria. I will honor you and fight for you. And I will slip you inside my heart, where I will protect you as long as I live."

The sudden sound of horses in the distance alerted them. Their time alone together was finished. Garic quickly lifted Arria back upon Iberian, and he jumped on Tiwaz. They readied to meet the riders as they burst out of the wood and up the path. It was no surprise when Drusus rode to the top of the knoll with Tarvistus and Vodamir behind him.

Magnificent as always, Drusus was dressed in full uniform. Trotting his horse toward them, his silver and bronze helmet reflected dancing flecks of light on the bark and leaves of the surrounding trees. His grim look bore a foreboding as he reined his stallion. He ignored any greeting and barked, "I was worried, Arria, that mayhem had befallen you and the barbarian."

"Were we gone so long? Besides, I am in the safe custody of the noble Garic."

"It may be so, but these woods are far too dangerous for a lady of your distinction to be about with only a lone warrior. I have come with these two men to make sure all is well. Your father would never forgive me if any harm was to come to you."

"How thoughtful, my lord," Arria replied tersely.

"The fault is all mine, Commander," Garic interceded. "I wanted the Lady Arria to experience the swiftness of Iberian and indeed she did. Iberian took to her command without hesitation, and unfortunately left me behind to contemplate my inadequacy as a rider."

"I hope for your sake that was all you both were left to contemplate."

"How do you mean, my lord?" Arria's eyebrow arched, instinctively.

Drusus grimaced, "Lady, it's hardly fitting that my betrothed ride alone unchaperoned. You cannot blame me for my concern."

"If you had not taken Samuel away as my attendant, I wouldn't be alone."

"I have need of your manservant. Samuel will acompany the two barbarians on this mission. Besides, I believe you are more properly served by the slave, Karas, as she is a woman. Cambria is a rustic fort. I don't wish to foster gossip among the men. Surely, you can understand my concern. After all, you are an envoy and aware of political proprieties, are you not?"

Angered by Drusus' innuendo, and his removal of Samuel from her service, Arria glared at him and answered, "I am well aware of my position, my lord, but proprieties at Cambria are not always what they seem; need I remind your slave of this?" Before Drusus could reply, she pressed Iberian's side and moved down the path.

Drusus eyed Garic with a confidant smile. "It's time that you be gone from here—and help to rid Gaul of these troublesome raiders. It's a shame that you'll have to find a new mount. Your horse Tiwaz is a beauty. Theobald the Visigoth, shall relish riding him. I too cannot wait to ride Iberian; however, I can assure you, I will make every effort to share him with my Arria. And of course, when you return, he'll be yours as promised." Familiar with the nuances of men's hearts, Garic grasped that Drusus hated him, and would never give Arria up. She might request the dissolution of their betrothal, but he would not agree. Drusus would destroy the object of her desire first. Garic recognized that in Drusus' eyes, he was a dead man. "Commander Drusus, the raiders might be only a small part of a bigger problem you may encounter, which time will surely reveal. Enjoy my horse, Iberian, he's a beauty, but if I was this noble beast, I would most undoubtedly prefer the soft, silky legs of the Lady Arria spread across me—they're so much lovelier." Walking his horse past Drusus, Garic signaled to Vodamir and the two barbarians headed down the path to the fort leaving Drusus and Tarvistus on the knoll.

Never taking his icy gaze from Garic's back, Drusus quietly hissed, "I *hate* that son of a bitch and I want him dead. Do you understand?" His lethal words and deliberate glance told Tarvistus that there would be no room for error. None. He was a man who sought vengeance. Survival for all the men on the mission would depend on presenting him with Garic's and Vodamir's hair. Failure would earn the same fate meant for the barbarians.

"It's as good as done." Tarvistus answered contemptuously and spat on the ground.

His voice vehement, Drusus added, "And not one word of Lady Arria's involvement with the barbarian to anyone, especially Severus. Is that clear, Tarvistus?"

"Very clear, my lord."

Chapter Eleven

FORTES FORTUNA IUVAT
Fortune favors the brave

THE MISSION

"Shhh ... ," Garic whispered softly, raising a finger to his mouth. Vodamir nodded his head and waited. The walls of their makeshift tent billowed in the wind. A twig snapped. Garic slid his arm from under his cloak, removed his blanket and with his free hand, gripped the sword at his side. Vodamir tugged on Samuel's leather tunic, whispering a warning. Samuel, instantly alert, gripped the knife Garic had given him. Vodamir reached for his axe.

Flickers of light danced from the dying campfire and mixed with the pale dawn. A light snow frosted the ground. Garic signaled Vodamir and directed him forward. Then he motioned Samuel to the far right; he would take the left. They must avoid being caught like fish in a net. Their enemy only needed to bring the tent walls down. Trapped, they would die unable to fight.

Crouched, the three crept toward the muted sliver of light outside the front flaps. A sudden heave and the rear support pole rose, yanked from the ground. The tent swayed and folded in upon them. Garic, Vodamir, and Samuel burst from the entrance and sprinted toward the fire, stopped and turned. Shoulder to shoulder they stood together eager to fight. They wouldn't run. Across the fallen tent in a line stood Severus, Tarvistus, and the four legionaries sent to track the Huns.

129

"You bastards!" Vodamir shouted. "This was your plan all along."

Severus' low chuckle mixed with his scowl. "You sons of a whore," he spat, "you're the bastards! How dare you insult the Legate Drusus and take liberties with his betrothed. Do you think he didn't know? Your kind isn't fit to breathe and live among us. You're animals." Severus glanced in Samuel's direction and ordered, "Step away, slave! Leave them now and you'll live. This isn't your affair. My orders are to eliminate the barbarians, not you. My Lady Arria treasures you."

"Step away, Samuel!" Garic commanded glancing over his shoulder, but not letting down his guard.

"I will not move," Samuel responded firmly.

"Don't be a fool, man! Step away!" Vodamir snapped.

"I will not move!"

"Samuel." The quiet command of his name forced Samuel to look in Garic's direction. Garic locked Samuel's eyes with a penetrating gaze. He moved his lips, mouthing the name, "Luthgar." Garic knew the shadows from the rising light hid his action from the Romans, but not Samuel.

Samuel glanced cautiously in the direction of the horses. He moved slowly backward several feet from the ring of glowing embers through the morning mist.

"You two dogs deserve a fate less noble than a dead warrior's journey to Valhalla," Severus declared.

"What are you saying?" Garic asked.

Silent until now, Tarvistus spat, "We've arranged for a life more fitting *noble* barbarians." Even in the yellow-gray light, his grimace and low chuckle showed his scorn.

"What demon speaks?" Vodamir growled.

"Roman demons!" Severus growled back. "Fight for your lives and you'll die. Surrender, and you'll be sold to the Huns. They value their warrior slaves, but attempt an e*scape* and you'll feel the hard edge of a Hun sword. Attila barters with allies and foes for his runaways and deserters. He delights in their tasting his Hun justice. What do you choose? Death or slavery?"

"We choose death, Roman swine! Prepare to meet Hel the bitch of the underworld. My cousin and I will take you there before we enter Valhalla!" Vodamir yelled back.

Severus' sinister laugh rolled through the line of men moving forward shoulder to shoulder. "Not likely. The last time I looked, you were outnumbered."

Tarvistus grinned in agreement.

Their legs spread and weapons raised, Garic whispered to Vodamir, "Move away, but stay in line with me. This will cause them to spread out as well." His quick glance behind the soldiers revealed Samuel near a horse, untying the reins.

A first legionary ran at Garic. He countered the soldier's blow easily and tripped him. The soldier, hands outstretched, plunged into the charred firewood quickened by small, orange flames and rolled screaming from the pit onto a patch of snow. Garic swung around just in time and blocked the descending blow from a second legionary's sword. With a solid kick to the groin, Garic brought him to his knees. The soldier groaned as he doubled over. Garic's vengeance unleashed, he kicked him in the face and knocked him out.

Vodamir, not far from Garic, fought Tarvistus, axe against sword.

"Follow the plan! Garic's mine!" Severus shouted at the two remaining legionaries and advanced cautiously toward Garic, sword in one hand, a whip in the other.

Severus and Garic slowly circled each other, their eyes locked—unflinching. They moved in a circle, neither making the first move.

Severus raised his whip and lashed out. The cracking hiss struck Garic's shoulder, ripping his tunic's sleeve. A red line seeped through the torn cloth around Garic's bicep, making Severus smile. "Come on, barbarian! Make your move!" he taunted.

"After you, woman!" Garic shouted unshaken.

Severus scowled. His hate flew on the tip of his lash, catching Garic across his neck, below his ear. The whip screamed and sliced the skin, making it well with blood. "If this continues, coward, you'll bleed to death while on your feet."

"Not before I cut my name across your dying heart!"

"Hah! Not likely!" Severus yelled, and the black coil snapped the air.

Garic raised his left arm across his face as the leather cord spun around his wrist. He swung his ready sword downward, freeing himself from the biting lash. Severus dropped his whip and advanced; drawing his sword. Severus licked his lips, and his sword rose in both hands. Garic's sword blocked and rang as metal struck metal. Fury raged in the tribune's contorted grin. This was a fight to the death.

The hilts of their swords rammed together, sweat oozed from their pores. Muscle against muscle, they strained for the advantage. A sudden energy rushed through Garic's limbs and he shoved Severus backward. A temporary reprieve, Garic glanced in Vodamir's direction. He fought Tarvistus, swinging his axe and inching him toward a row of buckthorn.

"Barbarian!" Severus bellowed, rushing back at Garic.

Garic dodged his thrust and crashed down on him. Unable to withstand Garic's force, Severus buckled and fell on his back. Garic lunged toward him.

Severus screamed, "Now!" and rolled away.

From the corner of his eye, Garic saw a web fly over his head. He turned and swiped at the net yanked closed by a third soldier who struck him with a wooden club. Garic struggled like a wild animal. Trapped and dazed, he watched as Tarvistus backed Vodamir into a second net wielded by the fourth legionary.

"Noooo!" cried Garic, forced to his knees by a kick to his side and a blow to his head. A burning pain raced from his skull down his spine. The hard ground rose to meet him. Painfully, he lay on his side and watched.

Jumped from behind, Vodamir was unable to maneuver in the mesh holding him prisoner. Tarvistus stepped on his neck and spat in his face. Vodamir squirmed and tried to wrestle free. The Romans stood panting, muttering obscenities. Each took a turn at kicking him.

"This is for my balls," cried the soldier felled by Garic's kick as he shot his foot into Vodamir's stomach.

"Yea! And this is for my face, you pagan pig!" cried the other soldier holding a clump of snow to his burned right cheek and brow. He kicked Vodamir in the ribs, then followed with several kicks to his face, while blurting, "And...for...my...pain!"

Tarvistus jumped in screaming, "For the beating I took at your camp from your chief, and *you*, trying to protect a fucking slave." He delivered a blow to Vodamir's chest. Vodamir rolled onto his back and groaned, his nose bleeding and eyes swollen shut. Garic's vision blurred.

Severus crouched over the unconscious Garic. Without looking up, he asked, "Where *is* the slave?"

Tarvistus and the four soldiers stood, catching their breaths. They looked blankly at one another and didn't answer.

"Where *is* the slave?" Severus asked louder.

"Not certain, Sir," Tarvistus answered lamely.

"Not certain? You're ... not...certain," Severus repeated and shook his head. "Then who is?"

Again the soldiers and Tarvistus cast opposing glances at each other, but didn't answer.

"Tarvistus, find the slave—now!" Severus ordered, clenching his teeth.

"Yes, Sir!" Tarvistus replied and scurried toward the horses.

Garic moved slightly and groaned. Vodamir lay silent.

"Get some rope and tie their hands. I don't want them escaping," Severus barked at the closest soldier, then looked down at Garic. "Such a fierce warrior; and yet, he's my prisoner. Hah! Not so strong now."

"Tribune, the slave is gone and so is his horse," Tarvistus reported, slightly out of breath.

Severus rose, a sneer on his face. "Taking one's horse in order to escape would be a logical move, don't you think, Centurion?"

"Yes sir ...very logical," Tarvistus shifted uneasily. "The horse's prints are headed southwest. That's away from Cambria. No doubt he's headed toward the Franks camp."

Severus pondered briefly. "The Franks are too far away to intervene. The Huns have been approached, and the raiding party will meet us peacefully in a few hours. They need allies of all kinds. Personally, I hate them as much as I despise these two bastards, but if we can fill our pockets with Attila's gold, why not? Are your soldiers with *you* in this matter, Tarvistus?"

"They were informed that volunteering for this mission would yield a benefit." Tarvistus faced the four legionaries. "What say you, men? A secret for a profit?"

Severus drew his sword, "Gold or death, which do you prefer?"

Tarvistus laughed, breaking the tension. "Balls! Take the gold, men. We're the ones risking our necks out here, not Drusus."

The soldiers looked at one another, then nodded in agreement.

"Good thinking, and much easier on everyone," Severus said dryly, sliding his sword into its scabbard.

"How do the raiders know where to meet us?" Tarvistus questioned Severus. "Let's leave it at ... someone in Cambria has a certain influence in all matters."

"These dumb bastards didn't even know what they were up against."

"Nor will they ever know. Take and hide their possessions before the Huns arrive, and Tarvistus, have one of these soldiers make us something to eat. I am hungry!"

The men dispersed, each preoccupied with his duty.

Kicking at Garic, Severus roused him to consciousness.

Garic's eyes fluttered open. He had to orient himself. His hands tied behind his back, he could barely move.

"You're awake. Good." Severus smiled above him.

Garic lifted his head and fell back in pain. His head pounded, and his neck and shoulder throbbed with a burning ache.

"What do we have here?" Severus lifted Arria's token, the gold cross, from around Garic's neck and over his head. It dangled in the light and he mused, "I thought you were a pagan? No doubt you stole it from a dead Roman soldier, wearing his wife's pledge. How beautiful and valuable. I will be happy to take this as payment for your life." Severus placed the chain over his head and tucked it under his uniform. "A wonderful addition to my gold collection, don't you think?"

Garic stammered through clenched teeth, "It's a woman's cross."

"You might be right. In fact, it will look better on the Lady Arria's neck than on mine."

Aided by pain and the thought of Arria's dismay, Garic feigned an angry response. "Drusus' woman deserves nothing of mine!"

"Quite the contrary, I believe she'll find it a wonderful gift from her dead husband's best friend. Yes, I am convinced, thanks to you. Arria will have this cross. Of course, I won't mention your name. I hope you don't mind."

Garic struggled with his bonds.

Severus crouched down and touched Garic's long golden hair. "I just love gold in all forms." Grabbing a long, thick strand, he pulled a short knife from his belt and cut a length two hands long. Then pulling some hemp cord from a pouch hanging at his waist he bound the end tightly and tucked the strand in the bag. Spying a hint of gold peeking through Garic's torn and bloodied shirt, Severus ripped at the cloth revealing Garic's armlet engraved with the Merovingian bees. "I think your gold band will also please Drusus and ensure for him your death. Before the Huns take you, I will relieve you of that armlet. If I don't, the Huns will."

Murderous hatred rose in Garic. He spat on Severus' boots.

Unruffled, Severus continued, "I must get your cousin's hair as well. I want my payment from Drusus. He wanted you both dead, but I see no reason not to double my earnings. This sale will rid him of you just as easily." Severus stood and moved towards Vodamir.

He sighed, "This has been a most pleasant venture—most pleasant indeed."

LUTHGAR'S CAMP

Samuel stood before Luthgar and Ingund who were seated on a small dais. A place to receive guests, it stood some distance from the dining tables to ensure quiet and undisrupted conversation. Torches burned brilliantly in the wooden hall and golden tapestries glimmered along the walls. Over the firepit, lazy streams of smoke rose from a roasting pig, enticing the senses of the hungry warriors and tribe's company.

Samuel's journey had been hard. He rode for three days and long into the night before resting. On the fourth day, he found his way into Luthgar's camp. Worn, hungry, and nearly frozen, he carried the news of the Roman betrayal and intended sale of Garic and Vodamir to the Huns.

"The *Wespe* will be needed." Luthgar thoughtfully stroked his beard and glanced at Ingund. "There can be no other course."

"Husband, it may not be the time to use them. Attila is close. We will need them here with us."

"I *need* my first counsel. Even his upstart cousin is valuable. He's an excellent swordsman, and who among us can throw an axe better? Garic is a brother to me and Vodamir a friend."

"With permission, my lord. Who are the *Wespe*?" Samuel queried with deference.

"The Lady Arria and Noble Garic regard you as a trusted servant. Will you vow to hold secret the answer to your question?"

"You have my word as a loyal servant who honors the nobles Garic and Vodamir, my lord."

Luthgar nodded his head, a satisfied gleam in his eyes. "The Wespe, wasp clan, is an ancient tradition in our tribe. Only the strongest male children at five years are chosen." Luthgar sat forward, intense in his explanation. "Warriors who comprise a clan within the tribe. These elite warriors supersede all our warriors in their ability to fight and execute missions that require a high degree of skill. They are the warriors of the Wespe."

"What determines if a boy is ready, my lord?" Samuel asked, amazed by this secret and Luthgar's confidence in him.

"First, he must reach sixteen years. At this time, he returns to his family and hunts and fights with the tribe's warriors. He must feel connected to the culture of the tribe. After a year, he rejoins the clan and is initiated. Franks who know of the Wespe understand with whom they are dealing if they see the wasp."

"Are they comprised of many?"

"The clan is highly selective because of what it requires. Garic fought with them. In his very first battle, we engaged Visigoth raiders. I am happy to say that my words of *encouragement* sped him to the point of readiness and understanding." Luthgar smiled as his distant look relived the past. "From that moment on he proved elite. Sometime later, he was asked to choose: counselor to a chief or distinction as a Wespe? He chose counselor and wears the medallion of the royal bee, King Meroveus' insignia, but he carries a black wasp tattooed on the left side of his chest. In truth, I believe he has the natural ability for it but not the heart. Garic has proven a wise counselor and a good friend."

"And to me as well." Samuel smiled, remembering the slave auction and Garic's plea to Arria that her new attendant should be a woman Samuel could love. Because of Garic, the beautiful Karas and her son, Angelus, had entered his life.

"We must rescue them!" Luthgar interrupted Samuel's thoughts. "I will never leave a Frank or friend on the battlefield. The Hun camp is a different kind of battlefield, requiring a different kind of warrior." He turned to Ingund and kissed her hand.

Ingund looked into Luthgar's eyes and sighed, "Your first counsel needs you, and I need you. But first you are chief, then husband. My lord, I will be your counsel. Take the strength of Wodan with you and bring back our Noble Garic and his cousin, Vodamir. I will offer my petition to the Valkyries that they return you to me victorious and unharmed. Call the Wespe, it's their time."

"And you, Samuel, will you join us or will you stay?" Luthgar asked.

Samuel felt an exhilaration rush through him. Vodamir and Garic were his friends now and needed his help. For the first time in years, his heart surged with pride and courage. He could stand tall and not be afraid, humiliated or governed by others. He would travel with Luthgar and the Wespe to the heart of the tiger, Attila's camp, and help save his friends or die fighting for them."

"Chief Luthgar, it would be my honor to join you."

Luthgar let out a booming laugh and slapped his knee. "Now then, Samuel, sit here at my feet and tell me of your homeland. Where are you from?"

"Palaestina, my lord—Palaestina," Samuel answered dreamily, but oddly for the first time in years, he felt as if he were home.

FORT CAMBRIA

"Mistress! Mistress!" Karas gently shook Arria's shoulders.

Arria's eyes fluttered open. Sweat beaded her temples and she swept a hand across her brow. In her dream, she had seen Garic's eyes flutter and close in pain. Was he hurt?

A week had elapsed since her race with him in the wood. She missed him terribly, but in the last few days her dreams of him had been strong and often. The night before, she dreamed of a room filled with hordes of men in strange attire. She searched frantically for Garic in this crowd, but only heard him whisper, "She cannot find me."

Tonight had been different—worse. Garic lay in pain, his golden hair streaked with blood and his handsome face bruised and swollen. His hands were tied, and he appeared to be dead. Her spirit floated above him. She could not touch him, only watch. Then her name rang out. She opened her eyes and Karas smiled at her. Arria awoke, resentfully. Her desire was to stay with Garic, even in a dream.

"Mistress," Karas said in her slow, accented tone, "allow me...wipe your brow with cool water. You cried in your sleep."

Pushing the damp cloth away, Arria sat up. "Leave me, Karas. I am distraught and I need to think."

"Then let me bring...a tea to calm you." Karas knelt at Arria's knees and gazed up at her.

Arria looked down at her beautiful slave and took her hands. "Do you think about Samuel?"

"Yes, always."

"Do you wonder where he is or if he's alive? Do you long for him?"

Karas tilted her head and repeated, "Long?"

Arria had forgotten there were words Karas didn't understand. "Do you wait for the day he returns home?"

Karas appeared thoughtful. "I think my heart can break...if Samuel does not return. My life has many cruel masters...since I am eleven years. I only know love...and friendship from one master, Angelus' father, a...merchant from Constantinople." Karas blushed, but saw the reassurance in Arria's eyes and continued, "His name is Tarlan...the first son of Oscan, a rich ... merchant ... who sell art and jewels. Tarlan is not...handsome...like Legate Drusus, but he is tall with dark eyes like Angelus, and...his face is strong...and his heart kind, and he loved me."

Karas looked away, suppressing her tears, while Arria squeezed her hands, reassuring her.

"What happened?"

"I come into Tarlan's life... a slave, but soon he make me...free... for our child. We marry...before our son is born. Our house sit on the land near the Bosphorus. We spend every summer there. It is wonderful. The summer...that Angelus become five, Tarlan left with his father for Thessalonika. They want to make bigger their markets for trade. Tarlan always leave men with weapon to watch the house... but this time...is not enough.

"One morning, we see a ship, but are not worried. Many ships from the Black Sea pass our way. Later, sailors come to our house.

At first, they ask for food. We give to them...in friendship, but they look at us. I feel not comfortable, but they thank us and go. That night, the pirates attack us ... when we sleep. They steal from the house...kill our man servants and guards who fight them.

"After they fight, hungry from killing, they force our old cook to fix them food. She scare them...when she say she make bad their journey...with magic words...if they kill any women or the childrens. The pirates laugh...like they do not believe. They take her and drop her in hole in ground. With the women and childrens and Angelus and me...we are twenty persons. They take us on their ship and sail to Athens where they sell us."

Karas gazed at the rays of sun, reaching through the windows and continued, but now more painfully. "The first night on the ship, the captain...he separate me from Angelus and the women and he...force...me." Karas winced. "The captain, he keep me for himself until we reach the port. He say he not want me...da .. ma .. ged. It not good for business or a big price."

Arria sat quietly. She still held her slave's hands. Karas took a breath, her eyes downcast and her blond lashes moist. "Samuel, he bring...how you say...new hope...in my life?"

Arria nodded in agreement.

"When I look at him, I feel safe." Karas' eyes shone. "His kind way and love is like his arms all around me."

Arria suppressed a giggle. "I think you're trying to say his love is wonderful."

Karas nodded and repeated, "Wonderful."

"It's about time you got back." Drusus demanded of Severus. "You've been gone for almost twelve days. Did *Januarius'* winds cause you to stray?" The tribune sat before him in his office chamber with a broad grin on his face. Was something amiss? It was hard to tell. Nine men had left, six had returned. The mission was accomplished. In fact, Drusus was surprised that the only casualties had been the barbarians and Arria's slave. Drusus thought that either Severus could be used to his advantage, or in time, he might possibly pose a threat. What to do? He needn't make any decisions now. What he desired more was the proof of his rival's demise. "Where are the tokens?"

"Drusus, won't you offer me some libation? We have plenty of time for business."

"You can have my finest barrel of wine. Just show me my prize." Drusus snapped his fingers and his slave approached. "Two cups and draw a carafe from the wine barrel just arrived from Turonum. Hurry! The Tribune has an immediate desire to quench his thirst."

The slave nodded and ran from the room.

"Satisfied?" Drusus continued. "My moment of revenge is far more immediate than my thirst. Show me now."

Severus reached for his pouch. "What will you see first, copper or gold?" Chuckling, he added, "I am rather partial to gold."

"First, the cocky bastard's hair."

A door opened and the slave entered with two cups of wine. Serving them, he then set a full carafe on the low table before the couches, bowed and left. Amusement shone in Severus' eyes as he raised his cup. "A toast is in order, don't you think?"

"I will not toast until I see both locks of hair." Drusus leaned forward. Cup in hand, he rested his arm on the round, purple bolster adorning his red couch.

Severus took several gulps and slammed the cup down. "To victory and a job well done, if I do say so myself!" He slowly pulled a piece of thin hemp cord from his bag. It held a thick lock of coppery strands. Like an ancient priest raising a holy icon, Severus extended his arm upward as the tail of hair swung at the end of the line.

"Excellent!" Drusus declared, his eyes gleaming.

"It's a beauty, that's for certain," Severus remarked, then smirking, he poured himself another cup. "It came at a high price. I almost lost my life. Those bastards can fight, but I was smarter."

"And they, of course, were outnumbered." Drusus reminded him.

Severus retorted, "Feeling sorry for the men who attempted to defile your woman?"

"Not in the least."

"Well then, it's yours to hold."

"The bastard's hair belongs in the fire," Drusus said, extending his hand, "but don't get hasty, I have a plan for it." He took hold of the bound tail and stroked the fine hairs. "Where is the one I really want to see?"

"I saved the best for last. For a man, his hair is quite thick and so gold."

"Perhaps, but he's no man. He's an animal."

"He was a man. Don't forget he's dead. You seem to hate Garic more. Why?"

"Beside insulting Arria, let's just say we had a major difference of opinion. He wanted something I own, and he was willing to steal it. The fool never figured on the consequences."

"Well, it's over. He's a fool no more, and I let him know that his death was your satisfaction." Draining his second cup, Severus reached into the bag and laid Garic's bound lock across Drusus' open palm. "How does that feel? Now that you have the Frank's hair, does it make the revenge sweeter?"

"You may never know how sweet; when its task is finished, this sweetness will pale in comparison to its final mission."

Severus looked confused, but shrugged and said, "Whatever your plan, I care not to know."

"As I care not to tell."

"Oh! I almost forgot," Severus grinned broadly. "I brought one more token to testify to the success of this mission." He reached into the pouch, still resting on his knee and pulled Garic's armlet into the light. Flames from angled torches decking the walls cast a glow on the gold band, intensifying the black bees etched on its surface. Tossing it on the table before Drusus, Severus said, "There! A gift from me to you. Now, if you'll be so kind as to pay me my gold. I must leave to find Arria. I have a small trinket for her."

"A gift from her father?"

"No, a gift from me in memory of Marcian."

Drusus hid his fury behind calm eyes. "Come, I will pay you," was all he said.

Chapter Twelve

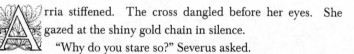

Frigida Solaque
Cold and Alone

FORT CAMBRIA
The month of Januarius, AD 451

Arria stiffened. The cross dangled before her eyes. She gazed at the shiny gold chain in silence.

"Why do you stare so?" Severus asked.

Unable to speak, she raised her eyes to him.

"What's wrong, Lovely? Don't you like it?"

Tears stormed the wall of Arria's disbelief and she bowed her head. Her heart raced. She must discover Garic's fate. "I love it," she lied. "It's just, it's been so long since I've been called Lovely. Aside from my father, only Marcian, at times, called me by this name. It touched my heart to hear it again."

Arria's emotions screamed inside her and threatened to weaken her resolve, but her will forced her words. "This beautiful gift. Wherever did you get it?"

Severus bent his head to her downturned gaze. He raised her chin and wiped a tear from her lashes. "Don't cry, Arria. This cross was meant to grace your neck. Does its origin matter?"

"Your gift requires no explanation. Thank you." Arria forced a smile to the corners of her lips, but her heart tore in two. "It's just my feminine curiosity and Roman vanity that desires to flaunt the source of craftmanship to an envious inquirer."

"If you must know, I brought it from Rome. I acquired it from a

Byzantine merchant who sells to the Empress Lucinia Eudoxia."

Struggling to maintain an outer ease, she ventured, "Why have you waited until now to give it to me?"

"Arria, why all these questions?" Severus answered, slightly impatient. "I am afraid you don't like it. You have yet to take it from my hand."

Arria reached for it and held it in her palm. "Quite the contrary, I love it. The etching on the cross is magnificent, and I am touched by your generosity." Arria ran her fingers over the Greek letters embedded in the gold. New tears welled and her throat tightened. "Severus...I never thought you capable—of such a gift." Behind her anguish, fear loomed. Garic was either hurt, or worse—dead. The possibility that Severus, a life-long friend, might have contributed to the demise of Garic, Vodamir and Samuel was unbearable.

Crossing quickly to a chair in the salon, she sat, pulled her crimson shawl closer and stared down at her hand. The gold chain laced through her fingers and gleamed delicately. Arria envisioned it around Garic's neck, lying against his bronzed skin, its sparkle peeking from the collar of his white linen shirt. *How could you, Severus?* she thought, and closed her eyes. *What have you done to them? This cross was my gift to Garic. What did you do to get it?* Horrible thoughts raced through her mind and she was desperate to discover Garic's fate. *Think! What should I say or ask?*

"I am touched that you would bring me such a beautiful gift." She feigned a girlish stance and teased, "Are you sure this wasn't meant for another? A lady, perhaps, who may have refused or bored you?"

"Arria, do you think so little of me?" Severus said, coming to stand before her. "Of course, it was meant for you. However, I must admit that with all the planning for the mission and the many meetings to prepare, it slipped my mind. Unfortunately, I am a soldier who thinks of my duty first, sometimes at the expense of a good friend." Severus paused, and hesitantly reached for her hands. "After being gone just ten days, I am struck by how lovely you really are. I always thought of you as precious, but time changes perception, and being older and...

wiser, in worldly ways, I feel like I am seeing you differently. No wonder Marcian thought of no one else. I envy Drusus. In this land, a finer and more beautiful woman doesn't exist."

Severus knelt before her and raised his hand to her face, and with his thumb he brushed away her one lingering tear. "Come with me back to Rome. I cannot see you with Drusus. He's ruthless and will never appreciate your beauty or character. Years with him will only bleed the life from you and leave you lonely, disillusioned."

Arria, taken back by the intimacy of Severus' words, softened. He was her friend, but he might also be the instrument of her sorrow. Had he done Drusus' will by slaying Garic? Or had events gone against the trackers, leaving Garic and perhaps Vodamir and Samuel simply victims? Arria was determined to find out. "I have a reason to be here. A messenger from the Hun camp has brought word that their envoys wish an audience with Drusus, and the Roman representatives, as well as the prime members from the Council of Warriors. You'll always have a place in my heart, but I cannot leave, not now. My betrothal to Drusus, at this point, is only that. He has yet to win my heart."

"I pray he doesn't. I can see only a disastrous end for you, and I couldn't stand to be a spectator to your unhappiness." Reverently, Severus kissed her palm, then laid his cheek in her hand.

Arria, touched by his devotion, softly stroked his hair, but persevered in her quest to discover the whereabouts of Garic, Vodamir and Samuel. "Severus, what was the purpose of your mission? Did you succeed? Have the Franks and Samuel returned with you?"

Severus pulled away, "So many questions, Arria. You're too curious for your own benefit, especially in these times. Discretion is much safer. Strong women are easily devoured by men threatened by an idea that is unfamiliar to them. Temper yourself. What took place on the mission or who returned is the commander's concern. If the well-being of your slave worries you, put it out of your mind for another is easily obtained."

Angered by Severus' stubborn resistance, Arria rose from her chair, leaving him on his knees and walked to the arched window facing the atrium. She wished she could see out into the land where Garic might lay dead, his discarded corpse food for wolves. She must know Garic's fate!

Arria turned toward Severus. He stood waiting, his gaze riveted on her. "Why would you tell me to suppress the person I am? Does no one understand? We sit on the verge of war with Attila, a cunning and aggressive ruler of men. Without the aid of the barbarians, Rome will be brought to its knees. I am an educated woman of Rome and a sanctioned envoy. I will be treated with the same respect that is accorded the other representatives of Rome." Softening her voice, she entreated, "Is it so difficult to understand why I question?"

Arria's passionate response called Severus to her side. He took her by the shoulders.

Arria gazed at Severus, intently. "I must do this. I know no other course."

Severus' words fell from his lips like a prayer, "Never before this moment have you seemed more beautiful. Your passion inspires me and wipes away any notion of a passive woman from my mind. Your fire..." he whispered, "inflames me." His fingers subtly grasped her shoulders a little stronger and his eyes roamed her face. "May God and Marcian forgive me, but you've kindled an awakening in my heart."

Without a word, Arria rested her hands on his outstretched arms that held her. With the deepest kindness and a blush in her cheeks, she replied, "Don't confuse, dear friend, a woman's passionate convictions for the passions of her heart. My love rests with only one." Arria heard Severus sigh and knew he thought of Marcian.

"Forgive me Arria, I was hasty and caught in a tide of emotion. I have no right."

"Dear friend, you have every right to feel what your conscience deems true. But tell me what I must know. What happened with the Huns and the barbarians?"

"They are dead—all of them. The Franks and your slave, scouting ahead of us were ambushed. My men and I heard their shouts, but when we arrived they were dead. We attacked and killed the few survivng Huns. Only Tarvistus, I, and the four legionaries made it back."

A sudden darkening gripped Arria at the words, 'They were killed.' Her fingers tingled and her vision blurred. Severus' arms caught her wilting body and lifted her off her feet as she slipped into darkness.

A dull, but cool sensation across her forehead pulled her back to the light. She saw Garic's smile; he waited to greet her. Arria felt the soft warmth of his lips and yielded to his kiss. Garic kissed her more deeply.

Arria whispered, "*Krieger.*"

"Arria?" The voice sounded confused.

Arria's eyes fluttered open. "Severus," she gasped. He knelt beside the couch where she lay, his face inches from hers.

From the open doorway, a sudden laughter filled the room. Marcella entered. A candle burning brightly in her hand, she spewed, "Ha! The mistress of Cambria who accuses *me* of harlotry is up to her own tricks—again. Is Severus your *new* victim? It seems your golden-haired warrior is barely dead and you've already replaced him."

Caught by surprise, Severus jumped to his feet. "How dare you speak this way to your mistress. It's not what it seems. I am at fault. But this is of no concern of yours, slave—leave us!"

"My concern or not,Tribune, our commander may find it very much *his* concern. As his *slave*, it's my duty to inform him, and I assure you I will!" Marcella hissed, then spun on her heel and walked out.

"Whatever does she mean, Arria?" Severus asked. "Who is the golden-hair...?" His words trailed off. "Who is Krieger?" he demanded.

Arria sat up and turned her gaze from Severus. Could she trust him, especially after his words and actions? She did not want to lie.

Severus grasped her shoulders, all tenderness gone. "Who is he

Arria? Say it!"

The man she loved and the friends she cared for most now lost, despair overcame her and she whispered his name, "Garic, the Frank noble."

"I don't believe you!" he hissed. "A barbarian? Marcian's enemies and murderers. You've lost your mind." Seeing the gold chain lying on the floor where it had slipped from her hands, he picked it up and gazed at it. Then, he tossed it at her breast. "Now I understand your tears; you knew Garic was wearing this cross, didn't you? It wasn't from the joy of receiving it that you cried, but rather, from your shock. Well, wear it now and know... I pulled it from his neck as he lay dead. I killed him!" Severus shouted, pointing his finger at his chest. A deep flush rose in his face and fury filled his eyes. "I, Arria!" he growled. "Your dead husband's best friend and your lover's worst enemy." A cruel smile broke from his lips. "But second only to another who hated him even more—your betrothed." Severus' words hung in the room like an axe poised over a condemned man's head. Giving her a bitter smirk, he turned to leave.

Arria sprang from the couch. Her hand tugged his sleeve and stopped him. "I know Drusus hates Garic, but Severus...did you bring back their bodies?"

"No, Lady. We buried them, a gesture too good for their kind. You'll never see your barbarian again. All you have is his cross and my word that he is dead."

Arria's grief broken inside her, she cried, "Did you bury them with their swords? Surely you know a warrior's honorable passage is beside his sword. Tell me you did!"

Severus laughed as he wrenched her hand from his shirt, "Ask your betrothed, Arria." Without another word, Severus bowed and walked out, his boots echoing his departure.

The final remnants of dusk's amber glow abandoned Arria. Left alone in the salon with her disbelief, Arria stood devastated by the news of Garic's death with Severus his murderer. Arria collapsed beside the silken couch and buried her face in the cradle of her arms.

She wept for Garic, for his fierce and loving heart, his warm caress, and his handsome smile. And she wept for herself, a woman alone in a cold dark room, in a cold dark world.

THE ROAD TO ATTILA'S CAMP

A gust of air barreled over Garic's wind-burnt face.

He tried to raise his head again, but another pain shot through his skull. He stopped, and rested on the wooden boards. He still wore his fur tunic beneath his cloak, with several blankets carelessly thrown on top, but the wind and the frigid air still ran through him. The incessant rocking of the cage aggravated his other wounds, especially in his leg. But one side of him felt warm. Garic realized that someone lay beside him. It was Vodamir.

Garic stretched his limbs and tried to assess if any bones were broken. His ribs, although badly bruised and sore, felt intact. Arching his feet, he spread his toes. They were quite cold but he still had feeling. This was good. A crippled warrior slave would not last long. A nagging pain in his left leg forced him to raise his head and look for wounds. The area above his ankle was swollen. He knew if it were broken he would be in serious pain; most likely, it was just badly bruised. Next, he felt his neck where the lash had hit him and then to his arm as well. Thick, dried blood clung to his fingers. He recalled the swipe of Severus' whip to his neck and then the cutting lash to his bicep. Garic looked beneath the rent in his sleeve, carefully pulling it aside. His armlet was gone, and now Severus' promise to relieve him of it came flooding back. *Bastard*, he thought. *One day, I will cut the hair from your head and rob you of your wild dog smile as my axe finds your heart. We will see how well a dying man gloats.*

The bloody wound wasn't deep. Wodan had been kind. A deep cut would need care that he knew he wouldn't get. Slowly he ripped the wool away from the wound. The air and the fresh sprinkles of snow would be better than his blood-crusted shirt. His mother had taught him that the best healed wounds were always clean.

He looked around. He couldn't see what was ahead of him, but he could hear the horses moving and laughter from voices not too many feet away. To his sides, he could see only trees. To the rear, he observed several riders—Huns with fur hats, animal skin tunics and boots to their knees. Each carried a bow slung across his shoulder. Deerskin quivers hung from their saddles. One Hun threw the other a drinking pouch. The drinker greedily swallowed and wiped the excess from his long mustache.

A screeching sound overhead drew Garic's attention to the clouds. He caught a glimpse of a hawk. The overcast sky made it difficult to know the hour, but it felt like morning. How long had they been traveling? He remembered being lifted on his horse and the feel of its mane, but that was his last memory before losing consciousness. His head still throbbed. Watching the Huns drink woke his thirst and made him run his tongue over his parched lips. He wiped the snow crystals from his coarse beard and the hair above his lip with a stiff hand. He wet his mouth, and then his tongue. Feeling some relief, he looked toward his feet and Vodamir.

His cousin's head rested against the rear bars of the narrow, squat cage. Vodamir's face was badly beaten. He had been the object of the soldiers' hatred, especially the centurion, Tarvistus. His right hand was swollen as well. Garic winced: Vodamir threw his axe, sharpened his sword and ate with that hand. He vowed to himself, Tiwaz, the god of war, and Wodan, father of the gods, to avenge this jealous and greedy treachery. He would survive and one day, he would find and kill Drusus, his lackey, Tarvistus, and Severus, the Roman thief. Nothing would stop Garic—nothing.

A slight moan broke from Vodamir's lips. His words were garbled, but Garic thought he heard him swear. This was a good sign. "Cousin," Garic whispered. "Cousin, can you open your eyes?"

A short gasp, then, "*Scheisse*! It...hurts," Vodamir growled in Frankish.

Garic almost laughed, but his bruised ribs kept him from the pleasure. Snow flurried around him and he too whispered in

Frankish, "Try to open them, slowly." He watched as his cousin blinked and attempted to raise his lids. Vodamir's eyes were slits. They fluttered for a moment, but closed.

"I cannot." Vodamir groaned.

"Don't force them. It will be all right. I can see. I will be your eyes."

"And the rest of me, as well? I cannot move," Vodamir croaked, his voice broken with fatigue.

"Just rest. We're in a cart on a trail in the forest. Where, I am not sure. I think the wind blowing over us is coming from the sea. That means we're headed north. The Huns are said to be camped there. Are you warm enough?"

"*Ja*."

"Can you talk? Is there a lot of pain?"

"*Ja*, but nothing I cannot handle to spite the bastards." His wracking cough stirred the silence, and Vodamir moaned, "Wodan, it hurts. *Scheisse*!"

"Keep swearing. It helps to relieve the pain," Garic quipped.

"So you're a healer now? Is that what love has done for you?"

"Pain seems to bring the humor out in you." Garic paused then said, "Vodamir, I am sorry."

"What's your regret?" Vodamir let out another cough.

"My love brought us here, Cousin. If I had not pursued Arria, we would be on our farms or at Luthgar's camp."

"Or maybe here, anyway. We're Franks and the Romans might need us, but they still hate us. They'll do anything for...money...or hatred."

"True, but it's more certain this was Drusus' jealousy; at least, that's what Severus led me to believe."

"What did that *dog* say?" Vodamir's hatred sounded even through his pain.

"That Drusus wanted us dead. He took our hair and my armlet to prove he killed us. We suspected something might happen before the mission was completed."

"Then, why are we here? Why aren't we dead?"

"Severus arranged this barter with help from someone at the fort. I heard them talking after we were netted. I know the Huns paid for us, but possibly something else might have been traded." Garic smirked, "We are great warriors, it's true ..."

Vodamir snorted, "*Ja*, so great we're broken, in a cage, and prisoners of the Huns."

"Don't tarnish our reputation. This is a small setback." Garic grinned with false assurance, then continued, "What if this sale is just a ploy hiding something more complex?"

"It doesn't matter. My pain won't let me think or care. I need water and to relieve myself."

"Where is your pain?"

"Everywhere. I feel sick."

"Try to hold on. I will help you," Garic said. He grabbed Vodamir's waist and rolled him toward the wooden bars. "Use your good hand. You haven't lost your aim, have you?" Garic gave a lighthearted laugh.

"Fuck yourself, cousin! The only way I would lose my aim is if I had no arms."

Garic didn't answer. He could see that Vodamir's wounded hand was in bad shape.

Weakly, Vodamir relieved himself. "Don't you have to piss after all this?"

"I'm waiting to piss on one of these Huns," Garic said fiercely.

"Not such a wise plan. In case you're forgetting, we're outnumbered."

"A problem for us lately. Right now, I thirst."

With some effort, Vodamir's eyes cracked open just enough for him to see his broken hand. He began to moan.

A Hun sensed the commotion and rode next to the cart. In Latin, he barked, "Quiet down! We will arrive at the camp soon."

"Some water," Garic responded to the order.

The Hun stared for a moment, then loosening the water pouch from his saddle, he tossed it into the cage.

Garic grabbed and untied it. Unable to sit fully up, he pushed himself as far down as possible. "Cousin, you must use your good hand and reach for it."

"Drink Garic, before I do, in case I drop it."

"There might not be enough. You need it! Take it!" Garic entreated.

"No, drink! There will be enough." Vodamir insisted.

Knowing Vodamir's stubbornness, Garic drank. The water, crisp as the outside air, washed down like the mercy of the gods and he savored the life giving sweetness and its restorative powers. After quenching his thirst, his head seemed to ache less. Then he reached and passed it off to Vodamir's weak and shaking hand.

"Don't drop it, Vodamir. Think of the axe throwing contest against the Visigoths. How your axe rose above all the rest and split a four inch sapling from twenty feet."

Vodamir's determination glinted through his half-closed eyes. Wrapping his fingers around the pouch, he dragged it to his lips. He drank greedily.

"Slower, Cousin or you'll be sick."

Vodamir, slowed himself, but drank it all. Then he fell back like a drunken man who can tolerate not a drop more.

Satisfied that his cousin was all right, for now, Garic, exhausted, slept.

FORT CAMBRIA
A secluded hallway

"What is your game, Marcella?" Severus caught up to her and roughly grabbed her arm.

"What is yours, Tribune?" she spat back, wrenching free. The torch in the hall cast a warm glow on them as Marcella slipped into the alcove. She blew the flame from her candle and placed it on the ledge.

Severus followed. "What will you tell Drusus?"

"Only what I saw, unless..."

"Unless what, you bitch? You'll not hold me captive."

"That's not what you said the night before you left on your mission—when I came to you in the dark." Marcella teased, giving Severus an alluring glance.

Unable to stop himself, he ran his hands over her breasts and lifted the soft fold of her gown. In the darkened alcove, he pushed her forcefully against the stone wall.

Severus hated himself for wanting her. Only minutes before he had tasted Arria's lips, but Marcella was beguiling, so hard to resist. Severus' pent up passions drove his hands to her soft, lush curves. Their eyes locked. Slowly, he ripped her silk gown to her waist. The rough coarseness of his knuckles brushed the creamy softness of Marcella's breasts, and her breath rose and fell vigorously. Severus grinned.

Marcella's smoldering look beckoned him. With a forceful command, he grabbed her closer. He wanted her to ache for him.

In this hidden alcove, Marcella the seductress was slave to Severus' passion. Running her hands over his chest, she bowed and lightly licked his nipples. "You're a beautiful man," her breathless whisper praised as she freed his hardened cock from the leggings trapping his loins. Marcella shuddered to feel him again and a smile pricked her lips.

With ease, he lifted her hips, pressed her against the wall and entered the warm, wet delta between Marcella's thighs.

Marcella clenched his shoulders. Her legs coiled tightly around his hips, welcoming each fierce thrust, while the cold, stone wall braced their lovemaking. Severus felt primal, a tiger caught in a man's body. Short of breath, Marcella stammered and whispered in his ear, "I cannot be ... without you. You're the only one who fucks me this way."

"I know," Severus hoarsely returned and kissed her deeply.

Severus' fingers dug into the roundness of her firm buttocks, while Marcella's fingers arched into his broad shoulders.

"Is this what you love?" He thrust one last time, "Or is it me, a soldier?" Severus rested his head against her breast

"You—both," she answered.

Severus chuckled as he lowered her feet to the ground.

Marcella ran her hands through the wet strands of hair clinging to his brow and looked adoringly into his eyes. "Am I not a better and stronger lover than your senator's daughter?"

He smiled and ran the back of his fingers over her cheek. "You're far better, but a bit less noble, don't you think?"

"She's never been a slave and forced to survive."

"Then, I could never be...the only one?"

'You could be—if it's what you desired."

"This depends on you, my vixen."

"How so, my lusty soldier," Marcella teased, taking his hands and cradling her breasts in them. The dark covered them and only a faint hue from a burning torch down the hall allowed them a faint view of their own features.

Severus caressed Marcella's hair and whispered, "You'll not tell Drusus what you saw."

Marcella let out a buttery laugh. "You and I are quite a pair, aren't we? I will not tell if you don't tell."

"I would never tell Drusus that we've loved," Severus said surprised. "How would that benefit me?"

"I meant the parchment I gave you to pass on to the Huns."

"The missive from Rome? I almost forgot." Severus cajoled, pressing his awakening phallus into the soft contour of her navel. "Let me see, our deal was, I get to sell the Franks in exchange for being a courier. Fair enough. I assume the missive was from our Master of the Soldiers, Aetius. He's a clever one. His skillful dealings with the Huns outshines even the Emperor, no doubt due to his boyhood years spent as their political hostage. Was I correct in my assumption? Tell me twin." Severus placed his hand on her neck and gingerly bit at her lips feeling his ardor rising even more.

"Twin?" She laughed.

"Didn't you say we're a pair? I think like the constellation."

"I know it well, Gemini. The goddesses love to rest there."

"So then tell me. Was it Aetius?" Severus continued to roam her face and neck lightly with his lips.

"I don't know. I received word to arrange the exchange. I am unaware of who gives the orders. There are men in high places who have a vested interest in the course Attila takes."

Severus stopped his kisses. "It must be Aetius. Surely, he would care the most. He loves Rome even more than that weak, mama's boy, Valentinian. Our greedy emperor will only bring Rome to its knees. Our only hope is Aetius. Until now he's been quite effective in dealing with these nomads. Times are crucial. With the Huns bearing down on Rome's borders, I fear Gaul is only the beginning. Italia will be next if Attila isn't defeated."

"That may be. All I know is that I was purposely sent to Cambria and Commander Lucinius to position myself in a location that would allow access to Attila if possible; however, I deal with intermediaries. I don't really know who's controlling this venture."

"If that's so, then how were you able to contact the Hun raiders?" Severus questioned.

"I have my own sources as well, and best left at that. I am just part of a chain." Sweetly Marcella pulled Severus to her and kissed him with longing. "Shall I come to you tonight?"

"Will Drusus not miss you?"

"Did I say he would? I must love him as well. It's my duty and protection."

"I wonder how much of it is your duty as opposed to your desire?"

A girlish laugh fell from her lips and Marcella cooed, "You're my desire, Severus. Drusus is but a rung on a political ladder. One that I can carry you up, leaving Drusus behind in this obscure outpost. It must be hard to believe that a slave woman can do this, but things aren't what they seem. Are you with me, or do you still prefer the Lady Arria who loves a defeated man?"

Severus bitterly remembered Arria's reaction to his kiss and the news of Garic's death. In the distance, Karas' voice could be heard calling to her son, Angelus. Aromas from the evening supper wafted through the hall reminding the pair that time was short. Severus looked intensely in Marcella's eyes, and rubbed his thumb over her lips. Then steadily he pulled her hand to his hardened manhood, and sensually whispered. "I am with you, *witch*,—with you!"

"And I with you, my twin," Marcella purred with delight. Triumphantly she kissed his lips, then slid slowly down his body to her knees, and seduced him, her Roman soldier.

Part Two

"But when her trembling red lips passed
From out of the heaven of that dear kiss
And eyes met eyes, she saw in his
Fresh pride, fresh hope, fresh love and saw
The long sweet days still onward draw,
Themselves still going hand in hand,
As now they went down the strand."

The Fostering of Aslaug

Chapter Thirteen

Castra Attilae
Attila's Camp

THE HUN CAGE

aric woke, but the dream of Arria still clung to his thoughts. She wept, alone in a dark room.

He pressed his cold, numb fingertips to cracked lips burnt by the wind's whipping lash and murmured, "*Mellitula*, I am not dead. Believe in me...Believe in me..." Garic repeated, his prayer giving him strength.

"Garic," Vodamir said, breaking his cousin's trance.

"*Ja*," Garic answered.

"How much longer, do you think, before we reach the Hun camp?"

"It will be soon. We've picked up the pace."

Welcoming shouts burst from the Huns surrounding their prison cage. Garic raised his head as galloping horses bore down on them. A troop of fierce-looking horsemen reined in and stopped before the raiders. The Hun driving their wooden cart halted. Hurried words passed between leaders, and the newly arrived Hun pointed south. They both laughed, then the leader of the raiders rode to the side of the cage. Kicking at the wooden bars, he peered in and snapped in crude and broken Latin, "Franks! We're a mile from your new home. Our world will shelter slaves who accept their bondage. Fight us or run away—die beheaded."

The Hun's horse whinnied as the rider tugged the reins. He turned and rode off shouting an order to his men.

"I'd rather be crucified than be their slave!" Vodamir spat through his swollen lips and half-shut eyes.

"Calm yourself," Garic urged. "Our goal is to heal and survive. We won't fight them. We will learn. Then, when the time is right, we will leave, but not one day sooner."

"That will take time. How long before Arria forgets you and marries Drusus?"

A sudden jolt of anguish shot through Garic. "It doesn't matter. I will make her a widow," he said harshly.

"She was widowed before by a barbarian. She might hate you for it."

Garic stared at his cousin. "If she does, I will change her mind. I will not live without her."

Vodamir grinned sheepishly. "Your resolve is something I could learn. I see why you stole her heart away from me."

Garic grinned back, "I didn't steal her heart, Cousin; I won it."

Vodamir's laugh turned to a cough and he grabbed his side. "Hel, the dark and ugly bitch, is the only woman wooing me with her malicious pain."

Garic glanced at Vodamir's red and swollen hand. "Hold on a little longer. I can see the tops of their tents," Garic observed, angling his head to the side and shifting his gaze to the far right. "Once we're there, I will find someone who can mend you."

"What else can you see?"

"A large corral of horses and the smoke from many fires. This camp resembles a village."

The prison cage lumbered and rolled up a shallow rise toward the center of the camp. In the distance, the sun's glow gleamed across the ice-glazed surface of the nearby river. The vision of cool running water left Garic thirsty. The aromas of roasting mutton and exotic spices filled his senses and his stomach grumbled.

All around men moved, carrying bundles of straw, wild grass gathered from beneath the melting snow, and hay, all fodder for the animals. Sacks of grain and dried fruits lay on carts. Spears and swords rested against wooden racks.

At the sight of their rolling cage, people gawked as their guards scattered the bystanders, allowing their passage. The leader of the raiders fell back to their driver and barked an order. The driver nodded and turned their rolling prison west. Garic looked up between the bars. The sun, a dependable time keeper, broke through the gray clouds. It was just past midday.

Lying on his side, Garic looked forward and saw a tent that seemed large enough to house fifty men. Its walls were made of sheep felt and horse hair. At the pinnacle of the dome roof flew a long, triangular flag whose amber color matched the striped cloth dangling from the tent walls. On it a painted emblem displayed a growling bear. From a slight opening, a woman stepped out supporting the arm of a limping Hun as the cart stopped.

The woman called to a male slave in Latin and ordered, "Help this soldier to his tent and make him lie down." Then taking the soldier's arm from her shoulder she addressed her patient, "Stay off this foot and rest. Tomorrow I will look to see if it's healing. Mind me now, or I will have you tied to your bed until I am sure your recovery is guaranteed. Do you understand?"

The hapless patient nodded and hopped off with the slave acting as his crutch.

The sunlight blinded her as she turned toward the cage. She shielded the glare from her eyes and peered into the wooden cage. "What's this?" she hissed in Latin, seeing Vodamir's face and hand.

The guard answered, but mumbled something in what Garic assumed was the Hun language, then laughed.

"Speak in Latin." she ordered, "Attila prefers a common tongue amongst our diversity." She turned her gaze toward Garic. "Ah, Frank prisoners," she said as she stared at them behind the bars. "New slave soldiers for Attila's army. From the looks of them, if they don't get some care, they'll be dead and worthless. Help me with them!" she barked at the guard.

The guard eyed her with disdain. He clearly did not appreciate her bossiness. "Step down and open the cage. Let's have a look at them," she said.

The guard grudgingly jumped from his perch and opened the cage door.

She stepped closer and was met by Garic's strong gaze. "Such vivid blue eyes, warrior," she said and leaned in warily.

Garic sensed her ready for any desperate act, even from a wounded prisoner.

"I am Basina, Attila's healer," she said, "Do you think anything is broken? Do you understand me?"

Taken by her commanding presence, Garic answered in Latin, "I understand. I suffer no broken bones, but my cousin, I think yes."

"Then let's get him out and in the tent and you as well. You both need those wounds cleaned and a bath. Attila insists that all his subjects bathe. He's adopted a few customs from his time spent with the Romans. Besides, it's cold out here." Basina threw one side of her shawl over her shoulder. "Guard help me move them. Ursula!" she called.

A woman slightly older than Basina came through the tent flap. Her purple tunic flapped in the breeze and her rough reddened hands helped Garic move his legs from the cage and stand up. He felt dizzy and tottered. The guard and Ursula each took one of Garic's arms. Walking him inside the tent to a low wooden frame spread with blankets, they helped him to lie down.

THE HOSPITAL TENT

Basina crawled into the cage and looked at Vodamir's face and mangled hand. She touched his fingers. Vodamir let out a moan. "It's all right. I am here to help you," Basina reassured him.

"Can you?" Taking a deep breath, he groaned despite his bravery and looked at her. His dark-blue slits fought to open fully but were too swollen.

Basina surveyed his face and assessed the swelling around his eyes

163

and jaw. She lifted his chin, then naturally moved her hands to his neck. Below his collarbone, she noticed the rays of a blue sunburst tattoo. "Your warrior totem is strong," she observed. She pressed his body, moving her fingers slowly across his chest and methodically downward.

"Will I live?" Vodamir forced a halfhearted grin to his bruised lips.

"You will live," she snapped. "We better get you inside. You need water and warmth."

"And food, I hope. Do Huns feed their slaves?" Vodamir taunted to lessen the pain.

"Yes, we do—so we can fatten and eat them if they're surly! Now be quiet. It's good that you're hungry, but I am afraid it's going to be soup for you. It'll be a while before you eat anything solid, and if your jaw is cracked or broken, even longer."

"Then, I will die," he answered, feeling weak.

"You will not die from lack of meat. I am an expert healer and respected by all. So you'd better behave and follow my orders or I will instruct the guards to take you to the river and abandon you there. Is that understood?"

"*Ja*," Vodamir muttered, feeling put in his place and not strong enough to challenge.

"What tribe of Franks are you from, warrior?"

"Luthgar's."

"You're unlike the Gepids and Visigoths. You wear your hair differently."

"We ... are nobles...called Long-Hairs. I ...Vodamir." He winced as a pain shot through his hand.

Basina called to the guard for help.

"Can you save my hand?" Vodamir's tone echoed his worry.

"I will try, Long-Hair. I will try."

FORT CAMBRIA

"Your appetite seems shallow this evening, *Carissima*. Aren't you hungry?" Drusus said, swallowing more wine. "Please, Arria, finish your meal. I have a special evening planned for us."

Arria glared at Drusus with bitter contempt and watched him feign a renewed interest in the plump mutton leg in his hand, but his downward gaze lingered on her breasts. She could barely eat. He sickened her, and refuge from his presence haunted her every thought. She felt a complete and utter disgust for these heartless killers: Drusus and her old friend, Severus.

Drusus had commanded Arria's company at dinner. She chose to defy this order, but Karas had persuaded her not to challenge Drusus. Arria reluctantly agreed. Garic had told her not to believe Roman news of his demise unless she saw his body, but she knew Severus to be a formidable warrior. Her fervent prayer was that somehow Garic still lived, even though Severus claimed his death. If Garic was still alive, he would come to her soon.

Down the table, Arria watched as Severus ate with a hungry appetite. If Garic was dead, how would the first counsel's death impact Rome's fragile alliance with the Franks? It was no secret that Luthgar's king, Meroveus, was for aligning with the Romans, but his brother had gone to the side of the Huns. Any insult to the Franks was sure to bring dissension to the Assembly of Warriors. These thoughts filled her with apprehension. She must remember her position and her father's trust in her ability to act as his representative. There was little time for tears or her personal desires.

"Arria, please join me in my quarters." Drusus interrupted her thoughts with a broad smile. "The braziers are lit and the room is warm with the expectation of your company. There's something special I need to show you."

Arria gave him her coolest gaze, "Whatever could you show me that would hold such signifigance?"

"Well, join me and find out. I guarantee it'll be a moment you will never forget," he answered, a hint of irony in his voice.

A chill shot down Arria's spine. Never had she felt such hatred, and it ran deep and dark. She would see this game through, no matter the cost. "Very well, I have some time before I retire." Arria beckoned Angelus to her side and instructed him to let Karas know she would be with the commander.

"Excellent! Take my arm, and I will guide you to the pleasure that awaits you."

A dread passed over Arria, but she gripped Drusus' arm.

"Ahh! It's been awhile since I've known your touch. It feels good."

Arria sensed his spite. The walk to Drusus' quarters seemed a hundred miles. If Severus told the truth, Drusus initiated Garic's demise. Had he paid Severus? What lie did Drusus tell Severus, or would hate alone make Severus a willing assassin?

Drusus had believed Marcella's accusation that she and Garic were lovers. The night in the stable, a spy had watched them. Arria realized now that their careless abandon had come with a price. One, Garic envisioned might happen—his death?

They passed Drusus' public office and continued down the torch lit hallway. "My bedchamber is much warmer and holds the surprise I've planned for you."

Arria stopped, feeling vexed. "My lord, the hour grows late. Surely this gift can wait until tomorrow."

"Quite the contrary, I've waited too long." Drusus whisked her along. "Please Arria, don't deny me this pleasure. There has been too much trouble between us." They reached his private door within seconds, and he raised the latch. With a sweep of his hand, he gestured for Arria to enter.

Over the threshold and into the bed chamber, Arria saw his table set with wine and cakes and a jeweled box placed squarely in the center.

Cautiously, Arria entered and approached the table. Tonight his dark curls clung to his patrician face and his falcon eyes pierced her and shone triumphantly. He harbored a secret that his excitement could barely contain. Was tonight about revenge?

"My lord why have you brought me to your private chamber? It's not proper that I should be here."

"I realize it doesn't have the comfort and propriety that the stable can provide, but I have tried to make it accommodating."

"What do you want from me?" Arria countered bluntly. A dread rose inside of her.

"I want to know why you would make love to that barbarian rather than me?"

"I didn't make love to him."

Drusus clutched her wrist. "Don't lie to me, harlot!" he hissed, "Tarvistus saw you together and gave me a very descriptive report. How dare you betray me in my own compound for all to witness!"

"As you've betrayed me with your Egyptian whore!" Arria spat back.

"Is this about your jealousy?" Drusus looked surprised, then threw back his head and laughed. "Are you so determined to be my equal that you would spite a commander and legate of Rome by soiling yourself with Garic's uncivilized seed? Have you gone mad?" Grabbing her waist, he pulled her to him. "I didn't realize your feelings for me ran so deep. But I am finding it difficult to forgive your wantonness. Maybe you could coax me."

Arria pushed Drusus away. "You arrogant bastard! Do you think I would stoop to such an action? I don't love you, and I will never marry you!"

Drusus walked to the table and poured a cup of wine. "Sit. I have something to show you."

"I prefer to stand," she said, raising her chin.

"Sit!" Drusus screamed, knocking the cup from the table and shattering it on the floor. "Sit!" he screamed again. A sudden composure washed over him. "Or I will *make* you."

Arria ran for the door but was not quick enough.

Drusus pounced on her like a leopard on his prey. Covering her mouth, he blocked her scream and dragged her to the bed. His weight against her body gave him control and he began to kiss her roughly, brutally, bruising her lips. Unsatisfied, he ripped her gown and clawed her breasts.

Arria broke her lips free from his and gasped, pushing on his chest. Every ounce of self-protection rose within her being and without fear, she slapped his face.

A shocked look spread across his face and he growled, "That won't stop me, you little bitch."

Arria cried out, pummeling his head and chest with her fists.

Drusus gripped her wrists and forced them down on the bed. He watched her. Her flushed, heaving chest, her lips parted and breathless. Drusus sneered and licked one breast, then the other.

Arria struggled to bite him.

Locks of his hair fallen on his forehead, Drusus grew rougher.

Arria struggled under his weight, fighting to free herself from his iron grip, but he was too strong and she was tiring.

"My lady, the lioness, likes to fight. Drusus, the lion, will be your lord; like it or not. Or else, others will suffer for your lack of respect and—support." Lifting to his knees, he released a wrist and slapped her soundly across the face. "Play rough with me and see what happens? I will get all the rougher."

Arria burst into tears and held her face, too numb to respond.

"Do you understand, my lady?" Drusus grabbed her hair and pulled her mouth to his, but before he kissed her he said, "Your servant, Karas, and her boy will survive depending on your...desire. If you choose to leave me, I will either have them sent as slaves to the silver mines in Hispania, where they will surely die. *Or*, I will use them as target practice for my primary bowmen to hone their accuracy. Better yet, have you ever witnessed a hanging?"

"You bastard!" Arria hissed, "I hate you!"

Drusus straddled her, sitting back on his haunches. "Now is that any way to talk to your betrothed? Addressing me as *My Lord* will be sufficient. You will love me day or night, or whenever I call you. In fact, you will love me tonight, now! My loins are aching with desire for you. Be as cold as you like. It only excites me more. I will have you and you will comply in *whatever* I desire. Is this clear, *Carissima*?"

Arria tried in vain to stop her tears as she stared back defiantly.

Drusus gloated, "I will lick the tears from your eyes," and glided his tongue over each lid.

Arria blurted out, "Pig!"

"Come now, my darling. Think about your servants, Karas and Angelus. Don't be selfish and think only of yourself. Think about me as well. You have so much love for everyone else. But not a drop for your protector?" Drusus gazed down at her and a cloudy mood spread across his face. He spoke with the sudden intensity of a wounded child. "You should love me, Arria. It would be wise. I am the best man for you, I am."

Arria stared, his shift in manner taking her by surprise.

Drusus seized the moment. He lifted her dress and spread her legs. He ripped at her undergarment, then freed himself. Poised over her, he whispered, "I am the victor. You are the vanquished. Yield."

Arria gazed past Drusus as he penetrated her with a jabbing force. An angry bull, he rode rough and hard. Arria gazed up toward the ceiling and counted the small tiles that formed petals in a bouquet of flowers. The thrust of his hips against her aching thighs intensified, until his spurts and gasps of release completed, he dropped himself without control upon her body and let out an exhausted grunt.

"I've desired you for so long," he said, clawing at her damp and fallen hair. "Your punishment has made my satisfaction even stronger. Now, you are mine. Just as much as you were the barbarian's. He has nothing—not even his life—and I have everything...I have you."

"You will never have me," She spat and turned her face away.

"We shall see. The lives of your servants depend on your love for me. It would help them...if I were convinced. Kiss me deeply," he commanded. "Come, Arria, kiss me with feeling." He ran his fingers over her lips and smiled, confident.

Burn in hell, you evil bastard. I will never love, nor forgive you. Arria thought bitterly. Drusus' forceful taking still ached through Arria's body. Hard and angry, his sex had left her weak, humiliated. Every muscle ached. All the hatred in the world seemed to loom inside of her, but her love of Karas and the boy was greater. Drusus waited for her kiss.

For a moment, Arria allowed herself a childhood memory. She had jumped from the garden wall. Landing harshly, she cried that she couldn't walk. Her mother, now beside her, said, "You can do it. Just get up."

Arria raised her lips to Drusus and kissed him with Garic's face in her mind. Drusus kissed back even deeper with a hurtful intensity. Then, abruptly, he stopped and pushed her down, "You bitch! You are kissing him. Are you not?"

"No, my lord," she lied. "Why do you doubt me?" It was imperative she protect Karas and Angelus.

"Do you still love Garic?"

Arria hated the way *Garic* sounded on his lips. They soiled the beauty of her love's name. "Give me time...I will love you." Arria winced with the last word.

"Then prove it, won't you?"

"How?"

Drusus rose from the bed, grabbed her hand and dragged her to the table. Arria clutched her ripped and soiled gown as he forced her into the chair. Taking the jeweled coffer in both hands, he slid the box to the end of the table where she sat. "My first gift is a pair of pearl earrings I had made for you in Rome. I meant to give them to you on our wedding night, but now is a more appropriate time. After all, tomorrow we will announce that in a fortnight, the third week of *Februarius*, we will be married. Choose the day and make preparations."

"My lord, *Junius* is the marriage month, and these times ... Attila's threat."

"The vows will require little time and Attila is yet distant. My mind is made up. Besides, your slaves will appreciate your cooperation, Arria."

"What is your second gift?" she responded, ignoring his veiled threat.

"Oh! This is rare. Not likely to be seen in the possession of a lady of your standing, but it's a rustic token that you might enjoy for its cultural value and as a reminder of your purpose for being here." Drusus walked to the box and slowly lifted the lid. He raised Garic's golden armlet from the case. "Look at the craftsmanship. The bees stand out boldly, almost as if they're flying, don't you think?"

Arria's horrorified reaction was a window to her soul. She covered her eyes with her hands and muffled a sob. Garic must be dead. How else could Drusus have his armlet?

"Stop your crying!" Drusus bellowed, but his stormy tone only fueled her flood of tears. "Lady, have you no pride? Let this be a reminder of what happens to those who dare to steal what's mine."

"You don't own me and never will! I would rather die a horrible death than love you!" "Death can be arranged...for many, if that's what you prefer." Drusus replied, coldly. "You don't understand, my lady. What's mine is no one else's, and certainly, no barbarian who's just found his way out of the forest, will ever possess a Roman aristocrat such as you. We were meant to join our blood lines. You will give me a pure Roman son. I've written your father and informed him of your momentary insanity and trifling with the Frank noble. It will be curious to see his response. I also informed him that I would save your honor, and his, and marry you despite your imprudence and, I might add, lack of good taste."

"I want to leave now," she commanded.

Drusus replied, undaunted, "You may leave, but wait, you have yet to see your final gift. I saved the best for last."

The box was big enough to hold many things. Fear gripped Arria like a dying person's last words. Her heart was a hollow grave and she was looking in it. There was no escape. How could she continue living among Drusus, Severus, Marcella and Tarvistus? Every time she came near them, she would have the vision of Garic suffering at their hands.

"Are you ready for your last gift?" Drusus prodded.

Forced from her thoughts, Arria focused on his hands. She sat staring like a drunken soldier, waiting for the innkeeper to pour another cup, and watched as Drusus, his gaze filled with menace, raised at first what appeared to be a horse tail. But as it rose higher and her vision became less clouded, she looked upon a copper-colored strip of hair. Something familiar about the red strands of hair struck her. As it rose higher from the box it was apparent that there were two tails, one copper and one blond, braided together and fitted into a leather strap with a buckle on one end. She instinctively denied what her mind told her was the truth. "What's this?" she asked.

"Don't you recognize it?" Drusus asked casually.

"It seems to be a belt made of animal hair."

Arria's quizzical look only enhanced Drusus' excitement. "Precisely, it's your favorite animal and his cocky cousin."

"You jest!" she gasped.

"No. It's real. Come...come touch it. Actually, take it in your hands. It's my gift to you. I will expect you to wear it every day; that is, until I tire from seeing it adorn your slender waist. Of course, I caution against wearing it around Luthgar or at the Assembly of Warriors. It could start a war, though Severus, your friend, might enjoy a war. As you've discovered, he hates barbarians. They killed his best friend, Marcian. Have you forgotten, Marcian?" A slow chuckle, cruel and biting fell from his lips. "This gift is meant as a warning to those who dare to cross or harm me. Is that clear?"

"How did Vodamir or Samuel ever hurt you?"

"That impudent fool, Vodamir, dared to challenge me on more than one occasion, and Samuel, a slave of no account caught in the middle warfare. He can be replaced."

Arria took a breath and felt her eyebrow arch. "If you believe that I betrayed you, why haven't you killed me?"

"I need you, Arria, more than you realize. Together we will create a legacy. One that will carry us to higher places. Your intellect is to be admired, but it needs to know its place. That place is behind me wherever I go."

"How do you know I won't avenge Garic's death?" Arria asked.

"Let's see." Drusus gazed upward in thought. "For two reasons.

First, in time you will forget the Frank. He had no power or influence. You would have lowered yourself being with him. Think of the time your father spent educating you. For what? To live on a farm among pigs? Really, *Carissima*. Think on it. What a waste of your talents."

"And the second?"

"Not as thoughtful as the first, but realistic. I've made arrangements for your father to suffer the same fate as mine, if an untimely or mysterious death should befall me."

"You...you wouldn't dare," Arria stammered. "He's a senator!"

"He wouldn't be the first senate official to die—quite suddenly in his sleep. Pray I stay healthy for a very long time. Anyway, I think you haven't the stomach for murder. Most women don't."

"Your slave woman, Marcella, does."

"True, and that's why I value her. She would kill for me." Drusus turned the belt in his hands. "So many lives rest in your hands. Is it worth the price of your hate? Can you realize your duty to Rome and to me? It's up to you, Arria." He extended his hand. The coils of hair hung defenseless. "Now take your belt and wear it... for your shame and for those who dare to cross me. Wear it for the benefit of father and slaves. Wear it for me, Arria." Drusus waited with outstretched arm, the belt dangling in the air.

The room glowed crimson as Arria reached out her hand and watched Drusus place it in her palm. She did not flinch, but tightened her grasp on the soft, smooth strands of hair. Before Drusus and unabashedly, she raised the belt to her lips. She let her kiss light upon it and said, "It would be my honor to wear this in remembrance of Garic and Vodamir. They will not be forgotten. This, I can promise you."

Chapter Fourteen

Medica
The Healer

THE HOSPITAL TENT
The last days of Februarius, AD 451

Girls! Will this bickering ever cease? Enough!" Basina reprimanded. "Only one woman, at a time, is required to nurse the Frank warriors. We have other soldiers that require your attention."

The eldest attendant, Adika, tried to suppress a grin. The younger, Tisza, stared nervously at her feet. Basina glared, then swung a perplexed look from the two sisters, standing before her to Ursula at her side. "Ursula, you must straighten this out."

"I would Basina," Ursula defended as she shooed the girls to their duties, "but they go behind my back or when one leaves the long-hairs the other is quick to grab her place. The one they call Vodamir is quite the rascal and talks sweetly to all who help him."

"How can they understand him—them? Their Latin is weak."

The sisters have learned a few more words in Latin with...umm...his help. Besides," Ursula added hurriedly, "the girls can speak my Goth German well enough, a strain the Franks can reasonably understand, and a few Visigoth mercenaries and one other Frank in here help to translate when needed." Ursula switched the pitcher of water she had in one hand to the other, then rested it against her body. "The Franks don't bark orders at the women or use profanity against them like our own tribesmen. Vodamir tries to learn our language and makes them

174

laugh with his poor pronunciation." She grinned, "I must say, he's rather appealing and his cousin, too."

Basina rolled her eyes. "You, too? Do I have to sequester these Franks to save them from their caretakers?"

Ursula ignored Basina and continued, "Garic is much the same. He cooperates and is quiet, but seems to shelter a deep hurt."

"He was sold into Attila's service, Ursula. Far and wide soldiers know the consequences for Hun vassals who desert. We must tend to his transition as well."

"True." Concern welled in Ursula's eyes. "He insists on walking the borders of the camp along the river every day. He's restless when he comes back."

"And his healing? Are you keeping his ribs bandaged tightly?" Basina queried.

"His ribs are mending. It was as you suspected, not broken only badly bruised. His shoulder wound is mending as well. You did a fine job of sewing him up."

"Good. I think you and I are going to have to take over their care. The sisters can nurse our own sick and wounded. That should keep them from clinging to the long-hairs and practicing their *Latin*. Our soldiers are healing and don't require my constant attention. In fact, activity has been rather quiet in here, since we crossed the Rhine. Spring approaches—pray it comes quickly. I will even welcome warm rain above this drafty cold."

"Basina. I was wondering...if...well, would it be possible to find something for the quiet one, Garic, to do while he recuperates?"

"Such as?"

"Perhaps he could help the bowyer, Kadam. There are bows to be made. He might also help the fletcher by carving shafts for arrows."

"An infirmary is not a place to make weapons, Ursula."

"What if he went to the bowyer's workshop? He could work for several hours, then return to rest."

Basina glanced over to where Garic lay. His arm behind his head, he gazed ahead, lost in thought. "Very well, the distraction might do him good. I will ask Master Kadam tomorrow. Now go and tell Adika and Tisza they have a new duty. I will go to Vodamir."

Ursula arched her brows and smiled wryly. "I am surprised, Basina. You remember the long-hair's name?"

"Why? It's not a name easily forgotten." Basina snapped imperiously and walked toward the Frank.

Vodamir watched the woman called Basina kneel by his bed.

"Your eyes are less swollen today, long-hair, and I see the semblance of a fine, long nose. Only battered not broken. And see here?" She lifted his hand. "Binding each finger to a pine splint and the hand to a board will make them heal straight, if kept still and secured."

Vodamir strained for fuller vision as she examined his hand. Basina's long strands of black hair, the color of the crow, hung to each side plaited and bound with dark-green ribbon tied at the tips of each braid. Her oval face came to a slight point, while soft, thick lashes rimmed eyes warm and brown as the clay of his land.

Beneath her exterior, Vodamir sensed a strength and acuity that lent a regal quality to her stature. Once, as a child, he had seen a slave woman come through his camp. The woman's master had tied a silk rope to a thin leather collar around her neck and led her like a prized horse he was afraid might bolt and break free. Yet this slave walked as if she were a queen. Basina had the same proud bearing. Like the slave, Basina knew what it meant to be free.

Vodamir's interest piqued, he stared at her. His own mother was an exceptional healer. Had the gods blessed Basina in the same way? A caretaker was easy enough to come by, but a true healer was harder to find. Would she be able to heal his hand and jaw completely? His curiosity brought an unexpected grin to his lips, despite the pain. Basina noticed his smile, he could see it in her eyes, but devoted herself to inspecting his jaw.

"The swelling has decreased measurably in these seven days since your arrival. The right side was extremely bruised and I was concerned that it might be fractured, but it was your torso and hand which received most of the beating. Feeling a bit better than when you first arrived?"

Vodamir grumbled, "Yes, and hungrier. When will I get some meat in my belly?"

"As soon as I know you can chew without injuring your jaw," she said flatly.

Vodamir frowned. "Woman, give me at least some bread, or are you trying to starve me? I am a slave warrior, not a prisoner."

"I am not your woman," Basina answered sternly, rolling his blanket to just above his groin. "It's not our custom to refer to the healer as a subordinate. Your well-being is in my hands now. There are no more girls to wait on you and bend to your liking." She placed her hands on his chest just above his heart and carefully felt her way to his ribs. "When I touch you, how badly does it hurt?"

Basina's fingers on Vodamir's skin unnerved him. He winced as she examined her way slowly down his chest to his pelvis, but he couldn't deny that her touch pleased him. It had been too long since he had felt the warm, delicate touch of a woman's hands on his skin. But his aching pain pushed away any other pleasure he felt and her stern attitude streamed through him, a cooling effect on her warming touch. "I feel like...ahh...a sack of pain."

"I am sorry," she replied.

Vodamir flinched, but asked, "May I call you Basina, Queen of the Healers?"

A skeptical look flashed across her face. "Is this long-hair humor or perhaps sarcasm? I don't understand your Frank culture."

Unable to suppress another grin, which he could see annoyed her, he answered, "You remind me of a woman I once saw when I was a boy. I thought her to be a queen, or to have the character of one. That's all."

"The only queen I will ever be is of this tent, and don't you forget it. *Basina,* will be sufficient." Gently she brushed his lips with her fingers. "Your lips have healed nicely, allowing for their insolence." A harsh cough sounded from Garic's bed. Basina asked, "Vodamir, I know what troubles you, but what troubles your cousin, his captivity?"

"Garic has many private thoughts. Even I know only a few. But what man would welcome the loss of his home and family? Attila should return home and rule his land. He should forget about conquering Gaul."

"I am afraid it's too late. Attila's desire and that of his chieftains for treasure has grown strong. He craves the power that is Rome's. He has found the *Sword of God* that legend claims was once lost to our people."

"What legend is this?" Vodamir asked, intrigued.

"It tells how the Huns and a neighboring tribe, the Magyars, won a sacred sword from the Scythians in battle. When the land became too small for both tribes, we searched for a new home. But who would possess the sword? After some debate, the two tribes decided to give it to a blind man who would twirl around with it seven times and then let it fly. Just after the seventh spin, the Sacred Sword was caught up by a rushing wind that swept it toward the west until it was lost from sight."

"And Attila has found this Sword of God? How can that be?" Vodamir responded skeptically.

Basina moved in closer, her voice just above a whisper, "It's true! One night, Attila dreamt that he flew through the sky over all the land, wielding a sword. When he told his dream to the shamans they prophesied that he would find the Sacred Sword and rule the world. Within days of this prophesy, a shepherd boy discovered a sword buried in the ground and dug it up and brought it to Attila. King Attila believes it's the Sword of God. He's convinced that it's a sign he should rule the world."

"Do you believe this to be true, Basina? Do you believe he will rule the world one day?"

"He'll not stop. His army is in the hundreds of thousands. Men who were once slaves of Rome and now slaves of Attila can work their way to freedom and profit more. You will see in time. If you're loyal—If you stay."

Basina's guard had dropped with the mention of Attila's name, and words fell from her mouth like water flowing over pebbles. "I came to Attila's attention as a small child. I was found orphaned and alone in an abandoned Goth settlement. Most likely, I had been bartered for food in order for my family to survive under Roman rule. When the Huns invaded, the Romans fled. I was not important enough to save. The Hun warrior, Irnak, Attila's youngest son, took me to his lodging where I became a servant and companion to his children. I was treated well."

"How is it that a slave girl became Attila's healer?"

"Lie still and I will tell you," Basina said and raised her head proudly. "Over time, my desire to learn the nature of plants and herbs grew, so I asked our shaman, Kama, to teach me. He laughed at me and said, 'A girl as healer?' I answered, 'One who is called to learn from the master.' Years later, after he had taken me as his apprentice, he revealed to me that he had seen my very words in a dream. And so I was accepted by the tribe, and our Lord Attila. Although I am a woman, no man treats me lesser. The gods have blessed me, and Attila has favored me."

"Then, I was right, Basina," Vodamir responded sincerely. "You truly are Queen of the Healers."

Vodamir's words caused Basina to laugh, but swiftly it faded. She seemed shamed. Picking up the jar of ointment beside his bed, she stood abruptly and all her laughter gone, said, "I must check on your cousin. Tomorrow, I will feed you some finely ground mutton to help your strength and disposition. Now rest."

As quickly as Basina had appeared, she was gone. Left wondering what had angered and caused her to leave, Vodamir let his thoughts linger momentarily in the gentleness of her touch and closed his eyes. Her presence had stolen the harshness of his pain and discomfort. Alone, his pain now surfaced, making him weary, and yet, in an odd way, he felt stronger.

"The bowyer will not want me, Ursula. Would he trust me?" Garic asked, sitting up from his bed of blankets and furs and placing his feet on the wooden floor.

"You're one of us now," Ursula assured and seated herself beside him. "Kadam will watch you, I am sure, but for the few hours you're there, it'll be fine." She lifted and checked the bandage on his neck and then his shoulder dressing. "They can always use the help. Do you know how to use a bow?"

"Of course, I am a *Wespe*." Garic caught himself too late, and winced inside.

"You're a...it sounds like wasp? What do you mean?"

"How is it you understand?" Garic asked trying to deflect the issue.

Ursula smiled. "I am a Goth. Our language isn't that different from Frankish." She paused, then looked at Garic with a glimmer in her eye. "So, will you tell me? What's a Wespe?"

He tried to hide his unease. "It's nothing important. Just a totem for our tribe."

Ursula looked at him shrewdly. "Is this tied to the tattoo on your chest? That's a wasp as well."

Garic realized what was hidden to others had been revealed to her as his nurse. In fact, there was no part of him she didn't know. Ursula had not only dressed his wounds and bathed him, but she had held his hand when Basina sewed his shoulder and she had spoken to him as he struggled through the fever that had gripped him for days. It was hard not to trust her and talk openly with her. The wisps of gray running through her hair, although slight, told him she had seen possibly thirty and some years, but he felt attached to her calm stability in a natural way.

"I am a warrior. Warriors in all tribes have their signs. Mine's the wasp," Garic answered as if it were of no consequence.

"Is your sting so sharp it should be feared?" she teased.

"What do you think, Ursula?" he replied. "Have I been sharp with you?"

"No, but I am not a warrior and I mean you no harm."

"True." He smiled shyly. "Your careful attention has brought back my strength. I could never hurt you." Ursula met his eyes as if she had fallen into his gaze. Garic thought she searched for something deeper.

"I sense a brooding sadness within you. Maybe, if you tell me what troubles you it will help."

"Sadness will live with me as long as I breathe. My heart is where I cannot be. I am a slave now. Fate has denied me my desire and unless I challenge it, I will be defeated."

Ursula rose from the edge of the bed. "Unless you rest, circumstance will deny you your health. Tomorrow, we will see about the bowyer and some work for you. Come raise your legs onto the bed and lie back. Dinner will be ready soon. Tisza has made soup." Covering him with a thick wool blanket, Ursula encouraged, "Rest now warrior wasp; think only of tomorrow."

LUTHGAR'S CAMP

"We must leave soon, but *Februarius* makes traveling difficult." Luthgar warmed his hands over the Frank training ground camp fire. "Too many hazards. We must wait until the weather breaks. My scouts tell me that Attila's army has just crossed the Rhine and is camped on its shore. They report around one hundred and fifty thousand men. It'll be quite difficult to enter the camp, but once we're in, we should easily blend. Attila's army is comprised of many races. The question is how many Wespe should go?"

Samuel stood wrapped in wool and wolf skin. His curls lifted in the breeze and the wood javelin in his hand gleamed in the morning sun. He listened attentively to Luthgar, then respectfully asked, "May I speak, my lord?"

Luthgar looked puzzled, "Of course. You need not ask."

"My lord, it's my habit."

Luthgar's gaze lingered on Samuel's earring and the scar above his left eye. "I suppose, but not here. Now speak up. What is it you wish to say?"

"I fear a force stronger than ten will attract attention. Every day, traders must enter and leave the camp. It would be far easier to disperse and search for Garic and Vodamir in smaller numbers. Can any Wespe speak Hun or Goth?"

"Amo's father fought with the *foederati* in Pannonia. I believe he's acquainted with the Goth tongue."

"An older man who speaks Latin and Goth may help deflect suspicions. Especially, if we present ourselves as traders. I am a Jew; most of us live as merchants. I also have a knowledge of Greek. There are sure to be other traders from the East who rely on Latin or Greek. I can help you in this subterfuge."

Luthgar stroked his beard thoughtfully. "Your idea merits consideration. Amo's father is called Rudiger. He's seen almost fifty years, but he's strong and able. He was a Wespe in his time. I will consult with Amo, but your suggestions are well taken. A force comprised of Amo, Rudiger, you, and I plus four soldiers might be enough to ensure success. With good men behind me, it's hard to fail. Help the men to gather the supplies we will need. I like this idea of posing as peddlers. It'll make infiltrating easier and will yield us information quickly. We have animal skins and grains that the tribe will share with us. Ornate jewelry, herbs and linen will help to attract the ladies to get the best camp gossip. You know how women like to talk."

"It's but a fortnight until Mars, the old Roman god, claims his month and *Februarius* leaves us. We will soon find Garic and Vodamir and bring them home. I will inform Amo of our plan."

"My lord! My lord!" A voice rang out and a Frank messenger ran up before Luthgar. "My...lord," he panted and waited to be acknowledged.

"What is it, soldier?"

"An urgent dispatch from Cambria's commander." The messenger pulled a missive from beneath his tunic.

Luthgar took the scroll from the soldier's hand and dismissed him. Opening it, he read slowly, his expression grim. Within minutes,

Luthgar lifted dumbfounded eyes from the parchment. "The Hun ambassador, Orestes, representing Attila has requested an audience with Drusus and the leading chieftains from the Assembly of Warriors in seven days."

"What does Attila want, my lord?" asked Samuel.

"Perhaps, a tribute to keep him from sacking the cities in his path. Gold and treasure keep his hungry hordes satisfied. He also has a penchant for reclaiming deserters and those who have fled his rule for the Roman way. He might even desire an exchange of hostages."

"You seem unsettled. Is there more?" Samuel ventured tentatively.

"*Ja.*" Luthgar nervously rolled the scroll and tied its cord twice around the parchment. "Two other matters. Drusus regrets to inform me that Vodamir and Garic died in a Hun ambush."

"The lying dog!" Samuel scowled.

"And the Lady Arria is to be wed to Drusus. The nobles are invited."

Samuel gasped, "How can this be true? The marriage is set for *Junius*. Besides, I believe her love rests with Garic. Arria could never love Drusus, the cold-hearted jackal."

"All I know is what's written in this missive. The wedding is to take place at the church of St. Stephan the Levite in Cambria's village in a fortnight on the third day of *Martius*."

"I should go to the lady Arria and tell her that Garic is alive."

"We have no assurance that either Garic or Vodamir lives. But if they do, we must get to them as soon as possible. We cannot stop what Rome has sanctioned for their lady envoy. She must find the courage to save herself."

"Warn her. That's all I ask my lord. She'll know what to do."

FORT CAMBRIA

Since learning of Garic's death, Arria found it difficult to converse with anyone. Like a phantom, she rose each morning, bathed, dressed, and tended to her household administrations. In the evening, when the household rested and before the Commander of Cambria might demand her audience and more, she wrote letters to her father. She hid her anguish to safeguard his life and the lives of her servants, but wished she could tell him about Garic; the love lost to her; of Drusus, the man she despised and now must wed; and the betrayal of her old friend, Severus. So often as she wrote the reed pen felt heavy in her hand. Even the air she breathed felt heavy.

"Lady Arria, Tribune Severus is at your door, requesting to see you. He says it's important," Angelus announced and looked at her expectantly.

Arria worked valiantly at avoiding Severus, but his persistence was unnerving. Often absorbed in a task, she would look up to find him nearby, watching her. Her loathing still strong, she would leave. Arria imagined him now, standing on the threshold of her salon waiting for her to receive him. Why couldn't he leave her alone?

Arria hesitated a moment, then stuck the needle into the canvas and laid it down. "Tell him that I will see him. Oh, Angelus," she called him back as he scampered to do her bidding, "offer him a chair and stir the coals."

Karas asked, "Lady, what does the tribune want?"

"I am not sure. I feel I cannot even speak to him—I hate him so. Yet, I cannot forget what he meant to Marcian and me. Friendships that die are difficult to live with and sometimes without."

Arria walked into the salon.

Severus rose. A crisp, white tunic accentuated his rugged demeanor. "Arria, thank you for receiving me." Relief shone in his face.

Arria waited, hands locked together.

"Arria, please hear me. I've hurt you. I am sorry, but I cannot say I regret what I've done. In these times, men must struggle to survive. There are few guarantees that one will see tomorrow."

"Honestly spoken, Severus, but your hand killed the Franks and my slave. I cannot forget. I loved you once as a friend and confidant, but no longer. It's best you leave. I will pray for your murderous soul." Arria felt a knot grip her stomach.

"Save your prayers for the worthy, Arria," Severus answered wearily. "Perhaps one day, you will smile on me again. I bear no ill will toward you, but I will never understand what possessed you—not in the matter of the long-hair."

"It may be difficult for a man like you to understand, but that is no longer my concern. Excuse me, but I must attend to my duties."

Severus raised his fist over his heart, bowed his head and turned to leave, but stopped. "I came to settle with you, Arria, and I did, but I also bring a message from Drusus. He requests your presence in his official quarters as soon as possible."

Without another word, Severus left, his fading steps a reminder of the friendship they once knew.

Ushered into the commander's office, Arria waited. Drusus examined a large map on his wall. Methodically he traced his finger over the Moselle River running north through Gaul. "Tonight Arria, we meet with the Hun ambassador, but tomorrow you will accompany me to the village." He turned. Noting her grim expression, he added, "Whether it's your wish or not. In fact, I prefer you be festive and wear your brightest silk with my favorite belt over it. A harlot should wear the adornments that suit her, don't you agree?"

Arria's brow arched with his insult, and a heat rose in her cheeks, but she answered calmly, "I pray the Lord will forgive you for your cruelty."

"As he should you for your bold indiscretion. Don't forget that I was the one wronged, and your behavior towards me will reflect on your servants."

"I will not forget, but it won't keep me from hating you less. You may have my body whenever you wish, but never my heart."

A fire leapt in his eyes and Drusus pounded his fist on the desk. "Come to me—now!"

Arria moved cautiously before him, afraid to refuse.

He grabbed the back of her neck and pulled her face inches from his. "Listen to me carefully. If you want your friends to live you will strive to love me and have me believe this is so. I will not stand a woman who shows open disdain for me. I own you, Arria. The game you've been playing with me is over. I alone control your future, and I say your destiny is *me*. Do you understand?" Drusus relished the fear, Arria knew he saw in her eyes. "If you ever look at another man, I will have him killed, regardless of his rank. It'll be his undoing to have you favor him. This is just the first rule for you to learn; others will follow. I musn't rush your—let's call it—schooling; even though, you're known for being an apt pupil."

"There is nothing in the village I need," she said, breaking free and moving away from him.

"Oh, but there is. We will look for a marriage token. I imagine when your father arrives in the summer, he'll bring your dowry, but I want to buy a gift befitting my bride. I thought a ruby ring, to match our passion for each other, will complement your betrothal band. All who see it will know you're the wife of a powerful man. What woman wouldn't want the prestige?"

"Will your gift also ensure your fidelity?" Arria shot back.

"I am faithful to whom I choose. I need not prove it," Drusus said icily and tossed a parchment resting on his desk onto a stack piled on the floor. "Now, let's consider the events of the night. The Hun ambassador has arrived with several chieftains. You've done a fine job, ensuring their accommodations are pleasing and comfortable. In the same manner, I will expect that the banquet is lavish and the food cooked to perfection. No mistakes. Also, every slave should know his place."

"Does that include your slave, Marcella?"

"Ah! Arria, your jealousy belittles you. Why must you mention her?"

"Jealousy is not my mistress. She is a *slave* is she not?"

"Marcella serves a very definite purpose."

"So the entire camp has noted."

"Wagging tongues of women and men idle from war are of no value. I choose to ignore certain tales told behind my back. After all,

I am the commander and a topic of discussion for every legionnaire. Soon you will be my bride and they'll have much to say about you, if they haven't already." A sarcastic sneer escaped Drusus, "I advise you pay less attention to the words of others and more to mine. Is that clear, *Carissima*?"

"My lord, the..."

"My lord, my lord! Call me Titus. It's what pleases me."

"I believe I was to address you as 'my lord'?" Arria answered with steely resolve.

"I've changed my mind—for now. Between us, address me as Titus, and in the bed chamber, *my lord*.

Arria's jaw clenched. "Titus. The Frank and Visigoth nobles will arrive shortly. Does Luthgar know that Garic and Vodamir are dead?"

"Luthgar has been informed that they were casualties of a Hun ambush. Is that clear, Arria?"

"Perfectly. Will this council meet before or after the meal?"

"There are no outside guests in attendance. We will discuss matters at the table. It's imperative that everyone is prepared. The Huns are shrewd. No doubt, they are looking for tribute. This morning, I received word that they attacked Argentoratum just below the Rhine. The city has been sacked and burned. Only a few have survived. The report claims that the stench of death reaches a mile away."

Arria gasped and sought a nearby chair. "What is to be done?"

"My soldiers are trained. All we need is Aetius to lead us. Until now, he hesitated to leave Italy. He was unsure of where Attila would lead his invasion. He needed to protect Italy in case Attila chose that path. Four days ago, I received orders to make ready the troops. Aetius knows that Attila has entered Gaul. As we speak, Aetius is negotiating with Theodoric and the Visigoths for their assistance. It seems they are afraid to leave Tolosa defenseless and in the hands of only a few nobles. Besides, there has been enmity between Theodoric and Aetius.

"Aetius' political ally against the Visigoths has always been Attila.

Now two enemies stand together against an old friend. You know how friendships shift in our Roman world. Tonight, we must obtain a measure of assurance from the Huns. We need to buy some time, while we wait for Aetius; otherwise, Cambria and all the cities in Attila's path will be defeated."

"Is that possible? Attila cannot defeat Rome and Aetius," Arria replied, defending the Master of the Soldiers and her friend.

"Attila almost took Constantinople. If it weren't for a plague that rendered his army weak and depleted, he would have succeeded. Scythia, Germania, Pannonia, and lands closer to the northern seas have come under his rule with little struggle. We must maneuver for time. It's crucial. Aetius needs it and Cambria needs it."

Arria pondered his statement, then said, "Who is Attila's ambassador?"

"It's Orestes, Attila's chief advisor." Drusus walked to his couch, sat and covered his eyes, obviously vexed.

"Oh...a precarious position," Arria mused. "Hun wolves and Roman boars, fighting for the same prizes—power and Gaul."

Chapter Fifteen

Magnum Opus
A Great Work

ows mounted on cedar racks filled the tent. Each stand reached eight feet toward the vaulted dome and spanned the length of the tent. The curved weapons layered one on top of the other and their vertical stands, one after another, reached to a solid wall far from Garic's first step. It was a sight Garic had never seen. The smell of resin, wood and dried sinew filled his senses and warmth spread through him and strengthened his resolve.

"Ah! The wounded warrior has arrived. Such yellow hair. Are you the Sun God's child?" Kadam chuckled over his own peculiar humor. His wide smile touched ears that peeked beneath tufts of silver-gray, crowning his brow. His short stature and pleasant manner seemed contrary to his status as master bowyer.

Garic stared at him blankly; then he glanced at Ursula, standing beside him.

Ursula laughed and said in Hun, "Master Kadam, excuse me for saying, but at times you're quite the rascal. It's lucky he doesn't understand you."

Kadam nodded, a wry grin still on his face.

"Is your apprentice here?" Ursula queried.

"Ah! my beauty, is it Donatus you wish to see or me?"

"I prefer you, of course, but your apprentice can speak Latin."

189

Kadam replied, "Fair Ursula, bowmen roam for what they need. Because of this, Latin comes quite naturally to me. Donatus' attempt to communicate with the barbarian will provide an amusing diversion."

Ursula laughed, "Master and trickster can you help the long-hair learn this craft, while he recuperates. His hands are strong and his mind is keen. He works hard and will benefit your labors, I am sure."

"How is it you know him so well, Ursula the Goth?"

Ursula blushed. "Kadam, a mischievous light shines from your eyes. Please find Donatus and entrust Garic to his care. You will not be sorry, he's a good man."

"Maybe so, but when he leaves *your* care, will you be sorry?"

Ursula glanced coyly at Garic and fidgeted with her shawl. "Old father, more questions? Do your eyes reach beneath the skin? Is my heart so apparent?"

"Yes, my dear. A liveliness besets you." Kadam's eyes twinkled.

Garic looked from one to the other as if he could follow their words, but his face remained expressionless.

"With all respect, let me tend to my own heart," Ursula replied. "Soon the soldiers will be calling for him, and Basina wants him healed."

Kadam gave her his warmest smile. "I am thinking of your happiness. Stay a moment while I look for Donatus. That young scoundrel is probably out gambling somewhere. When I find him, I am going to box his ears! Or better yet, I will let the Frank do it!"

Ursula turned her gaze toward Garic. He knew his eyes held a mild amusement when she asked, "What do you find so humorous?"

"That was quite a lengthy conversation for a simple introduction," Garic said and folded his arms. "I heard my name and the bowyer's left. Is there a problem?"

"Not at all. Kadam is looking for his apprentice, Donatus, who will act as your interpreter and teacher. Although he is young, his skills excel. A bow made by Donatus is highly respected."

"But I thought Kadam...?

"He is the Master Bowyer. His bows are used by the chieftains, princes and Attila. His are the very best."

Garic ran his fingers through his hair and thought for a moment. "How long will I be expected to stay?" he asked.

"When you are tired, Donatus will bring you back. Will you be all right?"

Garic nodded and lightly touched Ursula's elbow. "Thank you for your kindness."

"Is the Master here?" A thin, gangly youth with broad shoulders, blurted out in Latin as he burst through the entrance. Strands of black hair fluttered from the leather headband cinched at the nape of his neck and his sweaty face winced with a deep breath, "I've ... heard, he's threatening to box my ears," Donatus addressed Ursula and Garic, but his eyes roved past their shoulders as he spoke.

Ursula laughed at Donatus. "You've just missed Kadam. You speak Latin very well."

"I'm to have a new assistant, a Frank warrior who speaks Latin. Master told me I must practice."

Ursula glanced at Garic. "Well then, greet your pupil and begin right away before Kadam gets back. It might save your ears!"

Donatus eyed Garic and shot back, "Why would a Frank warrior want to make bows? He fights with an axe. He's not a craftsman."

Surprised by the boy's candid demeanor, Garic remained silent and let Ursula speak.

"He has many talents," Ursula said firmly. "Besides, it isn't your concern boy. Do as you're told."

"I am not a boy. I am fifteen."

"I am sorry. You're a young man—one who already has too many vices, I might add. I've heard about you and the Syrian trader's daughter. You'd best be careful. A Syrian father can cause a young suitor many problems. Nevertheless, we must not be rude." Ursula gestured toward Garic and the boy, respectively. "Garic, this is Donatus, the master's apprentice and your teacher. Donatus, Garic the Frank."

To the boy's amazement, Garic bowed. Standing taller, Donatus bowed in return.

Garic turned to Ursula and said, "Thank you for the introductions. I'm sure working with Donatus will enlighten." Garic gave them his best smile and Ursula blushed.

"Donatus, when Garic tires, please escort him to the infirmary." The boy nodded in agreement. Ursula returned Garic's smile and left.

An awkward silence fell between warrior and apprentice, but Garic spoke first, "Are you a fletcher as well?

"Yes," Donatus answered.

Garic approached a quiver of arrows for a closer inspection. "Which craft do you prefer?"

"I cannot say. Both arrow and bow interest me. However, Master Kadam would be angry with me if I didn't say the bow. He says bow making is where my true talent lies."

"I see," Garic said. Well, I know little about either. In my tribe, some men use a short, wooden bow to hunt small animals, but Franks fight with the axe and the sword. We are expert handlers of the *francisca*. The axe is our strength. However, on occasion, I've observed the bowyer in Cambria at work and found it curious." Garic was swept back home to Luthgar and Arria. Where was she now? If he had to learn this trade to find his way back to her he would. "I am willing to learn," he said, subdued by his memories.

Donatus cocked his head. "You appear apprehensive. It's true, it's not a craft one learns easily. Even I have failures. But not many," he added quickly.

Garic suppressed a chuckle, "From what I see around me, it's obvious that you and your master are quite talented. May I handle one?"

Eagerly the boy lifted a bow from the rack nearest them. The beauty of the painted weapon shone with a dark purple lustre.

Garic took the weapon and turned it in his hands. "Tell me,

Donatus, what makes this weapon so strong?"

"The core is from a supple maple and sits between the inner belly of goat or ox horn. The outer back is dried deer sinew. Bone overlays on the grip adds to the bow's strength and beauty. After final shaping, the bow is wrapped spirally with thin layers of birch bark for protection against moisture. It's called the composite bow for its layers." Donatus glided his finger across the belly of the bow. An earnest pedagogue, Donatus' eyes filled with excitement. "As you can tell, nothing of this process can be seen, only its painted beauty. Most bows are painted and those made for our nobles and chiefs usually have thin sheets of gold applied to the siyas and grips."

"It's a beauty," Garic admired. "How long did it take to make this one?"

Donatus returned the bow to the rack. "Almost a year."

Surprised, Garic said, "It must take many craftsmen to make so many, considering the time it takes from start to finish."

"The more assistance we have the more bows we complete."

Donatus spied Garic's glance rest on the bows made for the elite members of the tribe. "This one over here is for the chieftain, Aveek." He walked to a rack with only a few bows ornately decorated and positioned in the center of the tent. "This one is special. It's been inlaid with six round rubies on the face of the bow, three on each side and centered between the grip and siyah tips. Here, look." Donatus held it for Garic to fully appreciate. The rubies burst with a fiery brilliance across shiny black paint. Laced between each ruby, spirals of gold-leaf danced around the precious stones.

"Did you make this one?" Garic admired. He started to reach for it but caught himself.

"No, Master Kadam made this one." Donatus nodded and extended the bow forward. "Aveek would have no other craftsman. He paid a handsome price for this bow, but there is none like it."

Carefully, Garic lifted it from the apprentice's hands. "Did it take your master long to craft this one?"

"It's not that simple. Kadam works on fifty or more bows a year.

As master, he lays the sinew himself; it's an important step that merits his attention and talent. Laborers and apprentices such as myself pound and shred the fibers to prepare the sinew. This bow took longer than average because the bow was passed to the goldsmith for detailed gold gilding and ruby sets. It was completed three days ago. Aveek has yet to retrieve it. He's gone from the camp. Master said, he went on a diplomatic mission to a Roman fort."

Garic asked, nonchalant, "This fort, is it far from here?"

"I don't know. I seldom leave the protection of the camp."

"Well, if it's not too far, this chieftain, Aveek, should be back any day."

"It's hard to say. Sometimes men never return. In our camp, warriors and chiefs, peddlers and envoys arrive and leave daily. If Aveek shouldn't return, there will always be an archer anxious to barter or pay for a Kadam bow of such quality."

Garic nodded pensively. Light filtered through open spaces between the cinched canvas walls. "Donatus, I forgot to ask Ursula one thing."

"What do you want to know?" The boy teacher queried.

"Can I earn a bow made by Kadam?"

Donatus stammered, "I ... I don't know. You must ask the master, but just a word of advice, if I may?"

"Please, speak," Garic answered, and looked down at the bow in his hands. The rubies transported him to the roses that adorned Arria's window and he saw her face.

Donatus continued, "He's the wisest and the wiliest old fox you will ever meet!" Chuckling over his own words, Donatus suddenly shouted in pain.

Garic's gaze shot toward the boy.

The master bowyer stood behind Donatus, both hands ricochetting off his apprentice's ears. He was obviously annoyed at finding the boy back in the tent. He pointed to Aveeks bow and grumbled a tide of words, while his brow creased with displeasure. His objections completed, he crossed his arms and waited. In which Donatus gave an equally lengthy reply. Kadam then barked an order at the boy who turned to Garic.

"Master is angry that he searched for me and found me here. He also did not give his permission for anyone to handle Aveek's bow." Donatus rubbed his ears, looking cowed. "I told the master that I've begun your instruction. Master says, I should show you where everyone works. I told him you want to work for a bow."

"Does he agree?" Garic asked and glanced at Kadam.

"Master says, it's Attila's custom to make loyal followers by providing all who serve him with the spoils of war. Our king believes that rewards encourage loyalty. However, if you want a bow, you'll have to prove yourself."

Garic could tell that Kadam was not impressed by his expectation. "Tell your master I will work hard for a bow of such quality."

Carefully, Donatus relayed Garic's words. Upon hearing this, Kadam broke into his wide smile and said, "Good!"

Garic understood even before the boy said the word. He bowed toward Kadam and followed Donatus outside of the tent. The day was still young, and he was anxious to start. Every minute spent learning and preparing was a moment closer to freedom, Arria, and home.

FORT CAMBRIA

A hush settled over the Roman commander's dining table. Drusus understood well the consequences of Orestes' proposal. Diplomatic hostages were common exchanges of fealty, but things were precarious between the Romans and Huns. Roman hostages might keep the Hun camp safe, but would it keep Attila from Cambria's doors?

Drusus considered his most obvious option. He needed time. Attila was painfully close to Metis. Drusus had word that the city was barricaded and ready for the Hun assault. It figured that the jackal, Attila, would send his best man to reconnoitre the Cambrian garrison in the guise of diplomacy. These endless deceptions required a cold and calculated shrewdness. Drusus smiled. "Noble Orestes, now might not be the time for tributes or hostages. Matters are strained between Rome and Attila."

"Nonetheless, Legate Drusus, Valentinian has refused to recognize the betrothal of his sister, Honoria, to Attila. We hear he has married her to the old senator, Herculanus, as punishment for her traitorous attempt to wed Attila. My king has been dishonored and cheated. He has cause to take the lands that would have been his, if he and Honoria had been wed." Orestes smiled and continued. "King Attila is prepared to, shall we say—*welcome* the cities that open their gates to him, but those who don't...well." His final word dissolved into the silence that surrounded them.

Drusus and his executive officer, Eugenius, along with Severus stared back and contemplated Orestes' words. The barbarian representatives sat silently and listened.

Arria sat several seats from Luthgar and Thorismund, the son of the Visigoth king, Theodoric. Luthgar seemed restless. Earlier, when Luthgar and Thorismund first arrived, Severus had welcomed the two men, no doubt on Drusus' orders, keeping her from them.

Arria gave Luthgar a discreet glance. Luthgar beckoned a slave quietly to his side, the boy bent to his whispered words. The slave moved on and filled the guest's cups with a spiced wine, working his way to Arria. As he poured her glass, he relayed Luthgar's desire to meet with her in private.

Spurred by Luthgar's request, Arria announced, "Gentlemen, excessive political talk during the meal will only hurt one's digestion. Tonight, my lord, Drusus, has arranged a special evening for your entertainment." Arria signaled the musicians. They struck up a celtic melody whose haunting edge reflected the ancient sounds of Gaul.

The Huns listened mesmerized, while low-burning braziers added to the room's glow. Gradually from beyond the dining room and down the hall the single beat of a drum was heard. All heads turned toward the entrance.

A dancer appeared, a thin veil across her face. A brass fan topped with flickering flames crowned her head and she led a line of seven women clad in pale gold silk. They strutted toward the center of the room and stopped before the tables. All the onlookers gazed, fixated. Two dancers moved beside the leader and ceremoniously removed her crown of lights.

The leader twirled seductively before the warriors, dropping her veil. Arria recognized that smile, black eyes and the snake armlet that adorned her arm. Marcella danced before them. The silver chains slung beneath her belly tinkled as her hips rocked back and forth with every enchanted beat of the drum. Hun, Roman, Frank and Visigoth alike gaped.

Marcella swayed her hips and turned in a slow circle. She gracefully raised her arms and spun faster and faster. Her hair fanned and rose in the air with each revolution, while the corps of dancers encircled Marcella and fell on their knees. Hands locked together, their bodies pulsated like seven beating hearts ignited by the drum's rhythm. The cadence climbed higher, while the room reeled with a bacchic energy. The audience watched transfixed. Then abruptly, the music ceased.

Silence and subtle gasps spilled through the dining room from guests and dancers. A Visigoth banged his cup on the wooden table and broke the spell. All the men followed and slammed their silver cups repeatedly on the table, thundering their approval. Marcella glanced triumphantly at Arria.

Arria rose and with authority raised her hand in the air and dismissed Marcella and her dancers. Graciously, she invited the Huns, Luthgar and Thorismund to visit the stables and see the beautiful Iberian stallion that was a gift to Drusus.

Even beneath her charcoal paint, it was obvious, Marcella seethed. "My lord," she addressed Drusus, boldly, "if our dancing has enticed you, allow me to further please. My dancers and I will delight in entertaining your guests."

The chieftain Aveek could not hide the lust in his eyes as he dragged his gaze from Marcella and leaned toward Drusus, offering a few words. Drusus listened, his eyes dark and deliberate, while Severus sat beside him his fingers clenched around his cup.

Drusus called to the musicians to play a low tempo and then addressed Arria. "My lady, please show the Chieftains Luthgar and Thorismund to the stables if they so desire to see the Iberian. Orestes, Eugenius and I will meet privately for a short time. The Noble Aveek and the chiefs have decided to stay and enjoy the dancing. Severus, of course you will stay as well. I know how you love this music." Arria suspected Drusus cared not to leave the Huns alone with the women or unattended to conspire.

Arria looked at the barbarians. Thorismund sheepishly expressed interest in staying as well. It was apparent that he was smitten with the troupe's red-haired dancer, a slave girl in Eugenius' household. "And you Noble Luthgar, have you too lost interest in seeing a magnificent stallion when you can watch beautiful women dance?" Arria asked.

Luthgar stepped forward. "Beautiful women are a sight to behold, but nobles and lady, I believe my wife would encourage me to view the stallion." A small ripple of laughter ran through the men. Luthgar grinned. "My Lady Ingund wisely understands that a horse does not make a comforting bedfellow."

The men let out a raucous laugh, while Arria smiled at Luthgar's humor but was secretly satisfied with the results. She and Luthgar would be alone.

Drusus shot Arria a glance, then averted his eyes in Severus' direction. Severus stared back at him. It was clear that Drusus and the tribune had the same thought. "Arria, please one moment before you leave." Drusus ordered a slave to fetch his lady's cloak, while Marcella lounged on a couch sipping from a cup of wine offered from Aveek's hand.

"What is it Titus?" Arria asked demurely. Beneath her calm manner she was anxious to leave.

"Remember, the security of Rome rests on your discretion at all times. To reveal the truth about Garic and Vodamir's demise to Luthgar may prove imprudent. Your diplomacy also protects those whom you love, as well as your country and your betrothed."

"My lord, you needn't remind me of my duties. I am aware of my responsibility to my country and friends *at all times.*"

Drusus stared. "Very well, Arria. Don't stay too long. We shall reconvene in a hour." He placed the cloak handed to him by the slave around her shoulders, while Luthgar waited patiently by the door. "Now show the barbarian *my horse,* but remember, be careful."

Arria spun on her heel after the words "my horse" fell from his mouth.

"Where is your wife tonight Lord Luthgar?"

"She is at our farm with the children. I leave warriors there at all times to protect them."

"I would have enjoyed a visit to your farm," Arria said wistfully.

"You speak like you never will."

"I will be married soon. Drusus would never allow it."

Luthgar stopped and took Arria's hands. "Lady there is something I must say. Time is short and there is much to tell."

"If it concerns Garic and Vodamir's death do not worry. I discovered the truth a short while ago. My heart is broken and I fear it will never repair."

Luthgar looked anxiously around. "It's cold, my lady, we should hurry." He locked her arm in his and urged her along the path to the stable. At the door, a slave handed Luthgar a lantern. With a quick step, Luthgar opened the door and they stepped inside. "Come and sit, I have much to tell you," Luthgar said and led her toward a bale of hay.

Arria gazed at Luthgar somewhat surprised, but followed him to the straw bench and sat. The yellow hay brought Garic's golden hair first to her mind, but then, an image of his cold, blue corpse flashed before her. She stiffled a cry.

"My lady, are you ill?" Luthgar stood in front of her, his face worried.

Oh, no...it's just...sometimes when I think of Garic, I cannot help but picture him lying in a shallow grave, so still and prey to animals with no one to protect him." Arria began to weep. Tears ran down her face as she swiped at them with the palms of her hands. "Forgive my womanly tears. They are for a noble warrior."

"One which you loved with your whole heart it seems," Luthgar said, placing the lantern on a hook bracketed to the nearest stall.

"Is it so apparent?" Arria smiled through her sadness.

Luthgar grinned, "Mistress, would a Roman woman shed a tear for a barbarian unless she loved him? Lady, my news will heal your broken heart."

Luthgar crouched in front of her and whispered, "Garic's alive."

A sharp tingle ran down Arria's spine as soft tears filled her eyes. "He's dead. I've seen proof."

"It's not true. Your slave Samuel is with us and trains with us daily. He escaped the ambush Drusus planned for them and came to our camp. The last he saw, Garic and Vodamir were trapped, beaten, and bound as slaves for sale to the Huns."

"Both Severus and Drusus say they're dead," Arria said, astonished. "Drusus gave me Garic's armlet and a belt made of both Garic's and Vodamir's hair."

Luthgar squinted, "That bastard did what with their hair?"

"He made a belt to shame me."

Luthgar let out a low breath and grit his teeth. "Before this is over, I will make a belt from the hide of his rump, I promise!"

Arria feared Luthgar's deadly resolve. Now was not the time for revenge. Inwardly, she prayed it was possible. "Tell me again. Where were they taken? Are you sure they're alive?"

"Drusus sent me a dispatch, claiming they were killed in a skirmish with the Huns, but Samuel believes they could be Hun slaves."

"Drusus wanted them dead because of me. Why would he spare them?"

"I don't know, my lady. Maybe for money or a brutal revenge."

Arria's heart beat faster, there was hope. "What can I do?"

"You must not tell anyone they are alive, not even Samuel's woman.

My men and I, have a plan to find them. No one is to know, do you understand?"

That she might see Garic again was a dream too incredible for words. And so she cried, smiled and cried some more.

"My lady, you must fight your tears," Luthgar insisted. "Your red and swollen eyes will betray us. Drusus will know our conversation has been more than about horses. You want to help Garic don't you?"

"What can I do? I will be married in a week."

"Can you prevent the marriage?" Luthgar asked.

"No. There are circumstances surrounding this union, too complicated to explain."

"You must find a way! Garic told me you're the smartest woman he's ever known."

Arria rested her hand on Luthgar's arm. "Then, I must prove him true and discover a way to avoid this marriage. Please find them!"

"I will, or I will breathe my last breath trying!" Luthgar stood and extended his hand to her. Small blades of hay clung to his boots, while a horse nickered in the stall beside them. "My lady, it's time we return," he said and reached for the lantern.

Arria firmly grasped Luthgar's hand and rose. The bond of his vow and strength forged through her. Now, more than ever, she knew what she must do.

"What would it take to have the pleasure of your company tonight?" Aveek the Hun, his black hair adorned with silver corded braids, stood over Marcella who reclined on a couch plush with pillows. The evening's festivities ended, the guests were left to quiet conversation, while Drusus met with Orestes.

Marcella brazenly stared at his rugged frame and weather-hardened face. "My company is not for sale, but if my master was to order me to entertain you—then I must; for, his happiness is always in the center of my heart."

"As is his lust?"

"From the way you leer at me, I suspect yours has awakened as well. Whether it stirs my—heart...will remain to be seen."

Aveek threw back his head and roared. "You excite me Egyptian! I will speak with Orestes, and he will speak with your master. If it's acceptable, I will come to you tonight. We have much to *entertain*," his voice was deep, "but let's not waste this time on what's to come. Call for another cup of wine, no make it a flask, I am feeling like a warrior after a battle." Firmly Aveek pressed Marcella's thigh as he motioned a slave to bring more wine.

"What magic do you know, Egyptian?"

"Why do you ask?"

"Because the Roman fool at the table is staring at you like a mad sick bull. What spell have you put on him priestess?"

"Severus is a mighty warrior with mighty passions, but he does not own me, Drusus does."

"Will Drusus share you with a Hun?"

"He may or may not. He is often mercurial in his discretion, but you intrigue me as well Noble Aveek. I can feel a power runs through you. I would desire that power in me."

Aveek chuckled softly and moved closer running his hand up her leg. "If it's power you want then power you shall have. My quarters are simple, but they are my own. Come to me tonight, priestess, and I will fill you with all the power you can tolerate. That lovesick bull of yours will seem lame and daft. Will he pose a threat?"

"He'll not bother us."

"Good. Then I shall wait my beautiful Egyptian goddess." Taking her hand, Aveek asked, "Is your land beautiful and the women as enchanting as you?"

Marcella purred, "Rainbows crown the river Nile in spring and our temples seem to touch the deepest blue of the desert sky. All the women, enchanting and plain, could not resist a man such as you my lord. Like me. The women of Egypt would be slaves to your desires."

Aveek leaned in and brushed his lips against Marcella's silk covered nipple.

"Marcella!" Severus snapped, breaking their spell.

Aveek raised his narrowed eyes toward the tribune. "What do you want?"

"Drusus is ready to reconvene. He wants that Marcella find the Lady Arria and inform her to return."

"There's a bitter cold outside," Marcella protested. "I will not find her. She knows her way back. Besides, she has the Frank as an escort. You know how much she likes them."

Severus gave her a warning look.

"Very well," she pouted.

Chapter Sixteen

Per Ardua Ad Astra
Through Hardship to the Stars

ATTILA'S CAMP

The silence was broken by a hundred cries, or so it seemed. Outside the infirmary tent, the sound of tin bells and bleating sheep filled the air. Garic focused his glance off the side of his bed as he watched Ursula bend and ladle water from a bucket into a small basin filled with clean strips of cloth. Every morning she came to him with a smile and her patient care. The redness had disappeared into his skin, a good sign she had told him, and the stitches had been pulled. Now all he needed was the special salve that Basina made from swine and goat grease to make it heal completely.

"Good morning, Long-Hair, did you sleep?"

Garic lied sincerely. "I did." Ursula's womanly curves caught his attention. Embarrassed, he darted his gaze to his bicep.

Ursula set the bowl of water on the floor and reached for his arm. "This is healing nicely. The scar will be small." Her gaze on the bandage, she unwound the cloth. "How is your work going at the bowyers? Is Kadam keeping you busy?"

"Very. Donatus is teaching me how to pound and shred sinew. It seems to be getting easier. I cannot say that my work is good, but they appear pleased; in fact, Kadam looked surprised when Donatus showed him how well I bundled the glued sinew for the wood core. Today, they will demonstrate how to make a bow string from hemp so it's sturdy and will not snap."

"I am glad working with the bowyers has helped. Maybe this occupation will keep you from the battlefield."

"Has this been your plan all along, Ursula? Are you a Valkyrie here to save me?" Ursula blushed and reached for a wet cloth to clean the wound. "A warrior goddess I am not, but thank you. Your recovery is all the gratitude I need." She looked up and held his gaze.

Quickly, Garic swung his legs to the opposite side of the bed, pulling on his leather breeches, then grabbing his linen shirt from the nearby chair he lifted it over his head. He knew Ursula watched. He could feel her gaze penetrate his back. It made him feel alive, but then guilt consumed him. Where was Arria now? Was Drusus watching her? Garic had a sudden urge to breathe cold air. "Ursula, you're too kind." was all he could manage. "Come, let's find Vodamir. He and I could do with a walk. The morning sun calls to me."

"Sit down!" Basina demanded.

"No!" Vodamir shot back.

"You must rest!"

Vodamir stubbornly folded his arms in a defiant gesture. A resolve emanated from his eyes, warning Basina that he wouldn't be budged. "Woman, you will not keep me here all day in a bed. I am a man. I need air and to be outside!"

"I told you, I am not your woman and I will decide if you can leave. Your face is still badly bruised and your ribs are on the mend. Is there no pain in your body?"

"There is, but I need to breathe. I can stand a little pain, and the air will do me good."

"And your hand?"

"Wrap it for me, Basina, in a cloth to hold it secure to my body and protected. I will do nothing foolish, I promise. I want it to heal as quickly as you do, but I am restless and I need to be outside."

"It's still cold. The dampness will not help your bones or your sides."

"Then help me to find a warm cloak. Is there no one here who owns one?"

Basina looked helplessly about.

"Please, Queen of the Healers, let me walk and I will forever be in your debt, if I am not already."

Exasperated she planted her hands on her hips. "Under one condition will I let you walk. I must accompany you."

"How you torture me," he said smiling wider. "If you must, fine, but will you be able to keep up?"

"Keep up!" Basina snapped. "You can barely stand. I will be forced to support you and move slowly."

Vodamir smirked. He was looking forward to this walk more than ever. The prospect of her arm wrapped around his waist appealed to him. Basina appealed to him. She was unusual and bold, and this aggressive quality excited him.

"Cousin, are you being an irritable patient?" Garic walked up to the pair.

"We were just discussing the benefits of a walk out in the fresh air. I want to walk among the traders." Vodamir sat himself on a nearby chair, while Basina shook her head and threw up her hands.

"We have no coin or goods to barter. What can you possibly buy?" Garic puzzled over Vodamir's desire to roam the cluster of peddlers.

"I will search for the axe that I will acquire once I am fully healed."

"Is that all you can think of?" Basina groaned, and secured a wide cloth sling across his chest. Deftly, she placed his hand and arm in the cradling support. "You've been on your back for weeks due to a cruel beating and your first thoughts upon venturing out are about procuring a weapon?"

Vodamir's roguish nature grabbed him. "Well, actually, I've had other thoughts as well."

"I will find you a cloak," Basina stammered, and hastily retreated.

"Don't be so hard on her. You're always demanding something." Garic reproached Vodamir.

"I need some air. You're not complaining. You have your work with the bowyer."

Lapsing into the safety of Frankish, Garic said, "Let's begin to walk the perimeter of the camp if you can. We must get an idea of the size of Attila's forces."

"Basina will accompany us. Will she suspect anything?" Vodamir replied, his eye on Basina as she sorted through some cloaks and coverings.

"It doesn't matter if she does. She knows we're helpless. The more information we have, the better our chances are for escape."

"I hope you're right. I see years ahead of us in Attila's camp. That is, of course, if we survive."

"I don't have years, Vodamir. And neither does Cambria and Gaul. Attila is here."

"What will we do?"

"I am not sure, but I might know a way out."

"What is your plan?" Vodamir stood and braced himself with the back of the chair. Garic moved closer to him and extended a hand. Vodamir waved it away. "I am fine. Tell me more."

"I will earn a bow from Kadam and become an archer, a good one. This will take some time, but I will lead us out of here. You must heal!" Garic insisted.

"We may be here a long time. For your sake, I hope Arria's love is loyal."

"She will wait for me, Vodamir."

"I wish that for you, Cousin." Vodamir smiled as he saw the lithe figure of Basina approaching. Her shiny, black hair hung in braids beneath a cap trimmed with otter and she wore a jacket of mink pelts that hung to her knees.

Basina came to Vodamir and helped put the cape around his shoulders. Gently, he touched a braid as she fastened the brooch closing the cape. "Do not take liberties with me, Long-Hair." Her voice was low and she glanced away.

Encouraged by her lack of anger, he said, "I am sorry, Basina, it's not my right to touch you, but your hair is so black. When I look at it,

I see the blue blackness of a crow's wings. Forgive me, I momentarily forgot my place."

"You are different," Basina answered passively. "You don't act the warrior. Are you sure you can fight?"

Vodamir chuckled. "I assure you, more than one man has felt my axe. This is why I stand before you. Our ways are different, you're right. I hope I haven't offended you. Will you still walk with us? I feel myself beginning to tire."

"Your cousin will support you from one side." Basina said and called to Garic who wisely had moved to the entrance to wait. Garic wrapped his arm in Vodamir's, while Basina walked beside her patient, her arm lightly around his waist and her hand beneath the sling.

"Basina."

"Yes."

"I will be well again won't I? I mean my hand, it will open and close and move like before, won't it?"

"Long-Hair, I promise you I will do everything in my power to make you well, just so I can bring calm to my tent once again."

"Don't be cruel to me, Queen of the Healers. Make me whole again."

The bruises under Vodamir's blue eyes had dulled. He was on the mend. Each day Basina noticed a beautiful man rising from the monster that had devoured him. Facing Vodamir directly, she said, "I can heal you. I know it's a jest when you call me "Queen of the Healers," but I will prove to you that I am. You will live to fling your axe another day and better than before! Then you will never call me *woman*, do you understand?"

Vodamir sighed, the corners of his mouth curled lightly in a grin. His glance met hers, and he answered as if he spoke a vow, "Never, will I call you *woman* again."

FORT CAMBRIA

Luthgar and Arria left the stable with rekindled hope, and Arria prayed that Garic was alive and safe as she hurried through the atrium toward the dining hall. The long table was set with bowls of fruit, delicate sweets, and decanters of wine. Slaves scurried about as Marcella approached Arria. With a slight petulance, Marcella removed Arria's cloak and moved toward a servant's bench against the wall. Marcella had come in search of Arria and Luthgar. She had tossed at them Drusus' command to return, then spun on her heel and headed toward the festivities.

Arria and Luthgar took their seats.

Orestes addressed Drusus, "A political hostage, or as I like to think of it, an envoy exchange, would soothe any reservations our King Attila might have at this moment." Orestes folded his hands before him and gazed steadily at Drusus. "Our encampment isn't far from here. Your representative might prove the necessary balm to Attila's already wounded pride. A show of trust on the part of Cambria and an envoy willing to live with us as our guest might prove useful to all. Don't you agree?"

Drusus leaned back in his chair and rubbed his fingers slowly over his thumb. Arria recognized the gesture and knew that Drusus was calculating his best move. "If an envoy was selected to join your camp for a short period would this guarantee a halt to Attila's invasion?" Drusus ventured and fixed his gaze on Orestes.

"It would certainly ensure against any aggressive action that would harm both sides as well as the hostages." Orestes countered.

"Who should these hostages be? Who among us is so important as to stop any thought of attack from both our sides." Drusus queried.

Orestes continued boldly. "There is one who has come to mind quite unexpectedly. This person would prove most worthy in Attila's eyes."

"If you are thinking of the Tribune Severus, I am afraid I cannot part with him at this time. He's a valuable officer."

"I am thinking of another."

"Who is it you want, Orestes?"

"The Lady Arria."

Drusus froze and Severus seated beside him gasped, while Aveek's eyes betrayed amusement and Orestes gazed calmly upon the Romans.

"She is the daughter of a Roman senator!"

"Precisely. She is a worthy hostage to our king. And much more valuable as our guest than any soldier," bowing his head in Severus' direction, Orestes added, "no matter his reputation."

"This is incredible. I will have none of it."

"But I will." Arria interjected to the surprise of all the guests. "My lord, I accept."

Drusus turned in Arria's direction, burning with rage. "Leave us now, Arria. It's unthinkable and out of the question!" he snapped.

"Why is that, Titus?" Arria said and rose from her chair. "It makes perfect sense and is much to Lord Orestes credit. I am the perfect hostage. It's known that young boys of noble birth are preferred in matters of political exchange for diplomatic assurances of good faith. However, this is Cambria and choices are limited."

"Need I remind you that we are to be wed within days," Drusus bristled.

"We can be wed upon my return, my lord. As an envoy it's my mission to foster diplomacy in times of tense negotiations," Arria said with a soft confidence. She knew that Drusus seethed inwardly. The path this negotiation was taking was definitely not to his liking. He had planned to buy Cambria's safety with a monetary tribute until Aetius arrived with his army. He would view her interference as bold and embarrassing.

Drusus sat silent, but shot her his blackest look. He glanced once at Orestes and said, "Very well. My lady, you may accept this *invitation* if you wish, but I must add to this game of lots. The wife of Drusus will make an even better hostage. Arria, we will wed in two days and you may leave in three. However, after one month you must return when the outcome of this truce is decided. Do you agree, Orestes?"

Arria looked to Orestes who bowed his head toward them. "As you wish, Commander," he replied.

Her mind raced with thoughts of how to avoid the marriage. She had taken a bold chance by manipulating the negotiations in her favor and publicly against Drusus. It had been her plan to offer herself as a hostage, but Orestes and good fortune had seen it through. However, she could see no other recourse to the marriage. She let her careful glance find Luthgar who blinked his concern. *What will you do?* his eyes asked. What could she do was the better question? She would travel to Attila's camp, not only as an envoy, but in hope of finding Garic. Tragically, she would have to go as Drusus' wife. No longer would she be free to wed Garic. Arria consoled herself with the sad idea that her joy must spring from finding him alive and freeing him from Attila's bondage, even though as a husband, he would be lost to her. "It will be as you wish, Titus; however, I have one request."

"My lady, if it's within my power, I will grant you anything you desire."

"Your generosity is overwhelming." Arria said with a gracious nod. "I would request that Karas and Angelus accompany me as well as the *talented* slave, Marcella. Her dancing and obvious charms are sure to entertain King Attila. Do you agree, Lord Orestes?"

"Most certainly, if this is your wish, my lady."

Drusus interjected, his expression grim. "An excellent idea, *Carissima*. In fact, to ensure everyone's safety, I will dispatch Severus as your escort along with several soldiers. Once he has delivered you safely within the confines of the camp, I will expect his prompt return. Orestes, I hope you find this acceptable."

"Legate Drusus, we are here to be agreeable. We can guarantee the safety of your envoy and her traveling party, but why not make it safer with the added presence of your soldiers."

"You're most considerate. Thank you, and thank King Attila. My future wife's safe passage to your camp is of the utmost concern to me. Now, I suggest we retire for the evening. It has been a strenuous day for us all. Please, have one more cup of wine if you desire. My servants will show you to your quarters. Arria, I will escort you to your chamber."

All the guests stood as Drusus rose. Quietly, they said their goodnights. Aveek extended his cup to an approaching slave with a full container of wine and looked at Marcella now risen to stand beside a pillar, an odd smile on her face.

Drusus extended his hand to Arria. She placed her hand in his. His grip tightened immediately around her fingers and she caught her breath. All the men swallowed their last drops and moved from the room, their talk filled with the affairs of the coming days.

A scowl brandished his face as Drusus leaned toward Arria and whispered, "It will not be so easy to rid yourself of me. I anticipated a possible delay in our nuptial. Several days ago, I sent a missive to my former commander, Governor Lucinius, in Turonum and requested that he ask Bishop Ignatius to wed us as soon as possible. He will arrive tomorrow."

Arria, numb and expressionless, nodded. There seemed no other recourse than to marry Drusus. She must protect Karas and Angelus and had secured their safety by requesting they attend her on her mission to the Huns. Married or not, she would find Garic and help him to escape. In his freedom, she would find her happiness.

"Why did you maneuver Marcella into your entourage?" Drusus asked, shattering her thoughts.

"I think that Marcella's charms will prove useful among the Huns. She bears remarkable similarities to them. I am sure she'll feel quite comfortable among these barbarians. Will you miss her?"

Drusus halted abruptly in the corridor leading to her room and faced her. "Never contradict or manipulate me to your advantage, especially before others, again. I will not be made the fool!" he hissed. "My influence is what keeps you safe. The Huns may want an envoy, but you can perish—if things go wrong."

"Ah, a good reason for our marriage. A dowry followed by an inheritance?"

"I've told you what I want—nobility, an heir, and of course, your love."

"I thought you loved another."

"Marcella is my passion. I am a man with many appetites. Why begrudge me what most men claim for themselves? You will be the mother of my rightful heir and this prestige, Marcella or any child of hers will never know."

Disgusted by his cold appraisal of their life together, Arria pushed passed him, but Drusus grabbed her arm.

"Let me pass, Titus. I would go to my room."

"On the contrary, you will come to mine instead. I now can see some benefit from you as a Hun hostage. This insight stirs my mood. In fact, I'm feeling quite amorous."

"And I, tired and unwilling."

"Reconsider. There's a little boy I know who would look pitiful hanging from a tree with his mother hanging beside him. Can you picture it?"

"You disgust me!"

"Follow me, or I will have you here in the hall. A prospect you might enjoy when considering your preference for open lovemaking; the stable comes again to mind." His firm, smooth fingers raised her chin. "Will it be the corridor or my room?"

"Your room," Arria whispered tersely.

"Good. Let down your hair."

Arria pulled the pins from her hair and her long tresses fell over her shoulders.

Drusus grabbed the back of her neck and pulled her mouth to his. "Tonight will be a night you will never forget. In two days we will be wed, and you will be mine—forever."

Chapter Seventeen

Praemonitus praemunitus
Forewarned, forearmed

THE FOREST
Month of Martius, AD 451

A sudden silence and a distant snap roused Luthgar's drooping lids. "Huns. Wake the men," Luthgar whispered, his voice urgent like the great river they slept beside.

Samuel nodded, and snaked his way to each man. Cloaked by the night, Luthgar and his men stood ready. The hunt for the enemy had begun. Divided only by the fire pit, they dispersed into two separate and close-knit groups. Heading north a hundred paces, they instinctively knew the count.

The Wespe always fought this way. They trained in the night, the cold and the fog. They learned to blend with the forest and knew it better than most men. A warrior wall, they silently moved forward. The group reached the perimeter of their paces. They would circle back and flank any Hun scout south of them but north of the river. It wasn't long before Luthgar heard cursing and a clash of swords coming from the direction of Rudiger, Amo's father and Farro, the youngest. Luthgar whistled for Samuel and Amo, and they sprinted toward their companions. Metal rang against metal as Rudiger and Farro fought two Huns. Snorting grunts burst from the Wespe veteran and novice, like wild boars their tusks tangled in struggle as they killed the Huns.

The risen moon shone on the soldiers caught in combat. A sudden hum shot through the air. An arrow buried itself in Farro's neck. Luthgar screamed into the darkness, "Find the archer! Find Farro's killer!" They would drive the archer and any remaining Huns against the river, leaving them no escape.

Outnumbered, the last remaining Huns fired a few desperate arrows, then ran. The river acted as their beacon. Instantly, they shed their swords, quivers and bows and dove into the frigid water.

Amo called three of his fighters from the left flank who met him in the clearing. Strong swimmers, they shed fur vests, cloaks and weapons as they ran towards the river. Into the ink black water they plunged, following the fleeing Huns.

Samuel, Luthgar and Rudiger crouched on the edge of the shore. "Will they stop them before they reach the shore?" Samuel asked Luthgar.

"Four men cannot fail." Luthgar fixed his gaze on the water's surface.

Luthgar and his men waited anxiously on the shore as the swimmers furiously stroked and faded into the darkness. Amo rose from the water first, clawing patches of river grass with his hands. "They are dead," he stammered and stumbled toward the rekindled fire. The other warriors emerged behind him, shivering and exhausted and followed Amo.

The Wespe settled down for a few hours of sleep, but rose early to salvage bodies. Dawn's pink light spanned the horizon as Luthgar made his way back from the river with a skin filled with water and approached Amo. "When the sun is up, we will bury the boy on the rise overlooking the water. The river spirits can sing Farro praises for his valor."

Amo kicked the stones beside his foot. "His honor will be spoken of by the elders and his proud parents."

"Farro will rest with his sword but carry his shield to his mother."

Amo grunted his approval. "And what about the Huns?"

"Let them rot. Just strip them before we leave."

ATTILA'S CAMP

"Where's my bow, Donatus? I placed it on the rack closest to Aveek's." Garic looked down the rows for the maple shaft.

"Kadam will tiller it for you. You've learned quickly, but don't be over zealous. Your bow will twist, which can be very dangerous."

"Is tillering that difficult?"

Donatus' grin grew serious. "The bending of the limbs is a difficult process—a skill that the master and only a few possess. Kadam can usually tiller a bow in several days, but this step requires experience." Donatus lowered his eyes respectfully. "An ability you lack, although you show promise. Until your bow is finished, you may practice with one of mine. Pack your quiver with many arrows; but don't worry, in time and with my guidance, you will shoot an arrow as well as you swing an axe. If I found an axe, would you teach me to throw?"

Garic found Donatus refreshing. At times, he saw himself in the boy's sensibility and his willingness to take a risk. "Sounds like a fair trade. That is, of course, if you're as good an archer as I can wield an axe."

"I can split the limb of a young ash tree at thirty yards. Can you do the same with an axe?" Donatus challenged.

"Thor's hammer, I can!" Garic asserted. "It's settled. We're evenly matched and evenly taught. And tomorrow our training begins."

Kadam appeared unexpectedly beside them and piped, "What happy news. You both have formed a friendship, but time demands we make bows and arrows. Our warriors can't wait. King Attila will move in a few days to strike again."

Donatus smirked. Garic was taken by surprise. Kadam had spoken in accented but clear Latin.

"You speak Latin!" Garic blurted. Donatus grinned mischievously.

"Of course I do," Kadam responded gruffly. "I am a master bowyer who's traveled far and wide."

Garic demanded politely, "You kept your knowledge of Latin a secret. Why?"

"To observe what sort of man you are."

"What have you decided?"

"I can respect you. Now can we get to work? Attila has ordered the camp to join his troops in less than a week. You will assemble arrows and bows. It's a pity the other long-hair's hand is still not healed, or I would draft him into my service, as well."

Garic seized the opportunity. "Vodamir could carry wood, make glue and gather any materials you might need."

Kadam deliberated for a moment. "We certainly need the help ... but as you know, it's a docile job."

"One that will teach him patience, a talent he lacks at times."

Kadam seated himself and commanded his apprentice, "Leave us, Donatus." The boy trotted off without hesitation. Kadam motioned Garic to the stool beside him. He handed him some reeds from a woven basket to strip and sort for shafts. Grabbing some arrows, he inspected the fletching. "I hear the fiery Basina has had her hands full with your cousin. If he *was* inclined, a little attention sent in her direction might help to soften her."

Garic grinned. "Master Kadam, in my tribe you would be called matchmaker, a practice of older women, not a weapons maker."

"Should I feel offended, Frank?"

"Anyone who brings a man and woman together should never feel offended."

Kadam paused his inspection and looked at Garic. "I sense a connection between your cousin and our healer. Basina might resist, but that should not deter the long-hair."

"Would this be wise?" Garic queried.

"Some wouldn't approve, the Shaman Kama for one; however, it doesn't hurt to have love in one's life. Friends in camp would also be beneficial, don't you agree?"

Garic wondered if Kadam could be trusted. The old fox was smart. He nodded. "It never hurts to love, and it profits to have friends."

"Which brings me to Ursula. She can be an asset to you, as well. She is strong, able, and sensible." Kadam reached for an open box filled with arrowheads. Looking a moment, he chose one, placed it in his palm and ran his finger over its point. "A sensible companion can prove a strong ally. Just like the spiked tang that unites head and shaft, making the arrow complete."

Garic felt a heat rise in his neck. "I respect Ursula. She has been my salvation...but I am not free."

"You have a wife?" Kadam's eyes narrowed.

"Not yet, but I will one day."

"She must be a beautiful woman to have such devotion from a mighty warrior, and as I hear, first counsel to your tribe."

"My lady is rare indeed. I can love no other."

"I once felt that way. It was worth every moment. Then hold fast. Your love will carry you back to her one day. Destiny has no other option."

"If this is true, then I will find her again," Garic sighed. "It's an honor to work for you, Master Kadam."

A devilish smile lit up Kadam's eyes. "Will you and Vodamir work for me until battle calls?"

"We will stay until ordered elsewhere." Garic slipped a reed between his teeth and grinned. The wily fox had drawn a secret from his heart, and at the same time bartered for their labor.

Kadam flashed a smile of approval.

Garic plucked the reed from his lips and ventured, "Master, I have one request."

Kadam nodded.

"I wish to set two pink gems on the face of my bow as Aveek did with the rubies."

"These gems represent something?"

"Pink roses," Garic said softly. "They remind me of my lady and give me strength."

"We will find these gems, Long-hair. Are you prepared to work your hardest, first for me, then Attila? They will be expensive."

"I will work and fight hard."

"Will you fight against the Romans and your own people?"

"I will fight to buy my freedom, and my cousin will join me."

"Well spoken if you wish to survive here," Kadam said bluntly. Standing, he walked to the wooden rack nearest him and reached for the unbended maple shaft. "When your bow is finished, we will search for the pink stones. In the meantime, fetch your cousin and return. There is much work to be done, Garic, apprentice to Kadam."

Garic bowed respectfully, raised the tent curtain and stepped outside.

The spring air carried bird song from pines. Ground squirrels dodged Huns on horseback. Children ran through the crowd of craftsmen, laborers, and soldiers yelling the news that Orestes and the chieftain, Aveek, were riding into camp. Garic speculated that now he might meet the mighty warrior and judge for himself if Aveek was to be feared.

A deep rush of emotion suddenly surged through him. Unnerved by its power, Garic took a quick breath. He turned and gazed at a caravan arriving in the distance. He saw nothing unusual. He shook his head and walked toward the infirmary, reflecting on his escape plan. His only allies were his cousin, possibly Kadam, and the days ahead. As he reached the entry of the hospital, he turned and looked once more at the caravan. Garic felt drawn to it. Feeling foolish, he pushed the thought away and stepped into the tent. Once inside, he was met by the smell of goat grease, pine boughs, and the aroma from smoldering pots of witch hazel. In the dull light of the infirmary, he thought he heard in the distance, beyond the tent walls, a semblance of Arria's laugh. Her face loomed before him. Ursula tugged his sleeve and called his name. Garic focused on Ursula's face and asked, "Have you seen my cousin?"

"He went with Basina for his daily walk." Ursula answered. "Are you all right? You stared as if the night spirits paraded before you."

"Do you believe in destiny?"

His sudden question lit Ursula's eyes with surprise. "At times I do, but certainty evades me," she answered.

Garic watched as joy lit her face. She seemed to bask in his willingness to share his thoughts.

Ursula placed her hand on his elbow. "Let's not talk of the future. Come. I think I know where to find them."

"Where?" Garic asked, letting go his thoughts and parting the entry curtain. Together they stepped out from the infirmary into the afternoon air.

"Basina's tent on the edge of camp."

Garic raised his brow.

"Are you so surprised? Vodamir's gaze has followed her about the hospital for a month."

"They cannot be lovers. There's no time." Garic scowled and ran his fingers through his hair, then placed his hands on his hips and looked around.

Ursula winced, but continued, "Love and time have no master. They rule themselves."

Garic gazed at Ursula's wind-blown curls and pretty profile. "Time is a thief that steals from lovers."

Ursula smiled in an odd, almost sad way. "Come, Long-Hair. Time is also a taskmaster. The day grows short, and there's much to do."

Garic nodded and walked beside her, but the laughter riding on the wind forced him to listen and remember.

"That's disgusting! I refuse to empty her privy pot! I won't!"

"The mistress called for you to do it," Angelus retorted.

Cuffing him soundly on the head, Marcella grabbed his collar and said, "You will do it for me or I will curse you and your mother. I will ensure that your private parts, even as a man, stay as infantile as they are now, and that a rash risen from the jaws of the goddess Sekhmet will inflict your beautiful mother's face. Do you understand?"

Defiant but frightened, Angelus freed himself from the Egyptian's grip and screamed, "Whore!" while dodging her attempt to grab at him.

"Do as I say, or you will suffer you little bastard!" Marcella shouted after him.

A low chuckle rose from within the coach designated for Arria's female servants. Stomping up the few stairs, Marcella stepped into the dimness of the interior and brazenly hissed, "What's so funny? I refuse to do Arria's bidding!" Impulsively, she threw a nearby incense pot out the wagon door and crashing on a tree stump. "That's a lower slave's job. Tell her to get her Greek handmaiden, Karas, to clean her mess. I won't!" Marcella fumed.

"You'd best be careful," Aveek drawled and drank from his cup. "Your lady might have your head for your impertinence." He laughed again, which only made her angrier.

"If she takes my head, my mouth and body will be of little use to you, as well as my knowledge. I wonder, are there many Hun women who can do what I do? If this is so, then why bother with me?" Marcella's crimson robe hung open revealing her voluptuous body.

"No one can do what you do, priestess. I am a man with a large appetite and I cannot get enough of you," Aveek answered from the covers of her bed his bare body bronzed from the sun.

Marcella smiled, her lips pursed in a feline grin. "If that's so, then you must intercede for me. Request I be removed from her service while we're here and moved to yours. Drusus will not sell me, but he might concede to this arrangement to avoid any domestic issues at such a crucial time."

"Well spoken, and a proposal worth considering, but time grows short. I long to slip you beneath me and ride you until we both tire."

Aveek sat up and grabbing her wrist, he wrapped his arm around her waist and pulled her onto his rock hard body. "Come here and talk no more."

Aveek gave a final bellow and clenched Marcella's hair. "I know... why Drusus...keeps you," he panted, his eyes closed and arms outstretched, "despite what his men think...and wife wishes. I will send a missive asking that you move into my tent, while you live here."

Marcella gloated with satisfaction. "You will not be disappointed, my Lord Aveek.

"I will send my request back with your pining tribune, Severus. He will never suspect that he carries the missive that will land you in my arms whenever I desire." Aveek kissed her and rose from the bed.

"Why do you hate him?" Marcella asked as she watched the Hun chieftain pull up his breeches.

"I don't hate him," Aveek said, reaching for his woolen tunic and pulling it over his head. "He's just an adversary. A Roman who thinks he's more civilized and more entitled to rule. Attila is the Lord of the World, and he shall rule all of Gaul, then Italia. Very soon, priestess, we will be the masters of the spoiled and arrogant Romans." Aveek slipped on his final boot and donned his deerskin vest. Kissing her one more time, he pulled a thick, gold band from his vest. He clasped it on her wrist and said, "Attila's token. Protect it with your life." Aveek opened the coach door and easily jumped the stairs. He faded into the camp, his happy whistle trailing behind him.

Marcella watched him disappear. She gazed at the bracelet. A gift from Attila? Why? The center held a raised gold heart surrounded by blood-red rubies. Enthralled with its beauty, her fingers caressed the surface. To her surprise, the left side of the heart revealed a tiny hinge. Marcella pressed her nail into the seam and the heart popped open, disclosing a small hollow set into the thick band. A thin piece of folded parchment rested within the recess. Marcella's heart raced. Lifting it gently from it's hiding place, she opened the note.

Arria kicked the privy pot onto its side and into the tall grass edging the perimeter around her wagon, then stomped the ground with her foot. "I hate that woman. Marcella listens to no one and struts around here like a queen. How dare she ignore my command. She's a slave!"

Karas placed a folded blanket on a chest and approached Arria. "My lady, I will take care of you, please," she coaxed, her words accented and slow. "You are married. Anger does not help, especially after...drinking the monthly potion. Pennyroyal demands peace with its power. Calm yourself ... or maybe you find yourself with child."

Arria sat on a nearby boulder. She tugged her green veil from her curls and rubbed her temples. "You're right, Karas. The witch upsets me. I have never known hate until Drusus and Marcella. I feel powerless. My lord, Garic, brought me happiness and strength. Karas, I miss him so. Do you believe we will find him in this camp?"

Yes, my lady. I am sure," Karas said, and knelt beside her. "The stars are in...agreement. Your lord is here. I can see this...at night into the sky."

"Tell me, do the heavens predict Luthgar's arrival and our rescue?"

"I cannot be sure. A bloody mist ... covers the stars. War and death," she whispered.

"Will Luthgar rescue us? And Samuel?"

"You fear for Samuel, but Luthgar claims he's grown into a strong warrior. He's found what he's wished for—freedom. Samuel and Luthgar will come and help us find Garic and Vodamir. When we're gone from here, Samuel may take you and the boy away."

Karas winced. "My lady, you ... allow this?"

"I promise. Your freedoms are earned."

The sudden sound of hooves forced both women's eyes in the direction of their coach. Severus, dressed in shining brass and a red cloak rode up beside them. "My lady, greetings. Excuse my intrusion, but I carry news. King Attila requests your presence at his table, tonight. He's most eager to meet you. He loves entertaining and is partial to many Roman customs." Hesitating, Severus added, "I must escort you this evening. After tonight, however, I return to Cambria."

Arria shielded her eyes from the sun's glare and replied curtly, "Is King Attila concerned with protocol and the welfare of his hostage?"

"It appears so. Orestes, Attila's advisor, asked that I carry his king's welcome and invitation to you," Severus answered.

"Thank him and forward my request. I desire a private tent and additional servants to secure my comfort. Only after these necessities are provided will I concern myself with dinner and our introductions."

"I will inform Orestes. He brings all important matters to Attila's immediate attention."

"Very well." Arria answered and stared at him.

Bowing his head, Severus trotted his horse in the direction of the slave coach and Marcella seated on the steps.

Chapter Eighteen

Dum Spiro Spero
While I breathe I hope

BASINA'S TENT

Your hair is so black. The lustre lives on the wings of the crow and raven. It's beautiful." Vodamir grinned, kissed Basina's lips and tenderly caressed the strands falling across her breasts.

Basina kissed him a second time and snuggled closer under the heavy fur blanket, "Did you know I can fly?"

"I thought you were a healer not a shaman."

"It's much simpler than magic."

"How so?"

"When you kiss me I feel myself lifting off the ground and when you love me my spirit is above me and flying."

Vodamir aroused by Basina's compliment rolled on top of her. Kissing her slowly and sensually, he grasped black strands of hair in his fist. "Then let me lift you to the heavens, again."

He easily slipped inside her welcoming passion. Gently, he rocked his way higher to her heart.

Short gasps escaped her as she held his gaze with her eyes.

Vodamir rose to his knees and sat back on his haunches bringing her along, never breaking free. Basina instinctively moved with him. They were two bodies joined in one fluid motion each knowing what the other would do and wanted.

From the north a wind rolled over the dome of Basina's tent, forcing the lovers closer. A hawk screamed above the land and

Basina, cradled in Vodamir's lap, gasped. Every thrust drove him deeper. Every nerve within her tingled. She pressed her lips urgently against the coarse shadow of his beard as she clung to his hair. His strong thighs beneath her legs excited and soothed her. In spite of the moisture on her skin, Vodamir's lips burned on her neck. Her arms held him tightly. Lifted, Basina winced with ecstacy as Vodamir drove himself deeper. Like the hawk circling in the sky, Basina's spirit soared. Then without warning, a burning heat washed over her and surged through her body, causing her to cry out. Vodamir grabbed her tighter, talking softly, whispering words she didn't understand. With the strength of the fighter she knew him to be, he gave way to his lust and let himself go. *Meine Geliebte*, my love, huskily fell from his lips, caressing her cheek, and trapping the heart of the hardest of the Hun women, Basina, "Queen of the Healers." Vodamir, the slave warrior had won. She was in love.

Satisfied and exhausted, Basina languished beneath the blankets.

A banging on the outer step of the tent's platform interrupted the moment, and they both turned toward the sound in surprise.

"Who is it?" Basina called out. "What do you want?"

"It's Garic, and I've come for Vodamir. Master Kadam awaits us."

Basina turned to Vodamir, "I cannot let you go," she said plaintively.

Vodamir chuckled, "You must, we are expected. I will return, tonight." Vodamir cupped her breast in his hand and kissed Basina one more time, then jumped from the bed. As he pulled on his clothes, Garic banged the door even harder. Vodamir crossed the room, flung open the door, and smiled at a perturbed Garic. "How did you know where to find me?

Garic frowned. "Where to find you?" His tone mirrored his disapproval. "The entire infirmary, even the sickest man would know where to find you! Basina and the long-hair warrior are the talk of the hospital and by now the camp. And Kadam wants us both right away. Attila is planning to move. His advisor, Orestes and his strongest chieftain, Aveek, have returned from battle. They arrived early this afternoon, but how would you know? You're too occupied with your healing!"

"Settle down, Cousin. I am ready and can explain."

"Save your explanations." Garic shoved a quiver in his hand. "You'll need some arrows. Before the sun sets, archery practice at the forest's edge." He walked briskly and spoke, while Vodamir followed closely behind. "We must stay focused. I like Basina, but she's a Hun."

"Arria's a Roman," Vodamir snapped.

"It's not the same," Garic returned, harshly.

"Hel, the bitch, it isn't? Loki's confused you."

Garic stopped and faced Vodamir. "Do you want to get out of here, alive?"

Exasperated, Vodamir crossed his arms, but nodded. *"Ja."*

"Then follow the plan, and don't fall in love. It'll be your undoing. Do you understand?" Before Vodamir could answer, Garic spun on his heel and left him.

Vodamir glanced back at Basina's tent. Slim curls of smoke rose from the roof's vent giving it a warm, protective feeling. Then turning back toward Garic, he followed in pursuit.

ATTILA'S TENT

"Preparations for welcoming your guests are on the way, my king." Orestes, advisor to Attila, bowed respectfully, then pushed back the hood that protected him from the moist, *Martius* breeze.

Attila's long black hair, the sides knotted at the top, revealed angled features and narrow eyes that slanted upward toward his temples. He sat on a high-backed and ornately carved oak chair. Etched in the wood just above Attila's head, horsemen rode, their bows in hand. Attila's throne signified his sovereignity and the Hun way.

"I want the banquet to be lavish enough to impress," Attila ordered. "The Roman envoy is our hostage and our guest. Aveek claims she is comely. Is this true?"

"Yes. Her eyes are quite striking. They're green as shore washed pebbles, and she's lively. Drusus has his challenge." Orestes chuckled recalling the night Arria, contrary to Drusus' wishes, agreed to come into her enemy's camp as a hostage.

"How intriguing." Attila handed a scroll to Orestes who immediately opened it and began reading. Orestes' brow wrinkled, "Valentinian's sister, Honoria, has finally married the senator, Herculanus. The man is Valentinian's lackey and is easily manipulated. It seems he's found a more *stable* bridegroom, my king."

"Meaning?" Attila frowned, but amusement played in his eyes.

"Only that Herculanus is old and no threat to the emperor."

"I must admit, I do feel driven to roam and conquer." Both men laughed as Attila reached out for the scroll that Orestes placed back in his hand. "Valentinian is a fool!" Attila spat as he perused the parchment. "He doesn't even recognize that it's Aetius who keeps his empire safe from me. Or maybe he does, which cannot fare well for my old friend. However, Rome's security is soon to change. I want the Romans in camp to return to Cambria tomorrow. We will keep the Lady Arria as planned. She might prove to be more valuable than we anticipated. In four days, on the first day of *Aprilis*, we will advance on the city of Metis. I will shatter it to the ground. Not a man will be left standing. The plunder will more than please my people."

Attila motioned to a servant girl standing nearby. "Wine!" he called. The girl nodded and went for the refreshment. Attila's gaze followed her backside. Glancing at Orestes, whose eyes followed her as well, he grinned. "Orestes, never give a Hun a reward that holds no value for yourself." Attila smiled. "Do you like the girl? If you want, she'll be my gift to you."

A sharp grin seized Orestes, "Thank you my lord, she's quite tempting, but if my *Roman* wife discovered my indiscretion, you'd find yourself with one less advisor."

Attila chuckled. "Knowing Roman women, and your wife, a sudden and fatal affliction most likely would be your fate. A Hun is more fortunate. We can bask in the love of more than one woman. But

228

remember, Orestes, a clever man will always find a way to hide his mistress from his wife."

"Well spoken, my king. An idea I will surely entertain."

Attila motioned Orestes toward the chair opposite him. "Come now, sit! The girl will be here for you if you wish. We have more pressing concerns."

Orestes seated himself and gazed at his king with admiration. Attila's wisdom and determination to unite his Huns and any man, woman or child who joined him made him not only formidable but great. Attila sighed and extended his wooden cup, a preference and well-known reminder of his humble beginnings. The servant, having returned, filled their cups to the brim.

Attila took a sip and stared into the wine as if it held a vision. "It's a wise ruler and chieftain who shares his riches with men who show loyalty and are willing to stand beside their leader. For this act of generosity, they'll be willing to follow him even into the underworld if he asks." Looking sharply at Orestes, Attila continued, "Never underestimate the ability of the Romans to gain the support and even loyalty of Huns we fail to rightfully reward. This must be clear to the chieftains. Very soon Valentinian will realize that I, Attila, am the conqueror of Gaul and one day—Rome."

"May I gently remind my King that Lady Arria is now the wife of Titus Claudius Drusus. They married before she left Cambria. The Legate Drusus might come after his bride."

Attila flippantly waved his hand in the air. "And if he does, how will a paltry legion stand against an army ten times its size. Drusus isn't so noble. In the end, with little resistance, he let the Lady Arria act as my hostage, didn't he? He gambled that his woman's political standing and her presence here would stop our advance, until Aetius was further into Gaul. Fortunately, he miscalculated. How interesting. What will Drusus gain if Arria dies?"

"Under Roman law, the Lady Arria's dowry. Her father, Senator Felix, is quite wealthy. Also, I'm informed that before Drusus, she was widowed and childless. She solely inherited from her late husband as well."

"Perfect. All the more reason to keep our pretty hostage. She is quite valuable." Attila rose from his chair. He walked to a table spread with a map. "It's incredible that the Romans with their indulgent habits have ruled so far and so long. The only one of them worth anything is my old friend and commander, Aetius. It's ironic, don't you think, Orestes? Aetius spent several boyhood years as a political hostage in my father's camp; we were friends."

"Alliances change—it's the way of men and empires."

"True, but an alliance with Theodoric must involve some distress for Aetius. They've clashed often. Yet, if it means guarding Rome's interests....perhaps a price worthy of payment."

Orestes reached for his cup, his conviction firm. "We all must protect ourselves."

"At times, though, the task proves bitter," Attila replied. "Our advantage may spring from their mutual hate." Orestes smiled back.

Attila stared pensively at the map stretched before him. "Hate and friendship—an interesting combination, don't you think?"

"Indeed, my king and I hope one that weakens our enemy."

Attila returned to his chair, sat and raised his wooden cup. Orestes followed and held his golden goblet even higher.

"To friendships," Attila said, softly.

"Friendships," Orestes echoed. They both chuckled, drank, then laughed some more.

The Wespe arrived on the edge of Attila's camp. A breeze rustled the manes of their horses and swept past gnarled trees with early buds.

"Now take care," Luthgar said firmly. "We're merchants who met in Rome. We decided to join our ventures and travel this far north. Samuel, you'll act as the spokesman. A Jewish merchant traveling from Palaestina lends credibility to our group's size. Rudiger, you can claim to be a Chamavi trader who covers a great territory with his three assistants." Luthgar added, then pointed at Witigis, Denis, and Theudebert. "The hair bound on top of your heads, and the braids hanging on the sides of your faces is most convincing—good job." The men chuckled and made a few disparaging remarks aimed at the other. Luthgar raised his hand and they fell silent as horsemen rapidly approached them. "We've come to trade with Attila's great Hun soldiers and people. Is that clear?" The men nodded. With only time for a quick wink from Luthgar, the Hun guards were upon them.

Four Hun riders pulled beside them. "What business do you have here?" the leader spoke in Latin.

Samuel answered. "We are merchants come from Rome. We've heard of the greatness of Attila and the many opportunities that reside with your people for business and trade."

What goods do you bring?"

"A variety that will please both men and women. Would the young captain like a gift for his wife or lady of his affection?"

The Hun leader eyed Samuel warily. "Are you armed?"

"It might please your soldiers to know that we've come with a good quantity of Rome's finest spears, swords and axes." Samuel smiled with confidence.

The Hun captain turned to his left and motioned two soldiers forward. They jumped into the wagon and knocked baskets, stacks of wools, bolts of silk, and fur pelts aside to reach the long wooden boxes beneath. One drew his knife and cut the leather straps on one that held the lid secure and yanked it open. Spears lay piled in rows. Pleased, the Hun soldiers yelled to the captain and jumped from the wagon.

Samuel met the leader's gaze. The Hun inspected his scar from eyebrow to cheekbone. "Captain," Samuel offered, quickly, "allow me to share a small token with you, so you might appreciate the quality of our goods."

The captain reined in closer.

With an easy motion, Samuel lifted from his cloak a leather strip that dangled a silver and amber pendant. "Please accept this token as a sample of our wares. Speak of us to your men. We welcome the business."

"Why so many merchants?" The captain plucked the necklace from Samuel's hand, gave it a quick look and dropped it in his belt purse. "Who are the others with you?"

"My associates are Chamavi merchants. I am from Palaestina."

"A Jew?"

"And a merchant of some repute, especially in Rome. Have you not heard of Samuel Ben Zachariah? My two assistants are Franks. Three horses laden with goods and a wagon filled with weapons necessitates protection, especially in these times."

The Hun captain looked at the two brothers who drove the wagon. "What do you do, besides drive?" He asked the brother who held the reins.

"My brother and I hunt and cook for these merchants. They have very hearty appetites, but know only business."

The captain mused for a moment then drawled, "Very well. We will lead you to the marketplace in our camp. There you will find some open ground. In the morning, you may sell your wares. Avoid disputes, or you will be happy to leave with just your lives. Is this clear?"

"We are honest merchants, Captain," Samuel assured.

"See that this rings true." Turning his horse, the Hun captain signaled two of his men who rode to the rear. Advancing forward, the officer led the merchant train into the camp.

Samuel gently urged his horse to follow. At the same time, he looked at Luthgar who gave him a guarded grin. They were in.

KADAM'S TENT

"Attila has left!" Donatus ran yelling the news into the bowyer's tent.

Vodamir, bent over an arrow, looked at Garic who was laying bone overlays onto the bow grip before him. "What does this mean?" he whispered.

"It means trouble for the Romans and our people in his path. The Huns are on the move. They've been readying themselves for days.

You've seen it. Two days ago, Aveek came for his bow. I knew they would leave soon."

"Who's Aveek?"

"One of Attila's top chieftains. He's a fearsome warrior," Garic said, and continued working. "I stayed to the back of the tent when I saw him enter, but he presented himself before me. He had heard of two Frank warriors new to the camp. He ordered we train, while he is gone. On the next march out, we will join him. He said Kadam can find some young boys to teach and take our places. And that working in the bowyer's tent is the same as hiding behind a woman's skirt."

Vodamir's eyes narrowed. "What did you say?"

"What any man in our position must. But first, I stood up and looked down at him."

"And?"

Garic paused from his labor and chuckled. "I told him that we would be honored to fight beside him and for him, and I would fight with the best axe man in the land—my cousin, Vodamir."

"Thank you, Cousin. It seems you're determined to hurry me to my death alongside yours."

"Would you have me go alone?" Garic asked, and laid the last of the sinew in place and held it firm.

Vodamir grimaced. "Never! But must you rush us there?"

"I will not make Aveek an enemy. However, I can see he'll be no friend."

"Maybe he won't return."

Garic set the bow aside. "Maybe, but in the meantime, we will practice with bow and axe. Your hand must be strong again. The time is coming. We will have to fight...either for or against the Huns. Which do you prefer?"

"Against."

"Even though you love a Hun?" Garic rose and walked to a stack of arrow shafts waiting to be fletched. Carrying them back, he divided them and gave half to Vodamir, then seated himself and dragged a basket of hawk and falcon feathers between them. Reaching for a nearby glue pot, he passed it to Vodamir who grudgingly took it from Garic's hand.

"I am no man's slave,"Vodamir responded, indignantly. "Besides, I will bring Basina with us."

Garic felt his eyes widen with the news, but calmly said, "Is she aware of *your* plan?"

"Basina loves me. She'll come."

"Are you so sure? These are her people. She ranks high among them. Our escape will be dangerous and difficult." Garic's throat tightened, and he looked earnestly at Vodamir. "We cannot risk Basina knowing. It may jeopardize our escape. Do you understand? I cannot keep you from her bed, but you must not speak of our intentions."

Vodamir gazed at a cluster of ram horns suspended from the ceiling. A ripple of laughter echoed in his ears as Donatus, off stacking arrows, joked with another apprentice. "I promise you, Cousin, I won't say a word, but when the time comes to leave, I will go to Basina." Vodamir gazed directly at Garic. "I realize, I am asking her to leave all she knows and loves to be with me. If she says no, then our fates will be in her hands."

Garic cringed, inwardly. "Cousin, you're talking crazy. Have you ever left your life in a woman's hands? You must know how she will answer, even before you ask."

"There's a chance, she'll come. She loves me. I know this."

Frustrated by Vodamir's stubborn refusal to accept that Basina might threaten their plans, Garic switched his position. "Preparations for escape is when the army leaves the camp. We must go to the market for provisions, while the camp holds only a few soldiers. A few days ago, Kadam helped me purchase the pink gems I set in my bow. He introduced me to merchants who ask few questions."

"Do you trust Kadam? He's liable to sense something."

"He's too busy to keep a watchful eye on every craftsman and apprentice. He'll be busy replenishing arrows and bows for the next skirmish. Aveek boasted to Kadam that the shrewd Attila attacks only cities that promise substantial wealth. After Metis, if Attila succeeds, Ambiani, Tricasses, and Cambria stand naturally in his path. "

"Then let us go to market. Basina has given me some coin. I need a stronger knife and leather breeches."

"At first light tomorrow, pull yourself from Basina's arms and meet me at the edge of the wood. We will start with a hunt. Practice is over. It's time to see if I am a bowman or not. I am wagering, we will have pheasant to trade, maybe even a hare or two for the midday meal."

"I will take that wager—bow against axe."

"Accepted. Afterwards, we will shop the market and bury our supplies in the forest. We will not get far on foot. When the time comes, we will have to steal horses. If we're forced into battle under Aveek, then we will take our horses from dead men."

Vodamir nodded, then added, "Will you sleep alone tonight, First Counsel?"

"Why would you think otherwise?" Garic answered, perplexed.

"Ursula, I believe would be more than happy to keep you warm."

"Is pleasure all you think of? How do you know that Ursula favors me?"

"A beautiful blackbird with shiny wings."

"What does Basina know?"

"Only that Ursula would follow you, if you wanted her."

"I cannot ask for what I cannot return. My heart belongs to another."

"You're so wise, and yet, you cannot see that the woman you want has a different destiny as well. Maybe Ursula, who cares a lot and demands little, in the end would bring you happiness."

Garic grabbed and ruffled through the basket of feathers. "My thoughts rest with escape. Don't you want to go home, Vodamir? While I breath, I hope to see Arria again. I don't want to die on the battlefield, a slave of the Huns and a victim of the Romans."

"Our homes and people seem so far away." Vodamir looked

wistfully down at his hand. It had healed miraculously along with his jaw and ribs. His face was once again familiar and he owed it all to Basina's healing touch.

"Think with your head Vodamir. We must leave."

"Yes," Vodamir replied, "we must leave."

Out of nowhere, Kadam appeared before Garic and Vodamir. Startled, both warriors looked guardedly at one another.

"The camp will be moving very soon," Kadam informed them. "A messenger arrived this morning. Metis is under siege and Attila smells victory. We're to prepare. In a few days, we will join our king." Turning on his heel, Kadam moved through the tent with the news.

"Do you think he heard us?" Vodamir absently stroked the fine beard which had grown around his chin since his arrival in Attila's camp.

"He might have, but something tells me that he's sympathetic to our plight. Nevertheless, we need to get ready. We will have to make our move soon. Pray Wodan, we will be successful."

"Wodan and Thor and anyone who'll help us!" Vodamir grinned and stuffed a handful of ready arrows into the quiver at his feet.

Garic smiled, cocked his head and checked the feathers on his arrow for assembled precision. "We can do this, Cousin. We know the land. The spirits of the forest will protect, and our people call us. We cannot disappoint them. We must go home."

"*Ja*," Vodamir sighed. Looking pensively at Garic and then at his hand, he slowly clenched it in a fist. "Home."

THE WESPE

Twinkling lights burned throughout the camp, torches everywhere. Samuel tossed a stone into the embers and watched the sparks dance upward, disappearing into smoke, rising in lazy ribbons of flight. "In the morning, I will shop the market and inquire discreetly as to Arria's whereabouts."

"Be cautious," Luthgar offered. "Amo and I will scout the camp to

236

see if Garic and Vodamir can be found. We will leave Rudiger and the men to sell the goods and weapons. Rudiger will know how to ask his customers for the answers we seek," Luthgar paused and his eyes filled with merriment, "while he takes their money."

The men looked at Rudiger who dozed contentedly. "Isn't that so, Rudiger?" Luthger laughed as he kicked at Rudiger's boot. Rudiger snorted, "What!" His bewildered look and his ready response caused the men to laugh even harder.

"Father, our chief is speaking confidently of your abilities and you sleep!" Amo smiled fondly, although his words were stern.

"I wasn't sleeping, *pup*, only resting my eyes." Rudiger grumbled.

"I think it's time we all rest." Luthgar snapped a few twigs lying by his feet and tossed them into the flames. "Our time here will be fraught with danger. We must take care and be ready for anything."

The men nodded their agreement and stretched out beside the fire. Each had a weapon by his side. When sun rays sprinted across the ground, painting morning shadows on the wagon's wheels, Samuel awakened the men.

Approaching Luthgar, Samuel crouched beside him. "I will leave now. I won't be long. I will look for bread and cheese."

"Look for some wine or better yet a good mead. I am in need of a strong drink to relax me. I've never taken residence in an enemy camp before."

"I've always lived among the enemy, Lord Luthgar, that is until now. If we make it back...if I make it back, my lord...will you allow me to stay with your people? I see your Franks as my own.

"Our tribe is your tribe, man. There is no question."

Samuel stood as Luthgar rose from his blankets. "Go now...and Samuel?"

"Yes, my lord?"

"Bring back good news."

Samuel gazed toward the sun, then turned to Luthgar, "May your gods guide your search as well."

"That's what the gods do best...they guide," Luthgar replied

"There is only one who guides me," Samuel smiled and pulled his hood over his head, "May mine and yours be with us in the days to come," and walked toward the smell of fresh baked bread.

Chapter Nineteen

Nil Sine Numine
Nothing Without Providence

ATTILA'S ARMY

Attila raised his blood stained glove and the rear column of soldiers and horse archers halted. The scent of burning wood filled the air and smoke billowed from the devastation behind them. Among the ranks, the lament of a captive woman could be heard. Metis had fallen.

Attila spat, recalling his generous offer. The city's arrogant defiance sealed their destruction. He left nothing standing—not a man, animal, or home. Only the riches and belongings of the townspeople escaped the fire, plundered and piled into carts or thrown over saddles. The soldiers, drunk on victory, carried wealth and drank the best mead and wine Metis had to offer. A profitable and glorious day. Gaul loomed ahead, large with wealth and purpose. Nothing could stop Attila's horde.

"Bring my camp to me, Onegesius," Attila commanded his chamberlain mounted beside him. "My Huns smell the blood of wealth. There's no stopping them! With our allies, we're over one hundred thousand strong. Neither Ambiani or Cambria, nor the rest will stand against our strength. We will march through Gaul toward the kingdom of Toulouse. Let Aetius come. No army can compare to mine."

"No one, not even Aetius is as strong as you, my king." Onegesius bowed his head.

Attila glanced at the noonday sun. "You're a wise and loyal vizier. Go to my son. Tell Ellak that the more tribes we absorb, the more discipline must be maintained—at any cost. Have the new tribes quarter their livestock and preserved foods within the storage holds of the camp. Able warriors, remaining in the camp, must bring to the front any siege engines left behind. Ensure the infirmary holds no one but the very ill."

"And if Basina will not let her patients leave, my king?"

Attila drank from his water pouch and wiped his mouth with a back hand. "I command any warrior fit to carry a sword or bow join me. Advance the camp forward to support the army. Protect the rear with a contingent of fighting men. Newly acquired warriors or those freshly healed will comprise this unit. Is that understood?"

"Yes, my king. Who shall lead this task?"

"Send Aveek. Basina can be unruly when her mind is set on something. He knows Basina well. He has a way with her."

"As he does with most women." Onegesius joked.

"That news has reached my ears as well." Attila led his horse to shade.

"It seems his new interest is a slave called Marcella, belonging to the Lady Arria. She's the perfect servant, so I hear."

"How perfect?" A wry smile escaped Attila. Even in his most serious moments he could manage some levity.

"So perfect that Aveek can be heard moaning and snorting like a bull throughout the night."

Both men laughed and Attila added, "How intriguing. I would meet the woman, but now is not the time for diversion. I want all the Romans gone except for the Lady Arria. Has she any close attendants?"

"A woman and her son."

"They may stay. It's only fitting, she have her attendant, but the rest must go. Roman soldiers, the slaves and that includes this remarkable...what is her name?"

"Marcella, the Egyptian."

"Interesting. An Egyptian with a Roman name. Tell Aveek that she must leave—now." Attila ran his hand over the steed's soft muzzle. "He'll find her again among the spoils of a ruined Cambria. If my calculations are correct, within days he'll have her on her back and spread across his furs."

"I will inform Aveek immediately on *all* matters."

"He must hurry; I need his expertise in battle. Durocorturum has most likely heard of our victory over Metis. Our success depends on our ability to move quickly, enforcing one strike after another. "

Onegesius bowed. "As you wish, my king."

Attila mounted his horse. His soul burned with determination. "The gods have blessed my hands with the Sword of Mars, Onegesius. By the prophecy and its power, the Shamans have foretold my victory."

Onegesius leaped into his saddle and turned toward the rear of the column. His voice rose above the wind, "The Roman priests and people call Attila, *The Scourge of God.* Metis and the cities trampled in your path know this truth—I know this truth. Very soon, the mighty Attila will rule the world!"

Attila answered the accolade with a raised hand met by his chamberlain's firm grip. Hands clenched together, they reinforced their purpose. Then Onegesius prodded his horse and rode in search of Aveek.

ATTILA'S CAMP

"Aveek has just come! He's searching for you and Vodamir." Kadam frowned as he gazed at Garic. "I sent him to Basina. I told him that you both were at the infirmary or hunting."

Garic stood in the doorway of the bowyer's tent, Vodamir beside him. Two fat hares hung from the cord in Garic's hand, while several birds dangled from Vodamir's belt. "Did he say for what reason? Is the battle for Metis won?"

"Attila's forces were victorious and the plunder beyond their expectations. They're on the move and the camp must join them.

241

Aveek needs you both to protect the rear with other healed soldiers from the infirmary."

Garic glanced at Vodamir whose gaze returned a warning. "We will go to Aveek, but not before I show you my prize." Garic raised the hares before Kadam.

"Such beauties and fat too!" Kadam's eyes gleamed. "You've learned well, apprentice. I hope you valued your time here."

"Master, how can I repay you? I can craft and shoot a bow and will go into battle a stronger warrior. Your instruction has awakened in me an unexpected passion."

Kadam nodded. "Your skill will bring your people honor."

Vodamir rested his hand on Garic's shoulder. "We must go. I wish to find Basina before Aveek finds us."

Kadam lifted the curtain that covered the doorway. "Until we meet again. May the spirits of battle carry you safely."

"And may the gods, wily master, bring you much fortune!"Eager to find Basina, Vodamir nudged Garic. Garic eased them from Kadam's presence with a wave of his hand.

"Will we ever see Kadam again?" Vodamir asked Garic as they took the path to the infirmary. "I hope so, he's a friend. However, if we see battle and don't return, in the after life, he'll be but a distant memory."

Vodamir huffed, "A not too pleasant thought."

"*Ja*," Garic responded.

"For now, if we're to protect the rear of the camp, we will not see battle. I believe, Basina will secure our position in the rear guard, at least for a while."

"It will cer..." Garic froze. Through the dull, gray morning, the figure of a man came toward them. His curly black hair tossed in the breeze, and in his arms he carried round loaves of bread.

"It cannot be," Vodamir gasped softly.

"By the stars...Samuel!" Garic shouted and in several strides he had his arms wrapped around Arria's slave, knocking the bread to the ground.

242

Right behind Garic, Vodamir jumped in and greeted Samuel with a vigorous slap on the back then gripped his shoulders. "How is it you're here?" he demanded.

Joy filled Samuel's face, but still wary, he motioned them behind a nearby tent not far from the river's edge.

"How is it you're here?" Garic blurted out as they rounded the tent wall facing the water.

"I am not alone. I've come with Luthgar and others—Wespe. We've come to help you escape! We're posing as merchants."

"You're a true friend, Samuel. Your bravery, my kinsmen's bravery..." Garic's voice trailed off.

Vodamir interjected. "Thank the mighty Thor, you found your way to Luthgar's camp, but how is it you came with the Wespe?"

A huge smile livened Samuel's face. Without a word, he tugged at his cloak, opened his vest and lifted his shirt. A wasp tattoo, deep blue, decorated his chest.

"A Wespe! Loki's madness. Eight months ago, you couldn't handle a sword!" Vodamir slapped Samuel on the back.

Garic laughed and shoved playfully at Samuel. A hawk screeched overhead, bringing them to a sudden seriousness.

"We must go." Garic reminded. "We're to meet with the Hun chief, Aveek."

"Where can we find you?" Samuel grinned in reply. "Our wagon sits on the perimeter of the market circle. When will you come?"

"Tell Luthgar, Attila has ordered the camp to mobilize and join him. We will find you later, eager warriors looking to buy weapons and supplies."

"A perfect pretext. We have what you need," Samuel reassured.

Garic motioned to the birds hanging from Vodamir's belt. Vodamir unfastened and offered the game to Samuel. "Choice birds for your dinner tonight. Hopefully, we will share them."

An unexpected movement between the tents brought their conversation to a halt. A lithe hooded figure, looking away from the men, moved towards the water's bank. Walking quickly past the trio, but sensing their presence, the figure turned to reveal a mass of golden curls adorning Ursula's pretty face.

"There you are!" Ursula admonished. "Please come! Aveek awaits you both at the infirmary. He will send soldiers, if you do not appear within the hour." Ursula caught her breath and eyed Samuel suspiciously, "Who's your friend?"

"A merchant who trades in *special* items. He has a weapon that I desire."

Samuel bowed. "My lady."

Ursula, give us a moment and we will join you," Garic said, and addressed Samuel with formality, "Merchant, the prize axe you boast of had better be all that you claim, or we will go elsewhere. In battle, a man needs to know that his weapon is ready, otherwise he will fall."

"I agree my lord. A reliable weapon promises a warrior's success." Samuel placed his hand upon his chest.

Garic's neck prickled. Covering the wasp tattoo signaled a message.

"My lord, a thought before you leave." Samuel's voice, soft and direct, continued, "A priceless weapon is like a flower that blooms in a foreign land. Although one might not possess this treasure, it does exist. The sharp edge of this axe cleaves the air with the same speed that a flower's fragrance fills a mist. The weapon you seek, my lord, is here. It's called *The Rose*."

Garic's mind raced. What was Samuel implying? Who or what was the weapon? Surely the rose could only mean Arria. Calming himself, he returned, "I am very interested. If ever there were a merchant with the *heart* for selling, I suspect it's you. I will come to your wagon later. I expect a fair price, or you will have no sale."

"My lord, my prices reflect my generous nature. I await your arrival."

"Until then." Garic motioned to Vodamir who remained quiet. They walked away with Ursula who kept looking back at Samuel.

"He's an odd sort," was all she said and followed dutifully behind them.

"It's no matter—his manner, if he has what we need." Vodamir replied, with a defensive edge.

Ursula stopped, which commanded the men to stop.

Garic faced her. "What concerns you?"

"Aveek will order you into his service. I am worried. Sad that you must leave."

Garic reached for her hand. "We can never repay you, the sisters, and Basina for the care you've given us. We are in your debt."

"Will you fight for Attila?"

Garic and Vodamir glanced at each other.

"We will do what we must to survive." Garic cradled Ursula's small hand in his and gently squeezed. "Do you understand what this means?"

Ursula nodded and raised her hood higher. The sun's last rays broke through the clouds as she turned toward the infirmary. Vodamir held Garic back.

"What did Samuel mean?" Vodamir whispered.

"I can hardly contain myself, Cousin. I believe Arria is in the camp!"

"Impossible."

"But his message—the rose, the weapon. Arria and I? Come. Let us face Aveek and discover his intent. Remember, no matter what, we will comply. He must trust us. We need the freedom to find Luthgar. Understand? Now is not the time for outbursts—right or wrong."

"I want Basina; she owns my heart. I will not jeopardize our happiness."

"If your love is true, then take care...and Vodamir, ensure Basina's love is real. Our success depends on your conviction."

"She'll not betray me, despite your doubts. I trust her."

Garic clutched Vodamir's shoulder. "Then I trust you! Come, Aveek awaits us."

"Tell me, Basina, what do you know!" Aveek's iron fist clenched Basina's long, black hair.

Basina punched at his face.

Aveek caught Basina's fist and forced her to her knees. Crouching beside her, he tightened his grip and whispered, "A rumor thrives that the Hun healer has debased herself by sleeping with a slave. You could have had any chief you desired. You could have had me!" he growled. "Our alliance rising us higher—making us stronger. Are you loyal to our king?"

Basina met his gaze and forced through her fury, "My loyalty cannot be questioned. Attila has known me since I was a child in his son's house!"

"Then beware. There's talk that your healing powers will diminish now that you've spoiled yourself with the Frank's seed."

"Don't threaten me with your lies, Aveek," Basina spat. "My powers are as strong as ever. It's no secret in the camp that you've ignored your wives for a foreigner. Your wives came to me, seeking a potion that would diminish the Egyptian's power and enhance theirs. You have no right to judge me."

Aveek shoved Basina onto her chamber floor. She leaped to her feet and moved away. "My wives should tend our children and know their places," he snarled and stood. "I am the strongest warrior in the camp. I do as I please."

"I am Attila's chosen healer and I will also do as I please," Basina returned, raising her chin. "Never touch me again. Is that clear?"

Aveek's grin only partially hid his malice. "Basina, your threat is wasted on me. We're not that different. We share a loyalty to Attila. Who knows, the Franks might prove themselves worthy subjects. Anyway, the first battle will tell if, of course, they survive."

"Take care that nothing befalls Vodamir by Hun hands or your fate will turn for the worse."

Aveek winced. "If I discover any intrigue on the part of your Franks or that you've lied—healer or not—shaman or not—you will suffer a fate worse than anything you could inflict on me. You will suffer Attila's wrath and I will be his executioner. Soon we will need every man. The scouts report that Aetius is coming from the south.

We will meet him in battle. Our destiny rests on our strength and victory."

"Every man you shall have. The Franks can be trusted. You have my word."

Basina glared at Aveek and rubbed her aching fingers, a painful reminder of his iron grip. "Ursula has gone to find them. When they arrive, you will see that they are willing subjects."

The curtain shielding Basina's doorway parted held by Aveek's guard. Ursula addressed Basina quietly, demonstrating where her loyalty and respect resided, "They have come. Will you see them now?"

"Yes. Send them in." Basina's face told Ursula not to hesitate and she swiftly summoned Garic and Vodamir.

"Ah! Finally, the two slaves who act as free men in a Hun camp." Aveek's eyes narrowed with his scrutiny. "Your long hair distinguishes you from many of Attila's loyal subjects. Yet, you've both managed to avoid battle."

Garic stepped forward. "Chieftain Aveek, we are under your command as long as we live among the Hun people."

"You are the one called Garic?"

"I am. This is my cousin, Vodamir." Vodamir moved beside Garic.

Seeming discomfited by Garic and Vodamir's towering height, Aveek seated himself with the posture of a king. His chin held high, he continued, "In time, you will consider us your people and help lead us to victory over those who stand in our way. Even your King Meroveus' brother has seen our destiny and has joined the great Attila. While under my command, think of yourselves not as slaves, but rather as warriors who can win riches and honor. The wealth that awaits us is indescribable."

"My lord, may I speak?" Garic addressed. Aveek nodded his agreement. "Much wealth exists in the cities of Gaul. However, many believe it belongs to those who dwell within their walls."

"I see the time in the infirmary has softened you. When has any barbarian or Frank ever forsaken an opportunity to plunder and steal? Have you not retrieved the swords and axes of the men you've slain on the battlefield, or a pair of boots, a fur? Gold ornaments from a town or tribe you've pillaged?"

Garic chose his words, "I have done all those things, and now we will do it for you. My hope is that you will be generous."

"Generosity is one of my better qualities, especially toward warriors who please me." Aveek placed his fingers on the golden ring he wore and slowly turned the ruby encrusted band. Even on his calloused fingers, its fiery brilliance was hard to ignore. The assembly of jewels set in the triangle pendant hanging from his neck confirmed his station as chief and successful soldier. "Fight hard and follow my orders and you will fare well under my command. Huns live by laws learned from childhood. If we break them there is little tolerance. The first law is loyalty to your leader, no matter what he asks. You will act as part of the rear guard along with all the capable soldiers from the infirmary."

Basina stirred in her seat. Aveek glanced in her direction, but placed his hands on his knees and regarded Garic. "Long-Hair, it has also come to my attention that you've become quite the bowman. This is good. It will strengthen your position among my men. We are the finest horse-archers in the world. Shooting an arrow standing is a small feat compared to shooting an arrow from a moving horse. I encourage you both to train and make ready. The Romans are moving north to meet us. When we engage, the reckoning for the Empire will take place, and Attila is destined to win."

"Roman strength doesn't concern you?" Garic ventured.

"Attila's one hundred thousand soldiers far surpass the strength of the Romans. We sleep on our horses and move easily from place to place as our ancestors did before us. We are ready to conquer, and we *will* be victorious. Bring your hearts to the battlefield, Long-Hairs, to fight for the true ruler of the Roman Empire, Attila, and your *rewards* will be great."

Garic caught the implication as Basina blushed. He was sure

Vodamir had as well. Garic also sensed the chieftain's lingering distrust. "Noble Aveek, we will honor Attila with our service as long as we stand on his ground. To whom do we report and when?"

"Report to Uptar in the morning. He was a prisoner of Rome and despises them. He fights hard." Taking the riding gloves from his belt, Aveek slid them on his hands and rose from his chair. "Remember, Long-Hairs. Everyone's safety is dependent on your loyalty." Glancing quickly toward Basina, he walked out from her quarters, leaving them alone.

Garic and Vodamir silently approached the merchant campsite. Samuel, Luthgar, and the Wespe soldiers sat gathered around their fire. Orange flames crackled and sparked thin traces of smoke, rising into the night. Garic heard Theudebert joke that if he died tomorrow, he'd enter Valhalla laden with enough coin to buy the choicest spot at the warriors banquet table.

Their laughter followed and filled the air. Garic snapped a twig. Alerted, Amo rose and peered into the surrounding pines. Each Wespe put his hand to his weapon. From the trees, Garic and Vodamir emerged grinning. Garic exchanged an urgent glance with Samuel, but news of Arria must wait.

The Wespe soldiers stood, feigning a protective stance, while Luthgar welcomed their first counsel and his cousin. Greetings exchanged, Garic announced, "We brought some meat for your evening meal. In the hope your weapons will bear a reasonable price!" The men laughed and reclaimed their seats on several javelin crates positioned around the fire. Garic pulled a few partridge and a quail from his leather bag, while Vodamir held up a gangly hare. Muric and Bede accepted the offerings and began preparing a hearty meal.

Garic sat beside Luthgar who claimed a fallen tree trunk further from the fire. "My chief, you honor me with this rescue attempt."

"You're the brother, I never had and my best friend," Luthgar replied, his tone warm. "The Huns will not swallow you in their ranks!" He stroked his beard, then chuckled, "Besides, I need all my warriors. I've given my word to Theodoric and Aetius to fight by their side. The jealous snake, Drusus, ordered your death; but fortunately, Severus had his own plan. Greed often wins over hate."

"Severus is *still* a bastard!" Garic snapped, remembering the tribune's cruel beating.

Samuel, carrying two cups, approached Garic and Luthgar, drawing their attention. He sat beside Garic and served them a honey mead. Garic slaked his thirst, then observed Samuel's demeanor. Arria's slave was different. "You've changed Samuel. You speak our language well, and an iron resolve fills you. You've been our salvation."

Even in the light from the fire, Garic saw a flush rise in Samuel's face. "My conscience gives me strength, and I will fight for my friends. You and Vodamir helped me find my freedom, hope and purpose."

"To live and fight as a Wespe is a sacred honor among our people. You are a Frank now and will always be free." Garic placed his hand on Samuel's shoulder and a heartfelt look passed between them.

Luthgar coughed and slapped Garic on the back. "All this admiration is making me cry!"

Garic playfully shoved Luthgar from the log, then immediately offered him his hand. Luthgar hopped to his feet. "Careful Counsel, once back on our own ground, a wrestling match awaits you; there is no doubt, I will be victorious."

"My lord, I serve *you* always, but when this challenge happens, you will serve *me* with your cries of surrender."

"You've always been too clever for your own good. Beware, Counsel!" Luthgar taunted and brushed himself off.

Garic's laughter faded, he could wait no longer. "My chief, Samuel's message, the rose and the sword can only mean Arria. Have you seen her?"

"No. We arrived in camp only yesterday, but I believe she's here." Luthgar scowled. "Almost seven days ago, Attila's advisor, Orestes, came to Cambria at Rome's request to negotiate terms for a temporary truce. Having the advantage, Attila requested that Drusus secure their agreement with a political hostage. I was present when Orestes requested the Roman envoy, Arria, be sent. She accepted. Oddly, Arria demanded that the witch, Marcella, accompany her. The reasons for this action are unclear. I know well that Arria despises the Egyptian."

"What do you imagine?" Garic asked, feeling his brow crease.

"She most likely thought it a poor idea to leave the slave alone with Drusus. Arria's absence would allow Marcella to conspire against her even more. There's something else. I hesitate...to say."

Panic gripped Garic. "Tell me."

Luthgar's somber voice hesitated, "Arria...is married. Her message, 'I am wed to Drusus,' arrived one day before she left for the Hun camp."

Garic's fingers slowly curled to fists. He stared at Luthgar, then Samuel in disbelief. Despair waved through him and dragged his heart to an empty sea.

"Noble Garic, are you well?" Samuel asked.

Garic stood. "Drusus does not love her. He covets only her wealth and the prestige her position affords him. Arria vowed to free herself from their betrothal. Why would she consent?"

Luthgar shook his head confused. "On the night that Drusus met with the Huns, Arria and I spoke. When you and Vodamir did not return, Drusus proved your deaths to her with a belt woven from your stolen locks of hair. I shared my conviction that you and Vodamir lived, captured by the Huns. Upon hearing this, Arria shed her sorrow and promised to free herself from Drusus."

"I know my lady's heart; it rests in your hands." Samuel added softly, looking at Garic. "She cared not for Drusus. I believe, my lady had no choice."

From the fire, an unaware Bede called the men to dinner.

"Come!" Luthgar interjected, assertively. "Food and drink will do us good. We will find your lady, First Counsel. Then, you will know the truth."

A quiet hiss from the men around the fire alerted them to the approaching soldiers. Denis, Witigis and Rudiger ate, while Amo casually stoked the fire. Bede offered Luthgar a chunk of quail skewered with a twig.

Luthgar took the meat and walked nonchalantly toward the warriors who entered the camp. "How can we help you?" Luthgar asked and wolfed down the steamy morsel. "We're done selling our wares for today, but we might be able to accommodate you with a robust wine from the vineyards of Toulosa."

A grizzly looking Goth with his hair braided to one side, striped leggings and a heavy wool tunic stepped in front of the five men with him. "We seek the warriors called Long-Hairs. We were informed they came here to purchase weapons."

Vodamir stepped up. "My cousin and I are who you seek."

"We are to escort you to the banquet tent. New soldiers from various tribes have arrived, and order needs to be maintained. Uptar, your commander, desires your attendance—now." The Goth paused, then growled, "How can you buy goods if they aren't selling their wares this night and only offer wine?"

"We have already purchased what we need," answered Vodamir. "My cousin and I thought to taste their wine and throw some dice. Why not join us?"

The Goth looked to the rest. Garic suddenly stood. "I will be the first to toast our King Attila. Will you join me?"

Most of the men look interested but watched the reaction of their Goth spokesman. "If you're paying, Long-Hair, we will all join you for one."

"I will pay, if you drink." Garic ensured.

"Then get your wine and pour the cups, but we have time for only one. It's not wise to disregard Uptar's orders."

"We have more than enough time. Surely, Uptar won't begrudge his men a cup of wine."

Vodamir lightly rested his hand on Garic's arm. "Cous–"

"Who's in charge of the wine among you merchants," Garic said roughly, moving away from Vodamir.

Luthgar grimaced, but spoke up, "I have a wine that will warm your bones."

"Hurry then merchant." Garic chided, "The banquet grows anxious for our presence and my thirst is strong."

Forced to comply, Luthgar signaled Amo who jumped into the wagon and grabbed a large leather strapped *butticula,* wine bag, and some cups. The cooks brought additional cups resting by the fire.

"Pour!" Garic commanded.

Luthgar poured each man a drink and when he finished Garic raised his wine and claimed Attila as the greatest king that ever lived. The soldiers led by the Goth drank in unison. Before their cups were emptied Garic extended his cup toward Luthgar. Unable to say anything, Luthgar slowly poured him another. The warriors, anticipating a long dutiful night, gladly seized a second opportunity to warm themselves with drink.

"Long-Hair your thirst is strong, but tomorrow the camp will join Attila in the field for his next conquest. I assure you, wine will flow with his victory and you will drink, provided you live." Uptar's soldiers laughed and started toward the far side of the camp and in the direction of the banquet tent.

Vodamir nodded toward Samuel. Garic snatched the half-filled bag from Luthgar's hand. He slung the strap over his shoulder and stomped off, trailing the Hun faction. Samuel followed. He would report back to the Wespe.

Luthgar shouted, "Take care Long-Hairs. The devils of the night hunt for the mighty."

Garic only offered a bitter laugh.

Chapter Twenty

Amor vincit omnia
Love conquers all

ATTILA'S CAMP

vercome by the late hour and noisy guests, Arria suppressed a yawn. Music, wine, and merriment swirled through the senses of the men and women in attendance. But not for Arria. Fatigue coursed through her limbs, leaving her sleepy and a bit lightheaded.

Earlier in the morning, Aveek had brought news—all Romans must return to Cambria, except for Arria and her attendants, Karas and Angelus. In the mid-afternoon and without her mistress's leave, an arrogant Marcella rode by Arria's wagon, escorted by the few attending soldiers and Aveek by her side. A defiant gesture aimed at Arria.

Aveek had informed Arria that her attendance at the evening's festivities was required. The banquet Arria glanced at Garic. In that moment, they kissed good-bye.

would honor the chiefs from the new tribes assimilated by Attila's invasion westward. Arria thought Attila as clever as claimed. Who better than the Roman envoy to return to Cambria with tales of allegiance and the swelling numbers of warriors added daily to Attila's ranks.

Wine flowed freely and the smell of roasted meats: fowl, venison and boar filled the room. Tonight, Arria supped with the fiercest warlords in the world. More than a few eyed her with bold mischief or muted contempt. She strove valiantly to carry herself with the grace and dignity befitting a Roman senator's daughter and envoy.

"Would my lady care for some wine?"

"Yes, please." Arria raised her golden goblet to Uptar's waiting hand. Steadily, he poured the Pannonian wine almost to the brim. Arria took a long sip. Uptar's conversation faded as the smooth liquid warmed her and a slight tingle pricked her ears. This place— this moment, seemed familiar. Perhaps, in a dream.

"My lady?"

"I'm sorry, Uptar. You were saying?"

"I merely inquired about your appetite. Your food goes untouched. The venison is quite good but possibly too rustic for your palate. I can call for roasted pigeon, or if my lady relishes oysters, the way I hear most Romans do, I will order them. Our proximity to the sea makes for their abundance and quality."

"Your concern for my comfort is quite gracious. I am fine, just a bit weary. Tell me, will the camp leave at dawn to join your king? Do you know of Attila's plan for me, or if my husband, the Legate Drusus, has sent me any missives?"

"After tonight, I doubt few will be roused at dawn, but by mid morning all who are coming will be ready. I hope my lady finds this hour to her liking. As to my king's plan for you, I am not aware of it other than to escort you to his army. To my knowledge, no missive has arrived from the Legate for you, but if one does, I will deliver it right away. I hear that my lady is a new bride."

"Yes, several weeks."

"Drusus is fortunate to have such a beautiful and distinguished wife. Your separation, unfortunate."

"Quite," Arria responded impassively and gazed into the crowd amused by the variety of dress and manner of the many guests. To her right and toward the entrance, a commotion caught her attention. A cluster of men pushed through the opening; a man's wheat colored hair shone above the rest. Uptar spoke of the Hun campaign in Constantinople, but her gaze darted past him back to the entrance.

Uptar noticed Arria's distraction and turned toward the disturbance. He rose and Arria followed. They watched as the crowd backed up, leaving an open circle where the two warriors stood locked together in a vicious hold. Unable to see clearly, Arria directed Uptar, "I will move closer." The Hun officer obeyed and made way for them to the front of the crowd.

The tall, blond fighter dressed like a Hun with his back to her, held a grisly looking man in a head lock. The crowd cheered as the red-faced warrior gritted his teeth and twisted in Arria's direction, wrenching the blond man's arm with all his might. Arria recognized Theobald, the Visigoth, with an instant dismay. The blond warrior quickly countered and circled to maintain his hold. Arria gasped. Long, blond strands dangled over Garic's face, but they couldn't hide his handsome features. A tremor surged through her body and she grabbed Uptar's arm.

"Do not fear, Lady Arria, no harm will come to you," Uptar said, raising his voice above the din, a keen expression on his face.

"Stop them please, they'll be hurt!"

"They are young lions and it amuses everyone to watch. It's a manly diversion difficult for a lady to understand."

Arria bristled and swung her gaze back toward the fight. The red-faced Theobald, shot several quick elbow punches into Garic's side. Arria cringed and looked away, her glance resting on the mass of cheering men.

From the onlookers, the faces of Vodamir and Samuel emerged. They stepped to the front of the crowd. Arria gasped. She felt the urge to wave her arms and signal them, but Uptar's presence reminded her of the need for secrecy.

A sudden roar and a hoarse bellow caught Arria by surprise. Garic and Theobald barreled through the crowd in her direction. Uptar jumped sideways, reaching to pull Arria with him, but failed. Garic's charging body knocked her to the ground.

Only an hour before, Garic and Vodamir had gone, as ordered, to relieve the night sentries at Attila's banquet tent. Swallowing the last drops from his wine pouch, Garic had tossed it into the night and let the news of Arria's marriage dig deeper into his heart.

As Garic approached the entrance, he passed, to his surprise, a drunken Theobald. The Visigoth in the Hun camp meant he was double-dealing with the Huns. The Visigoth warrior sneered at Garic, but he ignored him, took his post, and checked three new guests for concealed weapons. Theobald, next in line, wobbled forward and stood before Garic, a smirk on his face. "Look at Noble Garic, once Chief Luthgar's first counsel, and now Attila's doorman!" he taunted. A chuckle ran through the ribbon of men behind him.

Garic lunged for Theobald, but Vodamir yanked him back.

Theobald mocked, "The counsel who needs his cousin to guard him and tell him when to fight! Ha!"

Garic broke free and punched Theobald, knocking him to the ground. Theobald sprang to his feet and drew a knife hidden in his boot.

Barbarians and Huns, milling around the entrance, crowded to watch. Garic drew his knife and tossed it to Vodamir. He shouted for all to hear, "Attila's doorman will fight you hand to hand and let you live. I once gave you my prized horse to protect a noble woman's honor. Now, I give you your life to protect my honor."

Theobald's face reddened and he charged. Garic side stepped and grabbed Theobald's wrist with both his hands. He twisted Theobald's arm behind his back and slammed the Visigoth's fist against his rising knee, knocking the knife from Theobald's grasp. His arm quickly locked around the Visigoth's neck. Theobald gritted his teeth and struggled to break free, propelling them through the entrance and into the banquet hall. Garic stumbled, but circled, regaining his hold. Theobald twisted and elbowed Garic's ribs; he pushed his weight against Garic's torso with a bellow and forced them through the crowd of jeering spectators.

From the corner of his eye, Garic saw a wave of chestnut hair and felt a figure fall with him ....

Garic's body slammed the ground. The earth pressed hard against his back as he lay there and caught his breath. Theobald moaned beside him. Garic struggled to his knees. Was he dreaming? A swift kick to his ribs and a blow to his head sucked the air from him.

"You *will* let me pass! I am the Roman envoy to Attila, " Arria ordered the guard, standing before the one room wooden structure and makeshift prison. She raised her lamp closer to her face. The light burned strong despite the breeze. "Or must I summon Uptar to speak for me?" Arria held his gaze.

The Goth guard shifted uncomfortably for a second and looked around. Clearing his voice, he said weakly, "My lady, I have orders to keep both men contained."

"I didn't ask you to free them. I just want to tend to the long-hair's wounds, physical and spiritual. It's my Christian duty to care for those in need. If you know your king, then surely you realize that Attila wouldn't deny me the practices of my faith?" With a calculated firmness, she added, "Uptar will not relish this insult." Her chin raised, Arria stood her ground.

Uncertainty played in the guard's eyes. "All right! but you mustn't linger," he blustered, "We will release the long-hair tomorrow. He's assigned to the rear guard. Your good friend, *Uptar*, needs every soldier fit for duty." He scowled as he lifted the timber latch on the door of the prison, built for drunks, fighting men, and those accused of larceny or murder.

Holding her lamp high, Arria stepped into the dark. The flickering light painted Garic's huddled body in a soft rosy hue. She swung the door closed and knelt beside him. Arria placed the lamp on the cold ground and turned Garic on to his back.

She lovingly brushed the hair from his face. "*Krieger*," she whispered. She shook him gently, "Krieger. It's Arria." Her hand still ached from the fall she suffered at the banquet, but her desire to caress Garic's warm lips and cleft chin beneath blond stubble burned stronger. Joyful over finding him alive, Arria pressed her lips against his. Her breath caught in her heart, and she kissed him. "Krieger, wake," she murmured.

Garic's eyes blinked and he focused on her face. He smiled weakly. "Melli ... tula," he murmured and tried to raise his head.

Arria's delicate strength stopped him. "Rest."

Garic's smile grew stronger. He engulfed her in his arms and kissed her with a suppressed hunger that reflected her own.

"By the gods, you're here," he said, huskily. His hands held her face and he kissed her again with a boyish eagerness.

Arria gazed into blue eyes deepened by the shallow light and read a happiness to mirror her own. "For days, I thought you would return, but Drusus insisted you were dead. I couldn't accept you being gone...forever. He showed me locks of your hair and Vodamir's. I felt numb and empty." Arria drifted her fingers over his hand. "Now, I am alive again."

Garic caressed the fallen tresses resting on her cape, and then her cheek. He kissed her again, and brushed away her grateful tears with his lips. "*Mellitula*, I will never leave you," he said with conviction. "We will escape. I promise you!"

With a loud rap on the door, the guard growled, "Finish your prayers now! It's time you leave!"

"Let me help you to your feet." Arria whispered. "It will help to stand. I must go. Vodamir waits along with Samuel. It's best that I'm not seen in Vodamir's company. When Uptar pulled me from your side, he ordered a soldier to carry me to a couch. Samuel volunteered to bring me water and the soldier agreed. We were able to speak. You must make it to the rear guard in the morning. I will be in the large green coach. I will instruct my driver that I am fatigued from my fall and to go slowly. This will allow us to lag to the rear. Tomorrow, as soon as I wake, I will request from Uptar several bodyguards to protect me. For my safety and by virtue of the Roman and Frank association, I will insist they be you and Vodamir, the two long-hairs I've been told serve in the rear guard."

"Come on, lady! It grows late." The guard called through the door.

"One more minute, please, we're almost done praying," Arria answered. Turning back to Garic, she said, "Morning is soon here. Kiss me Krieger, now I have hope!"

Garic kissed her, then she helped Garic rise to his feet. He winced and grabbed his side. Arria knew that since the night Garic fought to save her and Samuel from the drunken rage of Centurion Tarvistus and his soldiers, his side was weakened; yet, he never complained. The well-placed kick, he received in the banquet hall, had revived his injury.

"Are you all right?" Arria touched below Garic's ribs and he gasped.

"*Ja.*" Garic responded softly and pulled Arria to him. A bit hesitant he whispered, "Is it true?"

Arria knew what Garic meant and nodded. "Yes. I am married."

"Why," he demanded hoarsely, "because you believed I was dead?"

"No."

The creaking latch rose warning them that their time was finished. Garic dropped his arms and they parted. Arria stepped back and faced the door.

"Lady! You must leave now before the morning light rises and the day sentry appears," the guard barked. "Do not even think to visit the Visigoth this Frank fought. It's too late. And bring the lamp. Prisoners can have no light."

Arria gazed at Garic one final time.

"Thank you, Lady Arria. Your...kindness will live in my memory." Garic's sad smile and broken words mirrored his confusion and unwillingness to part. He reached down for the lamp and handed it to her. Garic's lips mouthed, *I love you.*

Arria turned and stepped out into the misty fringe of night. She anticipated meeting Garic come daylight when the camp would journey to Attila. Destiny had brought them together again, and she thanked the Lord for this gift.

She watched the guard close the cell door and drop the latch into place. Turmoil raced through Arria.

"There's a wind picking up," the guard said gruffly. "Take this torch. You will need a stronger light."

She suppressed the urge to cry. The door closing on Garic's cell brought a dread that Arria carried with her down the path to where Vodamir waited. Overcome with fear, she stopped and looked back. She took a deep breath and turned again to the path, looking into the night.

Arria raised the torch. In the near distance, Vodamir and Samuel approached.

"Arria!" Samuel called. "Hurry! You must return to your tent before dawn."

Reaching Arria's side Samuel took the torch from her hand and wrapped his arm in hers.

"Yes, we must hurry. Where will you both go?"

"At dawn, I become the merchant again," Samuel responded to Arria's query.

"I am the rear guard," Vodamir chimed in, "but I must visit someone first."

Arria saw only the illuminated contours of Vodamir's face, but his tone revealed his secret. "From the urgent sound in your voice, my instincts tell me a woman waits for you," she replied.

"Not just a woman, Arria, but a healer as well."

"You admire her. How fortunate for her—for you both." Arria's affection shone through her sincerity. At the same time, she grasped the tenuousness of their situation and a sudden lump rose in her throat and she said softly, "Go to her Vodamir. Make the best of your time."

"I want you and Samuel to know... I am bringing her with me."

Samuel stood by and listened quietly. "We would never deny you your happiness, but the escape will be difficult."

"Her love must be strong to leave her people...and position," Arria added.

"It will be difficult, but she loves me and I love her."

Arria stopped and gently squeezed Vodamir's arm. "Love precedes us in whatever peril or hardship we encounter. It conquers all. Go to your woman. Samuel will see me back."

Wrapped in Basina's arms, Vodamir released and cried out. Basina dug her fingers into his back, lightly bit his bicep and moaned; then taking a deep breath, she hugged Vodamir and stretched her limbs.

Vodamir slid beside her, his chest against her back. Basina purred her satisfaction as Vodamir danced his hand over her buttock and playfully pinched it. She reached behind, slapped at him, but turned in his arms and caressed his weary shaft. A low chuckle burst from his throat, but he grabbed her hand.

Basina giggled. "It seems my warrior is not spent after all."

Vodamir clutched her to him, kissed her, then whispered, "Come away with me."

Basina met his glance.

"Garic and I—we're going to leave."

Apprehension washed over Basina's face. "Has Aveek assigned you to the ranks?"

Vodamir caressed Basina's cheek. "We are leaving Attila. Going home. Come with me. We can marry."

Basina squirmed out from under him. "Leaving the camp? What demons plague you?"

Vodamir raised himself and rested on one arm. Lamplight filled the sheltering Yurt and framed Basina's delicate face. "No demons haunt me. Only you," Vodamir teased, then he entreated, "Come with us! We know the forest. I will bring you safely to my home and my tribe will welcome you as my woman."

Basina rested her hand on his chest. "As your woman? I am my tribe's healer and in your tribe, what shall I be?" She tugged a strand of his hair and demanded, "Tell me."

"You shall be my wife," Vodamir said, kissing her fingers. "We can have a life together. Trust me. I love you."

Basina shook her head. "I cannot leave, Vodamir. Stay with me!"

Vodamir took her in his arms. "Fight your fear, Queen of the

Healers. You will heal my people. Think on it."

"Don't leave," Basina pleaded.

"Then follow me, and I will never leave you—I promise."

Basina lay back down and closed her eyes. Vodamir slowly mounted her. He loved her with tenderness and she him, but beneath her silky skin, he sensed her discontent. If his escape plan was discovered or failed, her knowledge of it alone would count as treason. If she joined him and they were caught, she would die. Vodamir chased these thoughts away and responded to her passionate kiss. Her guttural cry drove him deeper, and they rut frenzied, until both exhausted, they collapsed and curled together bathed in sweat.

Vodamir nestled closer to Basina and matched his breathing to hers.

"I feel the chill in the air," she whispered.

Vodamir drew the fur blanket over them. "Are you warm enough now?"

Basina didn't answer; she was asleep.

Basina loved him, and would choose him over the Huns. He must be patient, let the idea grab hold of her heart. If she refused to go with him, he would leave her behind. The thought was grim, and one he was reluctant to entertain. Basina must follow him. They were in love.

"Sleep for a while, Queen of the Healers, I will bring you safely to my home where you will be accepted and loved," Vodamir said. He heard Basina sigh.

FORT CAMBRIA

"Aetius is here? When did he arrive in Cambria?" Marcella drawled.

"Yesterday."

Marcella rose barefoot from Severus' lap clad only in her shift. Severus in a brown tunic sat in the chair adjacent his bed. She placed a well-shaped knee between his legs and ran her fingers through his hair, while his hands caressed her round backside. "What's he like?"

she asked.

"He's Master of the Soldiers. He's strong. An excellent horseman. His face is noble and he commands everyone's respect and that will include you. Do you understand?"

"You don't have to remind me," she said, petulantly, pushing him, "I know my place."

"That's what worries me. Tell me. Who is really your master?"

"You bother me with such boring questions. I have said Drusus is my master and you command me beneath the sheets. You seek my attention. That's why you ask questions whose answers you already possess."

Severus scowled, "Will anyone ever command you? Just be careful with Aetius. He's part man and part fox."

"His fox to my vixen. Isn't that what you call me?" Marcella grinned. "Aetius and I may have much in common."

"Stay away from Aetius, Marcella."

"What will you do if I don't?" she asked, feeling her power over Severus. Marcella lifted her gown and revealed long, silky brown legs. She straddled his lap. "The same thing you did to Aveek? You accepted our being together." Her warm flesh against his groin made him throb, but condescension filled his rugged face.

"You bitch! Go back to Drusus!" Severus spat, and rose abruptly, pushing her onto the carpet. "Have I not given you my heart and more? I tolerate your promiscuous behaviors, but must you taunt me? You cannot imagine the rage I felt, watching Aveek slide his dirty hands across your skin. Killing Aveek would bring me pleasure, but not at the risk of endangering Rome and all who live there. Go!"

"Aveek provided information and kept me from serving Arria. I hate her! Never be jealous. It's you that I love."

Severus pushed past her and approached the window. He stared at the atrium garden below. "Did you learn anything from your time spent with Aveek?"

"I only received a bracelet that concealed a note."

"What did the note say?"

"I don't know. I cannot read Greek."

Severus turned toward her. "Let me see it."

"It's been delivered."

"By you?"

"Yes. I was met on the road to Cambria. We were resting, when a passing merchant asked to show me some expensive silk. As I examined his fabric, he spoke to me the secret word, then asked for the Hun bracelet."

"Did you give it to him?" Severus asked perplexed.

Marcella nodded. "Of course, it's why I'm here. But ..." She hesitated.

"What?" Severus laughed. "You don't trust me?"

Marcella's heart stirred and crushed her momentary doubt. "I memorized the letters in the event I must give up the bracelet."

"Show me."

Walking to an unlit brazier, Marcella scooped some of the cold ashes from the bowl with a cup that rested on a nearby table. Spreading the cinders on the floor, she wrote the letters as she remembered them. Severus joined her and watched. The Greek letters were familiar to him. In the moment Marcella finished writing, she gazed only a few seconds at the ashes and then blew them across the tiles.

"Why did you erase them?"

"It's dangerous. Perhaps, you should not know too much."

"I can protect myself. Besides, I read the words."

"What did it say?" she asked, unable to contain her curiosity.

"Ah, now I have your attention."

Marcella bristled, "I've let my feelings for you interfere with my duty more than I anticipated."

"And your ambition?" Severus spat back and returned to the nearby window.

Marcella came behind him and rubbed his shoulders. "Tell me. What was the message?"

Still angry, he shrugged her off. "It said, Plan for the wedding night."

"Of whose wedding does it speak?" Marcella asked, surprised. "Arria is already wed."

"Go to your master, Marcella," Severus spat. "He's been separated from his wife and you for more than a month. I am sure he'll welcome you with gifts. As for the game you're playing, be warned. This is all that I can offer." He turned on his heel, walked to his chamber door, opened it and waited.

"You're asking me to leave?"

"No, I am telling you. Go! I have plans."

"Plans more important than me?" Marcella insisted.

"I would say, just as important."

Fire flashed in Marcella's eyes. "Have you another woman?"

"I am your lover and I wish to be your man. I will try to purchase your freedom, if you agree, but I won't be your fool. Until you ask me to free you, I will find my diversion where I can. Now go."

Marcella raised her chin. Her face flushed, she marched from the room. The door to Severus' chamber closed behind her, the falling latch declaring his determination.

"Attila is moving in the direction of Cambria," Aetius announced, entering the study. Drusus quickly rose from behind his desk and relinquished his seat to the general. Aetius motioned Drusus to a nearby chair, "From here, he'll most likely move south toward Aurelianum. My troops are far south of here. You will take your legion out of Attila's path and join with my army. I will rest here one more night. In the morning, I will return to my troops."

"Aetius, I will pray for your safe return. The men in your guard are the finest soldiers in the Roman army and are led by one of the best generals Rome has ever known."

"Flattery always becomes you, Drusus. It has provided you with many rewards, beginning with the Lady Arria, one of the fairest ladies in Rome. To my dismay, I've been informed that your wife is a political hostage."

The conversation having shifted, Drusus hid his nervousness with

266

a dutiful reply, "I only honored Attila's request that Arria represent us."

"My old friend, Attila, might not honor his word as he once did, considering the circumstances. Send five of your best soldiers, versed in diplomacy, on my behalf to request your wife's return—unharmed."

Aetius stared pensively for a moment then returned to perusing the ledger on the desk. It contained details and figures concerning the affairs of the fort. "I must say, for a newlywed you seem quite composed." Aetius glanced at Drusus.

Drusus rubbed his fingers together and replied, "I keep my personal feelings in reserve."

"An admirable trait," Aetius remarked. "We should all be so able. I have known Arria since she was a child. Senator Felix is a friend. At his request, I taught her to ride and to handle herself in times of threat. On occasion, I assisted her with her mathematics."

"That doesn't surprise me, General. I've heard that Valentinian relies on your counsel for his many financial matters."

"True, I've a natural ability and respect for numbers. However, I also respect that you will work diligently for your wife's safe return. Arria is priceless in my eyes."

"And in mine as well." Drusus pursed his lips, suppressing a frown.

"Good." With a measured firmness, Aetius closed the ledger and rose from his seat. "I will retire now. Surrendering your chambers for my comfort is hospitable, thank you."

Drusus rose and nodded. "You're most welcome, General."

Halfway to the door, Aetius turned. "I expect to see Arria again. Is that clear?"

"Very," Drusus answered, tersely.

"Goodnight, then."

"Goodnight, General. Sleep well."

Chapter Twenty-One

Alea iacta est
The Die is Cast

ATTILA'S CAMP
Month of Aprilis, AD 451

A faint ocean breeze and the budding countryside drifted past Arria's coach as Attila's camp moved north. Arria sat beside her driver and watched as a rider cantered down a grassy knoll.

Uptar drew rein and nodded respect. "Lady Arria, I received your message, requesting protection. I've appointed the two Franks to oversee your safety."

"Thank you, Lord Uptar."

It's only fitting that the Lady Arria feel safe under Attila's wing. We will join the army by nightfall. The king has ordered me to inform you that he regrets that you've waited days to meet with him and looks forward to his audience with Rome's envoy and most respected lady."

"Please inform your king that the honor is all mine, and I will await his summons."

"Assuredly, my lady. I will come for you in the evening after we've joined the forces and made camp. Enjoy the morning." Uptar bowed, nudged his horse and rode away.

Arria raised her shawl over her curls, shielding her skin from the sunny spring day.

"My lady looks as beautiful as the flowers that fill these fields!"

Garic declared, reining in beside her.

Arria's heart burst with joy. "Noble Garic, comparing me to one of God's natural wonders is too generous."

"Undoubtedly, your God modeled these flowers from the beauty He bestowed on you."

Arria laughed, "The flowers have existed long before me, my lord."

Arria turned to the driver. "Halt the coach. The Frank will relieve you. Go to the luggage cart, you can rest there."

"Thank you, my lady," answered the driver.

Garic tied his horse to the coach, climbed into the seat and grabbed the reins.

"How do you feel today, my love?" Arria asked, concerned.

Garic looked around. "This is the best I've felt in months." For several moments there was a peaceful silence between them. The breeze glided past them and Garic cleared his throat. "Tell me now, Arria. Why have you wed Drusus?" Garic's quiet demand filled the air as he fixed his gaze on her.

Arria looked away. Could she say what her heart denied? "I have a duty to Rome and father and to those who depend on me."

"And your promise to us? After all we've been through...how could you marry a man you don't love?"

"It's not that simple, in my world. There are reasons that go beyond love."

"Then trust me enough to tell me."

"I trust you, but will you believe what I am going to say?"

"My love is strong."

"I...married Drusus because he threatened to kill Karas and Angelus, and my father—if I refused. I feared for their lives."

Garic's face steeled. "I believe the bastard would hurt a slave, her child and even force you into marriage, regardless of your feelings, but does his power reach as far as Rome?"

"Drusus is very powerful; however, only a few know this about him. I am one."

"I swear on Wodan's sword, if ever again I see him, I will cut him down without one merciful thought."

Arria stared toward the low rising hills. "Drusus' death would free me. I've thought of it often. I hate him, but, I cannot condone his murder." Arria turned to Garic, her voice faltered, "There's ... something else...that no one knows, not even Drusus."

Garic encouraged her with a nod.

"I am not all that I seem." Arria glanced down, seeking protection from his gaze.

"What do you mean?" Garic prodded.

"I came to Cambria as an envoy, but also...as a ..." Arria took a deep breath.

"A what, Arria? Say it."

"A courier. I am a courier."

Garic's surprise shone on his face. " A courier for whom?"

"I love and trust you, but I was sworn to secrecy," she said.

The wagons up ahead slowed as Hun horsemen rode past Arria's coach toward the rear. "Something is happening," Garic said.

Vodamir rode up beside the coach. "Aveek has ordered the rear guard to divide and encircle the army as perimeter support. I've been instructed to lead Lady Arria's coach among the merchants away from the soldiers, in the event of a surprise attack." Hailed by a Hun soldier directing men, Vodamir turned his horse about, "I must see what he wants. I will return, shortly."

Garic shook his head and looked at Arria with frustration. "Listen, for I have little time to speak what's in my heart. Whatever message you carry, you must be cautious. I will not ask you to break your oath. Just remember, I can help you ... us, if I know what is expected of you and who you represent. This evening, I will escort you safely to Attila and back to your coach, where I will remain as sentry." Garic paused, commanding Arria's gaze. "Vodamir will go to Luthgar to organize our escape. You must come with us. It has become too dangerous in Attila's camp. In two nights—we go. When I carried you from the fight in Luthgar's camp, I asked you then if you wanted me. I am asking you again, will you be by my side as it's meant to be?"

Arria said, "You would still have me, knowing I am married to Drusus?"

"I would have you even if you were the bride to one of Hel's minions!" Garic rasped. "We were meant to be together. Nothing will separate us, not Drusus, not even your duty. Trust me."

"I fear God will judge me too harshly. There's only hell for the adulteress."

"*Mellitula.*" Garic said in his quiet way. "Would your God condemn a pure love for one born from treachery and evil? I will help you divorce Drusus by the rules of your church and the law. I will embrace your God and marry you. You will have the dignity and honor that befits you, my love, I promise."

"To my last breath, I will trust you, Garic of Luthgar's Tribe."

Garic raised her hand from beneath the shawl and kissed her fingers. "You will not regret it Rome's jewel."

"The message you bring is most interesting, Lady Arria," Attila said. "I would keep the channel of diplomacy open with Aetius. At his suggestion, I had Orestes specifically ask for you as a hostage. Your presence serves your *master* and me as well."

Arria winced at the slight. "As you wish. I will convey to Aetius that there are factors delaying your decision in regard to his proposal. He would also have me reiterate that although reluctant to meet you in battle, he is confident of a victory. The towns that are destroyed will only incur the hatred of all Gallo-Romans and Aetius' soldiers."

"The warning is well taken, but need I remind Aetius that his adversary is *Attila*? I have a great army and in my hand the sacred Sword of Mars. Many tribes have fallen at my feet. I have no fear of Aetius—only a high regard. Besides, there are more players in this drama than perhaps he realizes. Now if you will excuse me, I must attend to other matters. Unfortunately, I cannot let you return at this time. Soldiers arrived yesterday to escort you back to Cambria. They were dispatched with my refusal and I might add, grateful to have their lives."

Arria's eyebrow raised, she knew betraying her anger. Quick to notice, Attila's eyes shone. Arria composed herself. "I was invited as a diplomatic hostage and came freely. Am I your prisoner?"

"You're far too lovely to be considered a prisoner. It's a pity you're another man's wife. Many of my powerful and wealthy chieftains favor Roman women." Attila's grin widened.

"Attila honors me by the compliment," Arria replied. "My husband will be quite upset to know I am not returning...as yet."

"I am afraid that even if I thought it wise for you to return that would be impossible."

"How so?"

"My scouts estimate that we are several miles from Cambria. Tomorrow, my army will march on the fort. In two nights from now Cambria will be under my domain. You may see your husband sooner than anticipated, that is, if he's wise enough to surrender as my prisoner."

Arria felt a flush rise in her face. "Then I fear I will be a widow. Drusus will never accept defeat."

"A pity. Orestes claims he's a shrewd man."

"In battle the shrewd often survive."

"You've a quick wit for a woman. Now I understand why you were chosen." Attila turned to his left. "Onegesius, call Uptar."

Onegesius, who sat several feet from Attila, rose and instructed an entrance guard to summon Uptar. Just beyond the raised curtain, Arria could see Garic standing to the side surrounded by the glow from the blazing torches.

Uptar stepped in and bowed. "My king," he said in Latin.

"Escort the Lady Arria back to her coach and see to her comforts. Does she have men to guard her?"

"Two Franks who came from the infirmary several days ago. Aveek ordered them to act as rear guards. They're proficient in Latin. One awaits her outside."

"Good. In the morning have these Franks set up a tent for my lady

272

and stand watch." Attila's intense gaze swung back to Arria. "Your safety is of the utmost concern. We wouldn't want any mishap to befall you."

A shiver ran down Arria's spine, but she forced a smile. "I thank Attila for his protection and pray that he sees the wisdom in Aetius' offer."

"I thank you lady for your devotion. No general or king could ask for more."

A nod from Onegesius signaled Uptar and the end of her audience with Attila. Uptar extended his hand toward the entrance.

Outside, Garic came to her side. No words passed between them as Uptar led the way to the coach.

"You and the other Frank will guard the Lady Arria," Uptar ordered, Garic. "Tomorrow, you will raise her tent. Protect her or pay with your lives. Understood?"

"If the Lady Arria is harmed, I will gladly give my life in return."

"The cold blade of a Hun sword on your neck is a guarantee," Uptar snorted. He bowed toward Arria and walked away.

Garic scowled and said, "No one, not even Loki in all his madness will get by me to harm you, Arria. No one."

Attila's gaze followed Arria. "Cambria will be ours in two days, Onegesius. From there we should easily move on the other cities in our path and finally, the greater prize, Aurelianum. As for our lady, she'll prove useful in the days to come. Make sure that Uptar keeps Aveek informed as to her whereabouts and condition. Let no harm come to her. She is most valuable."

"I will inform Aveek. May I say that Attila has acted wisely in this matter."

"You may." Attila's shrewd grin lit his face. "Now bring me the missive that the slave Marcella brought to the camp and gave to Aveek."

Arria climbed the two stairs to her coach door with the help of Garic's hand. Arria turned and faced Garic, their lips only inches apart. She sensed he wanted to follow her inside, but knew better.

"Tomorrow, I will raise your tent as Uptar has commanded, my lady. Any news from Cambria? This is Cambrian land."

"Drusus sent soldiers to escort me back to Cambria, but Attila refused them. They're gone. Tomorrow, Attila will march on the town and fort."

"I thought as much. The message you brought Attila. How was it received?" Garic asked, curiosity lacing his tone.

Arria hesitated for a second. Circumstances necessitated Garic's collaboration. His understanding was more valuable than her promised secrecy. "I brought him a...proposal...from Aetius."

"Aetius?" Garic echoed, surprised.

"Yes. Attila said he was not prepared to respond. Knowing the terms of the proposal, I was unprepared for his reluctance."

"Do you know these terms? I thought you just a courier?"

"A diplomatic courier with a good memory." Arria grinned.

"Garic chuckled and brashly wrapped his arm around her waist, "The perfect courier. A Valkyrie."

Arria took a deep breath and stepped back. "Think of what you're doing," she said, but felt the heat rise through her body.

"I am ... of what I could be doing, if we were alone." Garic bantered.

"We must be careful," she warned.

Garic whispered, huskily. "You will be mine one day, *Mellitula*."

A Hun on horseback trotted by and gave them a long look.

Arria wrapped her shawl tighter. "Our time is short."

"Tomorrow night, in the hours before light, we will steal away from Attila's Camp."

"Why not tonight?"

"I am certain tomorrow's campaign against Cambria will be successful. There will be celebrating. It will be some time before the Huns notice that we're gone."

"And if we're caught?"

"There will be only death. For you, at best, punishment and

slavery."

"Then, we must succeed!" Arria insisted.

"We will, *Mellitula*. We will."

Overcome with emotion and the truth of the situation, Arria kissed his lips.

Garic took her face in his hands and returned the kiss, but a distant noise broke the magic. Garic brought his lips to her forehead and said, "Arria, don't kiss me like that. It wears down my resolve. What has stolen your caution, my lady?"

"This dangerous escape has settled on me."

"I will protect you."

Arria lifted Garic's hand to her cheek and kissed his palm. "I will send Karas with Vodamir and Angelus. Let her stay the night in Samuel's company. Have Vodamir return with a Wespe to act as a guard in your place. Just before dawn, he should wake us so he might return unrecognized."

"Wake us?" Garic wrapped his arms around Arria and nuzzled her neck.

"Yes. Wake us."

"What of your marriage vow?" He whispered in her ear.

"Does an unlawful and forced vow have meaning?"

"It's just...if you were to feel regret, I ..."

"And if we shouldn't survive? My love is for you. The husband of my heart." Arria held tighter. "So many times you've asked me if I wanted you, I always have and still do. Tell me now, do you want me?"

"I wanted you from the first moment. I knew we would find a way to be together."

Arria spoke with resolve, "Go love, hurry! Find Vodamir. Karas and Angelus will make ready for the night. I am grateful that neither you nor your cousin will see battle tomorrow. The signs are right and I will trust God and your instincts to lead us."

"What lies ahead will be ..." Garic paused and stroked Arria's hair. "All that I ask from you is trust."

"You have it—and more."

"Time changes everything, Basina," Vodamir entreated. They sat on the edge of her bed and he stroked her long, black hair. "Come with me. Together we will build a life. I promise."

"I cannot leave my home...what I know." Basina gestured toward the surrounding comfort of her tent.

"You will build a *new* home. With me."

"Vodamir, whenever you're near me my heart is filled with fire. Why must you go? You're a great warrior. In time, you'll be respected here as well."

"I'm a slave warrior, and I don't believe in your king's lust for plunder and conquest, especially in my land. I want my freedom, Basina. I have a farm. It's not far from the sea. At night one can hear the gentle crash of waves against the shore. In the day, a breeze carries a freshness that dances on your skin."

Basina dutifully listened but looked woefully into Vodamir's eyes as hers began to well with tears.

"My tribe is strong. We will give Gaul a lineage that will birth a noble kingdom. There's a future with my people. Share it with me."

Basina began to weep. "Aveek will hunt you down and your death will be painful."

Taking Basina firmly by the shoulders,Vodamir gently shook her. "Stop crying and listen. By the time Aveek realizes that we are missing, we will have been gone for some time. Our plan will work!"

Basina fell into Vodamir's arms, accepting his resolve, but said through her tears, "You are my love, and I will...go...but I need some time to prepare."

Overjoyed by her decision, Vodamir held Basina close. "I too must prepare. We leave tomorrow, well into the night. I will come for you."

"I will wait."

"You will not be sorry. Trust me. We will escape!" Then Vodamir laid her down upon the bed where they sat. Unable to restrain himself, he feverishly kissed her mouth, then neck and her breasts that he laid bare with a strong sweep of his hand. With a fresh ardor, he freed himself, pulled her skirt to her hips and mounted her with an urgency that made Basina respond in kind. His victory expressed in his thrust, he felt strong when he was between her legs. Their cries uttered, Vodamir rested on Basina as she wiped a few beads of sweat from his brow. "I must go," he murmured, then hugged her, "but I will come for you tomorrow night when the moon hangs overhead. Be ready." Gazing into her clear but strangely bright eyes, he reassured, "You will not be sorry."

"I hope not," she whispered.

FORT CAMBRIA

A sweet scent followed by the soft rise of Aetius' bed covers awakened him. He reached into the darkness and found the neck of the intruder. Aetius heard a soft choke. From the feel and sound, he knew it was a woman. "Who are you?" he growled, placing the edge of his blade against her throat.

"Who are you?" The reply, although frightened, was firm.

Unwilling to play this guessing game, Aetius placed his leg over hers and wrapped the stranger in a head lock. "Let's find out together, shall we?" His eyes now accustomed to the waning darkness, he rose from the bed and dragged her to a side table. It held a squat oval lamp and a papyrus candle coated in beeswax. The dying embers in the nearby brazier were enough to light the reed, which he directed she take from the table's edge. His knife prodded her hand toward the wicks. "Light them!" he ordered.

Quickly she lit them, revealing her long, black hair and tawny skin.

"What sort of assassin are you?" Aetius demanded and tightened his grip.

"What have you done with the Legate Drusus?" she replied.

"Are we to play a game of questions? Answer. Who are you and why are you in my bed?"

"I am Marcella, a slave who serves Drusus. Where is my master?"

"Such a bold slave." Aetius pulled his knife from her throat and spun her around. He had not expected such beauty. "My friend, Drusus, does have a way of choosing only the fairest. If his successes on the battlefield match his successes in the bedroom, the legion will have nothing to fear from Attila," he mused.

"Where is my master that I might go to him?"

"Your master gave me his room for the night. I wager he did not mean to include you or did he?"

"My master summoned me and I came to where I thought him to be. I only arrived today from the Hun camp, and I have yet to see him."

"You a hostage? I thought the Lady Arria was Attila's hostage."

"She is. I serve her. But I should say little. My master might not approve."

"The stranger you're addressing is Aetius, Master of the Soldiers. And I order you to tell me all you know. Come. Light the fire."

"Master Aetius, what is it you wish from me? My master, Drusus, would want me to serve you in any way that pleases you." Marcella, crouched over the brazier, stoked the embers and added fresh coals. Marcella smiled up at him.

Clothed only in a loin cloth, Aetius felt Marcella's scrutiny. He knew his years showed through the gray at his temples and wrinkles that fanned the corners of his eyes. Long campaigns had sun-washed and hardened his face, but his sturdy frame yet housed a youthful quality. More than one scar marked his body to boast his bravery, and a stern demeanor seemed his best weapon.

Aetius eyed Marcella shrewdly. The slave's youth and good looks were quite appealing, but why was she here and not in Drusus' arms? "Your master would wish that you serve me—in any way? How generous of him and how keen of you to know what your master desires. A slave such as you is priceless. Why don't we start with what you saw in the Hun camp and if you serve the Lady Arria why aren't you there?"

"Attila ordered all to leave except the mistress and her closest handmaiden, Karas."

"Did you see his army?"

"I saw the camp that follows Attila's army. It's quite large and filled with men, women, and children from the many tribes he's conquered."

"And the Lady Arria? Is she treated well?"

"Well enough." Marcella's terse response betrayed annoyance. "Would the master care for a bath? I could call the servants to ready the bath house."

"A hard journey awaits me tomorrow. I am in need of sleep."

"Then let me warm your bed so you might sleep comfortably."

Aetius gazed at the sculpted features of her face and the way her breasts clung to the silk that draped her body. Why would Drusus send her to Attila's camp? She was too fine a prize to chance losing to a greedy Hun.

"You may warm my bed. I can think of no better way to follow Morpheus into the land of dreams than in the arms of a beautiful woman. However, I will arrest the guard you managed to slip by and add two more guards for a safe night's rest before I slip into your embrace." Aetius moved to the chamber door, opening it, he barked his orders then returned to the bedside and pulled Marcella to him.

"I am honored to be able to serve the great general."

"You already have my beauty." Aetius ventured.

"My lord?"

"You were given missives to carry to the Huns, were you not?"

Marcella blinked only once. Aetius, a veteran general and a wise politician, knew how to read the heart. Few deceptions evaded him.

"What does my lord know of this?"

"Come to me, Marcella. You are a most loyal and dutiful daughter to Rome."

Marcella slid into his arms and kissed him seductively. "I suspected it was you, Master, who enlisted my service. You are strong and powerful. Who else would dare such an action. Let me love you. You will not be sorry."

"I am sure you will be glorious." Slowly he undid her robe. With eager arms, she embraced him.

Aetius found his release intense and overwhelming. Marcella laid in his arms and massaged his scars with her fingertips. "You touch my wounds. Why?"

"I find them intriguing."

"And the missives, did you find them intriguing?"

"I must confess I did. However, I never broke the seal on any message, nor did I suspect my bracelet from Attila was meant for you."

Aetius accepted her lie with a mild grin. His soldier, Severus, had reported the bracelet's message to him. His gamble had paid off. He knew now that someone in Rome was talking to Attila. For what purpose, he had yet to discover. "Marcella, my flower, you've done me a great service...more than you know. I am weary now, sleep."

"Yes, General." Satisfaction glowed on Marcella's face and she slept.

A rooster's crow awakened Marcella from her dreams. She stared at an empty place beside her. Aetius was gone, but Drusus sat on the bedside chair, his eyes livid with anger.

"Are you happy now that you've bedded Aetius? Are there no limits to what you will do to advance your position?"

"If you were me, my lord, would slavery satisfy you?"

Drusus warned her with a raised hand. "I would aim to act more carefully, especially in the arena of powerful men, my love. I've learned to rely solely on myself and my strong intuition. Trusting no one has been the maxim that drives my ambitions. You would serve yourself better by adopting some measure of my thinking."

"I would serve myself better...the woman of the most powerful man in Rome, don't you think?"

"Your powerful man is gone and you remain here." Drusus said, his voice rigid as anger brewed in his gaze.

"My powerful man is not gone; he sits here."

Drusus eyed her critically. "Do you speak of me?"

"Of course. You are my lord and one day will be Master of the Soldiers. Why serve a master who is aging and stands on precarious ground? Valentinian cannot be happy and Aetius is working with many to secure and keep his control."

"What do you know?"

"A few things," she answered coyly, and sat up. Slowly, she removed her gown, revealing bare breasts flushed from sleep and lovemaking. Drusus' eyes flickered with desire.

He rose from his chair and approached the bed. "How unlike Aetius to reveal information to a slave. God knows, the man barely trusts himself."

"I know that...he corresponds with Attila."

"How do you know this?" Drusus challenged and flung the blanket aside, exposing Marcella's long, shapely legs.

Marcella slid to her knees, stretched out her arms and pulled Drusus to her. "I was brought here from Rome to act as a courier for an unknown source to Attila."

"Whatever do you mean?" Drusus postured.

"Periodically, I am contacted to be in a certain place. A missive is left for me with instructions on how to pass it on. Several scrolls have gone to Attila. I am sure they've come from Aetius."

"Why so sure?"

Marcella roamed her hands across his chest. "It is said that Aetius lived for a time among the Huns and knows their ways. That he had a friendship with Attila. As I lay in his arms he asked me if I'd read any of the missives."

"And did you?"

"Never."

"I see," Drusus mused. "So you're the courier for a great and powerful man."

"No, I am the lover to a man who'll one day be even more powerful than Aetius."

"Will you tell me if any more messages come your way?"

"I will."

"How clever of Aetius to choose you."

"Why do you say that?"

"No reason other than a slave such as you is so *flexible...in all ways.*"

"Always, my lord," Marcella purred and kissed his throat, his chin and his mouth. She wrapped her arms around him and laid her cheek on his. "Together, we will find riches and power beyond our expectations. We will make a dream that will make the dreams of others look weak." Marcella gazed at the sun bursting through the cracks in the shutters. It had worked. She would have preferred a liaison with Aetius, but Drusus would do for now, but had she deceived him?

"You are incredible." Drusus said and stroked her hair.

"It's my wish to please you, my lord."

"Then be happy. Your wish has come true, my vixen."

"Severus wake!" Aetius barked, nudging his tribune.

"General."

"It's barely dawn and we must ride. Hurry! I will not leave you behind. I've been on a hunting expedition and caught a fox. And a beautiful one I might add!"

Severus shook his head and rose from his bed. "A fox? You were hunting in the night?"

Aetius handed Severus the leather strapping for his armor. "I was hunting beneath the sheets."

"A woman?"

"An Egyptian and a rare beauty."

Severus stiffened.

"It seems Valentinian is up to his tricks. But I won't be undone. I have one of my own just as pretty and I wager a bit smarter."

"My lord, who does Marcella work for?"

"I cannot say, not yet, but I know Valentinian has his hand in it, I can smell him."

"Get dressed! We ride to my soldiers. Attila is only a day out from

Cambria. I want a head start on Drusus. You've been loyal and have served me well. Arria is in Attila's camp and the long-hairs are there to protect her. All has gone according to plan. I pray they escape, but if any have a chance, it's Luthgar's Wespe and the noble Garic."

Severus frowned, "I fear I may have beaten the long-hairs too badly."

"It had to be convincing. Drusus' man, Tarvistus was a witness."

"I lost my judgment because of Arria."

Aetius threw Severus his satchel. "Explain later on the road. Now make ready! We should be gone before the sun is fully awake. And Severus...for what it's worth, the Egyptian falls far beneath you. Find someone more deserving to love."

Severus watched his general turn and go. Aetius was right. He would leave Marcella rather than destroy himself from desire. But God help him; he loved her. Severus felt a cringing ache in his stomach as he donned his helmet, blew out the candle and left the room. The bloody battle that lay ahead would leave many dead. He might not live to feel the pain of Marcella's loss. He mounted his horse and looked toward the place where he knew Marcella slept. Severus gave one last glance at the window, then prodded his horse and rode to Aetius' side.

In the camp, somewhere among the barracks, a rooster crowed.

Chapter Twenty-Two

Esto Perpetuum
Let It Be Everlasting

ATTILA'S CAMP
Arria's Coach

The soft rap on the coach door told Arria that Garic stood just beyond the threshold. Arria gazed expectantly into her dressing mirror. She watched Karas run a final brush stroke through the chestnut waves, cascading past her shoulders. With Karas' help, Arria had readied the coach. Lilac and honeysuckle scented the room. Extra tapers were lit, shining a golden warmth on the surroundings, while fresh coals burned in the brazier beside the bed.

Arria smoothed her lavender silk nightgown and looked once more into the mirror. Karas laid down the brush and then stepped back. "May your night together be wonderful. You both have waited so long. Now is your time."

"Garic is the husband of my heart and tonight the bridegroom will love his bride."

"I will see to it that you are awakened on the edge of sunrise."

Karas opened the door cautiously. "My lord, your lady awaits you." Bowing her head, Karas slipped past him into the night.

Garic closed the door behind him and locked it. He turned and gazed at Arria. "You take my breath away, Arria. You are so beautiful."

Arria raised outstretched arms. "Come to me my lord."

284

Garic embraced her and then cradled her face in his hands.

"Is this real?" Arria stammered as his lips swept over hers.

"It is," he answered and led her to the bed. He sat on its edge and brought her before him. "This is the most real moment in my life. I ache for you like a man, but I worship you like an unworthy subject." With a boyish grin, he murmured, "Are you Freya, the Goddess of Love? Confess to me, and I will believe."

Arria gently ran her hands over his golden hair then cupped his face, her fingers resting on his chiseled jaw.

"I am only a woman who loves a warrior. Let me show you."

"How?" Garic whispered softly.

Arria took a small step back. Garic's eyes shined. Slowly she loosened the belt gathered around her waist and let it fall to the floor. She held his gaze. A sensual tug from her hand caused the gown to slip from her shoulders, revealing her ample breasts. Garic gasped. Arria's nipples hardened and her heart beat faster. She cradled her hair and raised the mass of waves above her head. She circled sensually in a provocative dance. Her back to him, Arria let her hair fall and tumble down her spine. She slid her hands over the fabric clinging to her hips. Swaying to a silent beat, the silk slipped down her body like a light spring rain. Arria looked seductively over her shoulder at Garic.

Stirred with desire, Garic siezed her waist and pulled her to him. He pushed aside her fallen hair and burned kisses up her spine. Then standing, he embraced her and cupped her breasts. With a feverish hunger, he kissed her ear, then neck; he ran his hands over her buttocks, caressing them. "My blood boils," he said huskily. "I cannot stop until you're mine."

Arria faced him. She slipped off his vest and helped lift his tunic over his head. Garic's chest glowed with vigor. Each muscle chiseled and perfect.

She knelt, slipped off his deerskin boots and rose.

Garic loosened his belt and slipped off his breeches.

A sudden shyness washed over Arria and she blushed.

Garic crushed her to him and whispered fiercely, "*Mellitula*, I want you now."

She brushed his lips with her fingertips. "Take me, my lord, or I will die from longing."

He swept her in his arms and laid her across the fur blanket. He covered her mouth with a deep kiss, his tongue gliding over hers hot and urgent. "Arria, tell me I am your husband," he insisted.

"You are my husband. God knows it and one day the world will know it." Tears welled in her eyes and she said softly, "Where you go, Caius, there I go Caia."

Garic's face shone. "Your Roman wedding vow speaks to me; I pledge, I will follow you as well." Garic kissed her again. Then he slid into her depths with a lustful strength.

Arria caught her breath and dug her nails into his shoulders. A faint moan rippled through her as Garic thrust deep down to her core. He brought her to an ecstacy she'd never felt. Together they rode the crest of their climax until it faded. Exhausted and wrapped in one another, their breathing calmed. Arria savored the warmth of his body pressed against hers.

"You're my love." Garic said and kissed her.

"You're my soul," Arria whispered. "I feel safe in your arms. Promise me, we will survive this escape."

Garic moved to her side. Pulling her close, his warm embrace enveloped her. "I promise," he said and toyed with the waves of her hair fallen across his chest. "Sleep love," he said, wrapping them in the fur and snuggling behind her. Arria sighed, and closed her eyes.

AVEEK'S TENT

Aveek sat on the edge of his bed, the white linens contrasting the bronze of his naked chest. Having just risen, he was undressed beneath his blankets. Basina's dawn visit had piqued his curiosity and he'd ordered that she be brought immediately before him.

"Up so early Basina? I thought a Frank warrior warmed your bed?

Apparently, the fire doesn't burn as strongly as it once did."

Basina glared back at Aveek as she approached and stood before him. "That isn't why I am here," she said, a cold edge in her voice.

"A pity. I thought you might have a taste for something just as exciting only a bit more familiar."

"Vodamir is the only man I want beside me," Basina countered with impudence.

Aveek suppressed a yawn and adjusted the linen draped across his lap. "I am bored by this talk. Why are you here?"

"I've come to make a deal."

"Curious. *You* make a deal with *me*?"

"Yes. Basina eyed Aveek shrewdly.

"Go on. What are you looking for and what do you have to offer?"

"First, give me your word you will not harm Vodamir. No matter what you hear." Basina demanded.

"An intriguing request," Aveek mused. "I agree. Now tell." He curbed his smile. He often felt a similar excitement before a kill.

Basina took a breath. "I have reason to believe that Vodamir's cousin, Garic, plans on escaping. He wants Vodamir to go with him."

"An escape? Hah! This is hardly surprising. I warned that you were a diversion for his restlessness."

"I am no diversion!" Basina spat. "Vodamir wants to marry me, but he's torn. His cousin wishes them to return to their tribe."

A servant with a bowl of steaming hot water entered the chamber. With Aveek's permission, he began to wash his master's chest and arms.

"What else do you want, Basina, and what more can you offer?" Aveek asked, gruffly. "You've revealed their plan. You've even put your lover in jeopardy. What are you proposing?"

"I will bring you the information necessary to stop them...if...you spare Vodamir, make him a warrior in your ranks and...sanction our marriage."

Aveek's scorn caught in his throat, and he countered, "And if I don't? I could accuse you as well as them."

"I will deny your charges. Do not forget, Attila favors me," Basina warned. "Your warriors will need a healer for the battles ahead. My love has strengthened my powers."

"How touching." Aveek smirked.

Basina ran her fingers over the rim of a cup sitting on the bedside table near her. "There are ways I can advance your status, Aveek ..."

"What's your plan?" Aveek barked. No woman had ever had an advantage over him before. He must be careful.

"I will let you know when we are to leave."

"We?"

"Vodamir asked me to go with him."

"Can I trust this traitor after his cousin is dead? I doubt he'll still cling to your bed after your betrayal."

"He will. We love each other. He'll not seek revenge. I've told you my powers are strong."

"They must be, which intrigues me all the more," Aveek answered with a quick wave of his hand. His slave ran a towel over his arms, then bowed away. "I will spare your long-hair. But I sense he is brash and might be more than you can control."

"Leave Vodamir to me." Basina's smile seemed forced, but she added, "Thank you, Aveek. I will not forget this."

"You certainly won't. A deal means both parties benefit. Let's see. My warriors get a healer for their wounds. Vodamir gets to live. Basina gets a husband. What does Aveek get? Hmm? I will tell you. Once a month, you will come to me in the night, and will love me. This will be our secret. None shall know, except for a few of my trusted servants." Now Aveek smiled.

Basina paled, then spat. "You disgust me! Is there no end to your malice?

"Mind your tongue, woman. Men rule this camp, Basina. And now it seems I rule you."

Infuriated, Basina attempted to leave.

"Stop! I didn't dismiss you."

Basina turned back. "I will return when I know the plan and when they're leaving. I must go with them to be convincing."

"If I'm to trust you, I need a gesture of *good intention*." Aveek said, and motioned Basina to his side.

With the eyes of a wolf, she trained her sight on Aveek and moved closer.

He slowly slid the blanket from his body and revealed his erection. "Now would be an excellent time to recognize our agreement, Basina. Our union will be the mortar binding us forever, aligned and formidable, in Attila's camp. My desire stems not just from a man's need. I also desire the power our indebtedness will generate in the days ahead."

"You would have me touch you even though I hate you?"

"Most of my wives hate me. Why not you?"

"Is there no other way to save Vodamir?"

"No. Mount me woman. Love me or not, this morning and in the months to come you'll be mine. This is what I wish. Your man's life depends on it."

Without another word, Basina dropped her skirt to the floor and stood clad only in her blouse. Aveek loosened the braid from her hair as she climbed onto his lap, her hate exciting him.

"Good morning, beauty!" Garic chimed as he approached Arria, handing her a bouquet of wildflowers complete with a hovering honeybee.

Seated on the coach steps, Arria smiled, but a sudden tear ran down her cheek.

"Arria, I thought after last night you'd be happy. It hurts me to see you cry."

"I *am* happy. That's why I am crying. I want to live with you the rest of my life, and bring you to my home. But I am afraid Attila will keep us from this, unless I get to Aetius. The information I carry can bring him victory against Attila and save many lives. I cannot run away with you."

"I am not asking you to run from your duty. I will get you to

Aetius, but first, you must come with me to my farm, *Wilder Honig*, Wild Honey. We will warn our families and regroup there; then meet the tribes gathering at the assembly and go south toward Aurelianum and Aetius. We have to trust, Mellitula, and yet, we need to be smart and understand the world that stands before us. Attila invades our land today, and tomorrow? There will be other tyrants to take his place. We leave tonight, when the eastern moon hangs high above the tree tops. The Wespe will have everything in place."

"Were you a Wespe once? The wasp on your chest."

"Arria, few know this, but...I still am." Garic hesitated, then held her hand. "I was called back into service by King Meroveus for...a special mission." Garic brushed the top of his fingers over her cheek. "I was assigned to guard a lady of prominence."

"This woman...is me?" she asked, feeling apprehensive.

Garic nodded, but his eyes searched hers.

"When did this duty start?"

"At the Assembly of Warriors."

Arria stared, baffled. "Why is King Meroveus concerned with my safety?"

"Aetius asked Meroveus for his best man to protect you. When I saw you, the mission changed for me. Goddess Freya, stole my heart and gave it to you...*Mellitula*."

Arria recalled the Assembly of Warriors when Garic invited her to sing. His deep-blue eyes had smiled at her, and her heart had smiled back.

Arria sighed, but Garic continued, "I understood the differences between our people and the importance of your status over mine. The nights in Luthgar's camp were grueling. I felt a man possessed. I went to our priestess and asked for a potion to shake you from my thoughts."

"Did she conjure one?" Arria asked, warily.

"No. She said our destiny was twined in the leaves that simmered in her bowl and the steam that rose from it was strong—there would be love."

Arria softened, but she raised her chin. "Your capture. Was that an accident? Severus and Drusus claimed you and Vodamir were dead?"

"To guard you well, I knew we must penetrate the Hun camp and then escape. There was a plan to sell us, but things went wrong, and we were badly beaten. I believe Drusus wanted us dead."

Arria looked up at the sky. The thought of Garic and Vodamir's suffering was painful. "A courier envoy and her bodyguard spy," Arria replied. "How much is my safety worth?"

Garic's brow wrinkled. "I will refuse it. Your love is my reward. Arria, last night was not a lie. My love is real."

"How much is my safety worth, my lord?"

"One hundred gold *solidi*, and land overlooking the sea."

Arria gasped and withdrew her hand from his. Returning her to Aetius would make Garic very wealthy. Was she not wealthy herself? Their union would ensure his prominence. "That's quite a sum, my lord."

Garic stiffened and his tone grew firm, "I have not betrayed you."

"What better way to protect me than to make me love you." Her heart ached, but she continued. "I am sure my father partnered in this deception with Aetius. They knew I would reject the idea of a barbarian guard."

Garic sighed and said, "Your fiery nature blinds you. They love you, *Mellitula*. I love you."

Arria felt the truth in Garic's words deep within her and softened. "I want to believe you," she whispered.

Garic stood and gazed at her. "Be angry with me for hiding the truth, *Mellitula*, but my actions were for your protection. Trust me, you are my life. I will not give you up." One hand on his sword hilt, he extended the other. "Come, Arria. It's time to prepare. Soon Uptar and his men will come to make sure your tent is raised and the guard is secure."

Arria did not rise. "My lord if you will, I require a moment alone."

Garic looked perplexed, but resolved to her wish. He spun on his heel and walked toward the coach.

Arria looked into the day. Life hummed all around her. Duty and the gravity of love had brought her to the brink of this daring escape. An escape led by the man she loved, and who had suffered horribly in order to protect her. Her decision to follow Garic into danger must be based on trust and her belief in their mutual destiny. Arria clenched her fists with resolve. She would hold on to Garic and have faith.

Instantly she was on her feet running. "*Krieger! Krieger!*" Arria called, but seeing a rider approach him, she stopped.

Hearing his name, Garic turned. He smiled, but the sound of horse's hooves alerted him to an approaching rider. Garic swung his attention toward the horseman.

Uptar's presence darkened the day. He reined in beside Garic and shouted, "Long-Hair! You and your cousin will stay behind today under my command. We number about fifty men. Is this the lady's tent?" Uptar pointed to the tent adjacent to the coach.

Garic nodded as Arria came to his side.

"Well done! Placing it next to the lady's wagon is more convenient for her. My lady, are the Franks treating you with respect?"

"They've been helpful and honorable," Arria replied.

The sudden sound of horns and a flurry of motion drew their gazes. A mass of men on foot moved toward the front of the camp. Horsemen carrying the banners of their tribes and chieftains rode swiftly by. Just outside the tent, Karas stood with her arms wrapped around Angelus. Samuel walked up behind them and gave Karas a quick smile. She nodded.

Uptar eyed the trio for a moment, then turned to Garic and barked above the commotion, "Make sure the lady rests easy, then join the men at the rear. Inform your cousin, he's to join us. When the army returns, you'll be relieved to guard the Lady Arria. Tonight will be a victory night. Men will fill themselves with drink and passion." Giving Karas a lecherous look, Uptar quipped, "Her pretty slave should stay confined with her lady as well. It will guarantee her safety."

"As you wish, Lord Uptar," Garic assured.

A few Hun soldiers rode up and saluted Uptar. With a raised hand, he signaled his men and rode in the direction of the moving troops, his warriors following behind him.

Garic moved closer to Arria. "Do you forgive me? Will you come with me?"

Arria nodded and smiled. "There's nothing to forgive." Taking Garic's hand, she squeezed it. "As long as I breathe, I will never leave you."

Garic grinned, "Then we will live and breathe together. This I promise you." Watching the wind float through Arria's curls, he spoke just above a whisper, "I will come to you tonight. Samuel will take Karas and Angelus to his wagon. The men know what to do. We will succeed, Arria. Don't be afraid."

"Tell me that our love and good fortune will help us."

"They will," Garic assured, then added, "If only I could kiss you now. Anticipate the evening when I will come and love you, then steal you away."

"I will be waiting my—love." Arria's last word hung in the air.

Garic mounted and gave her a last look filled with certainty and rode off.

Arria winced, and watched him retreat. She would meet whatever lay ahead with courage, but now she must rest and wait for the man she loved.

BASINA'S TENT

"Where have you been, Basina?"

Startled from her thoughts, Basina entered her dwelling. Vodamir was seated on the bed sharpening the edge of his axe. She smiled weakly. "I've been to the infirmary."

"So early? It was still dark when I left your side to meet with my cousin. I returned for one last kiss, but you were gone. Soon, I must report for guard duty."

Basina began picking up pieces of clothing strewn by the bedside to dispel her nervousness and guilt. "I missed you when I woke. You know how I hate not seeing you first thing in the morning."

Laying down his axe, he rose and taking one of his shirts from her hand, he tossed it on the nearby bench and embraced her. "Soon, you'll see me every hour of the day and most likely will tire of me."

"Never. I can think of no other." Basina replied, but glanced away.

Vodamir pulled her chin toward his gaze and said softly, "What's wrong, Queen of the Healers?"

"Nothing." She looked into his clear blue eyes. "I...just am fearful about escaping."

"Don't be afraid. We will be gone hours before anyone notices."

Only an hour before, she had stood before Aveek, revealing her lover's plan. In sad submission, she had bought Vodamir's life with her body, and her shame flamed her cheeks.

"Hmmm...Your body is warm and your face flushed," running his thumb over her lips he noticed, "and your lips...so red, almost swollen." Then with a low murmur of satisfaction, he whispered in her ear, "It excites me that you want me." Grabbing her tightly around the waist he fondled her breast and then slowly ran his hand to his haven between her legs.

Basina flinched and pulled away. "Don't love me, not now."

Vodamir's eyes widened. "What's wrong? Don't you want me? It inspires me when we love. I can go to the guard feeling strong."

"I wish to please you...it's just, I need to rest and prepare, so I can leave tonight feeling able. I must bathe and plan what items I will bring."

"Women and their planning," he responded impishly and stole a kiss. "Remember to pack light. I will buy whatever you want or need when we reach Luthgar's tribe." He rested his hands on the sides of her neck. His gaze was serious, but filled with affection. "I love you. Find courage in this fact. I, Vodamir, am your man. Wodan has favored us. I will return soon after the sun sets. Make ready and rest. Your new life awaits you."

Numbly, Basina nodded her agreement.

Vodamir kissed Basina one last time and left her tent.

Basina sighed and laid herself on the bed and stared toward the ceiling. Images of Aveek's cruelty flashed before her. Basina pulled back her sleeves to reveal chafing burns around her wrists. Fortunately, Vodamir had not seen the marks left from Aveek's ropes.

Now she washed her raw and aching bruises and rubbed a salve into all the places Aveek had violated. Then Basina lay down on her bed exhausted, despondent, her heart breaking. How could she have been so stupid?

Basina pensively ran her hand over Vodamir's pillow and inhaled his scent. His presence all around her forced her from her bed, pushed her out into the day and through the camp, back to Aveek's tent where she would reveal the details of the escape to buy Vodamir's freedom.

Chapter Twenty-Three

Ex Animo
From the heart

ATTILA'S CAMP

ambria is ours!" The shouts of the messengers riding through the Hun camp heralded the news. Shaken by the Huns' victory cries, Arria's eyes grew moist with tears, but she stood by and watched. All around, merchants and vendors spread the triumphant news: Cambria's coward commander, Drusus, having learned that Attila's forces outnumbered his soldiers ten to one had fled in the night. Only a few frightened store owners, unwilling to leave their possessions, and the very old and sick had stayed behind and perished.

Arria could bear no more and hurried to her tent. Once inside she dropped the pail and rushed to her mirror. She dabbed her tears with a cloth and took a breath. Now was not the time for emotion. She whispered a prayer for the people of Cambria and wondered about Drusus. Surely he had moved south to join Aetius marching his legions north.

The celebration thrived around her and the night was young. Garic was attending to duties, then would finalize their plan of escape. Her heart beat faster with anticipation and fear. She must stay busy!

"Lady Arria!" Samuel called, beckoning Arria to the entrance. She raised the flap and ushered in Samuel and Karas.

Samuel bowed. "My lady, we've sent Angelus to stay with Luthgar this evening. May we spend the night in your coach?"

For a moment, Arria couldn't speak. Her slaves understood what was in her heart for it was in theirs as well. "Our journey will prove difficult and dangerous. With my blessing, enjoy your time together."

Karas reached her arms around Arria and gave her an affectionate hug.

After Karas, Samuel embraced Arria. He whispered, "Thank you, Arria. May we all be protected and make it safely back."

"We will, Samuel," Arria assured.

Samuel looked at Arria and rested his hand over his heart like a true Wespe. Arria did the same. Then Samuel and Karas were gone. Within hours, they would all meet again, ready to make their escape.

Luthgar and his Wespe sat circled around the fire, Garic and Vodamir among them. "Let us meet here when the moon rests in the east above the trees." Garic said, and rose. He glanced at Vodamir, then to the rest. "Arria and I will come with Samuel and Karas. Vodamir you must be here on time with your woman. Is she ready?"

Vodamir nodded.

"Good," Garic answered. "Brothers, soon our backs will feel the wind and freedom. Our people, our homes await us!" Garic's conviction raced through them and they murmured their approval. Garic turned to Luthgar. "My chief, we will follow you once we escape the camp. Vodamir and I led you into Attila's lair, we will bring you out."

Luthgar acknowledged Garic's deference to his leadership and rose beside him. "The plan is set," Luthgar replied. "Travel home will take days. Get some rest; courage demands strength, sharp wits and a true heart."

To satisfy any spying eyes, Garic and Luthgar went to the back of the wagon. Angelus lay fast asleep, nestled between coverings and sacks of oats. Luthgar gently lifted the boy's arm, removed the sack and replaced it with a covered basket, trying not to disturb the child. Then grabbing a wine pouch, Luthgar tossed it to Garic and they returned to the men. Luthgar handed the grain to Vodamir. Garic gave their pretense meaning and produced some coins in payment.

"Thank you for your business," Luthgar laughed.

"Any time!" Vodamir replied and Garic grinned.

Garic and Vodamir left the light of the Wespe fire, walked a short distance and stopped. The moon shone overhead, announcing the coming days of *Maius*.

Vodamir handed the grain to Garic and said, "Wodan be with us, Cousin."

Garic placed his hand on Vodamir's arm and Vodamir did the same to Garic. "We will see our farms and families once again," Garic said.

"If not, we die trying." Night's white glow could not hide his serious tone.

"Whatever happens, we will see it together." Garic said.

"That we will." Vodamir answered, with equal conviction.

The light in the tent burned low. Arria rested in Garic's arms, the cold darkness drawing them together. Garic moved over Arria like Attila had moved over the land. "Are you ready for me?" he whispered.

"Yes, my lord," she whispered back.

He entered her with a lust that set her body in motion, in cadence with his heartbeat. "Your satisfaction is my victory," he whispered .

Arria's climax was long and deep. Garic held her closer. Their need for secrecy was essential. As her guard, his place was outside her tent not in her bed. Melded together, they panted and clung to one another, then rested.

"I wonder. Will we spend more nights in each other's arms?" Arria murmured.

"We will," Garic reassured.

"I love you." Arria said and stroked his hair.

Garic's heart filled. "I love you."

"You won't forget, will you?"

"Why do you ask me?" Garic held her tighter.

"I am just afraid, that's all."

"Don't be. Remember, you promised your trust."

"I did." Arria smiled.

"Get some sleep, Arria. Soon we leave and you will need your strength."

She closed her eyes.

Under the blankets and the cover of night lit by a pale moon, they were hard to distinguish. Arria's body lay closer to the entrance and her womanly form shaped the darkness. She dozed peacefully in Garic's arms, their departure only a few hours away. Before a mission, he never slept soundly. The wind blew mildly over the tent, but he was sure he'd heard a low, muffled curse. Alerted and awake, he waited for another sound, step or movement. Arria, fast asleep, was in a direct line of the entrance. Not wanting to betray himself, Garic held still. He lay on his side against Arria. The silence pounded in his ears as he waited for another sound. A low flare bounced from the brazier fanned by a waft of air and danced above them. The flap of the tent raised slowly. Garic could hear a man breathing.

"My lady," the intruder whispered.

Arria stirred, but didn't wake.

"My lady," the man said thickly and advanced a few steps.

Garic slid his arm toward the knife he'd hidden earlier beneath the blankets and grasped its handle.

"My lady...your slave... is who I want. I can do...much...for you. I'm Aveek's best man."

Arria raised her head. "What?" she asked.

Garic gently squeezed her shoulder. He felt her stiffen, but nod in the dark.

"Who are you?" Arria demanded.

"Uptar."

"Why are you in my tent? What do you want?"

The warrior's speech, slurred from drink, demanded, "Karas. She rests...beside you? I desire her."

"I cannot."

"Don't toy with me, woman. I'm stronger." Uptar's words fell thick and challenging.

"Karas isn't here," Arria replied calmly, while Garic's touch reassured her.

"Then who rests beside you?"

"I do!" Garic hissed, jumping from the bed and knocking Uptar to the ground.

Uptar smelled of wine, but a hardened soldier, he fought back. He floundered on top of Garic, then bellowed for help. Uptar's face only inches from his, Garic pressed his strength into motion and drove the knife downward. Breaking the Hun's grip, he plunged the cold metal into the warrior's chest. Even in the dim light, Garic watched Uptar's eyes blink—puzzled, then still. Flinching once, he huffed a short breath and a soft gurgle seeped from his throat.

The coals burned only red ash, and the risen moon seeped partial strains of light. Garic sat back on his haunches and exhaled.

"*Krieger?*" Arria whispered.

"Arria, light a candle," came from the shadow.

"You are safe." She sighed with relief and immediately felt her way to the bedside table where she grabbed a candle and moved to the embers. Lighting the wick, she came and knelt beside Garic and the fallen Hun. Arria and Garic, naked and stunned, stared at Uptar, Aveek's captain and the soldier in charge of Attila's rear guard.

"What will we do now?" Arria asked Garic. Fear filled her face. A short while ago, they lay wrapped in love and now they knelt wrapped in death. Uptar's drunken desire had led to his unwitting death.

"We must act—without delay." Garic said.

Arria nodded. "What will you have me do?"

"We must leave."

"It is not the hour."

"*Ja*, it is. Uptar's death has decided it. We must wake everyone and leave as soon as possible. I will go to Vodamir—he's the hardest to reach—after we join the Wespe. Dress. Wake Samuel and Karas. I will wrap Uptar and hide him beneath the blankets."

"Is it wise to leave him here?"

"It will not matter. We are criminals in Attila's eyes. I've killed his captain. Our only hope is escape. Arria, we must go now," Garic urged. "Ready yourself."

Arria flung her arms around Garic and they kissed one long last kiss. Turning away she rose, dressed and left the tent, while Garic rolled Uptar in a large sheepskin blanket and carried him to the bed.

The messenger bowed. "My lord, Aveek, the long-hairs are on the move," he said and waited.

When the moon was high, Aveek had risen from his bed and spent the night waiting patiently in the dark. No drink had passed his lips, nor the lips of his men chosen to stop the barbarians. In another hour or two it would be over. He planned to hang the quiet one from the highest pole and use him as a target for his soldiers' arrows and make Vodamir watch. This was sure to embroil his hatred. Aveek mused that Vodamir might become a drunk who would beat Basina, or let himself be killed in battle. Regardless, he would rid himself of this adversary without ever seeming the cause of the long-hair's demise. A clever plan and he was proud of it. When he took Basina against her will, a hunger was awakened that even now gnawed at him. He had not felt this much desire for a woman since the night he first saw Marcella.

The messenger coughed softly and shifted feet.

"Call my men to their horses," Aveek barked. "The Franks, where are they?"

"As instructed, my lord, I watched the Roman envoy's tent."

"And?" Aveek insisted.

"The tall, quiet Frank, the one called Garic, was assigned as the Roman woman's guard. He entered the tent, but never came out. After a while, another man entered her tent. The man resembled Uptar, but I cannot be sure. There were voices, but it remained dark in the tent. I snuck closer, but only heard muffled sounds. A dim light shone and there was low talk. Afterward, the lady left the tent and went to her wagon. She roused a man and a woman who left

301

with her."

"What of the Frank?"

"My lord, I followed the Lady and her two companions to a merchant's camp where they gathered with these men. Shortly thereafter, the Frank joined them."

"So this party is bigger than I was told. How many did you count?"

"Ten men, the Roman woman, a slave and a boy."

"Go to Basina's tent," Aveek ordered. "See what you can learn, then find me by the corral. We can track them easily. Let them gain a sense of false confidence."

Aveek watched the messenger leave, but his thoughts were elsewhere.

Vodamir gently shook Basina. "Wake love. We leave now!"

Basina looked up at Vodamir, and Garic beside him. "Now?" she questioned and wiped her eyes.

"It's time. Get your things."

Reluctantly, Basina struggled from the bed. What was happening? They were leaving later. This is what she had told Aveek. "It's early. Why must we go?"

"There's been some trouble."

"What sort of trouble?"

"Hush, Basina! Get your things. I will explain to you on the way."

They walked to the merchant camp, the cool air surrounding them. To Basina's surprise a group of men, two women and a boy waited.

Vodamir squeezed Basina's hand and said, "These are my friends and people."

Basina only nodded. Without words, the men helped the women mount. Basina watched as Garic helped a woman whose long dark hair escaped from beneath her hooded cloak. She resembled the Roman envoy that Basina had seen briefly at a few banquets. Things were getting more complicated by the minute. What had she done?

"Amo will help you to leave through the woods near Arria's wagon," Garic informed the women. "We will follow on foot. Once we're in the cover of the woods, we will ride hard to put some distance between us and the camp, just in case the Huns have been alerted by something or someone." Garic's bold glance toward Basina prompted her defiant stare.

Vodamir noticed and shook his head. "Can we go? It grows late," he urged.

"Have heart! We meet in the woods." Garic replied.

The men spread out and the women in single file followed Arria, who rode the lead horse. Angelus stayed by Samuel's side, but gave a small wave to his mother.

Basina's heart filled with anguish. Garic's hard look had unnerved her. What could he know? They were leaving earlier than planned. And when Aveek discovered they were gone, would he think that she had betrayed him? How could Vodamir's trust and love belong to her now that his people were involved? Basina realized the error she'd made. Many would suffer because of her stubborn determination to have her way. Vodamir had given her a choice. Either go away with him or live in her world without him. Now the ruthless Aveek would loose his vengeance on them all. What kind of healer could justify so much bloodshed?

They reached the edge of the wood as the darkness raised. Arria turned to check on the riders behind her and smiled at Basina. Basina smiled back, but tears welled in her eyes. Once inside the woods the women stopped and waited for the men. Soon they were all gathered and the men mounted their horses.

Luthgar moved ahead of the men and faced them. "We will head north, then to the west. This land is familiar, we should make good time. Each man will care for and guide his woman. Amo, you will guide the boy." Turning his horse, Luthgar led them at a gallop.

All followed but Basina.

Vodamir quickly noticed that Basina was not beside him. He stopped and looked back. She sat on her horse, looking at him. Returning to her, his concern grew and his words were hurried, "What's wrong?"

"I cannot go. I thought I could, but I cannot. I will always love you, but I cannot leave my people."

Vodamir held her in his eyes and didn't speak. His desperation filled the distance between them. In a thick voice he said, "You sit your horse like a queen and have never looked more beautiful, but you must choose. I will not force you to follow me. Go! Queen of the Healers."

Heartbreak showed on Basina's face.

Just behind him, Garic rode up. "Why do you delay? Time is crucial. Hurry Vodamir!"

"Basina will not come, she has chosen to stay," Vodamir said hoarsely.

"She'll betray us, Cousin."

"Will you betray us, Basina?" Vodamir asked, feeling empty inside.

"I love you Vodamir. I will not hurt your friends."

"Then go! Before Luthgar and the others return and they have no choice but to take you as a prisoner. Before *I* change my mind and take you as my prisoner."

Swiftly, Basina turned her horse and rode out of the wood at a gallop, a herald to the plight of lost love.

"She will bring Aveek!" Garic shouted.

"She won't!" Vodamir shouted back.

"Damn!" Garic cursed, and kicked his horse. Vodamir followed him off the path and north into the trees.

Rays of light welcomed Basina as she escaped the forest and entered the clearing. On the southern rise, the Frank merchant wagons sat, looking lonely. Basina peered at the pink opal sky and sighed. She loved Vodamir more than she could bear; but at the same time, she felt an urgent relief. She must go to Aveek and bargain with him. Her offer of marriage might ensure a safe passage for Vodamir and his people. Aveek's anger might be fueled by the discovery that the Roman envoy had fled with the Franks, but Attila would never know that Aveek knew of any escape if Aveek were smart. They could buy each other's silence.

Basina guided her horse toward camp. From off her right flank, thundering hooves shattered the morning silence. She halted and looked westward. Twenty or more Hun horsemen, one carrying Aveek's colors, descended the hill, riding in her direction. In the lead, she recognized Aveek, who she knew by now had spotted her. Seconds passed and a dread dawned over Basina. In the company of his men, he would save face and hunt the fugitives down. Terror and clarity gripped her senses all at the same time. She swung her horse around. She must go to Vodamir. She must find the Franks, warn them—join them. In a fraction of a second, her fate was decided.

Basina galloped at full speed for the wood. She knew the direction Vodamir took and would find him. Aveek and his horsemen fast approached. She must reach the cover of the forest. Into the cool light of the sheltering trees Basina rode. *Halfway there*, she thought. Just as ardent as her hope, a swift, rushing sound like wind through the leaves, hissed in her ears. A sudden jolt shot through her left shoulder blade, knocking her forward and slamming her face against her horse's mane. She cried out and gasped for breath. A burning sensation seeped through her left side as she tried to raise herself. To her horror, an arrowhead peeked beneath her shoulder connected to an inch of shaft. One of Aveek's bastard soldiers had shot her.

Searching frantically about, she found a grove of trees and hid. She quickly examined her wound. The bleeding was slow, but she must decide. Could she trust Aveek and his men to help her? No. She must find Vodamir. Only he could help her and if not, she preferred death in his arms than beside Aveek's feet.

The Franks were headed north then west. Listening for any movement, she left the cluster of trees and proceeded north. Weary and perspiring, she took the rope hanging from her saddle. With one hand, she tied it around her waist and then coiled it around the front horn at the top of the blanket-covered saddle. If she were to faint, she would not fall. Basina moved forward, cringing with pain. A cold sweat dampened her brow, but she rode as hard as she could.

Somewhere in the distance, she heard shouts. Basina watched the shadow of a bird's wing on the ground. A hawk circled overhead and screeched. She slumped forward and closed her eyes.

THE FOREST

"Basina!" Basina eyes fluttered. "Vodamir," she whispered and opened her eyes. Aveek's wide grin met her gaze. He bent over her. Basina recoiled, then raised her hand to the sharp burn beneath her shoulder.

"Would my wounded little bird like to confess the real plan of the Franks?"

Aveek's words filled her with dread, but she ignored him. She only grimaced in pain and touched her wound.

"A shot clean through. You're lucky, the shoulder will heal. I removed the arrow, with much pleasure, I might add and tended your wound. If you die, it'll not be by my hand but by Attila's or by the gods for your betrayal."

"Either way, you'd be pleased," Basina answered weakly. "I thirst. Give me water."

"Demanding will not help you. Beg me, beautiful healer!" Aveek hissed, his voice low and strong.

Too weak to resist him and too thirsty, Basina said, "Please, Aveek, some water."

Aveek motioned to the soldier beside him, kneeling over Basina as well. The warrior poured some water into Basina's mouth. She drank greedily, then gagged, the water running down her lips.

"Slower," the soldier barked and poured again.

This time, Basina drank slowly, but Aveek stopped him. "Not too much!"

The soldier rested her head back onto the blanket and she closed her eyes.

Aveek brought his lips to her ear and whispered. "If you cooperate and tell me what you know, I might try to save you—that's if you don't

306

die."

"I'd rather be dead!" she rasped and attempted to rise.

Aveek laughed and stayed her with a firm hand. "You're no good to me dead, healer, I like my women warm and alive."

"That's not what I've heard you bastard!" Basina winced, her retort heightening her throbbing pain.

Aveek laughed, but felt her sting. "Watch her!" he barked at the attending soldier. "I want her alive." He stood and stared down at her for a long moment, then moved among his men.

From the high limbs of the tree and a bright moon, Vodamir watched Aveek and his Huns as they camped for the night. He was relieved that the Huns were finding it difficult to track them. They were in Frank territory. Vodamir's eyes narrowed as he watched the Huns eat and drink around their fire. "I'd like to carry Aveek's head home as a prize," he whispered to Garic who sat in the branches beside him.

"Who would carry his stink?"

"You're right, but my axe itches for his neck."

"My arrow will go deeper."

"A compromise. First you bury your arrow in his ass, then I will sever his head," Garic murmured. Vodamir suppressed his laughter, not wanting to give them away.

Their levity passed, Vodamir asked, "How much longer must we wait?"

"As long as it takes. Their sound sleep will help us to steal her away."

"You left Arria with Luthgar to help me find Basina. Why? You don't even trust her."

"You followed Basina back to the clearing, even after she left you. I couldn't leave you, Cousin," Garic answered.

"I hoped to sway her one more time."

"Why does the most hardened soldier become recklessly foolish when a woman is involved?"

"Does that include you?"

Garic smirked, "What do you think?"

"Maybe Wodan wants a man to find his soul in the heart of a woman. They make us take risks."

"Like sitting in a tree at night over your enemy's camp, waiting to carry off their healer?"

"*Ja*, something like that," Vodamir agreed and grinned at the stars.

Within the hour, the Huns slept, while one sentry whittled a piece of wood and the other gazed into the fire.

Garic and Vodamir climbed down from their perch and closed the distance to the camp. Their knives between their teeth, they advanced on the perimeter where Basina lay wrapped in a blanket and isolated from the men. As they drew closer, Garic pointed to a log about five feet long. Vodamir helped him carry it to the edge of the wood. One of the guards, his back to them, glanced around as his companion left to relieve himself.

After the guard returned, the two Huns spoke in low tones. Garic nodded toward Vodamir, who went to Basina's side, quickly muffled her mouth with his hand and lifted her. Garic carried the log to Basina's place and covered it with her blanket. Safely tucked back into the cover of the forest, the two men darted through the trees with swift stealth. Within minutes, they reached their horses. Garic arrived first and held Basina, while Vodamir settled himself in the saddle. Vodamir reached out his arms and lifted Basina to him and held her close. She rested her head on his chest as he took the reins.

"You came for me," she murmured.

Vodamir felt her fevered brow. His determination grew even stronger. "Hush, Basina, rest. I am taking you home."

"I came back to warn you...too. Don't want...die alone."

"You're not going to die. I won't let you go."

Garic and Vodamir rode north and rode hard.

The dawn sentry awakened Aveek to the news that Basina was gone. A log rested in her bed.

Aveek jumped to his feet. "Mount up!" he screamed at his men.

He would kill these Franks and make Basina watch.

The Huns ran for their horses, but were taken by surprise. From the edge of the trees, the sound of flying axes sliced the air. Soldiers scattered as spinning blades buried themselves in the backs and chests of several warriors. Cries and shouts spilled from them as some fell and others tried to mount their horses.

Aveek jumped into his saddle, pulled his bow and looked for a target. A movement in the tree to his right caught his eye. He fired. A soldier mounted the horse beside him, but tumbled sideways, a hunting knife splitting his shoulder blades.

Aveek watched him fall. "Sons of bitches!" he screamed into the wood. "Your heads are mine!"

Deeper within the wood, Luthgar and his warriors fanned out on foot. Garic had reported that Basina was Aveek's prisoner, and he and Vodamir planned to rescue her. For Luthgar, no alternative existed. The Wespe would help, regardless of the risk. If their strategy worked, it would buy Garic and Vodamir the time to deliver Basina to the cave where the women and boy waited.

Surrounded by forest, the Wespe heard only their own breathing. Luthgar had counted twenty Huns before the ambush. Afterward, as they had collected their axes and enemy blades, five Huns lay dead on the camp ground. *Fifteen more will soon join them*, Luthgar thought, ducking behind a thicket. He whistled low. Amo came beside him. "Have Vodamir and Garic returned?" Luthgar asked.

"Not yet."

"When they do, have Garic perch in a tree with his bow and pick them off."

"And us?"

"We take them down like wolves—one at a time. Kill the Hun who falls behind or keeps the rear. Stay hidden. The Huns know open warfare best. They are good with the bow and they ride well, but tangled in the forest might prove their weakness."

"Let's find out!" Amo hissed. Excitement in his eyes, he pointed to the narrow path several yards ahead. "I hear them."

"Inform the men," Luthgar ordered, steeled and calm. A chill shot down his spine as a hand grasped his shoulder. Luthgar spun, his knife ready and faced Garic. "You flirt with death!" he whispered tersely.

"You didn't hear me?" Garic whispered, then chuckled softly.

"You're mad. Out numbered by Huns, you play?"

"Two to one. My best odds."

A rustling noise forced Luthgar's finger to his lips and Garic crept away and out of sight. Luthgar could sense his first counsel climbing the tree behind him. Luthgar watched the Huns approach. It appeared the Huns had decided to divide. The group drawing closer to Luthgar numbered seven from what he could see. He knew Amo and the Wespe had also broken into pairs and dispersed. They had their axes, javelins, and knives. Garic had a bow. This must work.

The first Hun on horseback passed, then the rest; all but the seventh man who lagged behind. Luthgar threw his hunting knife, propelling the blade into the straggler's back. The Hun slumped forward.

In unison, a spray of Wespe javelins pierced the rising light. Taking flight, each found its target in the torso of a Hun. Four fell at once. From a limb, Garic targeted one of the Huns and ran his arrow cleanly through his enemy's neck. The last Hun took a desperate shot at the treetop, but was knocked off his horse by Vodamir's hurdling axe.

"Of the twenty, twelve are dead," Luthgar whispered to Vodamir now beside him. "Eight are left. They may try to flank us."

"Two groups of four could prove fatal."

"Take Rudiger, Samuel, and the brothers. The rest come with me. Signal Garic to climb higher for a better view."

"How much for Aveek's head?" Vodamir bargained.

"An axe."

"Your chieftain's axe and no less!" Vodamir answered and crept away.

The Wespe divided and fanned with caution through the woods. Amo, acting as Luthgar's point man, signaled then pointed to a dried, narrow stream bed crossing their path. Four Huns on horseback, their arrows drawn, advanced in their direction.

"Perfect," Luthgar murmured.

The Wespe, waiting for the signal, crouched ready as their enemies passed before them. On Luthgar's cry, they charged the Hun horses, screaming and yanking the Huns from their saddles before any could launch an arrow. The horses frightened off, only the Wespe stood. The Frank warriors walked among the dead bodies, gathering weapons. Theudebert, his guard down, laughed and tossed a Hun bow at Witigis who jumped to retrieve it. Like a bird caught in flight, Witigis fell impaled by an arrow, rushing from the woods. Theudebert screamed. The Wespe scrambled and ran further into the woods. The four remaining Huns rode on their heels. Luthgar's group joined by Garic, Vodamir and the rest spread out and began to circle back.

Aveek pursued them, but abruptly halted his men; then he turned and rode away, his soldiers following behind him.

Garic nimbly climbed the tree beside him and took a breath. On the edge of the wooded hills, the clearing's panorama lay before him as the Huns broke from the trees and headed south. He drew back his bow string and aimed for Aveek, the lead rider. Instead, the northern breeze buried the arrow easily into a retreating Hun.

"Did you get that bastard, Aveek?" Vodamir demanded as Garic jumped down from the tree.

"One fell, but not Aveek. He smelled a trap and ran. Is everyone all right?"

Vodamir kicked the dirt. "Witigis is dead."

Vodamir retrieved the weapons and crouched before Witigis. He folded Witigis' arms across his chest, then wrapped him in his blanket. "A true warrior, who fought with courage." Vodamir stood tall and with a deep scowl announced to the men, "I pray I meet Aveek on the battlefield. I will kill him!"

"We'll see battle soon enough. These Huns have tasted plunder and the kindness of the land. They won't stop." Garic replied, then directed toward Luthgar. "Wilder Honig calls me."

"Our first counsel has spoken wisely. Retrieve the Hun horses." Luthgar ordered. "We will camp in the cave for the night, then return to our homes. After three days, let us meet with the Assembly of Warriors and our tribesmen; afterward, we join Aetius."

Nodding their acknowledgment, the men gathered their equine prizes, while Denis carried Witigis to his final ride. Luthgar watched the Wespe mount. He knew they dreamt of home. As secretively as when they first appeared, they now faded, ghostlike, into the cover of the trees.

Chapter Twenty-Four

Lapsus linguae
A Slip of the tongue

THE ROAD TO AURELIANUM
Month of Maius, AD 451

Roman, tribal, and *foederati* troops rallied as scouts galloped into Aetius' camp. Attila was moving on Aurelianum.

The messengers recounted the story of the young nun, Genevieve, who had bravely met Attila at the gates of Lutetia Parisii. Impressed by Genevieve's piety and bravery, Attila had ordered his Huns away from Lutetia Parisii, and had launched his attack on Tricassis and Ambiani.

Aetius grimaced. The destruction of these cities necessitated that his troops press even harder. His orders rang throughout the camp. The smell of rain and revenge clung to the damp air and their skin, as they swept across the verdant countryside to the tune of chattering birdsongs.

Aetius knew he must engage the Huns before the people of Aurelianum surrendered. Aurelianum provided Attila a bastion from which to protect himself. Aetius' legions would face more than a battle, they would brave a siege.

While the troops rested in the settling dust of sundown, Aetius directed Severus standing before him. "Go find Drusus. Inform him, he must come at once! There are matters I wish to discuss. In the meantime, Marcella can be of some use to me. She believes that I am the author of her secret messages. I need you to discover the truth. I must know who in Rome or elsewhere is corresponding with Attila, besides me."

"General, what does the message *Plan for the wedding night* the Greek words Marcella wrote in the ashes, mean?" Severus questioned Aetius, sitting in his tent with his dinner and an open map before him.

"I have no way of knowing, as yet; but, it must be the response to the missive you carried for her to the Hun raiding party when you sold them the Franks. If she knows what was in that letter—and told you, it would help us. Find out what you can and quickly. An empire might rest on the outcome."

"I did once." Marcella answered coyly as she crossed the rug covered earthen floor of her tent. "I only read one...the missive you gave to the Huns for me. Why do you ask?" Marcella pulled her silk robe tighter and sat beside Severus. He reclined on her bed, a wrinkled linen sheet across his naked body.

"Twice." Severus gave Marcella a grin.

"What?" she feigned surprise.

Severus loved her little self-deceits. He watched as she combed her long, black hair. It was her ritual after their lovemaking. She would position herself next to him and gently brush her long strands while they talked. And he enjoyed the beauty of it, but today he was caught up in his determination to satisfy Aetius' request. He had no choice, but it pained him. Marcella was his weakness. If she discovered his treachery, she would hate him. "Twice. You read the note in the bracelet, and now it seems you read the message that I gave to the Huns. That's twice."

"Oh! I suppose I did. I forgot," she pouted and brushed nonchalantly at a tangled lock she held in her hand.

"It's not wise for a courier to forget such important matters." Severus said lightly.

"Why do I tell you anything? This is not wise." Marcella teased and slapped Severus' arm with the back of her brush.

"How were you able to break the seal and restore it?" Provocatively he parted her robe, exposing her flushed breasts.

"The helping wedge of a knife's blade can be quite effective." With an ease that came from habit, Marcella resumed her brushing, ignoring Severus' admiring eyes. "Resealing it was easy. Some hot wax, a little pressure and the job is done." Her self-satisfaction was evident in her smile.

"I am assuming *this* message was in Latin?"

Marcella's eyes brightened. "It was."

The knowing grin on her face gave Severus confidence, and delicately he asked, "Why did you choose this particular missive to read?"

"I suspected that what it carried must be important. After all, I was ordered to get it into Attila's hands as soon as possible."

"And...was it?"

Marcella stopped combing and gave Severus a serious glance, "Oh yes."

"Will you tell me?" Severus whispered as he laid her brush aside, guided her face to his, and kissed her deeply, caressing her tongue.

Yielding to his touch, she closed her eyes while his kisses glided to her breast. "If I tell...it will cost you."

"How shall I pay?" Severus said huskily. He envisioned his tongue eagerly sweeping across her nipples as a reasonable price.

"I want an audience with Aetius," she answered a little breathless.

His temper sparked, Severus pulled away. "Damn you, Marcella! Why must you torment me with your ambition?" Frustrated, he sat up and leaned against the high back of the bed. "Isn't my love good enough for you? Why is it only power that you seek?"

Leaning toward him, Marcella rested her palms on his chest. "It was power that I sought until I realized...I love you. Now it's freedom I seek. Only Aetius can purchase and release me from Drusus' service. Once I am Aetius' slave, as a soldier of rank under his command, you can petition Aetius to buy me."

"And will you bewitch Aetius? If you do, he may never release you to anyone."

"If I bewitch him, it'll be for my freedom. I have slept with many, but I love only one."

"Can you love only one man, Marcella?"

"You're the one I love."

Softened by her words, Severus ran his hand over Marcella's golden arm band just below her smooth, brown shoulder. "Do you know the Roman custom where a wife wears a golden armlet engraved with her husband's name as a tribute to their marriage?"

"I do."

"One day, you'll wear my armlet." Severus pulled her to him. "I will get you your audience with Aetius." His fingers lightly touched the fragile line of her jaw. "Satisfy my trust and curiosity, love. Tell me the message." Then kissing her lips and fondling her breast he drawled, "Satisfy my lust. I am hungry for you again."

Marcella pulled the sheet from Severus' body and smiled proudly. Running her hand over his stiff, yearning skin, she leaned in and whispered in his ear, "The missive read, *Defeat the suitor and you've won the bride.*"

Closing his eyes, he basked in the satisfaction of Marcella's lovemaking, and the secret he would lay at his general's feet. He winced, took a breath and groaned. Then all else was forgotten.

"You're playing a dangerous game, woman. You've been talking and sleeping with Aetius!" Drusus snapped as Marcella entered his tent. He grabbed her wrist, forcing her to cry out."Let go of my wrist. I was ordered to go to him. What would you have me do?"

"What does he want from you?" Drusus strengthened his grip and forced Marcella to her knees and the Persian carpet spread across the dirt floor.

"What does any man want from me?"

Drusus fired a slap across Marcella's face and screamed, "He wants me to sell you to him." He backhanded her again and hissed between clenched teeth, "If I don't my career is ruined. Why does he want to buy you? You must be doing something more than keeping his bed warm, you whore!" Marcella took his punch to her stomach with a groan. "I was *once* willing to let you lie with him for reasons of state, but I will not lose you to him! You're mine! He took a deep breath, and with the back of his hand he wiped away the saliva gathered in the corners of his mouth.

Marcella looked up at him and brushed away strands of hair fallen across her face. A trickle of blood oozed down her chin. Crawling toward Drusus' feet, she wrapped her arms around his ankles. "My lord, I've never claimed to be anything different than what I am."

"What are you, Marcella? Tell me!" Drusus bent, grabbed her hair and pulled her face toward his.

"I am your slave. You're my master and I love only you."

"Can an alley cat love anyone? I should have known you couldn't be trusted." Tugging her hair, he leaned in and spat, "I vouched for your ability."

"To whom did you justify me, my lord?" Marcella whimpered.

"It's not your business. What's done is done. What have you told Aetius? If you don't tell me the truth, I will make sure your cuckold lover, *Severus*, loses his testicles. Would that please you? Never to feel him between your legs again? I know everything you do, Marcella. Think carefully, the stakes are high."

Drusus slapped her again and satisfaction shone in his glance. Her cheek burned as Drusus yanked her cowering body to her feet. Pulling her close to him, he inhaled her fragrance. "I will never sell you, *Carissima*," he hissed into her ear. He ran his fingers over her bruised and bloodied lips, then gently kissed them as Marcella yielded to his embrace, a rag doll at his command. "I will find a way to refuse Aetius," he said. As if the mention of Aetius had rekindled his anger, Drusus grasped her neck and dragged her to the table, sitting in the corner of his tent. With a quick snap, he struck her head on the wooden surface and rolled her onto her back. Marcella groaned. Drusus pulled a knife from his uniform's belt and put it to her throat and asked softly, "Now, my pet, what do you know of the messages you've carried? Tell me! Have you told anyone? Have you told Severus your secrets, too?"

Marcella's wit lost in her pain, she blurted, "You bastard, I haven't—"

"Bastard!" Drusus spat and inched the blade closer against her skin. "You bitch! You never knew your father. You're mother was a whore like you."

"I've spent my life searching for my father, and with help from a powerful person, I finally found him. I may not know the source, but why do you think I carry messages? I am more than just a slave. I too am of noble blood."

"Whose blood runs through your larcenous veins, Marcella? A wealthy farmer who performed his duty and sowed Roman seeds throughout the Empire?"

"A Roman far more noteworthy, my lord. A Roman to be reckoned with and among your kin," she whispered.

Drusus eased the knife at her throat and demanded, "You have my curiosity, especially when you speak of my kin. Tell me, or I will scar your beauty rather than taking your worthless life."

"You may regret knowing."

"I will take my chances."

"I am your slave and mistress, but Arria is my sister."

Drusus' stared passively, then scowled. "You lie," he whispered.

"Lie? What do I gain? This changes nothing. The noble and loyal husband, Senator Felix, had his youthful adventure. What he left behind was the tragedy, a woman shattered by his abandonment and a child, the victim of his Patrician world."

Drusus slowly removed the knife from Marcella's throat. "You constantly amaze me and your tenacity excites. Even now I want you, and even more for what you've just revealed. Arria is like the light, her position will shine on my advancement. You're a different prize. Your beauty rests in your darkness. And now...light and dark are mine." A low chuckle escaped his lips. "Can it be that two sisters belong to me? Did you tell Felix you're his daughter?"

"No. The trade for discovering his identity was my secrecy. I cannot betray this trust."

"This couldn't be better," Drusus gloated. "I've never been fond of my father-in-law. So, the honorable Felix, the senator concerned with welfare of the state even over his own ambitions has a past. Does he know he left a child behind?"

"I think not, but he left my mother and broke her heart."

Drusus, his mind racing, had another thought. "Who is your benefactor?"

"I am sworn to keep this secret."

"You're a woman of many mysteries...many indeed."

Lifting her skirt, Drusus commanded, "Open your bodice."

With a longing look, Marcella purposely pulled at the ties of her gown with a deliberate slowness.

Her breasts proudly exposed, Drusus gazed on her as he shed his uniform. Fully aroused, he grabbed her thighs and dragged her across the table to him.

Marcella held her breath as Drusus entered her with a fury.

"I will never...never...sell you to Aetius!" His words stumbled from his mouth between labored breaths. "I am your master. Tell me!" Drusus urged.

Despite her bruises, Marcella's body rocked in rhythm with each forceful thrust. Her legs wrapped around his waist, she tightened her hold on him. "I have only one master: Drusus," she moaned. Summoning all her beauty, she reached out to him. Drusus fell into her waiting arms. As he kissed her, she slid her hand to the knife at the edge of the table and raised it to his throat.

Drusus clenched her hips tighter. He eyed the blade at his throat, then Marcella. "You wouldn't dare," he snarled.

"A slave who kills a master is punished with death," she purred. "Even the most simple servant knows this. My concern is my beauty and welfare. I will not be beaten. You're my master, but if you ever strike me again, I will run away. I am confident, I will find someone to help and protect me."

Drusus gazed down on her. A low chuckle erupted from his throat and gently he pushed the blade from his neck. Marcella let it fall to the floor. "I will never strike you again," he said and thrusted himself deeper within her. "The only blows you'll feel from me—will be the ones ... I deliver between your legs," he grunted. "Does this please you?

"If your promise is kept."

"Then let me show you my sincerity." With a demanding kiss, he lifted her into his rugged arms and thrust until she cried out.

Marcella slid down his body to the ground. Victorious at Drusus' feet, Marcella looked up at her master. She had distracted him from what he hoped to learn. Never would she reveal her benefactor's identity or what she had imparted to Aetius; she believed the general himself was the author of the missives to Attila, and Severus knew through her the contents of the two messages. Drusus extended his hand to her. Marcella rose and wondered why Drusus was so curious about the letters, and why would he vouch for her and to whom?

"Come sister-in-law, slave, lover," Drusus teased, "there is much to do. Let Aetius play his games. I, Drusus, have a few of my own."

THE ROAD TO WILDER HONIG - WILD HONEY

"Say it again." Arria commanded sweetly. In the distance, through the grain fields, a farm house could be seen.

Garic smiled. "Vil...der ... Hoe ... nig. It means Wild Honey." Arria had tried to suppress the trill in her "r" and harden it, but her effort made him grin. No matter how well she said the name, her Latin inflection found its way into either a consonant or vowel.

"Veelderrr Hoeneeeg," Arria tried again.

"Vil...der...Hoenig." Garic repeated patiently.

Arria repeated, "Vil...der Hoe...neeg." Apparently satisfied, she nodded and flashed him a grin.

Garic decided to agree and applauded her. Up ahead the arched roof made from wattled hazel gleamed above the log walls of a house

320

under a broad blue sky.

Vodamir rode behind Arria and Garic. Next to Vodamir, Basina rested in a small, mule-drawn cart Garic borrowed from a tribesman farmer along their route. A little more than a week since their escape, Basina's condition had worsened, but they pushed on. Her fever lived in her like an unwelcome guest. At times, she was delirious and couldn't help with her healing. When she was lucid, she spoke of ointments that their travel couldn't provide.

"We must hurry if we're to save her," Vodamir entreated Garic as he moved beside him. Arria, riding beside Garic, listened attentively.

"We will keep her at my farm, Vodamir. There are too many miles between Wilder Honig and your farm. It's better that she rests." Garic spoke firmly, but with concern.

"She can make the five miles to *Silbereiche*, Silver Oaks," Vodamir insisted, glancing in Arria's direction. Returning to Garic, he said, "My mother can attend to her. We are to join Aetius after the assembly comes together. Basina needs someone who can care for her while I am gone. This morning, Luthgar said that we must meet at the tribal camp in two days."

"This is true, but Basina is seriously wounded. Travel will be slow."

"Cousin, I can make it to my farm and back to the assembly before our warriors leave to join Aetius. I know I can."

"You would be pushing it hard. Let Arria and Karas watch her." Garic glanced at Arria. "My older brother, Faramund, will stay behind. He will work the farm and protect you women. My younger brother, Tagus, will fight with us."

"My lord, I will not leave your side. I must return to Aetius," Arria said.

"No, Arria," Garic replied shaking his head. "It's far too dangerous. You might be caught in the battle."

"I must return to Aetius." Arria insisted, a stubbornness edged her tone.

"I will find him for you," Garic answered firmly. "After all, he knows I was chosen to protect you. I will be your courier."

"My lord, you cannot be my courier, you must advise Luthgar, your chieftain. You cannot do my job, nor can I do yours. Karas can attend to Basina. Her abilities for healing are far greater than mine." Arria retorted,

Vodamir, seizing the moment added, "I will only leave Basina in my mother's hands. I will take Samuel. He can ride with me. We will alternate carrying Basina on horseback and I will return in a day. Knowing she's in my mother's care will bring me peace of mind. As Basina is, it'll be hard to leave her."

"Go if you must. Bring her to your mother's healing hands. But be in Luthgar's camp with Samuel in two days, or we join Aetius without you. Is that clear?" Garic spoke gruffly.

"I will be there, Cousin. This is one fight I wouldn't miss. If I die on the battlefield my heart will find Basina's and my mother will see me in her eyes. If Basina dies as well, we will find the after world together."

"And if you live and she dies. Are you prepared for this?"

"A life without Basina has little purpose."

Vodamir's devotion touched Garic and he glanced at Arria. He knew that Vodamir's sentiments had found the same measure in Arria. Life without the other now seemed unbearable. "Go Vodamir," Garic said. "Let Samuel accompany you; but first, refresh yourselves with the noon meal my family is sure to have prepared. I will wait for you and Samuel to arrive at the Assembly of Warriors in two nights. Afterward, we will join Aetius and put an end to Attila. Franks bow to only one king—Meroveus."

"That is truth, Cousin." Vodamir reined his horse around and trotted toward Samuel.

Arria followed Vodamir's departure. "Your cousin once stood over my Chamavi attacker an axe in his hand. Then, I thought him cocky and impudent. Now, as he rides to save Basina, he has grown far nobler in my eyes." Arria reached and held Garic's hand. "I will pray for your cousin and my good friend that his woman is saved and he finds us before we leave Luthgar's camp."

"Arria your prayers are most welcome, but I don't think they will follow you to the assembly. You must stay here where it's safe. I won't be distracted by my concern for you."

Arria suppressed a response. She took a deep breath and cooed, "*Krieger*, we are tired. Let us reach your farm before the day grows late. I am hungry for some fresh bread and *your* wild honey."

Garic grinned, "As you wish, my lady. My honey is yours for the taking."

Turning her horse about Arria smiled mischievously, "Then I must go. My honey awaits me." With a quick nudge to her horse, Arria raced from Garic in the direction of the farm, with her laughter flying in the wind.

THE ROMAN CAMP

Aetius flipped the dagger with his fingers. His officers stood ready for an ensuing command, or outburst.

Aetius' thoughts jumped to Severus seated across the table from him. *What a soldier must do for his country and a beautiful spy*, he mused humorously to himself. Severus had succeeded in cajoling the coded messages from Marcella. Aetius had chosen his man wisely.

"Think Severus! *Defeat the suitor and you've won the bride.* Then later, *Plan for the wedding night.* The first message goes into Attila's camp, and the second comes out. Who's the suitor? And who's the bride? The author of the first missive, is it Drusus? Or Valentinian? I know it isn't me."

"General, if the message came from Drusus, would the bride be Arria?" Severus' brow wrinkled. "Why would Attila want Arria for a wife? Has he not plenty? Besides, her influence in Rome may be strong, but would an alliance with her house satisfy a tyrant such as Attila?"

"Drusus is a fool. He might posture for favor in the event we are defeated by Attila. Could Drusus be so despicable as to sell his wife for Attila's acceptance? No, Severus, as much as I love the Lady

323

Arria, I think she's not prize enough for our greedy warlord. I would wager that Honoria is the bride."

"But General,what would prompt Valentinian *now*–to barter his sister's hand in marriage? We will meet the Huns on the battlefield because Valentinian refused to give Attila, Honoria. What could Attila provide for the emperor that he would give such a prize? Attila's retreat? If so, why keep it a secret and from you, General?"

"All interesting questions. I wonder if Drusus has any answers? Severus, you must continue to spend time with Marcella. Let her know that I will take her from Drusus, but for now she must remain with him and be my eyes and ears. Reward her with gifts and gold— keep her happy." Aetius smirked ever so slightly then continued, "When I am ready, I will call her to me, but it would be better for now that Drusus thinks I've lost interest in her. That the demands of war take precedent over the demand for pleasure." Casually, Aetius flipped the point of the blade.

"Have you lost interest in her?" Severus asked, glancing at the dagger.

"I never was interested, other than to elicit information from her. My heart belongs to my wife. In the end, if we survive I will gladly wrench her from Drusus' arms and place her in yours. This reward will be only trifling and I hope for your sake, one you don't live to regret." A sage smile nipped the corners of Aetius' mouth. "You've served me well, Severus. I will not forget. Now get out of here and do as I ordered. I suspect Attila is the bridegroom, but who's the suitor? I have a hunch, but I must be sure."

"General, it's an honor to serve you. I shall not disappoint." Severus raised his arm in salute.

"I know you won't." Aetius waved his hand in acknowledgment and gazed at the dagger between his fingers.

WILDER HONIG

The matriarch moon held her lamp high among the stars, while crickets sang under the cover of darkness. Arria lay on a blanket a short distance from the house. Garic had spread it on the ground for her so that she might gaze at the heavens. Vodamir and Samuel were gone and Karas and Angelus had settled in the house loft for the night. Garic and his brothers made preparations for the protection of the farm and planned which supplies would best serve them in the days to come.

Lying happily on her back, Arria traced the constellations with her finger. The door to the house creaked open and Garic dropped down beside her. He gazed at her and asked, "Did you find your meal pleasing?"

"Yes, thank you. The fresh bread and honey was wonderful. The duck—roasted to perfection."

Garic moved closer and wrapped his arm around Arria's waist. "The stars of Wilder Honig are beautiful, aren't they?"

"The stars don't belong to your land. Your land belongs to them. The stars are for everyone."

"This is not so. My people believe that the stars that you see, no matter where on your land you stand, are yours. And you must fight any man or tribe that tries to steal them from you."

"Will Attila steal the stars of Wilder Honig?"

"We will burn the land, before we let Attila have all we've built. Under his rule, the stars will fade and die."

"Before you joined me, I was praying for my father. I miss him. But now, I will pray that Attila is defeated and we all live to come back to your beautiful home." Arria sighed. "You were right. I can smell the honey in the breeze."

Garic took hold of her wavy tresses. "The wild honey lies on your hair as well. It too desires to possess you." Garic kissed her.

Deep within their kiss, Arria knew that this time alone might be their last.

"*Mellitula*, my brothers sleep by the fire so that Karas and the boy might have the loft. Earlier, I made a place for us in the grain shed. We can sleep there."

Arria gazed at Garic. The silver light shadowed his high cheekbones but intensified his build and strength. She squeezed his hand. "It is my desire as well."

"Tonight will be our last time together before the battle. Tagus and I leave tomorrow."

"Krieger, you must take me with you," she insisted.

"I won't risk your life, Arria. I cannot lose you. Nor can I fight, worrying about your safety. When the battle is done, I will return for you. If we lose, you'll be safer here. If I die, Aetius will know where to find you."

Arria gasped and raised her forefinger to his lips. "Hush, you'll not die. Our destiny is together; fate has no other choice."

Garic took her fingers in his hand, kissed the tips, then her palm. "The gods have blessed me. Your courage commands me."

Arria wrapped her arms around Garic's neck. "Your bravery and our love will carry you home to me, *Krieger*. You'll return. Promise me."

"I promise. Come now the hour grows late, and I long for you." Garic rose and lifted her into his arms. "I want everything my lady has to offer."

Chapter Twenty-Five

Tempus omnia revelat
Time reveals all

ASSEMBLY OF WARRIORS
Luthgar's Camp, west of Cambria near the sea
The last days of Maius

What would you have us do?" yelled the Saxon counsel.

Garic stood and raised his voice so all might hear. "Join Aetius! We can wait no longer. If we hesitate, all of Gaul will feel the oppression and wrath of Attila's sword. Chieftains! Send messengers tonight to call all able-bodied men to join us! Together we will destroy the Hun army and their king who the Roman priests call Scourge of God."

Luthgar rose beside Garic. "My first counsel speaks wisely. Meroveus urges all tribes to follow him. What say you, Theodoric, King of the Visigoths?"

Theodoric stood. Garic had heard that Aetius had convinced Theodoric that the Huns would eventually find their way to the Visigoth Kingdom.

"I, Theodoric, pledge my life and kingdom as a faithful ally of Aetius for the safety of Gaul. My soldiers will fight for Rome against the Huns." Theodoric's wheat colored locks and aquiline nose enhanced his regal conviction.

A cheer went up from the crowded assembly. Luthgar answered, "Meroveus and Aetius will welcome you. Marcus Furius Severus who stands among us will carry the news to Aetius. The general awaits us that we may march on Aurelianum and save it from the Huns."

Tibatto, counsel to King Sangiban of the Alans, stepped forward to speak. "My lords, King Sangiban entreats you to make haste and come to the defense of Aurelianum. If General Aetius arrives with his forces in the next two days, King Sangiban will prevail."

Garic watched as Severus shouted, "I would speak" and worked his way to the open circle where he and Luthgar stood. Severus glanced harshly at Garic, but faced Tibatto. "Aetius entreats King Sangiban to hold fast. I assure you, Aetius will defeat Attila. Any loyalty shown by Rome's subjects will be rewarded."

"I will carry Aetius' words, Tribune, to my lord, Sangiban," Tibatto answered. "I must take my leave. King Sangiban awaits my counsel." Tibatto exited the hall.

The men's murmuring voices gripped the forum. Severus raised his hands high. "Noble warriors and men of Gaul! Tomorrow our long march begins. We join Aetius to drive Attila and his Huns from our land! All who desire victory say it now; for in the month of *Junius* Aurelianum will be ours!" Axe handles pounded the wooden floor and the crowd of men roared, drowning the hall in noise. Each hastened to prepare for the journey to Aurelianum and the inevitable encounter with the Hun hordes.

The hall now emptied of all except Garic and Luthgar, Severus swung to face Garic. Garic felt Luthgar move closer to his side. Garic had confided in Luthgar the grim details of his capture by the Huns and the part played by Severus. Garic had also revealed that King Meroveus had enlisted his service, but on this matter shared no reason. Garic assured Luthgar with a glance and a few words in Frankish that his reckoning with Severus would not be violent.

"Lords, please excuse me. My wife awaits me." Luthgar's eyes betrayed a slight twinkle. "There are some last minute details we need to discuss."

Severus nodded. Garic watched Luthgar leave, then shifted his gaze toward Severus. Severus met his glance and frowned. "I cannot say that I relish this moment. Much has gone between us. Arria is like a sister and Marcian was like a brother. I could never accept her being with you anymore than I can accept her being with Drusus."

Garic flinched amazed at Severus' candor. "Who would be acceptable in your eyes? Yourself?"

"I dare say, I think I know her best, but another woman commands my heart. Arria just needs time. A good man would come along. One who would keep her from all this madness."

Garic's eyes narrowed. "Say what you really believe, a better man than—a barbarian."

"Yes," Severus answered.

Garic shot Severus a wry grin and turned to leave.

"Wait!" Severus called harshly. "I need to set one thing right with you."

Garic turned back.

"I understood, despite Drusus' orders, I was to hand you and your cousin over to the Huns along with a message. I knew to make it convincing and the added reward of gold made it even more appealing."

"Some men find a satisfaction in beating and selling men they hate."

"I cannot forget barbarians killed Marcian."

"And because of this you hate me...and Vodamir? You almost killed my cousin. That wasn't the plan I knew. Weren't you concerned for Arria's safety? How could we help her if we were dead?"

"I was lost in my drunkenness that night. Before we left on the mission, Arria and I quarreled. It ended badly."

Garic scowled and glanced away.

"But... I came to say that it wasn't my intention to beat you both so badly. I don't like you, but for Arria's sake—"

"You will tolerate me."

"Something like that." Severus looked toward the entrance and said, "I must get back to Aetius, he's expecting me. Tell me if you will, where's Arria now? Is she here?"

"No. At my farm with Karas and the boy, Angelus."

"I imagine she'll be safe there."

"Arria's in good hands." Garic paused, then added, "If I die take Arria home."

"And if I perish as well, who will help her?"

"My woman is strong, she'll come and bury us both."

An ironic smile broke across Severus' lips. "It seems, First Counsel, you do know Arria after all."

AETIUS' CAMP
Month of Junius

Marcella believed in the old goddesses. To rise in a world of men she had called on the powers of Isis and Sikmeht. From their ancient magic, Marcella stole a man's energy and buried it deep inside of her, his essence reborn into a power she made her own, nurturing her hate and giving her strength.

Only her hate for Arria made her stronger. Arria had two weaknesses, the long-hair called Garic and their father, the honorable Senator Felix.

Marcella reclined in her tent tucked away from the afternoon's heat. Fanning herself, she contemplated her revenge on Arria—if of course, Arria were to survive Attila's camp—when a summons arrived for her sent by Drusus. She departed at once and entered the legate's tent. Informed by the guards that Drusus was unexpectedly called away, she informed them that she would wait. A lamp burned and papers laid strewn across his desk. Feeling fatigued, Marcella rested on his couch and looked around. Several swords hung on hooks slung over the frame, while his armor rested in an open chest where several tunics and a toga draped its wooden sides. A leather pouch, plain and unassuming rested behind the chest with a rolled parchment peeking beneath the flap.

Unable to take her eyes from it, Marcella looked out the entrance to ensure no one was coming. The guards knew not to bother her. Aware that Drusus could return at any moment, she crouched beside the pouch and quickly opened it. She lifted the parchment, delicately and observed the broken seal. She was in luck. With a determined ease, she unrolled it. In a bold Latin, the missive simply read, *A defeat will leave you victorious.* It was signed with the letters P.M.. Marcella's brows raised and she grinned. A sudden shift to attention by the guards forced her to quickly return the letter to the pouch. Drusus entered and found her with a fan in her hand and eating a pear.

"It's nice to know you answer my summons so quickly. You must be bored, Marcella. No one to amuse you? Oh, I forget. The lovesick Severus is away."

"My lord, your jealousy is unrelenting."

"All my drives are unrelenting, which brings me to a most important topic. The Visigoths, Franks and many more will join us against Attila. The march on Aurelianum commences tomorrow. Aetius will be choosing his battle commanders and laying his strategy. He likes to keep his maneuvers close to him, until right before the battle. Only a few of his field commanders are privy to his plans. Go to Severus when he returns and see what you can learn. With him it shouldn't be difficult. I also have reconsidered my attitude toward selling you to Aetius, at least I will pretend I have. This should guarantee that in this small victory he might indulge you with information."

"You seem smug today, my lord. What has precipitated your satisfaction. I thought soldiers before a battle were most often sober?"

"Let's just say that I've received some good news."

"Anything you'd like to share?"

"Not at this time. Now go my vixen. Use your charms and bring me information that in the end will benefit us both."

Marcella laid down her fan, rose and kissed his lips. "I will do my best."

"Your best is always sublime, Marcella. I will await you."

Severus rode into Aetius' camp late in the afternoon. "General, the Assembly of Warriors is united," Severus reported with satisfaction. "They've begun their march as we speak. In less than a fortnight, they will join you. I also met your courier on the road about mid morning. He informed me that Attila has just laid siege to Aurelianum."

"My scouts brought the news of Attila's army in the early morning. With the tribes joining us, victory favors us!" Aetius declared. "Get some rest, Severus. I will need you. At first light tomorrow, we march."

"Yes sir!" Severus replied, raising his arm in salute and departed. After corralling his horse, Severus walked through the camp. He attempted to shake some of the dust from his cloak when a voice rang out just beyond him.

He paused. Marcella sauntered toward him. She smiled enchantingly. "I think a warm bath would be in store for such a weary rider."

"A warm bath given by a beautiful woman would be even better."

"Then I won't disappoint you. Join me in my tent in an hour and I will wash away your fatigue."

His hand on his sword hilt and his helmet cradled in his arm, Severus frowned. "You seem very pleased with yourself. What games have you been playing while I've been gone?"

"Don't fret. Nothing serious. I have some interesting as well as good news that I am eager to share with you."

"Don't be coy, my pet, tell me now."

"I'd rather have you at my advantage," Marcella teased and turned on her heel. Glancing over her shoulder, she smiled provocatively and walked away.

"*A defeat will leave you victorious.* An interesting message," Aetius mused. He walked the perimeter of the field camp with his tribune, while two guards followed behind them. "It seems that Drusus is connected to this intrigue after all." Aetius stopped and rested his hand on his tribune's shoulder. "You have served me well, Severus. Does Marcella suspect that you're reporting to me?"

"No. She must never discover I've betrayed her."

"In the end, you will have helped the Empire and freed her. I will have my way with Drusus. He'll have no choice but to sell her and then God protect you, Severus, Marcella will be yours!" Aetius said and shook his head. "This missive is indeed perplexing. There is plotting against me and I can only believe that PM is Petronius Maximus. That greedy bastard won't be happy until he's Emperor."

"But General, Maximus lives so lavishly. His estates are numerous and his patronage is extensive. Why would he want the burden of being emperor?"

"Maximus aims to thwart me because he envies the power I wield. My drive is to preserve the Empire. His is to preserve his name in history."

"A point well made, General. When he erected a statue of himself in Trajan's forum, I did think it ostentatious."

"Indeed, serving as consul, then Prefect of Rome wasn't enough to satisfy his power lusting appetite. I know he poisons Valentinian against me. He must be the person behind the letters to Attila."

"I also learned that for a time Marcella was a slave in his household. She told me he helped her in a most vital matter."

"What could be so important for a concubine slave? Was she with child?"

"I don't think so. She was reluctant to speak about it, but I had the feeling that with Maximus' help they both gained in some way."

"I'd wager that the two together against anyone is more than frightening...it's dangerous."

Nodding in agreement, Severus added, "My dark beauty is formidable and ... ."

"Severus!" Aetius suddenly interrupted, "it's clear to me now!" His eyes gleaming, he continued, "The first missive, *Defeat the suitor and you've won the bride* finds its way into Attila's camp with your loyal assistance. The second missive, *Plan for the wedding night* finds its way out of Attila's camp, via Marcella, and most likely to Drusus who sends it to Petronius Maximus through the legion's messenger service. With anonymous couriers and Marcella as an intermediary, Drusus is protected. Nothing can lead to him, that is unless, you're dealing with an *intermediary* who's ambitious, self-serving and has a weakness for a certain tribune. All this time, I kept asking myself who's the bride? Now I think I know—It's Gaul. The *bride* is Gaul. Maximus wants Attila to defeat me, *the suitor*, and will convince Valentinian that Gaul is one less unmanageable territory to maintain. How perfect. Unlike the late Emperor Theodosius, the Emperor Marcian, refuses to pay Attila tribute. With a victory here and Gaul as his prize, Attila might turn back toward the Eastern Empire to exact revenge for Valerius Marcian's lack of respect and abandon any thoughts of Ravenna and Rome. Valentinian no longer would be dependent on my military expertise. How clever of Maximus."

"Emperor Marcian's experience as a senator has helped to make him into a prudent leader. He'll surround himself with the right allies. Attila would be sorely tested." Severus looked toward the east, their direction for this new day, and his voice softened. "It's sad that Lucius Marcian, couldn't have been by his father's side. Life would have been different for him and Arria."

"I've almost forgotten." Their walk finished, Aetius mounted the horse that his guard held ready for him, and waited for Severus who mounted as well. Aetius tugged gently on his horse's reins. "Senator Felix is beside himself with worry and is demanding to know how his daughter fares. Severus, send a dispatch right away. Let him know that you've had word that she is safe and under the protection of the Franks."

"As you wish, General."

"Now make haste, then meet me at the front of the army where I will lead our soldiers to Aurelianum." Having given Severus his orders, Aetius kicked his horse and cantered to Rome's battle standard.

CATALAUNUM

A gnawing hunger clenched Garic's stomach as he ruffled through his knapsack for the last remaining morsel of bread he'd taken from Luthgar's camp. Garic wondered if Arria was watching the same stars as he and longed to feel her in his arms. Like most men before battle, his mind traveled to thoughts of home. Would the land prosper if he weren't there to help tend it? Would his elder brother marry. Would they raise children who would carry on and nurture their land? Garic glanced at his younger brother beside him already fast asleep. He always said that Tagus could sleep through anything, even a battle right at his feet.

Garic stretched out on his blanket and let his mind drift to the army of lights spanning the night sky. He had traveled with King Theodoric to Aurelianum. Luthgar had left the Assembly of Warriors before the rest with most of the Franks and ordered that Garic stay behind to secure any final camp preparations.

Garic and the allied barbarians reached Aetius in the late afternoon ten miles outside the walled city of Aurelianum. Attila saw the cloud of dust raised by Aetus' army and shrewdly moved north. Aetius pursued.

Now, Meroveus and his Franks reached Attila's rearguard. Garic readjusted himself, propped up the blanket beneath his head and closed his eyes. In the distance, he could hear men yelling and he listened as the sounds came closer. He jumped to his feet, alerted. He grabbed his sword and moved toward a larger campfire among the Visigoths to investigate the disturbance. "What news?" Garic asked several men grouped around the riders. His concern was especially for Vodamir, Samuel and Luthgar.

"Soldiers are straggling in. The Franks caught Attila's heels and attacked him," one man replied. He was a Visigoth with a wine pouch in his hand. "More are headed this way. Most are on foot and slowed down by the dark. If you're hoping to find anyone, Long-Hair, stay close to the fires. That's where I would head after a battle."

Garic nodded and moved forward through the gathering crowd. He began searching among the newly arrived men. Garic cursed himself for having stayed behind. He never went into a battle without Vodamir and Luthgar. Together they always fought in a triangle of strength. What had happened, today? Was Meroveus so zealous?

"Do you know Vodamir? Luthgar?" Garic asked each man he encountered. He headed toward a large burning fire in the distance, where he found Amo on the ground, his leg torn and weakly bandaged. "Amo, man, it's good to see you alive!" Garic cried, kneeling beside his fellow Wespe.

Amo grimaced, "You're the best thing I've seen today. I'd kiss you from the joy, if I weren't in such pain."

"Where are the rest? Vodamir, Luthgar and Samuel, were they with you?"

"They were. We got caught in the stream. The Gepids fight strong in water, while the damn Huns shot down on us from the crest of the bank. What saved us was the sunset in their eyes. So many bodies filled the water that I couldn't move around them." Amo groaned and tried to move his leg. His words forced between breaths he continued, "Then, I took a bastard Hun arrow in my leg. I fell back under the water, but someone pulled me to the shore. I don't know who. I woke up with my face half in mud, the brothers Bede and Muric, dead, beside me." Amo's voice trailed away, he spat, then asked, "Have you got any wine? I am in pain."

"I will bring you some." Garic ran back to his brother and woke him. "Tagus, rouse yourself! I need you to watch Amo, while I look for Vodamir and the rest." Tagus rose sleepily to his feet and followed. Garic grabbed his blanket and his wine pouch and returned to Amo. Garic poured some wine on Amo's wound and listened as his friend complained that Garic not waste too much of this precious libation on his injury. "You will be fine with an attitude like that. Tagus will watch over you. I must try and find the rest."

Garic searched any horse or traveler who walked toward a fire. Once or twice he called out, but only a few laughs met his ears. Further into the camp, but closer to the stream caught in the battle between the Roman vanguard and Hun rearguard forces, Garic wandered. By a row of poplars, he saw a fire burning brightly and several women bent over pots brewing with the smell of soup. One woman was speaking sweetly and dressing the arm of a man slumped against her breast. Garic cautiously approached the woman, helping the wounded man. Vodamir beseeched this kind mistress to take care with his injury.

"I knew no Hun could kill you if it meant a woman to coddle you on her breast!" Garic said dryly, and placed his hands on his hips in exasperated relief.

"I knew nothing would keep you from finding us. So I thought I'd rest in these lovely arms for a while."

"Us?" Garic questioned.

Vodamir nodded to his far right. "Draw closer to that bunch huddled over there, fast asleep."

Garic walked up to the ring of men, one flat on the ground snoring, the others leaning in one way or another on the other. Luthgar's head rested on Samuel's leg while Samuel's arm crossed on top of Denis's arm who lay beside Rudiger whose breathing was labored and slow. There was no sign of Theudebert the close companion of the brothers Bede and Muric.

Garic returned to Vodamir and said sadly, "I saw Amo. The brothers are dead. Where's Theudebert?"

"I don't know. But he's never far from the brothers."

"In the morning, before battle, we will look for them. Are you in pain?"

"It's only a small wound. A Chamavi bastard's sword caught my arm as he was falling down to his death. It's probably no coincidence. I think they all know how much I hate them!" Vodamir scowled and his pretty nurse finished tying the cloth around his arm. Vodamir landed a kiss on her cheek and she pushed Vodamir away. Vodamir rose and walked a short distance with Garic. "I will sleep here tonight with the men. Come to us in the morning."

"How was it?" Was all Garic could say.

"Brutal. They'll not be easy to defeat. When we came upon them we could see a slim column of smoke rising in the distance over the ridge. Some of the scouts rode among us on their way to find Aetius. They claimed it was Attila and his shamans burning the entrails of

337

cattle to predict the outcome of the battle. In the morning when we search for the bodies, you will see just a little of what is to come. I hope that tomorrow night we will be as fortunate as we are now."

"Thor and Wodan are with us, Vodamir. And I will ask Arria's God to protect us as well. This would please her."

"I said words over the tokens my mother gave me before I left. One is my boar's tusk for strength and the other is Basina's ribbon, to tie us together." Looking into the dark ring around the camp fire, Vodamir mused, "It's frightening that Basina's life hangs on the whim of the Gods. My mother promised to do all she can to save her. She knows I love Basina." Vodamir looked at his wound and gently placed his hand on the bandage. "As both sides turned away from the fight, the light waning, I stumbled to the bank of the stream to cross. I gazed at the water and believed I saw Basina's face floating beneath the surface. I rushed in. As I bent to touch her vision, one last arrow flew over my head. I lost my balance and fell into the water—I bumped against a corpse. It was...a boy. They both saved my life...Basina and the boy.

"Cousin," Garic said softly. "It's best we put aside the thoughts of our women. Tomorrow we fight as Franks."

"That is the talk of a brave man." Vodamir said with a hollow tone, but a despondent edge curled around his words. "Tonight, I want to dream of Basina. Let my final hours in this world be wrapped in sleep haunted by my Queen of the Healers."

Garic understood Vodamir's struggle. Garic said kindly, "Cousin, my love is as deep. Arria is always with me."

Vodamir gazed at the fire and picked up a stone and tossed it into the flames. "Freya will protect us. She understands the hearts of lovers."

"Then we will paint Freya's heart and Thor's hammer on our shields. We will stripe our faces with lines of red ocher and drink from my aurochs' horn. Together we fight, die or survive. Perhaps Valhalla awaits us both."

Vodamir spouted, "I am your brother, but I refuse to give that bitch, Hel, one more man. I want to live, and I will fight to find my way back to Basina."

"Tomorrow, I stand beside you, Cousin. Let us send Attila and his bastard Huns to their underworld, wherever it is!"

"Not far from ours, I'd wager," Vodamir said, his cocky smile spreading across his lips.

Garic laughed, his cousin was quick. "You're probably right, but I don't want to find out!"

Vodamir grimaced with a sudden pain and touched his arm. "Neither do I," he sighed and moved to lie before the fire.

Garic watched him for a moment. Then he found his way to Tagus and Amo and stretched beneath the ceiling filled with a million stars.

A FOREST ROAD

"Lady Arria, we left at first light three days ago and the sun will soon set." Karas spoke trying to hide the worry in her voice. The horse she rode blinked its long lashes at an annoying fly that Karas promptly swatted away.

"You need not worry. Faramund cautioned us not to stray from this road. The night without a fire was a bit cool even for *Junius*, but we persevered, didn't we? We're almost to Aurelianum. I wish Faramund could have brought us all the way, but we wouldn't want to bring Angelus too close to danger. I just couldn't do this alone. Don't worry, we'll arrive unharmed."

"Mistress, you seem so sure."

Arria unclasped her cloak and laid it over her saddle. A quiet smile broke on her lips. "Years ago...my dying husband promised to watch over me from heaven. I know his word is true."

"The battlefield is brutal and not a place for a lady of status."

Arria frowned. "I searched a battlefield in Germania for my wounded husband and held him dying in my arms. I have seen the battlefield. I am ready to travel through the underworld, if needed, to find Garic."

A rise in the path loomed into view as they rounded a bend. With a quick nudge to her horse, she broke into a canter. They rode into the clearing and up a hill. Aurelianum sprawled in the distance with riders and foot travelers going in and coming out of the walled city. Roman soldiers guarded its massive gates.

A relieved sigh escaped Arria's lips, "Aurelianum at last, and all looks well! Maybe the battle is over and Attila is gone. Come, let's find our men."

Patches of barley stretched before them and a blanket of wildflowers rose to greet them as they descended a hill just before the city walls. They reined their horses several yards from the sentries who stood alerted at their approach. Arria asked, "Where is Aetius' army?"

"My ladies, where do you come from? It is unwise to ride alone," answered the older guard.

"I'm a Roman envoy. We are looking for Aetius and his army." Arria replied impatiently.

"They are in pursuit of the Huns."

"Who commands here?"

"Legate Drusus."

Arria looked at Karas. "Please bring me to him, I am Lady Arria, his wife."

Arria walked into the commander's quarters with Karas behind her. Drusus' slave approached her and bowed. "Betto, tell your master his wife is here."

Looking around, Arria spied a doorway that led to an atrium. She walked toward the entrance and was met by Drusus rushing through. "My God, Arria! You're alive," Drusus said, and embraced her.

"God has been kind," Arria replied and pushed away. "I stand here, because of Aetius and others."

"Arria, your judgment is harsh. I would do anything to save my—"

"My lord, where is the army? I must find Aetius."

"Why such haste?"

"It's a matter of state I cannot share."

"Not even with your husband?"

"I have no husband in you. Please, time is of the utmost importance. I need an escort to the army." Arria gave Drusus her most contemptuous look.

"You speak foolishly, but you're in luck. My command here was only until Legate Brucerius arrived. He rode in this morning. If it's Aetius you must see, then I will escort you." Drusus stretched out his arms to her. "Come now. Put your anger aside and welcome your husband with a kiss."

Arria bristled, "How dare you! When diplomatic relations with the Huns began to wander, you left me without any attempt to save me. I would rather kiss the backside of an ass! Now escort me to Aetius, so we might arrive before battle is engaged."

"Careful Arria, you need me," Drusus warned with a raised finger. "Deploying a garrison of men and abandoning my fort required a priority. A commander must make tough choices."

"There is no love between us. It's not a marriage, just a mistake."

"I heard the barbarian helped you escape. If lowering yourself is what you want, then so be it. A divorce will cost you money. But a union with the Frank will cost your reputation and good name. He's tarnished you for me. There are other women of status I can easily find."

"Then we're in agreement. Can we leave?"

"Don't worry, Arria. You will find all that you've bargained for... and more."

Chapter Twenty-Six

Qualis vita, finis ita
As the life, so the end

THE FIELDS OF CATALAUNUM
Month of Junius, AD 451

To Garic the camp moved like a living, breathing being. Soldiers marched in unison, while tribal warriors gathered and gazed at the flat plains stretched before them. Women, some with children, followed their men. Horses and animals, supply wagons and siege engines all moved into position. This flow and hum charged the air and brilliant summer day.

Garic finished folding his blanket. Time was etching this moment on history and this plain called Catalaunum. This ordeal would be long and bloody, Garic sensed.

Today, on the battlefield, King Meroveus and his Franks would support Aetius. Garic, Vodamir, Luthgar and the Wespe would stand among them, their courage sharp and their fear dispelled.

"We better find a supply wagon with water, I am thirsty and my pouch is empty," Garic said, approaching Vodamir with Tagus and a limping Amo.

Vodamir sat by the fire and nodded his agreement. "I won't drink from that bloody stream," he spat. Beside Vodamir sat Denis, Rudiger, Samuel and Luthgar. They greeted Garic and Tagus. Rudiger hugged Amo with such strength that his son almost lost his balance.

"How will you fight?" Rudiger asked the determined Amo who

stood on both feet but winced.

"From a horse, and demons take the man who tries to knock me off!"

"And if you find yourself on your feet?" Rudiger questioned.

"Then I will prop myself against the men fighting beside me," Amo fired back, a stubborn resolve in his eyes.

"The men fallen beneath you will drag you down. Leave this fight, son."

"Father, I cannot. I fight to live, not die."

Rudiger looked at Garic who felt compelled to answer Rudiger's plea. "Amo, promise us, the moment your advantage is lost, you'll move to the rear and help protect the women and children."

A grimace escaped Amo's lips. "Only if all of our men have dismounted or been brought down."

"What about Vodamir?" Samuel chimed in, pointing to his arm.

"A scratch," Vodamir replied, his manner flippant. "My sword will send many Huns to Valhalla to meet real warriors!"

Luthgar barked, "Let us prepare. Word has spread, Aetius waits for Attila to start this battle. Samuel, did you and Denis find the brothers or Theudebert?"

"Vodamir led us to the brothers, but Theudebert was not among them. We buried them and took their weapons. We found Muric's sword still in his hand and Bede's beneath him."

"If we don't survive, who will bring home their swords and tell their stories?" growled Rudiger.

"We must see tomorrow for their sake," Garic answered bluntly.

Luthgar broke the spell. "We chatter like women. King Meroveus has called all Franks to join him." A horn's low bellow drew their attention. "Meroveus is calling his troops." Luthgar solemnly extended his arm. One by one, the men covered their chief's hand with theirs. "My honor is to lead you. Whether our shields protect us or carry our fallen bones home, once again, they will rest beside our doors—free from the Huns who would kick them down."

"Victory!" they cried, and without another word, they mounted their horses. Axes, javelins, and round shields painted with stars and crescent moons hung from their saddles. Garic donned his helmet with a *Thor's Hammer* cross. They rode toward Aetius' left flank, their long hair, banners in the wind.

"Mistress, I am afraid we'll never find them," Karas lamented, trailing behind wearied by their journey.

"Hurry," Arria urged. "Soldiers are forming. We must find where the Franks are positioned. Perhaps with Theodoric and his Visigoths. Quickly, Karas! That horn calls the women and children from the field and behind the lines for safety." Arria stopped a young Roman soldier driving a supply wagon and asked, "Can you tell me where the Franks will fight?"

"Lady, I was ordered to bring my wagon behind the center forces to retrieve the wounded. General Aetius will command the right wing. That's all I know."

Disappointed but not discouraged, Arria moved through the crowd of men. She peered in every direction for the long golden hair she knew so well, fighting back her tears. Overwhelmed by the sea of warriors and camp followers, she stopped and turned in a circle. She pushed through the throng and up an incline. With Karas close behind, Arria skirted a wall of soldiers, standing in a rough formation, and suddenly found herself beside Marcella and Severus seated on their horses. Marcella and Severus turned toward the movement next to them and stared. Arria stared back.

Marcella caught her breath and sneered, "Well, it seems the princess has returned."

"I am your mistress. Address me as such!" Arria commanded angrily, but inwardly cringed. Now was not the time for quarrels.

"I have no mistress or master," Marcella gloated. She looked down at Arria. "I am no longer a slave; I am free."

Arria could not contain her astonishment. "Drusus released you?"

Marcella smiled and glanced at Severus. "Mistress Arria does not believe me. Tell her."

Severus frowned but answered, "It's true Arria. Drusus gave Marcella to Aetius who gave her to me. I freed her. We will marry."

Marcella's grin even larger, she leaned toward Arria "Just think, I am now a part of your happy family. Is not Severus like a brother to you? Now, I can be your sister!"

Severus barked, "Enough, Marcella!"

The sea of men moving forward interrupted Arria's indignation. She looked around.

"Get yourselves behind the lines!" Severus instructed the women. "Settle your differences after Attila is defeated, but now we must all try to survive. If the battle turns against us, move south with the remaining forces. The consequences for those who linger is slavery, rape, or death."

Severus grabbed Marcella to him and kissed her with a tenderness that confused Arria. She watched Marcella return Severus' affection.

Severus looked at Arria. "Fate has graced me with one final gaze upon the two women I love most. Pray that I return. If I do, I promise to protect and serve you both; hopefully, you will extinguish your hatred for one another."

Tears burned behind Arria's smile and she nodded. Marcus Furius Severus called to his centurion who called to the soldiers under Severus' command. The men urged their horses forward. Severus shot Marcella and Arria a last look, then pressed his horse forward and followed the column.

Arria shifted her attention to the now free slave and followed her gaze. Marcella watched Severus' back armored in leather strapping and bronze disappear over the crest of the hill. Marcella's eyes lingered only a moment, then she looked down at Arria and said, "Now I sit above and you stand below. Shall I offer you a ride to safety?"

"Offer me what you will, but I will not take it. You've bewitched Severus, but I know who you are."

"If you knew your anguish would be even more complete, but

there is time enough for that." Then turning her horse downhill, her haunting laugh trailed into the din already forming around them.

The battle was brewing. Warriors pouring over the hill filled the void left by Severus and Marcella. Arria fought against being pushed along, but it was impossible. A Roman soldier grabbed Arria and Karas by their arms and yelled, "Get down this hill or you will die!" Arria clung to Karas as they pushed their way to the safety of the camp.

"If we destroy Attila's horses, we can win," Aetius assured Theodoric and Sangiban.

"Are you certain?" Theodoric glanced at his son, Thorismund.

Aetius surveyed the barbarian warriors and Roman officers before him and spoke with conviction, "As a boy, I lived with the Huns. I know them. Their strength lies in their horse-archers. They attack with a fury of arrows, regroup, and attack again."

"Our men fight on foot. Can we withstand this assault?" Thorismund asked, his tone grim.

Aetius leaned over the parchment map covering the table. A crude sketch revealed the field and the Roman and Hun fortifications. "This battle belongs to whoever is strong enough to take it. We will force them to dismount!"

Theodoric's staid expression grew to a grin. "What is your plan, General?"

Aetius tapped his finger on a curved line. "I ordered my soldiers to prepare the hill. A hidden trench, fireballs of hay and my archers await. Theodoric, your men will press their left flank. I will swing my right flank around them. If they break through the middle and your Alans, Sangiban, our fireballs and archers will greet their riders. We will drive Attila back to his circle of wagons, and lay siege to his army. At all cost...Attila must not take the hill."

"A worthy strategy. My Visigoths stand ready."

Sangiban nodded. "The Alans stand ready as well."

"God's mercy, we all drink a cup together at battle's end,"

Theodoric extended his hand. Aetius and Sangiban covered it with theirs.

"Victory against Attila!" Aetius boomed. The officers and warriors around him echoed his battle cry.

THE FIELDS OF CATALAUNUM
The height of battle

Smoke floated over the battlefield. Garic inhaled and coughed. His throat and nostrils burned. The battle raged. He and Vodamir took to foot as ordered by Luthgar. Scores of men lay before them impaled by flaming arrows and fiery debris hurled from siege engines. Attila's forces had pierced the center column held by the Alans.

Warriors battled hand to hand around bodies fallen like broken trees. Garic and Vodamir fought their way through the carnage. Riders lay crushed beneath their vulnerable mounts; others lay hacked to death, their blank stares beset by flies.

Garic and Vodamir pressed forward. Garic's arm ached as his sword, swung again.

"Move toward the hill!" Garic shouted to Vodamir.

Inch by inch and back to back they moved cautiously toward the hill. All around, men fell as Garic and Vodamir continued to hack, sever and slash across the battleground.

A smoldering ball of hay resting at the base of the hill lifted with a sudden shift in the wind. Garic waved his shield at the smoky cloud and trampled past it, but stumbled upon a horse's head. He gazed down the length of the fallen mount and blinked. Propped against the horse's belly, the tribune Serverus slumped with a groan as Drusus thrust his javelin deeper.

"For stealing Marcella," Drusus screamed, then plunged the spear again.

Severus feebly attempted to remove the shaft as blood trickled from the side of his mouth, "Love her," fell from his lips in a final gasp. Drusus stabbed Severus one more time and spat on him. He turned to leave, but Garic blocked his way. Revenge brimming in his eyes, Drusus growled, "A perfect battle. Today, all my enemies will die, even Aetius, if I am lucky."

"A bold statement—coward!" Garic shouted back.

Drusus drew his sword as he spoke and lifted his shield. "A *coward* who's going to kill you. This one will be for Arria, my *wife.*" His lip curled and he lunged at Garic like a cat. Garic stopped it with his shield, rolled to his right and sprang to his feet. Garic felt a movement beside him. A quick glance revealed Vodamir. "Leave me! Drusus is mine!" Garic raged.

Garic bore down on Drusus. The air rang with the clash of his steel upon Drusus' sword, and the thudding blows upon their shields. A strange invisibility cloaked them from the battle as they pushed on, exhausted. Blade against blade, their eyes locked like the weapons in their hands.

In the distance, a horn sounded, calling the battle's end. Those who fought stopped, while some made their last killing blow. Garic would not relent. Parched with thirst and sweat pouring down his face, he pushed Drusus with all his strength.

Drusus tumbled backward and brushed against a Hun pony, its dead master at its feet. A moment's clarity flashed through Drusus' eyes. Spent, wet, and dripping, he smirked at Garic. "You son-of-a-bitch, I will kill you another day!" he shouted, then leaped onto the renegade horse and made his way up the hill away from their private battleground.

Garic turned and sprinted a few feet behind him. He crouched beside the horse, pillowing Severus' corpse. Just beneath the animal's fore leg, a bow rested on top of a smashed quiver. Garic wrenched the bow free and dropped to one knee. He snatched an arrow, nocked it and aimed at the fleeing Drusus. His weakened hand unsure, he shot the arrow into a dead man's body. A dark hate rose in Garic, crushing his fatigue. He quickly drew a second arrow. This time, he aimed the bow higher, drew the bow string with all his might and released it. The arrow sailed strong, but flew off course hit by a sudden breeze. A cry burst from Garic's lungs. He snatched the final arrow and struggled to his feet like a drunken man determined to fight. Almost to the hill's crest, Drusus wound his way through the maze of bodies. Garic drew a steady breath and aimed again. He would kill Drusus and free Arria. For an instant, he hesitated, but a steely resolve clenched him, and he let go of the arrow. It sailed swift and straight and buried itself in Drusus' back just moments before he reached the top. The Commander of Cambria slumped forward and his horse climbed onto the crest and disappeared from Garic's sight.

Garic dropped his bow and gazed after Drusus, his mind clear of any thought.

A sharp thrust stabbed his side and a sudden warmth filled its center. Startled, Garic looked down into the face of Marcella.

"You've killed the only man I ever loved," Marcella hissed, her eyes crazed.

"Drusus," Garic mumbled confused.

"You lying dog! You stole Severus from me! Now, I will steal you from her! Unwed widows we will both be with cold lonely nights and—"

Garic grabbed Marcella's wrist and pulled the knife from his side.

"Get away from him!" rang out from behind them as Marcella struggled free. Arria ran up with Karas beside her. Garic sank to his knees. His vision fading, he dropped the knife and fell on his back.

Arria screamed and stumbled to Garic's side. His eyes closed. His breath was shallow, but he lived. Arria ripped a piece of cloth from her hem and covered his wound.

Marcella dropped to one knee, snatched the knife fallen beside Garic and raised it to strike him again. Arria cried out and reached to stop her.

Karas, sprang between her mistress and Marcella, knocking the Egyptian backward and falling on top of her.

"Bitch," Marcella screamed and stabbed the knife into the soft hollow of Karas' neck, then shoved her backward onto the ground.

"No!" Arria shouted, scrambling toward Karas.

A desperate gaze welled in Karas' eyes as blood spread across the collar of her dress.

A vision of her servant's life seized Arria: Karas auctioned for solidi and silver, Samuel's happiness found in her company, her kisses on Angelus' forehead, her loyal attention. The images flickered before Arria like fireflies at sunset.

Karas' eyes fluttered once, then fixed.

"She attacked me," Marcella rasped, stumbling to her feet and dropping the knife.

Grief-stricken, Arria shouted, "You whore! You've killed her!"

Marcella's eyes narrowed. She turned and fled down the hill toward the camp, her hair flying in the wind.

Arria bolted after Marcella, knife in hand. An avenging angel, Arria shortened the distance and caught Marcella who swung a fist wildly in the air. Arria ducked and lunged, knocking her to the ground. Marcella fell across several bodies and hit her head on a slain man's helmet. It left her dazed but trying to rise. Arria straddled the Egyptian and pinned her elbows with her knees. Marcella made a futile attempt to kick, but Arria pressed the blade to her throat and yelled, "Don't move!" Karas' death and Garic's wound pounded through her temples and she inched the blade a little deeper. "How does this feel, Marcella? How does it feel!" she cried a second time, yanking Marcella's hair.

Marcella's eyes showed fear, but quickly turned defiant. "How does it feel to lose someone you love?" she spat back. "You're the spoiled daughter of a senator. What do you know of pain? Severus was my life and Garic stole it. Murder befits your family of jackals. Your father is a killer as—"

"Stop your babbling!" Arria cried, and tugged Marcella's long strands harder. "You know *nothing* of my father. I should kill you for Garic and Karas and tainting my father's name." Tears ran down Arria's face and she pressed the blade deeper.

Marcella caught her breath. "I know your father. So does my

mother. I am your sister!" she hissed.

Arria blinked, but hid her confusion. She lowered her face inches from Marcella and snapped, "You're an evil witch who lies!"

"Ask your precious father. He was stationed in Egypt...a young tribune. He loved my mother, then left her." Marcella stared at Arria with contempt. "Lost in grief, she gave me to temple priests who sold me into slavery. Kill me if you will...but in truth, I am your half-sister."

Arria read the gloating pride in Marcella's eyes and felt a hatred rise inside of her, but she could not murder, and Garic's plight beckoned her. She released Marcella's arms and staggered to her feet. Marcella sat up and rubbed the life into her limbs. Did Marcella lie? Arria's emotions robbed her of words. She lifted her torn and bloodied skirt and hurried up the hill toward Garic.

"It's true, Arria!" Marcella shouted after her. "I am your sister—your blood!"

Arria turned back. "If you know what's good for you, especially if Aetius is alive, you will leave now," she yelled. She found Vodamir, Luthgar, and Amo by Garic's side. "Does he still live?" she asked breathless, kneeling beside Garic.

"Barely," Vodamir answered. "We must move him to the camp. The light grows dim. He needs care and a fire to warm him."

"The Roman physicians will help us," Arria replied.

The men nodded, but looked depleted and shocked. They lifted Garic and started toward the camp.

On the ground, Samuel cradled Karas in his lap, lightly stroking her hair. Stunned and weary, he fought his anguish, but when Arria knelt beside him, he sobbed.

"Arria...the boy," Samuel managed. "How will I tell Angelus his mother is ... dead? She was his world. He was the first to rise in the morning and wake her. He loved to tease her and touch her hair. So many things. I cannot..."

"Tell him his mother has gone to heaven. The Lord has called her to Him, but his father, *Samuel*, lives." Arria's hand rested on his arm.

Her other hand held Karas' limp fingers. "She'll live in our hearts and memories."

Samuel pulled Karas closer and rested his cheek against her golden hair.

Arria rose and hurried to find Garic.

Aetius looked through the parted flaps of his tent. Blazing torches lined the entrance path, and a shadow stretched from a nearby wagon. He pondered the day's battle and outcome at his field desk. The sudden appearance of a guard startled him. He sat taller.

"General, a Hun, the chieftain Aveek, carries a missive from Attila."

"Bring him in," Aetius replied curtly.

The guard turned and beckoned past the entry and Aveek stepped through. Hun and general eyed one another for a tense second, then each gave a customary nod. Aveek gently tossed a rolled parchment onto Aetius' desk, then stood at attention. The heat clung to Aetius' tunic as he opened the message. A drop of sweat rolled down his back.

To Aetius, Master of the Soldiers of the Imperial Roman Army.

My old friend and now my enemy. Many men have died today. More will die tomorrow, if you choose unwisely. My funeral pyre will not burn tonight. It will go unquenched. I leave Gaul behind me. Do not follow. There are those who would see you defeated.

Attila, King of the Huns

Aetius read the missive a second time. Laying the parchment down, he reached for his reed pen.

To Attila, King of the Huns.

My old friend and now my enemy. Never is the hour ready for a king to burn on a funeral pyre, not even in defeat. There will be time for us to meet once more on the battlefield. Let us bury our dead.

Aetius, Master of the Soldiers of the Imperial Roman Army.

The parchment prepared, he rolled and sealed it. His gaze lingered upon the document in his hand. Then he stood and gave it to Aveek, who nodded and left. Aetius ordered his guard to call the dead Theodoric's son, Thorismund, to his tent. Aetius would convince Thorismund to return to Toulosa to claim the Visigoth kingdom before his brothers might intercede and steal it. Aetius knew Attila would now vanish into the night.

Aetius thought to summon Severus, but caught himself. Severus was dead. He had ordered his body prepared for a hero's burial. Aetius felt Severus' loss already. Another loyal Roman perished, but by whose hand? Arria had informed him of Marcella's actions and claim. Marcella had tried to avenge Severus, surprisingly, and in error killed Arria's helpless handmaiden and only wounded the Frank. If Garic the Frank could find the conscious world maybe the truth would unfold. If he died, the truth would die with him.

Aetius reflected on Arria and Marcella. How incredible, Marcella's assertion that they were sisters. *Marcella is finally free, but all alone,* he mused.

The guards announced Thorismund's arrival. Aetius needed the balance of Attila's threat to protect his position and value with Valentinian. He wouldn't abandon Rome to a spoiled and ineffectual emperor and his two power hungry courtiers, Heraclius and Petronius Maximus. Attila had suffered a defeat, and Attila knew it. A draw would serve everyone, even Thorismund.

Arria wrestled with sleep and a vision. Garic stood on the edge of a battlefield and called to her. Arria reached out and stumbled toward him across mangled and blood-drenched corpses. An abrupt gust of wind materialized a cackling Marcella who blocked her path.

Marcella raised a knife.

Arria opened her eyes. Beads of sweat covered her brow. She turned on her side and faced the fire. Not far from her blanket, resting against a cluster of stones, two red poppies lay on the grass. She stared, then looked around. The soldiers, women and children, except for the sentries, slept. Had the wind blown them there? The poppies reminded her of the Tuscian field where she and Marcian had made love; their bodies cradled in red and enfolded in the same heavenly scent that now clung to the air.

Arria sat up and inhaled the sweetness of the poppies, and the realization of this comforting gift brought tears to her eyes. She went to Garic. The physicians had cleaned and bandaged his wound, but pronounced he was deep beneath the veil of consciousness. She, Vodamir, Luthgar and the rest had resolved to bring him back to Wild Honey, even if it took all their strength. He would not die on this battlefield. "My love, Marcian has sent us a gift of hope. Awake so we might bring you home. Your brothers and I await you. The land of the veil cannot hold you, if you fight! Please Garic, leave and come to me." Arria brushed a long strand of Garic's hair from his shoulder. His features shone in the glow of the nearby fire. "Love, hear me," Arria whispered. "Always—I will be by your side...in the shadow or the light." Arria laid her head on his chest and closed her eyes at peace; this time she dreamed that Garic reached for her hand.

Chapter Twenty-Seven

Dum vivimus, vivamus
Let us live while we live

THE ROAD TO WILD HONEY

he road is endless and I grow impatient."

"Then why don't you do what your heart yearns for?" Arria responded quietly.

"And what is my heart yearning for?" Vodamir replied impishly, his complaint forgotten.

"To kick your heels to your horse's flanks and ride like the wind to Silver Oaks and Basina."

"You're as perceptive as you are beautiful, my lady. But you know I am torn. I am unwilling to leave Garic."

"Garic dreams and doesn't know you're beside him. Go to Basina. She needs you. Your presence will help her to heal. Go Vodamir! Samuel and Tagus will escort us to Wild Honey. Let love lead you. God speed you, Vodamir."

"The same to you Lady. Heal my cousin with your love. I want him back." Vodamir turned and kicked his horse's flanks. Arria watched Vodamir leave as Samuel trotted beside her and asked, "Is Vodamir going home?"

"Yes."

"Where is home for us, Arria?"

"My home is by Garic's side. Your home is wherever you wish. You've always been free in my eyes and you still are. Angelus will need you more than ever. Take the boy and decide if you will stay a

355

Wespe, or return to Palaestina."

Samuel's taut and bronzed scar wrinkled with his grin. "I will take Angelus and stay a while with the Franks. He needs some time to heal and know me better. Then, if he's willing, I will take him to my home in Palaestina. If there's one to go to."

"Home is like a parent, it claims us. Those whom you knew and loved...some will be there."

"The greatest gift the Lord could give me, Arria, would be to see my parents once more."

"God in his mercy is generous. Have faith Samuel."

A shout from Luthgar turned their attention to his farm visible on the horizon. With another whoop, he sped across the open stretch. Samuel shouted to Denis and Tagus and waved them on, "Make a bed ready for Garic! Luthgar will be busy!"

The men obeyed and galloped in pursuit. Left alone, with only Garic in the wagon driven by Amo, Samuel spoke candidly, "Has Drusus died and freed you?"

"His body was never found," Arria said. "I asked Aetius to have men search for him. Neither was Marcella found. Vodamir claims that Garic made an attempt to shoot Drusus with an arrow, but Vodamir was too engaged fighting for his own life to notice if Garic was successful."

"Do you think Drusus killed Severus?"

"I don't know. I won't believe that it was Garic. Despite what Marcella claims."

"Arria, what will you do now?

"I will nurse Garic to health. I will divorce Drusus, dead or alive, and marry Garic."

"If you're a widow you need not divorce."

"If I am a widow, then I must be sure. I will return to Tuscia. My father will help me."

"Will he accept Garic?" Samuel asked.

Arria knew Samuel held back what he thought, *If Garic lives.* "I am not sure, but he'll have no choice. I pray I am not forced to choose between my father and the man I love. Besides, I must know the truth about Marcella."

"These strange ironies, are they destiny or chance?"

"Does it matter?" Arria replied. "They happen and we live with them, cruel or not."

She had awoken the morning after the battle at Catalaunum to find Garic's hand resting in hers. Had she reached for it in her sleep, or had Garic found his way to her? She would never give up. Garic would find her again, and she would help him. "Samuel, we will greet Ingund and the children, but then we must leave. Wild Honey is only a few hours away. We must get Garic there as soon as possible. I will ask Faramund to fetch Vodamir's mother, Sunechild. Vodamir claims she's a healer."

"As you wish," Samuel replied and called to Amo.

Garic lay in a small corner room of the house. His eyes fixed on the beams and his hands at his side. Arria cried, but lovingly washed him and combed his golden hair. What had Marcella done to him? If only it was Marcella and not Garic, who slept in this dark prison.

As Arria sat at Garic's bedside, Samuel came running, calling Arria's name. The healer had come. Sunechild arrived in an open cart driven by Faramund with her shawl draped around her shoulders and a woven bag slung across her chest. The sun was setting and the last rays of light coursed through her gray strands, highlighting vestiges of her once-blond hair.

Arria ran to meet her.

Sunechild climbed down from the cart. "I must see Garic at once. Time is of the essence. Vodamir claims that he's caught in the world of the veil. We need to call him back."

Seated before Garic on his bed and surrounded by burning tapers to light his way and warm him, Sunechild peered into his fixed and open eyes. "I've brought something that might help pull him from the tether that holds him. Another healer as good as I, shared this with me just yesterday."

Arria nodded, but wondered if healers abounded in this region.

"Basina is well. She helped me to fix a potion. When heated, it will cast off a strong vapor that will travel into the dark depth where his conscious soul is held prisoner. You must talk to him Arria, all through the night. Talk of your life as a child, your hopes and dreams for the future, and the children that the gods will bless you with. If Garic fights his hardest fight—the battle to return to you—he can win."

Arria's eyes widened and filled with tears, but she quickly wiped them away. "I will not rest until I see his gaze focus on me."

"Then begin now. Let Garic hear you call."

Arria gazed at Garic and held back her fear. Her voice strong, she began.

A wild dog barking outside the house brought Arria to attention. Soft beads of sweat clung to her cheek, where it had rested on Garic's chest, and an eerie silence gripped her heart. The nearby candle, low in its holder, had lost its flame. -

Arria groped through the hazy gray blackness for the poker to stir the glowing embers, and heard a slight rustle behind her. She paused and listened. From the loft, she heard gentle snoring. Angry with herself for having fallen asleep, she hurriedly put the candle to the embers. The flame sprang to life, and her candle burned once again. With her palm, she shielded the light and turned toward the room where Garic lay. A shadowed figure loomed in the doorway. She gasped and almost dropped the candle. An early morning ray seeped through the window and lit the room. In the doorway, leaning against the frame with his head bent, stood Garic.

Holding his side, he rasped, "*Mellitula*."

Arria cried out, swiftly placed the candle on the nearby table and ran to him. "My love, you've come back," she said. Her kisses smothered his face.

"Where are we, Arria?"

"You're home. Don't you recognize it?"

"*Ja*," he answered and held her hand.

358

A low chuckle sounded from above and the couple looked up. A jury of sleepy faces, hanging over the banister, gazed down on them.

"Garic's awake!" Arria announced, joy pounding in her heart. She ran to the door and flung it open. "Come love, the morning beckons." Arria reached out her hand. "Let's rest beneath the willow that overlooks the stream."

Garic walked slowly toward her, and without a word, he crushed her in his arms. He reached up and tenderly took her face between his hands. "I'm alive because of you." Garic kissed her with the passion of a man reborn and then pressed his lips against her brow. A light breeze floated over them and Arria folded her arm in Garic's. Together they stepped into the day and the world awaiting them.

THE END

ACKNOWLEDGEMENTS

The completion and publication of my first novel is the product of a journey that began years ago when my maternal grandfather, Paris, and my father, Ariano, came from Italy to the United States before I was born. They dreamt of building better lives for themselves, and I am grateful for the opportunities their courage provided for me. My eternal gratitude to two very special women: my mother, Lillian, her gentility, kindness and love will live ever present in my heart, and Sister Mary Ernest who taught me to read and love books.

My deepest gratitude to novelist, Rosemary Edghill for contributing her excellent editorial skills to my manuscript, and to her sister and novelist, India Edghill, whose gracious review of my manuscript, support and friendship kept me focused on my passion and publication.

Many thanks to my publisher, Dana Celeste Robinson, founder, editor, and managing director of Knox Robinson Publishing. For all the teachers and experts who gave me their time and shared their knowledge, I wish to thank: the women of my novel group, Tamara Tabel, Janet Souter, and Susan Hines, excellent writers, editors, and members of the Barrington Writer's Workshop, Charlene Chausis for her computer knowledge, Latin teachers Christopher Mural, Christopher Condrad, and Latinist Timothy Paul Kowalski, and to Maries Huening for her assistance with German phrases substituted for Frankish. In addition, many thanks to Linda Hlavacek and Nancy Moran, my readers for plot and observations, to Sam Roebuck and the members of UNRV Roman Empire Forum, and Tim Caldwell, Bill Link from Germanic-L Forum, the Spertus Institute of Jewish Studies, The Jewish Theological Seminary, and also Adam Karpowicz and Bede Dwyer, experts in Asian and Turkish composite bow construction.

Last but not least, my heartfelt thanks to my family readers: my husband, Greg, who helped with battle scenes, my son and military officer Ryan, (who said, "Mom, I'm skipping the sex scenes.") and my daughter, Rachel, for her thought provoking questions. Thanks to my sons Collin and Patrick for their kind encouragement.

Omnia ad Dei gloriam: All for the glory of God.

AUTHOR'S NOTE

An avid reader of both fiction and history, I became fascinated with fifth century France and the world of the barbarian Franks, later called the Merovingians. My curiosity doubled when I discovered a different view of ancient Rome in this period and its interaction with European barbarian tribes. The Roman Empire was on the brink of collapse and into this gap stepped the barbarians. Gregory of Tours, bishop and sixth century historian, wrote in his work, *The History of the Franks*, of how the Franks rose from tribal chiefs and warriors to the acknowledged masters of Roman Gaul (France). Fascinated by this era of change and upheaval, I chose late ancient Rome and Gaul as the setting for my novel. I've endeavored to represent the events, places, and beliefs as closely to the historical record as possible, but I've also added my own interpretation to the lives of all the characters real and imagined.

Places in On the Edge of Sunrise

Fort Cambria is the fictional name for the city of Cambrai in Nord Du Pas, France (Ancient Roman: *Camaracum*). In the fourth century, with the Franks invading from the north, Romans built forts from Cologne to Cambrai and Boulogne located in the Roman province of *Belgica Secunda*. Although the Salian Franks took control of the town in 430, I chose to represent Fort Cambria (Cambrai) as a Roman controlled outpost situated in the Salian Frank territory.

Arria's home and villa is located in *Tuscia*, the Roman name for Etruria, the territories in central Italy originally under ancient Etruscan influence and in the past equated with the modern day region of Tuscany.

In regard to the birthplace of the character Samuel, a Jewish slave and Arria's trusted servant, I think it's worth noting that modern day Israel was known as *Palaestina* in the fifth century. It was the name given to Judea by the Romans after they crushed the revolt of Shimon Bar Kokhba in the first century.

To help recreate the Frank settings in the story, I referenced written sources and the site, *Musée des Temps Barbares: Parc archéologique de Marle*, a recreated sixth and seventh century Frankish village based on excavations made to Juvincourt and Damary.

History and People

By the third century, the Germanic Franks were a federation formed of eleven tribal groups, which included the Salian Franks and the Chamavi. They occupied the territory on the east bank of the lower Rhine valley (known today as Belgium and southern Netherlands) but then as Gaul and into the later centuries as Francia/France. Their political federation does not preclude the possibility that the groups and their chieftains warred as rivals. With this understanding in mind, I created tension between Luthgar's Salians and Ingobar's Chamavi, two Frank tribes in my story.

Merovingian, the title given to the Franks, derives from Meroveus/ Merovech.

Gregory of Tours mentions Meroveus as the son of Chlodio, the first king of the Salian Franks. Around 450, Meroveus went to Rome to gain support from the Romans for succession as king against an elder brother who aligned with Attila the Hun for the same reason. Priscus, a Roman diplomat and historian, wrote of Meroveus, "I have seen him, he was still very young and we all remarked his fair hair which fell upon his shoulders." This statement supports the idea that Frank nobles distinguished themselves from the commoner and other groups by wearing longer hair, despite the fashion, and were called 'Long-hairs.' The Roman Master of the Soldiers, Flavius Aetius, welcomed Meroveus and accepted him as a friend and *foederatus*

(Roman subsidized barbarian warrior). The Salian Franks fought with Rome at the Battle of Catalaunum (also known as the Battle of the Catalaunian Plains or Châlons).

The great Roman general, Flavius Aetius, referred to by some, as the 'last Roman' is a supporting character in my novel. He served as the *Magister Militum* (Master of the Soldiers) from 429 to 454 and had a long career as a soldier, general and leader. He won the Battle of Catalaunum against Attila the Hun in 451. After Attila's death, he diminished in importance. By this time, the emperor, Valentinian III, believed that Aetius conspired to put his own son, Gaudentius, betrothed to Valentinian's daughter, on the throne. Valentinian, influenced by the ambitious senator Petronius Maximus, felt threatened and stabbed Aetius to death as he read a financial account to him. With Aetius gone, the empire was vulnerable and left without a true defender. In 455, the Vandals sacked Rome.

From my research, I chose one scholarly theory among several for the outcome of the Battle of Catalaunum and the actions of Attila the Hun.

Religion and Artifacts

By the fifth century, most of the Roman Empire was Christianized, including many barbarian groups; however, reputable sources have recorded that the Germanic Franks were northern pagans in a Christian Roman Empire. Little evidence exists regarding their precise spiritual beliefs, especially in the fifth century. Yet, they were a Germanic tribe. The references to Germanic pagan deities that we have today illustrate some parallels to the Norse pantheon of gods of Viking Scandinavia.

Gods such as Wodan (Norse-Odin), Thunar/Donar (Norse-Thor), and Tiwaz/Ziu (Norse-Tyr) are thought to be Continental Germanic and Norse counterparts. One example, the South German Nordendorf Fibula (sixth century) has a runic inscription that mentions the deities Wodan, Donar and Logathore recognizable equivalents to the Norse gods, Odin, Thor, and possibly, Loki. For purposes of clarity and familiarity, I have taken the liberty of using both the Continental Germanic and Norse names in my story. For example, Thor is better known than Donar, but Wodan and Tiwaz offered a stronger Germanic tone. The goddesses Sif and Freya are Norse.

The cross necklace, a significant element worn by my heroine, Arria, was used as a show of Christian devotion. St. Clement of Alexandria and Tertullian (second century Christian scholars) wrote that the cross was a sacred symbol of Christ's passion and protection. After the Emperor Constantine issued the Edict of Milan in the fourth century, he eradicated crucifixion as punishment and advocated the cross as a symbol of Christian faith. Archaeologists have found cross artifacts from different civilizations, including fibulae, necklaces, rings and medals dating back to the fourth through sixth centuries and beyond.

Weapons and Warriors

I discovered a fascinating area when I decided to have my hero, Garic, learn how to use a foreign weapon. The Hun composite bow is a recurve bow made from horn, wood and sinew glued or 'laminated' together, in contrast to a bow constructed of a single piece of wood. The composite bow can store more energy and has greater power than a longer, simple bow. The smaller size of the composite bow makes it an ideal weapon for use on horseback. It plays an important role in my story and historically in Hunnic warfare as the long-range weapon of Attila the Hun.

The elite group of Wespe (wasp) warriors in the novel is a purely fictional creation but based on a legendary notion. A seventh century account in the *Liber Historiae Francorum* asserts that the Franks were descendants of the Trojan princes, Priam and Antenor. After the fall of Troy, the princes found their way to a land they called Sicambria, and there they set the stage for a great people and the kings of the

Franks. Aware that other barbarian tribes had elite levels within their midst as well, I created the Wespe, a special fighting unit within Luthgar's tribe of Frank warriors.

The fifth century is an era rich in drama and ripe for storytelling. I sought to bring my heroes, Arria and Garic, to life in an age not only changing in cultural perspectives, but one also caught in upheaval. *On the Edge of Sunrise* is a story about love and betrayal, politics and power—as an ancient world dies and a new one struggles to be born.

Cynthia Ripley Miller